In the hands of Ms. Golden, their path to understanding and renewal slowly reveals the strength of family, the power of love and the mystery of redemption."

—Pearl Cleage, author of
What Looks Like Crazy on an Ordinary Day

"Marita Golden's exceptional new novel takes an honest and unsparing look at the devastation Alzheimer's disease causes in even the most caring and accomplished of families. Remarkably, it also celebrates the meaning, healing, hope—and even joy—that may still be found in the lives of everyone involved."

—Jean Hegland, author of
Into the Forest and Still Time

"Heartbreakingly beautiful, *The Wide Circumference of Love* is filled with hope and happiness."

—Bernice L. McFadden, author of
The Book of Harlan

"Golden takes a frank and authentic approach to dementia's relentless and all-encompassing nature—losing one's dignity, forgetting loved ones' names, bewildering personality changes, disappearing friends—while also calling attention to the increased prevalence of Alzheimer's in the African American community. Indeed, any one of these problems and stories could be the plot of a separate novel, but Golden connects them seamlessly and compassionately, treating each with the prismatic complexity that defines family crises. In doing so, she makes each character's past an integral part of their present, as well as their impetus to move forward into a new and unexpected future."   —*Shelf Awareness*, starred review

"Golden's redemptive novel is a tale of family survival in which love softens the brutal edges of an insidious disease."   —*Kirkus*

The

WIDE

Circumference of

LOVE

Also by Marita Golden

FICTION:

After

The Edge of Heaven

Gumbo: An Anthology of African-American Writing

And Do Remember Me

A Woman's Place

Long Distance Life

NONFICTION:

Living Out Loud: A Writer's Journey

The Word

It's All Love: Black Writers on Soul Mates, Family, and Friends

Don't Play in the Sun: One Woman's Journey Through the Color Complex

A Miracle Every Day: Triumph and Transformation in the Lives of Single Mothers

Saving Our Sons: Raising Black Children in a Turbulent World

Skin Deep: Black Women and White Women Write About Race

Wild Women Don't Wear No Blues: Black Women Writers on Love, Men, and Sex

Migrations of the Heart: A Memoir

The
WIDE
Circumference of
LOVE

A NOVEL

Marita Golden

Arcade Publishing • New York

First Paperback Edition 2018

This is a work of fiction. Names, places, characters, and incidents are either the products of the author's imagination or are used fictitiously.

Arcade Publishing books may be purchased in bulk at special discounts for sales promotion, corporate gifts, fund-raising, or educational purposes. Special editions can also be created to specifications. For details, contact the Special Sales Department, Arcade Publishing, 307 West 36th Street, 11th Floor, New York, NY 10018 or arcade@skyhorsepublishing.com.

Arcade Publishing® is a registered trademark of Skyhorse Publishing, Inc.®, a Delaware corporation.

Visit our website at www.arcadepub.com.
Visit the author's site at maritagolden.com.

10 9 8 7 6 5 4 3 2

Library of Congress Control Number: 2017002225

Cover design by Erin Seaward-Hiatt
Cover image courtesy of iStockphoto

Print ISBN: 978-1-62872-990-0
Ebook ISBN: 978-1-62872-736-4

Printed in the United States of America

The
WIDE
Circumference of
LOVE

The words hurl through his lips with a familiar bad taste. His fingers clutch the cool, round object filling his palm. He twists it and pulls. Releasing the orb that he no longer understands is a doorknob, he kicks the stubborn thing looming before him, kicks it hard over and over, then turns from its unmoving gaze. He paces in circles, in straight lines, frenetic and relentless movement. This feeling, dizzying now, pumps into his blood, unearths a fury of words he cannot marshal. Words that are slimy, slippery, burn inside him like a house on fire.

The tattered calendar in his mind reads March 2, 1978. That day. A story that he sees in a million little pieces. There is no beginning, middle, or end to that day; there is only what he would say if he remembered.

He is late for the meeting.

He imagines Mercer cursing in that slow-cured Virginia drawl, "Where the hell you at, Slim? If I can get my black ass here on time, then I know *you* ain't making *me* wait."

Their proposal to design an office building in the U Street corridor—still boarded up, on its knees, and destroyed in the days after Martin Luther King Jr.'s assassination—is finally being considered. Today. Caldwell & Tate needs a break. A big one. He has to make this meeting. He has practiced what he will say. This is the project. He is ready to go.

A pain tightens his temples. To soothe the invasion, he rubs his hands over and over as though washing them and paces the wooden floor in slippered feet. The words now a mumble. Fatigue paralyzes each attempt to move and he slumps on the floor as the words dissolve into a creaky whisper. There is wetness on his cheeks. His mind is the devil. Tears.

He no longer knows what they are.

Chapter One

SEPTEMBER 15, 2015

The footsteps echoed all night long. Her husband, wandering through the terrain of the house they had shared for thirty-five years. A house that for him no longer held memories. A house that he no longer recognized as home.

Locked in the bedroom they once shared, Diane Tate lay in the dark listening to the stuttering dance of footsteps that revealed the path of her husband's halting circumnavigation.

Even at sixty-two, she still possessed a young mother's ears. Once able to hear three rooms away, a quarter mile in the distance, or among the voices of a dozen others for the singular cry of her children, Lauren and Sean, now with the same instinctive precision, she heard Gregory anywhere in the house. Silence was the fear now, for if Gregory was not beside her or near her, then he might be *gone*.

Midnight: his feet hit the hardwood mahogany floor in the den where he now slept. Twelve forty-five: a muffled stomping shook the carpeted floorboards of the living room, its side tables and mantel crowded with photos of the children Diane had borne and they had raised, faces imprinted with Gregory's high forehead and strong jaw. One o'clock: she heard the lighthearted jingle of the small bell attached to the front door as Gregory tried to leave the house.

Punching in the four-digit security code to impose a preventive lockdown was Diane's final nightly ritual, begun months earlier when her slumber was severed by a flood of premonition. A throbbing, cataclysmic knowledge had roused her and she'd run downstairs, opened the front door, and raced barefoot in her nightgown beneath a still dark, early morning April sky to find Gregory, his pajama-clad frame rounding a nearby corner.

Now, Diane tossed aside the lightweight thermal blanket and prepared to get out of bed when she heard the bell stop its tinny vibrations. The silence that followed was interminable until finally there was the sound of Gregory's defeated footsteps heading away from the door.

Diane granted herself a reprieve and slid back beneath the sheet and blanket. She surrendered to the embrace of the bed that was hiding place and refuge. Yet sleep was impossible as early morning raced toward dawn.

Two forty-five: the oven door slammed shut. Each evening before she went to bed she unplugged the microwave and the stove. Sharp knives were locked away in a drawer to which only she had the key, an action taken the day she found Gregory shaving with a paring knife, oblivious to the blood trickling down his neck. Three thirty: the gurgling, boisterous flush of the toilet down the hall echoed. This did not mean that Gregory had used the toilet. Four o'clock: the leather-slippered feet padded back to the den. She imagined rather than heard Gregory lay down. Half an hour later, sleep now firmly out of her grasp, she rose from her bed and walked barefoot down the stairs, past an array of photographs—their wedding in the sanctuary of Metropolitan AME Church; Lauren, back then bespectacled and toothy in her Girl Scout uniform; Sean at his high school graduation in black robes, his eighteen-year-old smile self-effacing and unsure, arms hugging Gregory's and Diane's shoulders; the framed *Washington Post* article about Gregory and his partner Mercer, standing before their award-winning signature building, the city's main library, only eight blocks from the White House; Gregory kissing Diane at the conclusion of her installation as a judge for the family court division of the D.C. Superior Court.

The photos trailed to the den where Diane opened the door and saw Gregory finally asleep, swathed in a wrinkled checkered shirt and khakis, an outfit he had insisted on wearing every day for the past week. She had consigned her husband to this room and slept behind a locked bedroom door ever since the afternoon he struck her, nearly giving her a black eye. The room's walls were filled with paintings bought during their travels, separate and together, masks from Nigeria and Ivory Coast full-lipped with feathers and carvings designed to evoke and invoke spirits springing both from heaven and hell. Mementos from Cuba, Turkey, and Israel filled the shelves along with the awards Gregory and Mercer had won over the years. A faded blueprint of the first building they had designed occupied one wall.

Diane padded over to the fold-out bed. Gregory lay asleep atop the rumpled sheets, mouth open, his lips caked with spittle. He snored, a volcanic staccato that seemed to threaten to choke him. His arms were wide—either in supplication or defeat, she could not tell which, for either captured what lay before them. She gently sat down on the bed, stunned as always, by the sight of his massive, thick shock of hair that had turned white in the four years since the diagnosis of early onset Alzheimer's. She buried her fingertips in the gray and white beard that she could not convince him to let her help him shave or trim. She gazed upon this stranger. This husband. Gazed at him in the early morning quiet with pity, love, revulsion, guilt, and shame, steeling her eyes shut for a moment to quell that reflexive storm of emotions that often singed her heart.

Scattered around Gregory like finds from an archeological dig were his "friends"—a small teddy bear with a checkered ribbon around its neck that had arrived last year with a bouquet of roses sent by a friend for her birthday, a pad of bright orange Post-it notes, an egg-shaped marble paperweight, an inch-tall wooden carved elephant, and a set of keys. During the day, Gregory obsessively moved the objects from windowsill to mantel to kitchen countertop.

The teddy bear was now odorous, dirty and soiled, with an eye and the nose missing, the Post-it notes on which Gregory had scrawled crude markings that resembled nothing more than a figurative nightmare, were scattered like crumbs around his body. Numbers and letters, the set of keys to his Lexus, his office, and this house were objects whose purpose he no longer knew.

The beginnings of dawn filtered through the curtains, warming the room. Diane sat and dared a long, courageous look at her husband. In several hours she would take him to Somersby where he would become a resident of the facility's memory care unit. She did not want to cry but felt the tears where they always began, in her groin, a tight-fisted, fierce tumult. She did not want to cry, was aghast that there were tears left, but just like that, her eyes were damp and she was bobbing in the undertow of a torrent of terror and sadness.

Chapter Two

Lauren stood staring out the floor-to-ceiling window that showcased the Capitol dome captured against the gray sky. All morning, since she'd risen two hours ago to meet this dreadful day, she had been cold and trembling, yearning for a warmth that had nothing to do with heat or temperatures.

She'd been spending twelve-hour days at Caldwell & Tate followed sometimes by twelve-hour nights watching over her father, protecting and feeding him, to relieve her mother, who had already performed her shift. Tying a bib around the neck of Gregory Tate. Wiping spittle from the lips of Gregory Tate. Leaning on the man who had held her up. Helping Gregory Tate remember a plate from a fork.

It was through his eyes that she scaffolded and defined her place in the world. He had made her who she was. Who she wanted to be. Daddy's girl, the architect. By the age of ten, she'd possessed an intuitive sense of the beauty in structures, how to judge it, how to know when it wasn't there. At sixteen, her father had taken her on a trip to Chicago where he was to make a presentation for a mixed-use development in Hyde Park. It was spring in the city, but winter had been unyielding and the lake was pockmarked with small islands of ice. A boat tour unveiled the elegance of the Chicago skyline, and as she sat beside her father, snuggling against him for warmth and love and approval, the skyline looked grand above and around them, each building in dialogue with its neighbor, their symmetry, color, width, and depth shaped into a perfect statement of intelligence and art. That was the happiest moment of her young life. A world of skyscrapers whose hold she never wanted to leave. That was the moment Lauren knew she would follow her father into his world.

A test in high school confirmed what she already knew, that she loved math and art and found them compatible and codependent. Her classmates read books, watched TV and movies; she drew floor plans for houses and rooms that bloomed in her imagination. Blueprints fascinated her—the minutiae, the hundreds of details on the page that represented everything from a door or a light fixture, to a wall or a screw an eighth of an inch wide. Creating them, she was intellectually fulfilled, sublimely lost and eternally found.

She told her father she wanted to be an architect and that's when they created a world of their own, in which she was daughter and mentee and he was father and mentor. A world that set them apart in the family circle. A world with its own language and vision, passions and rules. She listened quietly and studiously at the dinner table as her father talked about fellow architects, complained about shoddy workmanship, discussed the bids he and Mercer prepared. By her junior year in high school, he allowed her to sit inconspicuously in meetings at Caldwell & Tate where she watched him make presentations.

When she graduated from Cornell University's School of Architecture, the following evening over dinner at a restaurant in Manhattan's Little Italy, her father had leaned toward her, kissed her on the cheek, and whispered, "You aren't just my daughter now, you are my eyes, my memory, and all my hunger, too. Now you know who I am."

And who was he? She had indeed become his eyes, his memory, and everything else. And what she remembered about him from years before was hers alone, but what she saw now was too unbearable to claim. Yet she claimed it every day because he was her father. He gave her life. He'd given her his life. Eventually, she'd stepped into her father's shoes and joined his firm. She had to learn how to walk in his path.

Today, a phalanx of caretakers and strangers awaited her father at Somersby. This day was a severing that already felt bloody and raw.

Lauren reached for her cell phone on the kitchen counter, wondering if she had somehow missed her mother's call. When she checked her phone and saw that she hadn't, Lauren went into the living room and slumped onto the sofa. Her mind brought forth the day she found her father standing in the middle of the bedroom he and her mother then still shared. He stood urinating, staring in wonder at his flaccid penis, which he was shaking up and down to dislodge the final drops as they fell onto the carpeted floor. When he sensed her presence, he merely wiped his palms on his pants, left his member poking out of his unzipped pants crotch, and gazed at her in unmasked triumph. Lauren shook her head, but still remembered the twinkle in her father's eyes as he'd stood there, the puddle inching closer to his stockinged feet.

Closing her eyes against that memory, Lauren hugged herself tight. The feel of her own staunch embrace conjured thoughts of Gerald. She woke this morning alone but not *alone* like before. Her sheets, body, and bed were drenched in the perfume of what she had daringly begun to call love. Gerald had dressed and kissed her good-bye sometime around midnight. He was her lifeline. Until they'd met, everything had felt like the end. Every day an unwilling act of closure. In the past three months, he had given her the courage to think that nothing ever really ended. Every conclusion was finish line and launching pad. That's how he thought. That's how he talked.

"Call me as soon as it's done," he'd whispered last night as he kissed her good night and good-bye, leaning over her prone, sated, and sleepy figure. "Even if I don't answer because I'm in a meeting, text me. I want to hear how it went."

The shaved gleaming head, the gold earring in one lobe, the musculature primed by hours in the gym. All that poise and sensual assurance had been the first line of his offense when they'd met in a smoky, dark club in Northeast. One of those cavernous places, all noise, sound, sofas, and table islands—a setting for fake intimacy. She'd been there with Whitney and Marla. He'd been watching her, staring at her really, from the crowded circular bar. What had he noticed? The black sequined top she wore, low-cut and inviting, or her eyes, which Marla had made up so dramatically that Lauren had not recognized herself in the mirror?

Gray suit, black shirt open at the neck. He was friendly, almost brotherly, as he slid onto the plush purple sofa and introduced himself, asked their names, and repeated Lauren's several times as though testing it out before he extended his hand and asked if he could buy her a drink, if they could find, as he called it, "their own oasis" somewhere in the club.

Gerald had taken her hand and did not let it go as he navigated a path for them through the wall of bodies. Their oasis was in a patch of open space on the crowded balcony overlooking the warehouses, budget motels, and traffic along New York Avenue. They were outside, beneath a dark sky whose face, Lauren noticed as if for the first time ever, was flecked with a multitude of stars. They sat at a table being cleared by a dreadlocked waitress.

She hadn't had a date, a kiss, or sex in over two years due to the demands of caring for her father and her increased workload at the firm. All the men at Caldwell & Tate were married or already taken and she lacked the nerve for online dating. It was easier to be alone. Lauren had thought all of this as she settled into the seat facing Gerald. She was parched, on edge, self-conscious.

"So you know since this is D.C., my first question has to be what do you do?"

"Does it have to be?" Her heartbeat thudded at the sound of herself, ironic and sassy. Who was this woman?

"No, but that's as good a place as any to start, don't you think?"

"My mother would probably say a background check would be better."

His laughter was a thunderclap. She laughed in response and uncrossed her legs beneath the table. The waitress appeared, anointing them both with an intimate smile. Had she heard their banter? Did the waitress know that Lauren was nearly whirling inside with delight?

"I'll have a bourbon—and you?" he'd asked.

"White wine."

The waitress placed tiny white napkins before them both and went to the table behind them.

"I'm an architect."

"Damn, I'm impressed." Gerald's eyes had widened and

then narrowed. Lauren felt herself momentarily shrink and then she sat up in her seat, blossoming in the studied aim of his gaze.

"You're blushing. I can see you better now. I can see all of you."

"Really?"

"Really."

The statement, Lauren thought, was preposterous. If he meant, which she hoped he did, that he could see inside her, her longing for peace of mind, healing for her father, for love, for a connection with a man who could calm her perennial ache, then she hoped the preposterous words were true, even as she trembled at the thought. She hadn't wanted to talk about her father and how he founded Caldwell & Tate, but there seemed no way not to. And then she found herself telling him about her design work for a new children's museum at National Harbor, a contract the firm had finalized earlier in the week.

"I'll never look at D.C. the same way again, knowing you and your dad got your hands all over it."

"What keeps you busy?"

"I'm with an IT firm in Northern Virginia. We do a lot of cyber security work."

"If you told me the name of your clients would you have to kill me?"

He'd blessed her with a reprise of that laugh, a storm of happiness. "Believe me, we're not that deep, but we do okay. You come here often?"

"My first time. My friends brought me. Actually I hate places like this. I was afraid I'd feel invisible."

"I hope you feel seen. I hope you feel discovered." Gerald's fingers brushed her hand. "Why'd you come with your friends if you hate places like this?"

"We've been friends since high school. I'd run out of excuses, and they asked how I could hate someplace I'd never been. So I took a deep breath and got dressed. And they're always saying I work too much."

"Do you?"

"I have to. My father's been ill."

"I'm sorry to hear that."

At that moment the waitress placed their drinks before them.

Gerald had raised his glass and said, "Let's toast to the fact that life still goes on."

"Are you sure?" she asked.

"You wouldn't be here if it didn't."

Maybe her father no longer had a life. Not the kind of life he would have thought was his due after the years of work, dreams, and family. But Gerald had told her over and over these past three months, when they made love—her appetite for him, an astonishment—when he visited her at her office, that life went on, brutally, sullen with darkness and lit with grace. Life went on.

Just then she saw the call from her mother come in and answered it saying, "Mom, I'm on my way."

Chapter Three

"Do you think this will be enough clothing?" Lauren asked skeptically. Lauren wore tight-fitting jeans, a Cornell University football jersey, her copper-colored locks shaped into a bun—an outfit Diane thought more suitable for moving someone into the dormitory of a college campus rather than into an assisted living facility.

Toiletries, a week's worth of underwear, socks, slacks, and shirts on wooden hangers lay on the sofa. There was Gregory's worn chessboard and the sturdy chessmen (he would never play the game again, Diane knew, but it had once meant so much to him), a photo of the family gathered for Gregory's surprise sixtieth birthday party, and a stack of blank writing pads. Armed with the blank sheets of paper, he could spend hours drawing, though the wobbly, childlike sketches he produced now looked nothing like the designs that had been a signature of his professional life.

"You were there when they told us not to bring much. The

fewer choices he has to make about what to wear when he looks in that cubbyhole of a closet, the easier it will be for him."

"I want him to take this, too," Lauren said, as she walked to the mantel above the fireplace and lifted a picture of Gregory building sand castles with her on the beach on the Outer Banks in North Carolina. In the photo she was five years old, digging a moat around a sand castle in the shadow of Gregory's love-filled gaze.

Hugging the framed photo to her chest, Lauren said, "We still don't have to do this, Mom. I can move in here, work from home. Mercer and I have discussed me having a more flexible schedule." The words were a deflated life raft that inspired an annoyed shake of Diane's head.

"Lauren, we've been through this. You've done enough. I can't ask any more of you. I can't ask any more of myself."

"Daddy deserves better, he deserves more."

What *more*? And where would that *more* come from, Diane wondered, seething and offended. Would it spring from some secret reserve of resilience she had not tapped already? Turning away from Lauren, she began piling items in cardboard boxes and said, with an iciness designed to quell further discussion, "We all deserve better than this. We all deserve more."

"I know it's been hard on you, Mom, I . . ."

They heard Gregory's footsteps and turned to see him standing at the bottom of the stairs clutching the nicked and scarred leather briefcase Diane had given him as a wedding gift, which he had carried to work every day. Barefoot, his corduroy jacket on inside out, the legs of his pajama bottoms inexplicably rolled up to his knees, Gregory's face was luminous and expectant. He looked like a boy ready for the first day of school, a boy who was over six feet tall with white hair.

The incongruity and absurdity of what Diane saw set off a

seizure of flashbacks: finding Gregory's shoes in the refrigerator and a gallon of ice cream stored in the microwave. The sight of Gregory watering a large boulder in the backyard as though it were a flower. Suddenly laughter engulfed Diane, filling her chest, bursting through her throat. She sank to her knees, the raucous mirth astonishing her daughter but giving her a chance to breathe. *On my knees.* Perhaps that was the best place to be, she thought, vainly attempting to quell the outburst and wondering why she felt it necessary to derail what had suddenly steadied her. *On my knees. Maybe I should pray*, she thought and then decided that the laughter was more than enough.

"I'm fine, I'm fine," she whispered as Lauren helped her up from the floor. Diane walked to her husband, held him in her arms, and kissed him. She then stood back and gazed at his elongated face, the prominent, slightly crooked nose, and that damned beard. A face beautifully battered. A face bland and blank.

The tan corduroy jacket and striped pajama bottoms had been removed, and Gregory sat naked on the bed. The white tufts of hair on his still broad chest bloomed thick and unruly. At sixty-eight, Gregory's arms and shoulders had maintained a sinewy musculature. His member lay tucked between thighs beginning the descent into a benign flabbiness. And his legs and feet, which Diane had always found beautifully tapered, had grown somehow smaller. Those strong legs, those thighs had carried him so far.

Once they had walked early mornings and early evenings down Montague and the lovely surrounding streets. They'd walked for exercise—Gregory striding slightly ahead of her—for solace and relaxation, on springtime evenings, holding hands as Diane shared the details of a particularly thorny case or Gregory fumed about the impact of micromanaging neighborhood councils or bungling city agencies on Caldwell & Tate's projects. The streets of their neighborhood had called to them. How many hundreds of miles had they walked together over the years? Now, for Diane, the thought of walking with Gregory conjured the fear of him being swallowed up, evaporating into thin air if she turned away from him for even a second.

Kneeling before Gregory, Diane opened the legs of his boxer shorts. Gregory stepped into them, holding on to her shoulder. *Thank God he doesn't need diapers yet,* she had thought more than once, envisioning herself wiping Gregory's butt. And each time she allowed herself the thought, both brutally honest and shameful, she beat it into submission with the knowledge that she would wipe her husband's ass if she had to. Standing up, facing Gregory, Diane lifted his arms and helped him into a white T-shirt.

"Gregory, today we're going to a place where they'll help you feel better," she told him as though he could understand her lie. Running his hands over his chest, Gregory suddenly pushed past her and headed resolutely and for no apparent reason toward the bedroom door. She pulled him back into the room with the combination of force and gentleness she had now mastered. This was the tightrope she walked: communicating in a way that did not condescend, show anger, or impatience. Remaining poised because she had to be prepared for absolutely anything to happen—to be pushed aside, hit, squinted at, or walked away from, because those actions now substituted for a verbal response.

She handed Gregory a black shirt and watched him investigate the collar and the buttons for several moments before correctly slipping it on. As she watched him meticulously button the shirt and saw him gazing at his hands performing this act, she silently prayed that this ruse would work. What else could she say? What lie or half-truth would suffice to voluntarily get Gregory to leave this house for good?

Gregory had successfully stepped into his pant legs and now, with her help, was buckling his belt. As she held him around his waist, Gregory grabbed her hands in a suffocating grasp. His gaze was deep and empty and she flashed back to the moment when he had struck her.

He had burst into her study as she sat reviewing case files. That voice, that anguished, guttural scream, she sometimes still heard its echo:

"What did you do with my memories? My memories, what did you do? Why did you take them away?"

Then the blows, the slaps, her horror. Lauren miraculously entering the house in time to pull Gregory off of her. And the crater of distance that had engulfed them in the aftermath, a distance that led her to sleep behind a locked bedroom door. Since that day, every moment in his presence had been a breath-holding negotiation of unfamiliar, eerie emotions that had crept into the seams of their marriage. It did not matter that a sinister apparition now occupied Gregory's body, a force that tortured and enslaved him. Those blows had been the first ever between them.

"I'll be there," she assured Gregory now, looking away before the words had left her lips and Gregory freed her wrists. She was a lawyer and so had parsed the truth. Never once had she told him she would stay. But this was her husband, not opposing legal counsel. This was her bedroom, not a court of law.

"You look very handsome," she beamed, trembling, as her

hands brushed Gregory's cheeks. And he did. Looking at Gregory Tate, no one would suspect for even a moment what was happening to him.

∞∞∞

Diane sat in the driver's seat of her car watching Lauren walk with Gregory to the entrance to Somersby, their figures receding across the small parking lot. Lynette, a certified nursing assistant, waited for them in the lobby of the assisted living and memory care facility. While Lynette cared for Gregory, Diane and Lauren would unload the boxes and clothing. Diane placed her head on the steering wheel, eyes closed, and surrendered to this self-imposed moment of solitude. She breathed in and out, slowly, counting each breath, a trick she had learned to calm herself. Sometimes it worked.

But not a single breath quelled her fury at Sean. Sean, who had called last night and told her that today would be more than he could handle. More than he could bear. He couldn't and wouldn't go with them to take Gregory to Somersby. He simply couldn't do it. Tearfully, he had admitted and confessed everything. He was selfish. He was a coward. He was as terrified as she was, as was Lauren. But he wasn't there yet. Not where they were, able to face this day. But now sitting in her car, encased in a shell of anguish, breathing in, breathing out, there was nothing left of Diane's shattered heart to break.

Four years from the first signs, to the diagnosis, to this place—an odyssey of denial, drugs, "alternative treatments," dashed hopes, and unanswered prayers. If she could drive away now and not witness what her yearning had wrought, she would.

A blast of cold air startled her when Lauren opened the passenger-side door and asked, "Mom, are you okay?"

"I'm fine," she lied.

———— ∞ ————

Somersby masqueraded as an upscale hotel with its décor: walls in calming, soothing earth tones; wide windows that flooded the floors with sunshine and light. Somersby was nestled in a residential neighborhood near Silver Spring, Maryland, and Diane had been charmed by the name that inspired images of a country estate or manor. The movie theater, private dining room for families and guests, the library and computer lounge, and the cozy living areas with fireplaces all provided comfort and a quality of life designed, it seemed, mostly to assure the families of those who now called the facility home that at Somersby, elderly fathers, mothers, and siblings would not waste away.

When Lynette, a tan woman of commanding girth and compassionate bearing, opened the door to Gregory's room, she said brightly, "Here we are," as though ushering them into a palace rather than a room so small it resembled a cell or a dorm room. Diane had forgotten how small the rooms were, how pitifully tiny the bed seemed, and how inadequate the desk and bureau appeared to store the material objects of a life.

Lauren sat gently on the uncovered mattress, as though afraid the bed might break, and looked at her mother.

"It looks small, I know, but he'll spend a lot of time in the dayroom, the dining room, on trips. We keep them busy." Lynette's apologetic smile did little to lift Diane's sudden gloom.

Busy, Diane thought. Busy performing tasks that meant little to the residents but provided the framework for a reasonable facsimile of life, rather than a mere existence. She had been told about the memory exercises residents performed designed to stimulate what remained of memory, to beat back the disease even by an inch. But in the end, Alzheimer's always won.

Gregory's life had shrunk to the width and breadth of this room, the length of the hallway outside his door, the space of this three-story building. The anger and sadness Diane felt was as much for herself as for Gregory, because her life had shrunk into the tight parameters of this room as well.

Gregory peered into the room from the doorway, and Lynette said, "Let me take him down the hall, I'll introduce him to some other residents while you get the room ready."

Lynette gently steered Gregory away from the room and rested her arm on his shoulders, saying, "Mr. Tate, I'm going to do everything I can to make you comfortable here."

"So this room will be his life," Lauren said, the moment her father and Lynette were out of earshot.

"You heard what she said; he won't be in this room much. They make every effort to keep them out of the room, active and socializing with others."

"You sound like a brochure. Mom, this is a prison."

"What do you think our home was for me? For him? I can't do it anymore. I can't do and be everything he needs. I no longer even know what he needs."

"I was ready for this when I woke up this morning," Lauren said. "Sure, I could do this. Now it feels even worse than I imagined."

She marched into the hallway and began bringing boxes into the room. They took refuge from each other in silently unpacking clothing and filling the closet and drawers. The chess set and the photo of Lauren and Gregory on the beach sat atop the chest of drawers.

"Now it looks like a cell masquerading as a bedroom," Lauren concluded once they were finished, looking around in dismay.

Lynette and Gregory walked back into the room. "I was showing Mr. Tate the library. I think he'll like it there." Diane heard the soothing neutrality in Lynette's voice, designed, she was sure, to mask what was taking place.

Lynette's cheery aplomb set Diane's stomach roiling. She feared she would throw up, and took a deep breath, willing her body to halt its incendiary rebellion at the thought of what in this dreaded moment they were actually doing.

"Where is everyone? I haven't seen any other residents," Diane asked.

"They're in the dining room. Let's head there."

The memory care unit was both hermetically sealed and spacious. Residents' rooms lined a carpeted hallway that opened up at intervals to reveal dens, meeting rooms, an area with an open kitchen space, and several islands where residents often practiced setting a table as a test of memory.

This is where we will break bread, Diane thought, holding Gregory's arm as they entered the dining room. Here he would stay, among absolute strangers. People stranger than even she and Lauren and Sean were to him now.

A faux fireplace sat against a wall, plants hung from the ceiling, and a wide swath of floor-to-ceiling glass doors framed the facility's dormant garden. Autumnal beauty—mellow, radiant, and still—was rooted on the other side of the glass. She surveyed the faces, clothing, and demeanor of those sitting at the tables. Only a few people looked up as they entered; most seemed enmeshed in their own worlds.

Gregory gazed curiously around him and, at Diane's urging, slid into a chair beside her. Looking around the room at the wheelchairs, walkers, and faces that revealed everything and nothing, Diane told Lauren, "This is his new family."

"How will we fit in?" Lauren asked. Diane did not even attempt to answer the question.

"Hi. Welcome to Somersby. I'm Miss Shirley." The woman seemed to appear from nowhere, suddenly standing beside the table at Lauren's shoulder in a bright orange dress, cream-colored apron, and hairnet. Miss Shirley's voice was craggy with a smoker's velvet trill and she squinted through thick-framed glasses, smiling at them.

She handed them each a menu and explained that the residents were always given a menu from which they ordered their meals. Diane showed Gregory the menu and pointed to her choice for them both.

At a nearby table, four women sat chatting coherently and she could hear snatches of their conversation. Leah Temple, the director of Somersby, had told her that some residents had been placed here not because of severe mental decline but because they had wandered away from home, nearly been lost, and family wanted them in a facility that could ensure their safety.

Their trays appeared before them, brought by two young women in blue uniforms and hairnets. The meal was broccoli, baked haddock, and sweet potatoes. Diane reached over, cut Gregory's food into small pieces, and handed him a spoon. She watched him eat and felt a stab of doubt, second thoughts, but did not know why.

Lauren ate slowly and held Gregory's hand even when he repeatedly pushed her away.

"Daddy, I love you," she whispered over and over to Gregory, who sat contentedly chewing, wolfing down the food with a vigor Diane had not seen in weeks.

After lunch, Lauren left, telling Gregory, "I'll see you soon, Daddy. Be good."

Gregory waved good-bye and whispered the words, "Be good, be good," as she left the room.

Diane and Gregory walked the carpeted halls, passing the doors of the residents. Taped on each door was a photo of the man or woman who lived in the room and included a list of their hobbies and professions (teacher, fireman, bank vice president, social worker) in the lives they had left behind. After they strolled the halls, they napped. Diane lay spooning with her husband, grieving what they had lost, trembling at the thought of what lay ahead.

Three hours had passed. *Everything in place,* she thought. Everything except her emotions. What was there to say that would not upset the fragile web of subterfuge? Diane sat beside Gregory, watching a rainstorm beat against the window. The words in her mind were weights she was too weak to lift. She wanted to leave. Guilt made her want to stay.

Diane stood up. Gregory, roused by her movement, pulled Diane back onto the bed.

"Don't go. Don't leave." He had sat beside her quietly, nearly comatose, but now his banked bewilderment and terror inspired the plea that was a contagion seeping through his hand and fingers into her arm, which he now held tightly.

"Gregory, I have to go now."

"No," he demanded, yanking on her arm for emphasis.

Now she was afraid. Of him hitting her. Of her striking back.

"Gregory, I said, let me go."

He said nothing but tightened his grip in response. With her free hand, Diane pushed against his shoulder, but Gregory had morphed into a wall. Each push, each shove, lodged him more firmly in place. He sat beside her angry and implacable.

Exhausted, she whimpered, "Let me go, Gregory, please. I'll be back," she promised, though Leah Temple had asked her not to visit for three weeks, to allow Gregory time to realize that the facility was now his home.

"No." The tiny word was uttered with childlike, unreasoning truculence.

"I'll be back."

"No."

Diane managed to stand up even as Gregory held her arm. With one final push, she shoved him onto the bed. Now she would run. Looking around for her purse and jacket, she felt his hands on her shoulders pulling her back onto the bed. That's when she heard the knock on the door.

"Come in, help me, please," she shouted.

Lynette swiftly entered the room, cooing in disappointment. "Oh, Mr. Tate, what're you doing? What're you doing?" She placed her body between them, helping Diane stand up as she firmly but gently pushed Gregory down on the bed.

"Go, go, go now," she whispered to Diane, who gathered her things and ran from the room, from her husband.

Standing before the entrance door to the memory care unit, Diane remembered that it could only be opened with a security code Lynette had told her earlier in the day, a code that she could not now recall. A howl erupted from room 4B. The rank odor of guilt rose from her skin as she felt the warm palm of Jessica, one of the nursing assistants, on her shoulder. Jessica's fingers speedily punched in the numbers that set her free. A last look backward revealed that Gregory's door was now closed, but his moans rumbled down the hallway.

Diane raced to the parking lot, bumping into a couple walking toward the entrance. She opened her car door and sank into the driver's seat, breathless, her pulse a knotty drumbeat. Her frightened breath was the only sound she heard as she sat wondering at the bitter taste of this bewildering, terminal, new beginning.

Chapter Four

Looking at his watch, Sean saw that it was twelve thirty. His mother and sister had probably done the deed by now. He'd been looking at his watch all morning, hating himself for not reporting for the real duty that had called him today. The real work he knew he had been put on this earth to do. All morning he had been ambushed by thoughts about his father. But he had forced himself to remember where he was. He was at work, in a basement he was renovating, at work on a job already a week past its deadline.

This was construction as a work of art, he thought, looking at the bookcase Manuel and Steven were polishing. The shine of the finish on the case and shelves seemed sunlit. The bold, broad molding was flush with the ceiling of this three-story Victorian that dated back to 1912, and gave the impression that the stately, deep-hued, wall-length bookcase had grown like a sturdy limb from the innards of the drywall. Three more bookcases to go in this monster-sized basement. Sean looked from Manuel and

Steven to the pile of wooden planks stacked in a corner near the steps. Planks that had to be cut, sanded, finished, and handled at every step of the process as though they were building book-cases in their own homes.

Manuel, a five-foot-four pit bull of energy and focus, stepped down from the ladder and dropped his rag on the floor. He turned to Sean and smiled. His English was rudimentary, but he understood everything Sean told him and was so skilled that Sean called him "the house whisperer."

Steven, rangy and bearded, with a soiled painter's cap on backward, stepped back and said, "Man, I wish this was my house."

Sean's cell phone vibrated and he reached for it in his jacket pocket.

Archie's voice came in a sorrowful blast: "Hey, man, look, I'm sorry."

"Don't gimme that bullshit, Archie. We've been here since eight o'clock. I been calling you since eight thirty. Where you at, man?"

"Ima be there. Ima be there. Hold tight. I'm on the way."

Sean heard the familiar Monday-morning-just-came-off-a-bender slur in Archie's voice, a croaking whine that made every-thing Archie said sound like a hustle or a lie.

"You got one hour. I'm not s'posed to be doing your job."

"Okay, okay, I'm on my way."

Sean hung up and stuffed the phone back into his pocket.

"Sean, he can't keep doin' this. Why you let him get away with this? You gon' let *me* pull that bullshit?" Steven asked, hunching his skinny shoulders, throwing his cloth down, and storming past Sean out the sliding doors into the backyard.

"No good. No good," Manuel said, shaking his head. He

walked to a table near the fireplace and grabbed his keys. "I go for lunch now."

No, it wasn't good. And he didn't need Manuel or Steven to tell him that. A week ago, thieves had broken in and stolen all their tools. Now they were finally back on track.

This was his crew, and he was their boss. He got them work. He found the clients. And he was supposed to handle their shit, no matter what it was. Hell, he knew this wasn't good. But it was better than where he'd been a couple of years ago. Better than knowing what he wanted and being afraid to go after it.

Everything he knew or thought he knew about contracting he had learned from these guys. Steven, the young brother he'd taken on as part of a city-wide effort to connect ex-cons with jobs, had done five years for trying to be the marijuana kingpin of Simple City. Archie, the old head of the group, had nearly thirty years in construction working on some of the city's biggest projects. But when he got paid at the end of the week he dove into a fifth of scotch.

Usually it was just Mondays. What was it about Mondays that made them blue, bleak, and impossible for Archie to face? That made him resist the call to come back to the world?

Still, Archie was the boss when Sean wasn't there, and it was Archie who had taught all of them to honor a house, not to just repair or build it, but to work on it as though they were working on a cathedral. Guys who had fired Archie for drinking still gave him a good recommendation.

Manuel and Steven didn't know it, but it was Archie who had introduced Sean into the tight-knit, competitive world of the city's black contractors. He'd taken Sean around to work sites where Sean had observed how the men who'd been at it for years worked with their crews, managed a job.

Sean had been a contractor for three years now but remained in start-up mode, doing the same "see-me-hire-me" jockeying he'd used when trying to get his first jobs: driving by a work site, looking for whoever was in charge, asking for subcontracting work, anything—plumbing, floors, demolition, clean-up, painting. He had a crew or could get a crew to do any of it. All of it. Trusting he'd get good word of mouth when a client was satisfied. Giving out business cards at the Home Depot; calling real estate agents; tracking down city government contracts; bidding on jobs, calibrating what was too high, what was too low.

He'd never before been more aware of the power—and powerlessness—of money. Getting nearly ten thousand dollars for a week and half of work, and out of that having to pay salaries and deduct supplies. He dreamed about money at night. Nothing was for sure. Everything was a possibility he had to nail down into a certainty. But this was the price he paid to turn houses into homes, and in rare moments, turn craft into beauty as the backdrop for living a life.

Once in the early, lean days, sitting in Archie's truck in an alley behind a house his crew was demolishing, Archie had told Sean, "Youngblood, you can do this thing. Ain't nothing to it but to do it." Archie had leaned back against the driver's seat, adjusted the rearview mirror as though he was expecting a bill collector or an ex-wife to round the corner, and said, "You just got to keep doin' what you doin' that's all. Keep being hungry. Being broke is inspiration. Hell, that's the story of my life."

"Yeah, but look at your life. Archie; you could be somebody's boss. What the fuck happened?"

Archie had turned his rheumy eyes on Sean and said, "Sometimes the knockouts, everything you didn't see coming just happens to you and all you can do is try to get back up every time it knocks you down."

Archie was a conundrum, a shadow. Sean knew all about Manuel's family in El Salvador, the wife and children he had left behind and who he hoped would join him in America one day. Steven had told him about his two baby mamas and the boys he'd grown up with in Simple City, half of them now dead. But it was Archie whose story he didn't know, who had given him a way to imagine his own.

Still, he'd have to let him go, he knew that. Monday was as valuable a day of the week as any other. He'd let him go and soon. But not today.

Pissed, Sean slumped onto the basement floor, removed his jacket, and dipped a paint brush into the half-full can of finish. He stacked several sanded shelves and painted each one with the brilliant yet toxic gleam. Painting, he forgot Archie and his breathing slowed. Painting, he was encased in a zone impenetrable to even his own reliable, vexing worries. Painting, he had never told anybody, was how he prayed. But the brushstrokes merely kept pace with the onslaught of questions, embers glowing at the edges of his thoughts. How had his father reacted when his mother and sister said good-bye? What had his mother told him to get him to stay?

The good thing about living with Alzheimer's, Sean sometimes allowed himself to think—because he lived outside its grip—was that you had no idea when someone had failed you. The bad thing about having Alzheimer's, he knew—because it had stolen his father from him—was that you had no idea when someone had failed you. This was all bullshit rationalizing gleaned from the books and articles his mother collected and pressured him to read. To understand the ultimately inexplicable. To dive into the freezing waters of all this loss and somehow reach the surface, step onto the shore, and stand shivering but strong.

His father was moored in a world where he thought he was thirty-one or thirty-two years old, a bachelor, with all that he would achieve still a heartfelt desire. Was the fact that Sean found it harder and harder to look at his father a verdict on his love? Sean had allowed himself to conclude, unlike his sister and mother, that there was nothing left of the man he wanted to love, honor, and respect. But that void, and his insistence on it, offered Sean little he could use in acknowledging the man who remained and always would be his father. A ghost, a shell of himself, but still his father.

It had cost his mother all the love she had to decide to put his father in Somersby. He knew that, but all he could do on this day was pay his own price, his devil's due by bailing out.

As a recovering prodigal son, letting them down had become a reflex.

Caught in Georgia Avenue eight o'clock traffic, Sean checked his phone and saw a text from Valerie, a curt, four-word inquiry: *How did it go?*

Sean dreaded telling Valerie the answer to her question, even as he meditated on the reality that he was a grown-assed man in a grown-up relationship. It didn't get more grown than living with a twenty-seven-year-old widow whose husband had died in Afghanistan. He loved her, and that unfortunate soldier's son, too.

Sean had just passed the contractor's exam and given notice to the big-box hardware store where he'd been working when he met Valerie. She'd strode into his aisle, unsure what she was looking for, but she'd needed his help.

Valerie was a big-boned woman who wore her weight as an

embellishment, her size a sensual promise. She smelled of jasmine and both her reddish brown hair and freckled cheeks were girlish. Somebody he already knew he would want to take home. Her giggle was music, an invitation, when she became confused about her purchase.

When she came back two days later to return the bolts, washers, and faucet she had bought for her plumber, she was coy, lingering long after they found what she actually needed. Sean had asked for her number, but she'd shaken her head no and instead asked for his. He actually dreamed that night that she would call. In reality, she made him wait three days.

Initially, Valerie put her son Cameron between them. Their dates usually included the boy, as if she was testing Sean to see if he could love her and her son.

"I don't come unencumbered," she'd said. "We're a package."

She'd told Sean this as though she had practiced using the declaration as a scare tactic. But now, almost three years later, he'd moved in and they had begun to talk about marriage. No one in their families knew yet, but they considered themselves engaged. Even his dad, now forgetting everything, would be happy for him.

When Sean entered the apartment, he dropped his keys in a ceramic bowl on a table near the door.

"I'm home," he called. Greeted by silence, he was enveloped in the aroma of garlic and tomatoes. The living room had the look he loved: Valerie's shawls and the caftans she was knitting were piled on the sofa. Cameron's soccer ball, several Spider-Man comics, and video games lay on the floor near the television. He saw Valerie's and Cameron's plates on the table, littered with remnants of garlic bread. The kitchen stove and sink were a puzzle of pots, pans, and dishes. This wasn't disorder, Sean thought. This was a place where you could tell people lived.

Walking down the hallway, Sean passed the closed bathroom door. Behind it, he heard Cameron splashing and engaged in a muted but fervent conversation with himself. Or was he giving orders to action figures? Valerie was in the computer room manipulating a spreadsheet on her desktop. Sean placed his hands on her shoulders to claim her and to steady himself.

"How did it go with your dad?" she asked, turning around to face Sean, and in that swift movement severing his touch. Her eyes rested on Sean's face with an electric expectancy that would accept nothing short of the truth.

Sean turned from those eyes and walked a few feet away, sitting on a leather hassock. He sat examining his clasped, tense fingers, not looking at Valerie.

"You didn't go with them?"

"I couldn't. It seemed too much like saying good-bye."

There was her silence. Then his silence. What more did she want him to say?

"Sean, we talked about this last night." The words came in a whisper he had not expected.

That's what he loved about her and what he hated about her: the way she charged in, refusing to let a thing rest until it had been solved.

Gathering his will and his wits, he aimed the words at her. "You mean *you* talked about it and tried badgering me into saying I'd do something I knew I couldn't." He stood up in self-defense, to explain why he lost his nerve.

"What are you afraid of?" Valerie looked up at Sean from her swivel chair. The disappointment in her eyes stunned him like a blow.

"When I finally get my life together, he's gone. He can't see it, can't comprehend it. What I am supposed to do with that? You saw the last time we went to the house—that rigid, vacant stare. The stories he tells that make no sense and go on forever. Asking me over and over if I'm his son? That's what I'm afraid of. And it makes me feel like shit that you and Lauren and my mother don't seem to be as afraid as me."

He had said it, and now his heart bulged with regret and relief. His eyes glistened. He blinked back the onslaught. He didn't deserve the anointing they promised.

"I can't speak for Lauren or your mother. Sean, I know what it means to lose someone. To really lose them. Your father isn't gone. Love what's left."

After that, he had no appetite. Valerie shepherded Cameron through the rituals of preparing for bed before escorting the boy into the kitchen where Sean sat at the table studying the food on his plate rather than eating. The six-year-old climbed onto Sean's lap and hugged him good night. Watching Valerie and Cameron walk to the boy's bedroom, Sean plunged into all the thoughts that the searing moment of truth with Valerie had unleashed.

He had never told anyone how the impact of Alzheimer's on his father reminded him of his own continuing struggles with dyslexia. His father had lost the ability to read. *Reading.* Even now Sean saw numbers and words backward. Sometimes reading felt as exhausting as lifting weights. He knew in some sense what his father must be going through, how frightened he must have been the first time he looked at a page and saw nothing he could comprehend.

In elementary school, Sean had been teased for his halting, stuttering attempts to read. The words they'd used were branded into his psyche, and even now those wounds radiated their own special heat: *slow, different, special.* Words he had heard his parents use when he held his ear to their closed bedroom door. Cold, clinical words that sounded like the opposite of love.

When he looked at the pages of the books that filled every corner of his room, he saw shapes and sequences of letters appearing to move, disappear, or shrink, sometimes actually dancing across the page. The sight of all that induced a nausea that sickened him.

Eventually, he was enrolled in a pioneering school staffed by specially trained teachers, psychologists, linguists, and tutors with all the time in the world, all the time he needed, who crafted lessons just for him. There, he wasn't broken. He wasn't a problem. They told him his brain was healthy, it just took him longer to make the connections reading required. The walls of the bright, sun-filled school were plastered with posters of the pioneers of science, math, the arts, and culture who were dyslexic. He learned to read, write, and spell. But it was always laborious, and he still needed help, extra time on tests, and the forbearance of those in the real world beyond the borders of the special school. He was convinced deep down, in the place that was his alone, that he was a problem. The optimistic, experimental school couldn't stop him from thinking that.

He was still a Tate, the son of a man whose buildings were part of the landscape of the city, whose mother judged and decided the fate of others, whose sister became the son, he knew this, that his father had always wanted.

Visiting Caldwell & Tate projects with his father, Sean had been mesmerized by the sight of the craftsmen at work. How a wall was built, how a buildings' frame grew over time, became a massive skeleton that in his mind he compared to something spawned by the hands of Hercules or Goliath. This was the greatest show on earth.

One summer, he'd spent a part of every day watching a high-rise being constructed. He sat in a park in McPherson Square, across the street from the K Street building for three or four hours at a time, munching on the lunch his mother had packed for him.

He could read this; construction was a language he understood. Working with his hands had always felt like salvation. He was the handyman his mother never had to hire. Wood and brick, cement and stone were not inanimate but had sprung from the same soil that had given him life. But he wasn't like Lauren, who could tell their father all this and thereby seal the lock on their father's respect as well as his love.

If you were a Tate, you went to college, even if you didn't learn a damn thing. While Lauren studied architecture at Cornell, Sean had sweated it out at a junior college in Maryland. He'd graduated but he still had trouble spelling and writing.

After college, for nearly a decade, he'd done it all—even selling pot, until a close call with the cops had reminded him that he could end up in a courtroom next door to his mother's. He'd been a security guard in a building his father had helped design, worked on a construction site, washed cars, bartended, and driven a limo—anything where his weakness would not be exposed.

He had let the family down and he felt it every time he went to an obligatory holiday dinner, funeral, or wedding—rituals that even he could not avoid. None of them had told him he was a failure, they hadn't needed to. His own mocking chorus was ever-present in his mind. The checks his mother wrote when he was broke, the pep talks from his father to help him find his way, the encouraging calls from Lauren. So much love. So much faith in him. And for most of his life he hadn't felt he deserved any of it. Every family his mother reunited in court and every building Caldwell & Tate designed dragged him into the foaming undertow of self-doubt. It was hard to know which was worse: his father's nagging that he had to do more, be more, or his mother's seemingly patient acceptance of the leveling-off of his life. Both made him feel like shit.

Sean could hear the television in the bedroom he and Valerie shared but he chose to tackle the kitchen. At least he could do that. But neither rinsing the pots nor scraping the plates halted the rush of the longing for his father, the intrusion of the past.

"Haven't you learned anything from me?" his father had asked once.

Sean had been working then at the big-box hardware store. He'd actually liked some parts of the job: helping customers find bolts, screws, lumber. Tangible items they needed to repair, fix, and build. Working with his hands, he was secure.

But on the day his father asked him this, he'd been thirty years old, making thirteen dollars an hour. If he ever wanted to get married, have kids, exist, and be visible to others and himself, how would he do it? Some days he was lodged in cement, other days sinking in quicksand.

His father had come by his apartment that evening without warning and when Sean opened the door, he'd known Gregory could see the sink full of dishes, could sense the creeping despair in the boxy, drab efficiency apartment in a complex where there had been two murders in the last year.

"You could've called," Sean had said sullenly, sinking onto the dark-brown corduroy couch, picking up the remote, and turning up the volume of ESPN. Gregory had grabbed the remote from Sean's hand and thrown it across the room, the instrument grazing Sean's cheek.

"What the hell?" Sean sprang from the sofa, buzzed, belligerent, more angry at what his father saw than at what his father had done.

"So this is your life?"

"I guess it is."

Gregory slumped onto the matching corduroy love seat. "I'd slap you if I thought it would do any good. Your mother's worried about you. We both are. She wants to know why you don't call. She expected to hear from you on her birthday at least."

"Sorry, it's not about y'all. It's me; I need my space," he said, in a muffled voice directed at the television screen.

"You don't get to fire your family because you can't handle your life."

Sean had watched his father stand up and almost hoped he would hit him. He was ready to bleed. But his father had merely looked around the apartment and shaken his head.

"You think you're damaged goods. You believe life is hard for you because of dyslexia. Sean, dreams are blueprints, dreams are first drafts. I didn't raise you to be small. I'm expecting more. You're expecting more. You're just scared you can't hold it in your hands."

"You're ashamed of me because I don't wear a suit and tie to my job like you," Sean had shouted weakly, knowing the words were a blatant lie.

"I'm ashamed of you because you've sold yourself short. You're running from nothing instead of standing still and letting the thing that could ignite you and the talents you have catch up and claim you."

Sean laughed contemptuously. He watched his father turn to look at the television screen and saw a new and unfamiliar pall of age on his face.

"What do you want me to tell your mother?"

"Tell her I'll call her soon. Tell her I love her."

"And I'm supposed to make her believe that? You don't realize it now, Sean, but life is short. Whatever you do, you don't want life to get away from you. Nothing is guaranteed. Not your health, not even the next day."

"Dad, what's going on?"

"I'm just saying, I mean, I don't know what I'm saying. It's just that . . ."

The confused timbre in his father's voice. The withered, drawn look on his face. The shadows in his eyes . . .

"What's wrong?" he'd asked, although he did not want to know, was afraid to know.

"Nothing, nothing. It's just that I'm starting to forget things."

"Are you okay?"

"Health-wise, sure." He had shrugged. "It's my mind, my thoughts."

"Dad, you're strong. Whatever it is, you'll beat it," Sean offered, embarrassed by the hollowness of his pat response. He'd sat looking at his father wishing he had the nerve, the courage, to ask more.

Gregory had taken a deep breath and said, "Stop being a stranger."

Sean stood up and walked his father to the door. A space yawned between them that neither chose to close. He watched his father walk down the stairs and called after him, "Tell Mom I'll call her. I'll call her soon."

His father had not answered.

And Sean didn't call his mother that day. He couldn't. He knew he would have had to ask about his father. He would've asked and his mother would've told him what his father could not. His mother would have told him the truth.

Sean sat in the kitchen flush with all the emotions of that encounter. All the longing for connections he had been too fragile and fearful to make. They'd been through so much as a family since that day with his father, nearly four years ago. Alzheimer's had brought Sean back into the fold, stumbling, resisting as he was even now.

"You coming to bed?" Valerie called.

"In a minute. I gotta do one more thing."

Sean wiped the counter with a paper towel and surveyed the order he had brought to the kitchen. Then he pulled out his cell phone. He dialed his mother's number.

"Hello, Mom. How'd it go?"

Another sleepless night. But this time, night was frightening, nearly foreign. Diane had not imagined that on this, the first night of Gregory's absence—or was it exile?—that she would feel their house, their home, cast upon her so brooding and heavy. So accustomed was Diane to her husband's rambling expeditions through the house as she tried to sleep, that this new solemn silence was disquieting. The bedroom closet still held some of Gregory's shirts and slacks, the drawers were layered with excess socks and underwear. The sum of the life they had lived together pulsed in the air she breathed, lying in bed, in the dark, unable to sleep, able only to remember.

Sean had called as she sat downstairs in the living room watching the ten o'clock news, asking her, timidly, how the day had gone.

"We got through it."

In truth, the day had drained her: leaving Somersby and going to the superior court for two afternoon meetings, preparing for the next day's docket of cases, opening the door to her empty house at eight thirty. So although she had rehearsed a soliloquy that would vent her disappointment, at the sound of Sean's voice, the rage she had harbored and stoked felt inelegant and unnecessary.

"When you go see him I want to go with you," he said.

"I won't see him for three weeks. He needs that time to adjust."

"Mom, I feel like shit."

"Sean, you've spent too much of your life, too much of your time feeling that way. Your father wouldn't want that to go on."

"I let you, all of you, down."

"We've got an unforeseeable future of days ahead with your father. Days on which you can do what you couldn't do today. Give Valerie and Cameron a hug for me. Hold them close. Now you get some sleep."

Forgiving her son felt like the one thing she had done right today. The one thing that unequivocally made sense.

And now she lay in the dark. Unable to sleep. Too tired to read. It was three a.m. In the quiet, alien confines of her house, Diane's mind sifted, conjuring who she once was. How she had created and become Diane Tate. She found relief in the flashbacks that rained down on her in place of dreams. Who would she be without Gregory? How could she let him go and usher in even the barest outline of the woman she was bound to become? If she could not sleep then she could remember.

Chapter Five

1960–1977

Loving Gregory Tate had helped Diane reinvent herself, yet in some ways she would always still be standing in the doorway of her mother's bedroom, watching her apply makeup as if she were an actress preparing to go onstage.

Ella would glide over to her closet to choose the dress she'd wear to go six blocks down the street to Jim Dandy's, the neighborhood bar. Ella's skin was the brazen, polished color of a raven. She had high cheekbones and small eyes that were wary, unbelieving, and distant.

Ella's brittle laughter would rip open Diane's and Ronald's sleep when she'd come home with an "uncle." They'd enter the apartment like burglars, knocking over chairs and lamps, their hushed whispers and giggles erupting in the small apartment's darkened gloom. Her brother Ronald, two years younger but with a body that spoke its own language, more than once—pajama-clad and raging—had stepped between Ella and one of these men's fists. It took Ronald longer to learn his schoolwork than Diane, but he could size up the men their mother brought home in a glance—a skill that turned into a steady surveillance.

Then there were the days and nights when Ella went without sleep and whirled through the apartment washing, cleaning, smoking, talking frantically to Diane and Ronald, and chatting on the phone for hours, her antic, frenzied voice signaling the cliff on whose edge she teetered.

But Ella Garrison was more than those crazed days and desperate rendezvous with men whose names she could not the next day recall. She was a nurse at Freedman's Hospital, and over dinner, Ella often told Diane and Ronald about her patients, the ones she helped the doctors save and the ones they could not. Over time, she said, her patients told her everything: that they were afraid to die; that until this illness, this disease, they had been terrified to live; and that if God gave them another chance, they would live a full-blown life.

Ella witnessed the patients whose beds were surrounded by a steady flow of family and friends and those for whom no one came. And it was the lonely ones who sank into despair and refused to eat, that on her days off Ella would visit with Diane and Ronald in tow, bringing a get-well card purchased at People's Drugstore on the way and signed by each of them.

When Ronald protested that they didn't even know the people Ella made them visit, she scolded him, saying, "But *I* know them. I've emptied their bedpans, taken their temperature, and comforted them when their sickness made them mean and hateful. I haven't met a stranger since I became a nurse. You all are my children and no matter what you do when you grow up, I want you to take care of somebody."

Diane possessed faint yet stubborn memories of the father who had left them when she was five years old. She often rummaged through her mother's drawers trying to find a picture, anything that would give her an answer to the question of why he went away, to which her mother simply responded, "He didn't love me or you and your brother anymore."

But Diane would never be released from the childhood terror she'd felt after her father had left. Stationed at the living room window for hours, looking for him to round the corner. Wetting her bed, refusing to eat, throwing toys at her mother. All to make her daddy come home. And then as the days and weeks passed, Diane had surrendered to her mother's silence, her mother's riddle-like explanation. She surrendered to the only person who was left. Over time, the anger and sometimes hate her mother inspired in her congealed in equal measure. What could her father have done to deserve to be so stoically erased?

Loretta Epson, Diane's best friend in the fifth grade, visited her father at Lorton Prison in Virginia once a month. He had stabbed a man to death during an argument over a game of craps, yet Loretta was not denied the father who had committed what Diane learned in Sunday school was the greatest sin. Loretta's mother told her that her father was the only father she had, so she had to love him no matter what. Diane convinced herself that it was Ella and her fearsome, wild moods that had made her father leave. Maybe there had been "uncles" too, who drove him away. Her anger was neither childish nor transitory. When she grew up, she vowed, she would find her father, and just like Loretta Epson, love him in spite of his sins.

———— ∞ ————

If her childhood was one of concealment, her adolescence offered the equally searing pain of discovery. When Diane was thirteen and Ronald was eleven, Ella was hit and killed by a car speeding along Florida Avenue. The 1963 Volkswagen had been

stolen half an hour before by the three teenagers and then barreled through a red light as Ella stepped off a curb just blocks
from where she nursed the sick and the dying.

Aunt Georgia, Ella's older sister, swooped Diane and Ronald up and brought them to live with her. On Friday nights,
Uncle Harold and Ronald would sit in the living room together
watching boxing matches on television while Diane and Aunt
Georgia folded clothes, warm and tingling with static, from the
dryer. For Diane, there was a closet full of new dresses, and for
Ronald, a Schwinn bicycle and skates. For neither was there any
mention of their mother.

But when Diane was a senior at Roosevelt High School,
Georgia finally felt it was time. Diane was parting her hair and
pinning rollers tightly against her scalp when Georgia entered
her room that night. The stricken look on her aunt's face brought
Diane from the mirror to her bed where Georgia sat.

"You're almost grown," Georgia said, "and I promised
myself I would answer your questions about your mother and
your father when I thought it was time."

"Is it time?"

"I think it is."

Georgia cupped Diane's chin in her fingers, gazed at her
niece, and said, "You look so much like her, you always have. I
should've told you this years ago. I just didn't know how."

"I'll go get Ronald."

"No, I want to tell you first. If I can tell you, telling him
will be a bit easier." Georgia took refuge again in Diane's face
for several long moments and then said, "You were four and
Ronald was two when it happened. I was watching you both
for Ella that night. A man broke into your parents' apartment.
He had a gun. He tied up your father in the kitchen and raped
Ella."

"My mama was raped?" Diane clutched her stomach to still the queasy invasion of a lava of sickness slithering into her groin.

"Then he stole what little money they had in the house, the radio, and the television. Ella and Samuel reported it to the police, but they never found the man." Her aunt's voice, crisp, bloodless, charged on. Diane would do anything to make it stop.

"They were never the same. Neither of them. Your father started drinking, wouldn't come home at night. Ella came home from work one day and found a note from Samuel saying that man had taken everything. He had to leave. He couldn't stay."

Diane had always known there was more than the unadorned explanations her mother had offered, but this history, so intimate and so monumental, made her wish that she was mute so no words would be expected. All her young life, she had felt branded and did not know why. How had her aunt hoarded this story all these years? How had she said it aloud now?

"I was there the day she tore up every picture she had of Samuel and swore that she would never forgive him."

"Did you know about all those other men?"

"Yes, I did. I think she was looking for your daddy in them."

"And my father, he just left us?" Diane asked, her voice stiff and incredulous. She had lived through the loss but until this moment had not known its depth.

"Yes. He did."

"What about his family?"

"I've run into them sometimes and they don't seem to know much about Samuel anymore. I know he had a sister who just after a while got tired of Ella telling her she couldn't see you and Ronald."

"So she kept us from knowing about my father and the rest of my family?"

"Diane, she was hurt."

"If she was raped, why did she act like a whore?"

"That's the wrong question. How did she get up every morning and give another new day a try? I was her sister, and I could never figure that out."

"Why didn't she tell me what happened to her? Why he left?"

"You were thirteen when she died. Maybe she was waiting till you got older. Maybe she didn't want to risk losing you, too, by asking you to carry what she could hardly bear."

Her mother had been mangled and nearly destroyed by one man. Forgotten by another. Still, Diane could not quell the yearning for her father even as the lingering promise of even more discontent was embedded in it. Now she knew why her father had left. He was weak. He had let them all down. He had fled from her wounded mother and what had remained, Diane was now certain, of her mother's love.

—⦿—

Diane was an A student whose English teacher had given her paperback copies of *The Street* by Ann Petry and *Go Tell It on the Mountain* by James Baldwin, stories that they did not read in class. Miss Daughtridge, a silver-haired, long-legged, white woman who walked the aisles of class like a field marshal, asked Diane one day after class, "Tell me, what will you do with your gift for words?"

The question, like all the questions Miss Daughtridge asked, assumed that she was instantly due a reasoned and deeply considered answer. Clutching her books as she stood before Miss Daughtridge's desk, Diane had stammered, "I don't know. I can do lots of things."

Miss Daughtridge handed her the two books. "I think you can handle these."

The books filled her hunger not only for story but for a replica of everything that, at seventeen, she knew life could be.

She soon realized, however, that she did not want to use words like Ann Petry or James Baldwin, to tell stories that she knew were half lie and somehow all truth. She wanted to make words achieve what they never had for her mother or her father—to make things right. The joyriding teens who'd hit Ella with a stolen car had served three years in a juvenile facility, a punishment that embittered everyone Ella had left behind. Diane's favorite TV show was *Perry Mason*, and although she had never once seen him defend a person who looked like her, she loved his stoic yet unquenchable commitment to finding the truth, to law and order.

After high school, she ran, but never fast enough, from her mother's life and her mother's death. From her father's disappearance and his weak-kneed cowardly love. At Spelman College in Atlanta, Diane learned from her professors that she was there not just to get a degree but to figure out how to crack open a resistant world for her people. She imitated the confident demeanor and style of the black girls of privilege who were her classmates, yet snuck off campus to serve free breakfasts provided by the Black Panthers to children in the projects of Atlanta.

Then, in the middle of the fall semester of her senior year, Aunt Georgia called and told her Ronald had been killed in Vietnam. She'd come home from Spelman tight-lipped and controlled. At Arlington cemetery she sat beside Aunt Georgia watching her nervously pat the folded American flag that lay inert—and to Diane, obscene—on her lap. During the repast following her brother's burial she accepted everyone's condolences and the hugs of Ronald's friends—one or two headed to college and several to Vietnam themselves—and then walked upstairs to her room and wrecked it, tossing sheets, blankets, clothing onto the floor, ripping up the paperback books, the poetry of Gwendolyn Brooks, Maya Angelou, Nikki Giovanni, and yanking the posters of Gil Scott Heron and Angela Davis off the walls. If she'd had a match to strike, she would have immolated what was now debris, as well as herself.

Diane graduated salutatorian from Spelman and then she ran to New York University School of Law. The law, she was sure, would make her someone with more answers than questions. On her best days, she walked through the world remembering that her mother had told her to take care of somebody, pleased that she had chosen a profession dedicated to doing just that.

Yet the nightmare raging within her whispered, *Men leave, men rape, men die.* When Diane watched her lovers leave, she watched them go as Ella's child. Ella, who had shattered at night and gathered up her remains in the morning because she'd had bodies and souls to heal.

Diane returned to Washington from New York to work as a legal aid lawyer in D.C.'s public defender service, unique in the country for hiring graduates of the nation's top law schools to represent indigent clients. The courts were clogged with so many young black men on trial for everything from mayhem to murder that the black court-appointed lawyers began calling the pool "the chain gang."

She was by then a woman who saw her mother's face in hers, all the time and everywhere, for she had the same smooth, seamless dark skin, the same look of doubt that made some think that she could never be satisfied. But the look of calm certitude that gave her eyes a probing, meditative glow—that was her own.

Those eyes made her clients feel that she was on their side and assured her friends that she could be trusted with their secrets.

She sat face-to-face with her mostly young clients and listened to their stories of innocence, guilt, wrong place, and wrong time. Sometimes they had murdered, but Diane often learned that they had killed because someone was out to kill them or they'd taken a life to prove a decadent sense of manhood seeded in the very soil of their lives. They had stolen but also had nothing to lose. They sold drugs not just for greed, but for respect. Of the scores of those she was assigned to defend, only a few, she concluded, were sociopaths, criminals with no hope of salvation or redemption. Most of their stories circled back to barren and bleak childhoods that ensured they would end up just where they were, staring at a lawyer, considering a plea deal and wondering which of their friends they would be reunited with in jail. Until they sat across from Diane for the first time in the basement of the superior court, many had never ventured out of their decaying and forgotten neighborhoods—Anacostia, Barry Farms, Ivy City, Sursum Corda, Trinidad—never seen the White House or the Capitol, and couldn't imagine either of those buildings having anything to do with their lives. More than once, she had wondered if, sitting across from her at the nicked conference table, was the son of the man who had destroyed her parents' lives. She wondered if she would extend to her mother's rapist the compassion she found herself bestowing upon her clients. She was haunted by the knowledge that defending her clients was so much more than legal procedures and bargaining with prosecutors. The essential meaning of life, of crime and punishment, for her clients, for the society that had made them, were the questions and obsessions often obscured by the grind of never-ending cases. Only rarely did she have time to breathe in the renewing essence of those inquiries.

Increasingly burdened by a sense of futility as she plea bargained more cases than she tried or got a client off on one offense only to have him show up in handcuffs again months later, Diane began to think of changing to family law. Surely there she could make a difference, defend these young men as juveniles, steer them into rehabilitation services and treatment for the learning disabilities, post-traumatic stress, and emotional abuse that was the ticking time-bomb pulse of their criminal acts. If she couldn't do that, then the choice of law made no sense.

Chapter Six

1978

The night Diane met Gregory, he was an architect at a party full of lawyers, wore a dashiki—though, by then, even the Reverend Jesse Jackson had begun shopping at Brooks Brothers— and he interrupted a boring conversation Diane was having with a justice department lawyer. He dismissed the lawyer just by thrusting his hand at Diane, standing his ground, and saying, "Hi, I'm Gregory Tate."

"That was rude," Diane scolded him, astonished, as the lawyer quickly and quietly skulked away.

"Not really. I call it survival of the fittest."

"You're wearing a dashiki and throwing around an out-of-context Darwinian quote that's been used to justify racism, colonialism, and war. Is this nerves or balls?"

"Both." Gregory smiled, too confidently for her comfort.

She was a tall woman, exactly six feet, used to entering a room and allowing everyone to catch their breath, evaluate her, get comfortable with her height and what they imagined it might portend. Gregory was a few inches taller, though she was not sure why that mattered. His light skin, those gray eyes with a flicker of blue, the keen features and straight hair texture made Diane wonder if Gregory was one of those racial dinosaurs, more proud of and interested in the white ancestor who had bequeathed him that hair, those features, than of the scores of blacks whose blood flowed more generously in his veins. She knew him—or thought she did—could look at him and know what kind of neighborhood he had grown up in, what his parents looked like, what his values were. She had him down pat. Diane heard and felt the creak of a familiar curtain lower between them. She was on one side and he was on the other. Gregory Tate, she suspected, was the product of a world where skin tone and class were sometimes interchangeable bloodlines.

On her side of the curtain, Diane remembered Jeff Darlington, a boy from that world who she had met at fifteen in the D.C. Youth Chorale. They'd stood at the bus stop after the rehearsals and talked about folk singers like Odetta and Bob Dylan and the colleges they wanted to attend. He'd call Diane in the hour or so after she had finished her homework and before she had to go to bed and they'd talk in whispers and hushed laughter about the cliques at their schools which they hated, not because they had never been invited to join but because they knew there was so much more to the world and to them. Diane waited for Jeff to ask her out to a movie. She dreamed about going to see *Dr. Zhivago* with him. And then, one night after they had talked about his membership in the chess club and an article she'd written for the school paper, he'd said apologetically, "I like you a lot, but you're too dark. I couldn't have you as a girlfriend."

Those words changed everything Diane had felt for Jeff. He had defined her with a lethal casualness that was a stake she felt pulsing inside her flesh even now. In the weeks that followed, her growing coldness toward Jeff baffled and angered him. His indifference to the impact of those words for Diane drew blood. Was he joking? Was he stating what was in his world a fact? How could she possibly call him a friend? Fantasize about holding his hand? In the world she was now a part of, Diane often looked around the restaurants and boardrooms for Jeff, having practiced in her imagination striding over to him and asking coldly, "Am I still too dark?"

But the fact that Gregory had approached her, a six-foot-tall, dark-skinned woman still flouting a big afro when all her girlfriends had cut theirs down to a "sensible" height or begun once again perming their hair, made this man suddenly interesting, although she was certain she was not his type—and he wasn't hers.

Gregory formally introduced himself, asked Diane her name, and told her that he was a cousin of the guest of honor who had just graduated from Howard's law school. The party was held in one of the rambling Victorian houses surrounding the Howard campus, houses full of "character" that rarely hid the disrepair. It was August and the tiny sweltering living room where she and Gregory stood was packed. The tie-dyed covered sofa for six held at least nine and the steps leading upstairs were home to bodies prone and hunched over in intense, seemingly conspiratorial conversations. The drinks of choice were sangria and malt liquor. The drug passed from hand to hand was marijuana.

"So now that we've established you've got nerves *and* balls, Gregory Tate, please tell me there's more to you than that."

His laughter broke open his face, washed over her, and was so loud and joyous those around them turned to look. Gregory reached for her hand, leading Diane into the den where in the blue-light tinged room, couples were slow dancing to Heatwave's "Always and Forever."

"Actually . . ." she began, looking him dead-on as he positioned his palm on her lower back and moved in close.

"Shh," he whispered, gently pushing her head onto his shoulder against the musky, warm material of his dashiki. Diane relaxed and found that she was made for his arms to hold her like this, the instinctive movements of their thighs, pelvis, and arms entwined, and the gentle drag of their footsteps across the floor, lulling and delightful. When the song ended, she released Gregory, bothered and charged, a quiver of mindless laughter whirling in her throat. After dancing, they moved to the front porch among a procession of partygoers leaving and arriving, other couples leaning on the banister, huddled on blankets on the grassy lawn. They sat in a corner, sipping sangria, surrounded by others but both feeling entirely and happily apart.

He was the son of a "Gold Coast" family, one of the black families that lived along Washington's Sixteenth Street, home to the president of Howard University, black members of the president's cabinet, and the city's black upper crust. Gregory had not used the term "Gold Coast," but in the southeast neighborhood of her childhood, Congress Heights, and even in Petworth where Diane had lived with Aunt Georgia, Sixteenth Street was often referred to as though it were an Alpine principality, a mythical land whose black population breathed a rarified air.

Diane grilled Gregory until he told her that his father was not just a doctor but the head of surgery at Howard University Hospital, once called Freedman's Hospital, where Ella had been a nurse. And he told her he was an architect. His mother, Margaret, taught social work at Howard University.

"I won't stereotype you if you don't stereotype me,"

Gregory said after they had traded personal histories, his with references to summers on Martha's Vineyard and graduation from Wilson High School, hers with stories of growing up in southeast and Petworth.

"All that, and you don't want me to stereotype you?"

"Actually, no, I don't. Can you do that?"

"I don't know," she told him, the statement quelling the reprise of an unruly desire. "Why architecture?"

"I loved math and art and that's what architecture is. I looked at empty lots and wondered how the space could be filled." Gregory leaned back in the plastic folding chair, his gray eyes aflame with remembrance and satisfaction. "One of the most thrilling moments of my life was a midnight tour of the ruins in Rome a couple of years ago. My dream trip? Egypt. Now *that* was architecture." He sighed, like an unabashed lover.

"Do you know," he continued, "there's not a single building downtown, in the city's power center, designed by a black architect? I'm going to change that. My heroes are men whose names too few people know: Paul Williams, John Brent, and Louis Bellinger, early black architects whose lives and work I've studied."

Gregory's ambition and confidence was bracing and seductive and Diane felt the need to match his gift for revelation with more of her story. He went into the house to refresh their drinks and when he came back to the porch she took her cup and haltingly began, "My parents divorced when I was young. Then my mother died. My brother and I went to live with my aunt." The lie came easily. She had told it so often a part of her believed it was true. Couldn't you consider it a kind of divorce, what her father had done? Rarely could she admit how much it mattered what people thought of her. Of her background. Of her family. Of her beginnings. Law, with its specialized jargon of offense, defense, boundaries, and arguments, had schooled her in the art of creating and controlling her narrative. The truth promised conflagration if she ever spoke its name.

"I'm sorry, but I know you're more than what you lost. Tell me more. Now I'll ask you, why the law?"

"It seemed to promise a way to set some things right. For me injustice isn't theoretical.

I went to law school and worked a year or two as a public defender, and now I'm with a firm specializing in family law."

"Will you promise to tell me one day why injustice isn't theoretical for you?"

"I'm black. I'm a woman."

"But there's a deeper reason, and I hope one day I earn the right to hear what it is."

Gregory drove her home from the party and on the way they stopped at Ben's Chili Bowl on U Street and ordered hot dogs laden with a soupy stew of cheese and a mountain of fries. They sat in a booth in the crowded diner and gorged on the food and each other. Gregory pointed across the street and told her that he had an office in that building, which his family owned, though the rest of U Street was ghostly and treacherous, still scarred from the riots sparked by Martin Luther King Jr.'s assassination a decade earlier. The streets had been dug up and in daylight resembled the aftermath of a bombing, all as part of the work on the city's first-ever subway system.

They talked about the end of white rule in Rhodesia and the prospect of majority rule. Diane was optimistic. Gregory, as he lathered his fries with ketchup, wondered if black despotism would replace white tyranny.

"In the end, Nkrumah became a dictator," he reminded her.

He thought America had lucked out with Jimmy Carter as president and didn't deserve him and predicted one term. They both confessed with whispers and laughter to watching the nighttime soap opera *Dallas.*

Parked outside her apartment on Newton Street, Gregory asked Diane for her phone number and she scribbled it on the back of one of his business cards. When she reached for the door he lifted her hand away and kissed her, long, hard, and convincingly.

Diane had dated fellow attorneys, an ex-client who she'd gotten out of a charge of embezzlement, and a lot of men who were separated, unavailable, or brought with them messy emotional baggage. She was skittish, felt supremely orphaned as she carried grief for her parents and brother in her bones, despite the resolute face she turned to the world.

Gregory Tate was dangerous. He had stirred in her an original and unfamiliar desire not just for him but for a new version of herself. And besides, she thought, as she slipped into her nightgown that night, she was probably too dark for his family. He was Sixteenth Street, she was southeast. Still unsettled by Gregory's kiss, and by the memory of how her hands had held his cheeks, wedding his lips more firmly to hers, Diane fumed.

He was so sure of himself. That confidence, she decided as she brushed her teeth, was vanity and arrogance. The ghosts of her mother and long-gone father would surely walk with her into any room she and Gregory entered and upset everything. By the time she slipped beneath the sheets and plumped her pillow, Diane had convinced herself that she hated Gregory Tate.

The first call came on Sunday afternoon, twelve hours later. Elusive, fitful sleep had confirmed Diane's desire to overturn the decision to give Gregory her phone number, and with it, entrée into her life. When he asked her, in a voice full of expectancy, if he could take her out on Saturday, she simply said no.

"No? Why not? We had a great time last night. I know we did. I wasn't faking and I know you weren't either."

"I've had time to think about it and I'd rather we didn't go any further."

"I'm not proposing; I'm asking you out on a date."

"I have a right to my feelings."

"All right, if that's what you want." And he hung up.

Implicit in Gregory's parting words was a promise that he would not call again. But he did. He forced her to lie, to tell him she was preparing for a trial, that she had to go out of town, and he trapped her in the lies saying, "So it's not really that you'd rather not go any further?"

"Just leave me alone," she told him the last and final time he called, and then broke down in tears as she sat looking at the inert phone.

———— ❧ ————

He had not called in two weeks. Now Diane wondered what she had done.

"Put that little girl, the one scared to be loved, in check, Diane," Paula Briscoe said, leaning forward forcefully across her desk. "She's not who you need to be listening to right now." As usual Paula was multitasking, lecturing Diane with a withering stare, then standing to search for a law book on the shelves behind her desk.

"Spare me the psychobabble."

"Spare me the bullshit," Paula said, turning to face Diane, book in hand. "You asked me what you should do and I told you. Give the brother a chance. Unless you don't think you're good enough for him, that is."

"I never said that and you know it."

"I know what you said, and I've seen what you do. You're all tied up in knots. That little girl whose mother was raped and died too young and whose father disappeared, she gets no vote on this. If I can still believe in love, you can, too."

"I told you that in confidence, Paula, I wish you wouldn't use it against me."

"I wish you wouldn't hide behind it." Paula's secretary, Louise, entered the office and told her a client had stopped by unannounced. Paula, a small, wiry woman with her hair brushed back in a bun, cast one last long stare at Diane before she followed Louise, pointing a finger at her. "Don't move, I won't be long."

It was times like this that Diane resented Paula. Paula had established her family law firm in a house in Logan Circle, one of the first female-headed firms specializing in cases of spousal abuse and incest. Diane had mentioned to a friend, who had mentioned to another friend, that she wanted to leave the public defender's office, and they had arranged for Diane to meet Paula.

Paula had grown up in West Virginia, married at seventeen, and endured a decade-long marriage of brutal abuse. She'd finally gotten the courage to leave the marriage and move to Richmond, Virginia, where she stayed with an uncle and attended Virginia Commonwealth University and law school at the University of Richmond. It was a brilliant and inspiring story, one that Paula often shared with women's and judicial groups.

Eventually, Paula won a three million dollar judgment against the D.C. government on behalf of a group of girls abused in a juvenile detention facility. She wrote articles, gave speeches, and worked with a national group of lawyers to create the language and laws turning spousal abuse from a "family matter" into a crime.

As Diane sat waiting for Paula to return, she thought how amazing it was that this woman, eight years older, had become her colleague, mentor, and friend. It was Paula who had finally made her a lawyer.

Working with Paula had helped her to fully embrace family law not as an occupation but as mission. What else could you call standing up for children who had been abused, neglected, or forgotten? She had wanted this. To make an end run around the misery. To staunch the slide into disaster at its source. Not to get a client off, but to secure a space where the courtroom would not become a second home.

It was demanding work, navigating the nexus of bureaucracies designed to salvage children in need and children in danger and to connect those children with foster care, mental health programs, good schools, counselors, and support for their parents. As guardian ad litem, Diane would represent some children's interests in the courts for years, along with handling divorce and custody disputes, bloodlettings as awful as some abuse cases.

Paula's entrance broke into Diane's thoughts about a ten-year-old she was representing in court in two hours and about how she had come to Paula to lay down the weight of the enormous desire and fear Gregory had inspired.

"Where were we?" she asked. "Oh, that's right. I remember. You forget, I was at that party, Diane. I saw the man. Witnessed the chemistry between you, heard snatches of your conversation with him. I saw your face. Don't make him pay for something he didn't do."

Several weeks passed. One day, as Diane got off the bus and watched it groan noisily down Fourteenth Street, she looked across the street and there he was, sitting on the steps outside her office. Crossing the street, she clutched her briefcase and marshaled a formidable stride that belied her emotions.

"What are you doing here?"

"You left me no choice. I couldn't forget you. If I have to stalk you I will. I don't usually jump through hoops, but you have brought me to my knees. I'm not ashamed to say it."

There was only longing and desire etched on his face. It was the same longing and desire raging inside her, the same longing and desire so different than any other she had felt.

What was she afraid of? Whatever it was, she stood before Gregory fully in its grasp.

"You aren't used to being rejected, are you? To someone telling you *no*. Not in that safe, secure world you come from. Because of what you look like, who your parents are, who you know."

Gregory's skin flushed, anger warming his face. "I own a business, so forgive me, but I hear *no* all the time," he shouted. "'No, your firm doesn't have enough experience. No, you don't know the right person in the mayor's office. No, we can't trust you with a project this big.' What are you talking about?" Gregory stood up and gazed at her in befuddlement and disgust. "You *are* stereotyping me, putting me in a box, when I swore I'd never do that to you. And you don't even give me a chance to make my case. What kind of lawyer are you?"

As she watched Gregory walk away, Diane corralled her fast-fading strength, reached in her bag for the keys to the door, and entered her office. This was where she belonged. This was where she was in charge. Her desk was stacked with folders, and she tossed her briefcase into her swivel chair and placed her hands on the desk. She suddenly felt sick. She thought of his laugh—that big, bright, bold laugh—and the feeling of his arms around her waist and suddenly bolted out the door, nearly twisting her ankle running down the front stairs. But he was gone.

The next day, Diane called information and asked for the phone number of Caldwell & Tate.

"I want to see you again. Really, I do. I'll understand if you say no, if you think I'm crazy. It may not seem like it, but I couldn't forget you either." This was what she said instead of hello when he picked up.

"Should I tape this conversation in case I need it in the future?" Gregory laughed.

"I'd like you to come over for dinner this weekend. More than anything I'd like to start over."

"Why should I come? Are you sure you don't plan to poison me?" She heard the jest in his voice and nearly wept with gratitude.

"I have to tell you something. It's about my mother and my father. The night we met I didn't really tell you the truth."

The story was actually a simple one, and as she told Gregory what little she knew, and how long it had taken her to know it, the waters parted between them.

"Sometimes I feel like I'm the scar left from all that," she said. "The evidence that remains."

"And the man was never found?"

"No. I've talked to some local cops about the case but its ancient history to them, a cold case no one's trying to solve."

"I don't know what you're thinking, but I'm not that man who hurt your mother and I'm not your father. I just want to get to know you."

Chapter Seven

1978–1979

When she stopped blockading her emotions, Diane fell in love easily. Love like this was an unknown quantity. She had long assumed she would be an amateur in an expedition like this but soon proved herself a hardy explorer. Gregory and everything about him seemed so expansive. The way he had pursued her. The way he walked into a room with an unsettling flair. The large-scale smile. The handshake that felt like a confidence and a caress. The voice, deep, rich. One that, Diane soon learned everyone told him, belonged to a radio DJ or a crooner of "baby-making music." When Gregory introduced her to his friends, his arm around her shoulders, Diane stood with him beneath their private spotlight.

Still, she wondered if Gregory saw the flash of surprise on the faces of some of his female friends when he introduced her. Despite her credentials—Spelman, which counted for a lot because it was a famed HBCU, and NYU, because it was a prestigious white university—Diane despaired of ever possessing the sense of entitlement that Gregory and his friends possessed. They were black like her but their parents and kin had prepared them for the leadership of the race and ownership of their private worlds. It was only in Gregory's embrace that she did not feel like a tourist.

Still, in time, Diane settled into loving Gregory as though she had finally crossed the finish line of a marathon. *Maybe,* she thought, *I can be happy.*

Happy like Gregory, beloved by his accomplished family, certain that he would blaze a trail as an architect or die trying, and blessed with a friendship with his partner that he had told Diane had enlarged and ennobled him.

Of his partner, Mercer Caldwell, Gregory told her, "He is my brother." And although Gregory told Diane that they shared responsibilities in the firm, he also told her that he felt Mercer was the stronger designer. Mercer was a small man, almost petite, with large, languid eyes. While Gregory was often dressed with a casual ease in tie-less shirts, worn but expensive jackets, and scuffed shoes, Mercer was fastidious, in a business suit each time Diane saw him. His moustache clipped and shaped to give depth to his long chin and sculpted face, Mercer could listen so closely it would seem as though he was deep in meditation.

One day, Diane stood in the shadow of the steel loins of a Caldwell & Tate project. The new municipal office building would stand at the crossroads of one of the city's busiest neighborhoods. The showcase building would house the new offices of the city council, and the mayor had decided that he wanted it to be located in the city's once vibrant black core, as a precursor of what he promised were good times to come. A tailor shop, shoe shop, diner, boutique, jazz club, record store, beauty parlor, and liquor store all occupied the street where this building would stand.

Gregory had told Diane that he and Mercer were chosen from a pool of over two dozen architects. "We don't have a crown yet, but so far this is the jewel in it," he'd said.

Watching Mercer and Gregory consulting with the project manager a few feet away as workers drove cranes that hoisted beams into the air, Diane now felt a swell of pride knowing that someone she knew, someone she loved, was responsible for all this.

Gregory had unfolded the blueprint for the building on the hood of his Volkswagen Beetle and explained how what she saw on that paper would become a building. But it was unclear and unfathomable to her. All she knew was that a building would soon stand on this corner and that a sign on the site read: A Project of the District of Columbia and Caldwell & Tate Architects.

Afterward, the three of them walked across the street to a soul food restaurant. Today Diane had come with an agenda. She had met Mercer before, but they had not talked much and she wanted to find a way for him to tell her who Gregory was. As an attorney, she spent a great deal of time listening to her clients for what their words, their silences, and their expressions told her about their cases; to judges, whose eccentricities and personalities dictated their decisions as much as the law. She knew how to listen, and today she wanted to find a moment when she could ask Mercer questions only he could answer about Gregory.

They were just about to settle into a booth in the back of the restaurant when Gregory bounded out to visit with a friend he spotted parking his car outside.

"How did you and Gregory meet?" Diane asked. "He told me his version, but I'm a lawyer so I know there are always multiple versions of the same story."

"Am I under oath?"

"If you want to be."

"I studied in the architecture program at Howard a couple of years before Gregory. I had graduated by the time he came in, but I met him at an AIA convention. He and I were damn near the only black faces in the place, and believe me, there were a couple of thousand architects there. Somehow Gregory and I latched on to two other brothers and one night, the four of us skipped the panels and sessions and went up to my hotel room and played poker and ordered room service. We were doing our own networking, not just connecting with the white boys. We were trying to find a way to make a different set of connections. I liked the way Gregory played poker. He played it brash, yet smart. I liked his hunger. Wasn't too many men I knew who talked about what they were gonna do like they had already done it.

"I had a little architectural company in Philly I was struggling to make work when I met Gregory. After we met at AIA, I packed up and drove to D.C., stayed with him a couple of weeks till I found my own place, and we set up shop. Caldwell & Tate. I liked that he didn't just want to design and build, but that he wanted to make a mark, wanted to play in the same sandlot as the big boys. I'd felt the same way for a long time, but I gotta tell you, I hadn't gotten to the place where I could say it as smooth as Gregory, say it and not give a damn if other Negroes thought I was 'smelling myself' or thought I was better than them.

"Some black architects feel like they got to stay in the community and improve it one building at a time. They act like if you focus on major projects in a city center you're turning your back on *the people*. But Gregory could see that if we could get our name on a major project in the high-rent district, that would reverberate back in the places where our people live. Gregory didn't see any Mason-Dixon Line in the city. Except to cross it. He's got that 'I belong here, wherever here is' air and potential white clients like that shit. He's a glad-hander. I come in, slide in really, to close the deal, sign off on everything. And *he's* the better designer."

"He told me you were the better designer."

"I guess that's the hallmark of a good partnership. All I know is his motto is, 'Get the job. Get the job. Get the job.' He's made it mine. If you can't get the job, you ain't got a damn thing. I saw my daddy work for other people all his life, and he told me to be my own boss. Gregory Tate helped me put words to what I was feeling. What I wanted."

Mercer leaned forward animatedly, a wry, battered smile flickering across his face. "We decided when we set up shop we weren't gonna be only Georgia Avenue architects. We plan to leave our mark on this whole city, and especially on the real estate downtown. There's easily a billion dollars' worth of boarded-up housing and property in this city right now. All the decay and filth you see downtown, it won't be like that for long, and we want to be positioned for the turnaround. After being locked out of the action for generations, now we're getting some of the major building work in this town."

Mercer settled back against the booth and eyed Diane closely. "You gave him a real run for the money, sister. At one point, he was talking about *me* coming over to your office to plead his case. Vouch for him with references and such." Mercer laughed.

"I had some issues that really had nothing to do with him."

"Sister, we all got issues."

"Tell me something, just between you and me, that I should know about him."

"He's hungry. Hungrier than me. Like that building we're

doing. That's a big deal. A big *fuckin'* deal for us. In four years this is our biggest contract. Normally it would have gone to a white firm, although our design was solid and our bid low, that's just the way it has been. But Gregory's got something to prove. He's the youngest son, chose a profession you got to study and intern for almost as long as to be a doctor and without the guarantee of a steady clientele. Medicine's the family business. He wants to prove he made the right choice."

"What's he told you about me?"

"Damn, you're shameless," Mercer said, reaching for his beer. "That you're a beautiful woman of substance. But you don't believe that do you?"

"Is it so obvious?"

"Only to someone really looking closely. But he's right, and you've got the brother, long as he's what you want. And if he don't treat you right, my foot goes up his ass."

"Whose foot goes up whose ass?" Gregory asked as he rejoined them.

"I was just telling Diane here that I got her back."

"She'll be well taken care of."

"I just told her I'm gonna see to that."

———— ⬥ ————

"My goodness, young lady, you are quite . . . *tall*," Margaret Tate observed when she met Diane. Tall, that was the word, innocuous and harmless. But Margaret Tate, a slender woman with an olive complexion and dressed that day in tailored slacks and a white silk blouse, looked at Diane with a pinched smile that merely enhanced the disdain Diane was certain she saw settled in her eyes. She had said "tall," yet "orphaned, damaged, dark," was what Diane heard.

"Mother, this is Diane, the woman who has stolen my heart," Gregory said after Margaret had opened the front door and hugged Gregory as though she had not seen him in years (he'd told Diane he visited his mother and father every Sunday). Margaret then turned regretfully away from her son to look at Diane, who felt herself *looming* in the vestibule, waiting her turn, for what she was not sure. After the comment about her height, Margaret consumed every aspect of Diane with a practiced, glacial glance. In a few seconds, Margaret's eyes studied Diane's natural hair, her large hoop earrings, and her face, then receded.

The living room resembled a stage set, open and sunny with a profusion of plants and fresh-cut flowers in the windowsills and on settee tables. The sofas and chairs were overstuffed, startlingly white with deep brown cloths draping the cushions for contrast. The room felt open and closed at the same time as Diane sat in one of those white chairs and watched Gregory sit beside his mother on the sofa. Gregory had told Diane that Margaret and Ramsey Tate had hosted fund-raisers for Walter E. Washington, the city's first presidentially appointed black mayor, and for Marion Barry, the first elected mayor. *Probably in this room*, Diane thought, hearing in her mind glasses tinkling and the buzz of animated conversation.

"Help yourself," Margaret told Diane, pointing to the coffee table burdened with a full silver tea set, crystal teacups, and an array of small sandwiches cut in triangles.

"Thank you," Diane whispered, reaching for a teacup as Margaret filled it, suddenly uncomfortably aware of how tall she was.

"Where's Dad?" Gregory asked.

"Napping on the sun porch. Go wake him. He's been sleeping since noon, and he should come and meet your friend."

Watching Diane sip her tea, Margaret placed her hands on

her thighs, leaned forward slightly, and said, "Gregory tells me you're a lawyer." Diane now noticed the layer of pancake makeup and the rouge flowering on Margaret's cheeks.

"Yes, yes," she stuttered.

"And you're from Washington originally?"

"Yes, southeast, Congress Heights."

"And your parents?"

"My mother was a nurse at Howard Hospital back in the days when it was Freedman's."

"Was?"

"She died when I was a child."

"I'm sorry. I know that must have been difficult for you. My husband was once head of surgery there. I wonder if he knew your mother."

To that suggestion Diane said nothing, she merely reached for a sandwich for which she had no appetite. She imagined if her mother had known Ramsey Tate, if he might have been one of the many "uncles" she brought home. The thought made her place both the sandwich and the cup of tea on the coffee table in order to steady her nerves.

"And your father?"

"He and my mother divorced when I was very young and I never got to know him."

"You poor dear," Margaret said, her face creased with what seemed to be genuine concern. "That makes all that you've achieved that much more significant, considering where you came from. Come here sit beside me," she offered expansively, scooting over on the sofa to make room for Diane, who sat reeling from the sting of Margaret's condescending conclusion. She could hear Gregory talking to his father, and she wished she could telekinetically transport the two men into the living room.

Margaret coaxed out of Diane the story of her journey to

Spelman and law school. Sipping her tea, Margaret nodded in approval.

"Come, come closer," Margaret urged her as she reached for a photo album on the side table. "I want to show you some pictures."

The leather-bound album was a cavalcade of the history of Margaret and Ramsey Tate's families: An ebony-hued dark-skinned drummer boy who looked no more than twelve or thirteen, dressed in a Union army uniform and white gloves. One of Margaret's aunts wearing a high-necked dress of brocade and lace. She was president of the local chapter of the National Negro Women's Club organization. A photo of Ramsey Tate examining a little girl in a clinic in Greenwood, Mississippi. Margaret and Ramsey on the beach at Martha's Vineyard.

"Family is so important, and we're very proud of ours," Margaret said gently closing the album. "There are other pictures in that album I didn't show you. Pictures of my uncle who was lynched in Memphis because he owned some land and a grocery store and refused the money a white man offered him to buy it, pennies on the dollar for what the store and the land was worth."

The bitterness in Margaret's voice as she revealed this chipped away at the glazed veneer of welcome Diane had felt rising between them. If this was what sufficed for warmth, Diane decided, she would take it. Without warning, she found herself admiring this titanically self-possessed woman.

"So you're a lawyer. That's a good start. Where do you want to ultimately land?

"Land?"

"Yes, what have you set your sights on? A judgeship?"

Diane was satisfied with where she was but felt to say that to Margaret Tate would reveal an unforgivable defect. "Well, I have time."

"Do you? Are you sure?" Margaret shook her head in dismay. "That's the thing about *whites*. They never sleep, they're never satisfied."

"Mother, are you harassing my girlfriend?" Gregory asked as he wheeled his father into the room.

"No, it's just that I'm so impressed with her I could talk to her all day."

———— ∞ ————

Over the weeks and months that followed Diane's visit to Gregory's parents, she and Margaret built a kind of détente. One question from Diane and Margaret would launch into interlaced memories of her role as coordinator for a fund-raiser at their church for the work of Dr. Martin Luther King Jr. and the Southern Christian Leadership Council, her doctoral research on the political impact of black sororities, or the challenges and frustrations of chairing the department of sociology at Howard. Diane felt somehow anointed when, as the two women cooked dinner together for the regular Tate gatherings, Margaret would say as a way of learning about Diane's work, "I read about the most awful case in the *Post* this week. Are you working on that?"

Over the required second-Sunday dinners that brought Gregory's brothers, Bruce and David, to the house—Bruce with his wife and son, David with a procession of attractive girl-friends—Diane was slowly inducted into the Tate clan.

Ramsey Tate, at seventy-five, was twenty years older than Margaret. The vigorous, influential head of surgery at his hospital had, to everyone's surprise, begun showing signs of dementia several years earlier that eventually forced him to resign. Two years later, he suffered a stroke that left him, despite rehabilitation, wheelchair-bound with only partial speech.

Over those Sunday dinners, Gregory's father sat amongst his family, despite the twin challenges of dementia and the stroke, his eyes glazed with brightness, holding up his left hand when he wanted to speak, his voice hoarse and cracked and nearly unintelligible but still stubbornly vibrant as he weighed in on family gossip and discussions of politics. Diane watched as his wife and sons listened with patience and what seemed like gratitude to his halting, treasured words. She watched Gregory help Margaret place Ramsey in the lift chair that took him upstairs. She saw Margaret read him articles from *Ebony* and *Jet,* whole chapters from murder mysteries.

This was what families did, Diane thought. They cared for one another, loved even more fiercely the weakest among them.

Diane helped Gregory care for his father, laying out clothing for him as Gregory helped him bathe, sitting on the sun porch beside him when Gregory helped Margaret with errands, touched to the core when Ramsey Tate squeezed her hand and struggled to mouth and utter the word, "Daughter."

By Christmas, she and Gregory had begun talking about marriage as the assumed next step. Marriage would give her a whole new history; no one except Gregory need ever know how loss and abandonment had stained her. She had not been raised to walk the tightrope stretched across the terrain of Gregory's world and she shivered at the thought, wondered if she would fit in with grace and comfort. Her past told her she did not belong here but her heart told her she had come home.

———⚬⚬⚬———

They married a year to the day after the August night they met and Diane became a Tate, a member of a world that from afar had seemed ceremonial and self-absorbed. Dinners and dances, fund-raisers, galas, and more. In the summer, they'd spend two weeks in Oak Bluffs, a village on Martha's Vineyard. There was the beach and the round of parties, the salons hosted by the island's most celebrated black lawyer, doctor, or banker, or the next presumed black winner of the Pulitzer Prize.

She felt like an imposter. On guard for any words or deeds that confirmed her belief that she was an interloper in this world. Vigilant for slights, hiding behind disdain to prevent any unexpected strike against her or the ghost of her parents who stood invisibly by her side.

One night in the ladies' room of the Hilton Hotel, where Margaret was being honored by her sorority, Diane had taken refuge from her table of twelve. Suddenly, Margaret opened the door and strode over to her daughter-in-law. Margaret's gray floor-length gown hugged her curves and revealed a swath of her neckline and chest. A pearl choker clung to her neck and the matching earrings shone like surprised, tiny eyes. Neither woman spoke as they drifted over to the mirror.

"You're so sure we think we're better than you, but you've already decided you're better than us."

Before Diane could respond, Margaret forged ahead. "My son married you for a reason. He loves you. I'm glad he did. We have welcomed you into our family. But I feel your resistance to truly accepting us. Out there you see the final product. You don't see how all that was made. The grandmothers who were domestics and saved to put somebody through Howard or Fisk. The fathers who were Pullman porters and on-call, all the time, but who grinned and bore it. And yes, we like to think we've made it. Because we have. But we know we're black, and we hit the glass ceiling every day. My son loves you. We all want to love you. Let us. Get over it."

Diane stood, strangely relieved by Margaret's injured

soliloquy. It had slashed the skin of the barricade she had erected, that separated her from the world she had married into. That wall she knew, held off a famished longing and desire.

She wanted to ask but could not, "What part, Margaret? What part do I get over first? The father I didn't really know or the mother who was raped?" The whirlwind of Margaret's words had left her with a throat parched and aching and her eyes wet with stifled tears.

She wanted to tell her mother-in-law, "It's less about who you all are than who I'm afraid I'll always be." Orphaned and alone, no matter the depth of Gregory's love. That is what she tried to will herself to say. The words she mustered instead were plaintive, a stripped-down plea: "Just give me some time Margaret. Just give me some time."

Diane had brought it all into the marriage with her like some rancid dowry—her mother, her father, the grief sown into her fingerprints and her cells, and the fear that she would never be at ease in Gregory's world. That she could never make his world hers. Clumsily, callously, Margaret had called her out. How long, Diane wondered, had Margaret been preparing that speech, waiting for what she deemed to be the opportune moment? Was her discomfort tonight so obvious? Why had Gregory said nothing? *How could he have said anything?* It had to be Margaret; she was the only one who could have said those words. Perhaps, the only one in the family who had the right.

Margaret's palm touched Diane's cheek. "I didn't want to offend you, but I had to say something."

Flushed with a brokenness that was unexpectedly healing, Diane said, "Let's go back to the ballroom. There's an extraordinary woman who's about to be honored."

Diane and Margaret settled back at their table with Gregory, Ramsey, Bruce, David, and several of Margaret's sorority sisters. When the program began again, Margaret was introduced and walked to the stage to accept her award for her work mentoring younger members of the sorority and for heading the organization's community outreach programs. Margaret spoke of joining the sorority while an undergraduate at Howard.

"All the things that have come to matter most to me happened to me on that campus," Margaret said, clutching the crystal statuette. "I met my husband who gave me love and a family. And I joined this organization and found a sisterhood that ensures I will never, ever be alone."

Margaret gracefully wound her way back to her table through the ballroom full of women and men who had stood to give her an ovation, accepting the hugs and handshakes with a practiced generosity. When she reached her table, Diane was the first to stand, the first to reach out for her, the first to offer an embrace.

———— ❧ ————

Three days later, Ramsey Tate had a heart attack while napping one afternoon and died in his sleep.

Diane joined Gregory and his brothers in handling the multitude of preparations for the memorial and funeral. Planning for the kind of "home-going" befitting the life of Ramsey Tate allowed them to sideline the act of grieving. The memorial service took place at the Tate family church, Metropolitan AME, and was standing room only as fellow doctors, former medical students, patients, friends, and the scores of people who knew Ramsey Tate from his work with professional, civic, and political groups honored his memory.

That night, after she and Gregory returned to their home, to the house that Ramsey had made the down payment on, after a long day that had begun with the memorial, then was followed by the internment at Lincoln Cemetery, and a repast at Margaret's house that lasted until nearly eight p.m., they went to their bedroom and wordlessly undressed. Beneath the sheets, they held on to each other, silenced by the arrival of the mourning that had been stalled and by the presence of death that had entered the house with them.

"How was it for you when your mother died?" Gregory asked, releasing Diane and turning on his side to face her.

"I was so young. It somehow wasn't real to me. My aunt and uncle took my brother and me in and they felt the best thing was to go on. To not say much about what had happened. There was no one really that I could talk to about whatever I was feeling. I recall feeling disconnected from what I knew would be emotions like nothing I had ever felt before. So I tried to erect a wall between those feelings and the rest of me. I got pretty good at that."

"Well, this is real. And I feel it. The grief but not the sadness. My father was such a presence in my life, in all our lives. During Freedom Summer in 1964, he took me and Bruce and David to Mississippi with him to provide medical treatment for sharecroppers. He let me watch him perform an operation one time. He told me that he wished I'd become a doctor but that he envied the adventure I'd have as an architect."

"I wish I'd known him before. So we could have talked. Really talked."

"Y'know, in his spare time before he got really sick, he wrote poetry. He was no Langston Hughes, but reading it gave me another way to know who he was."

Her husband had lost his father and because of who his father had been, what his father had evoked and inspired in them all, Diane knew this moment would open and seal them, bound and bond them.

She kissed Gregory and told him, "Maybe this is the best moment, the only moment to tell you this. I'm going to have a baby."

"Thank you, thank you," Gregory said, holding Diane close, kissing her face, cheeks, lips in an unabashed display of pleasure. "He would've been so happy."

"We'll tell our child all about their grandfather."

"Who knows, maybe he'll meet your mother in heaven."

Diane laughed at the thought, so generous, brimming with a sincere innocence that made her want to love Gregory forever.

Chapter Eight

1980

Now that she was pregnant, Diane hungered for her paternal family. She was ready and willing to try to find her father. The day Georgia told her that Ella was raped, she had pressed into Diane's hand a phone number of another aunt, her father's sister.

Over the years, Diane had stapled that slip of paper to a page in her diary, under lock and key, and placed it in a music box given to her by a lover on Valentine's Day. She then put it in a safety deposit box in a bank downtown.

Her joy at being pregnant was clouded by thoughts of all the questions she would not be able to answer for her unborn child. Questions that revealed the emptiness of the family inheritance she had to offer. There was all that she did not know. And there was what she did: in the years that had passed since her father left, he had not reached back for her, and the aunts, uncles, even the grandmother and grandfather that she was owed had been rendered nonexistent.

The child she carried needed answers, perhaps even more than she did. Yet the knowledge that seemingly no one from her father's side cared to know her, search for her, was a blatant injury. Invisible to whoever remained of the Garrisons, Diane strained to be seen by the world. She owed this child answers, even if the search for answers only led to more questions. Friends had told her that having children filled you with focus and direction. Her baby wasn't even born yet, but it had already made her think that she could stand up for herself as she had stood for others.

Nearly all those she had represented as a public defender and in her family law practice had been erased by someone. Guilty or innocent, abused or neglected, her job was to give them a voice, to remove the cataracts of prejudice and indifference from the eyes of judges and juries. No one had fought for her, so she fought for those who had been disarmed.

And so one evening, she decided to tell Gregory all of this, slipping into a chair beside him in his office at home, where he sat making initial sketches for a home for senior citizens to be built in Rockville, Maryland. He finished a few marks, and when he looked up at Diane, what he saw on her face made him put down his pencil. "What's wrong?" he asked.

"I want to try to track down my father."

"Are you sure?"

"Why wouldn't I be sure? All these years, I've allowed myself the luxury and the lie of believing it didn't matter. That I could go on not knowing at least something about him, where he went, who he is. But with the baby coming, I feel like it's now or never."

"He and his family never reached out to you. I just don't want you to get hurt."

"Gregory, how could I get more hurt than I already am?"

"I'm afraid to answer that question."

"You've got family to give our baby. I only have my Aunt Georgia and Uncle Ray. How will I explain that?"

"Our baby won't need explanations, excuses, or apologies for things you couldn't control."

"But I can't be a mother to our child until I at least try."

The next day on her way to court, Diane stopped by her bank and retrieved the slip of paper from her safety deposit box. Later that afternoon, she returned to her office, closed her door, and made the call. Her aunt's name was Marcia. Was her aunt still alive? Was this still her phone number? What would she do if the number had been disconnected? If no one answered, would she call back? The onslaught of questions gave her a momentary reprieve. Then Diane felt the movement of the baby in her abdomen, a slight, gentle roll, a shift that brought the child closer to her heart. She picked up the receiver and dialed the number.

"Hello?"

The voice was hoarse and resonant with age. She knew this was her aunt Marcia. And Diane, who had not thought of her father in a specific, concrete way, who had only imagined him as a figure fleeing her mother, her brother, and her, realized that her father would now be a man in his late fifties or sixties. He might be sick. He might be dead.

"Hello?" the voice asked again.

"Hello, my name is Diane. My father is Samuel Garrison, and I'd like to speak to my aunt Marcia."

"You Sammy's girl?"

"Yes. Yes, ma'am."

"Lord have mercy, I was hoping this day would come. My brother run away. Left town like *he* was the criminal. Like he was the one who done wrong. And then he did."

"Yes, ma'am. I know it's been a long time but I'm trying to find him."

"He ain't never tried to find you, did he?"

"I don't know."

"I get a call or a card from him every couple of years. If you looking for him all I can do is give you the last address and phone number."

"I would like that. Could we meet somewhere? I'd like to meet you, connect with you."

"I ain't seen you since you was three or four years old."

"Where do you live? Could I come to your house?"

"Naw, honey, you don't wanta do that. I live in Sursum Corda."

Just the name conjured images of drive-by shootings and open-air drug markets. On its streets, children were regularly killed in the crossfire of bullets aimed to settle scores, to exact revenge. During her time as a public defender, Diane had several clients who had lived in the complex which sprawled over several blocks, resembling a barracks or a prison. The place had its own police station.

Instead, she met Marcia in Chinatown. After arriving fifteen minutes early, Diane was so nervous she vomited in the restaurant bathroom. She sat sipping a tiny cup of jasmine tea when Marcia came through the door. It was a blustery day and Marcia told Diane she'd be wearing a red leather jacket. The ferocious winds that whipped along the streets propelled Marcia through the door. Diane saw her aunt, a small, shriveled woman the color of nutmeg, look around the room and finally meet her gaze.

Her wide smile erased years from her face as she closed in on Diane, who stood and leaned forward and hugged the woman. She was tiny, her face was ruined, the only question was: *Had it been crack or heroin?* Addiction and ill-health had ruptured her skin, pockmarking it with scars and leaving her brown eyes overcast with a milky film so thick that Diane wondered how well she could see.

Marcia removed her jacket and revealed a linty black turtleneck sweater, the sleeves of which she pushed up her arms. She folded her bony fingers and settled her hands on the table.

"You turned out beautiful, just like your mama."

"Thank you. I'm glad you came. My mother's sister said my father had other siblings, too."

"Your two uncles are twin brothers. One's in jail, the other got an auto repair shop in Oxon Hill, Maryland," she said matter-of-factly. "You look like you made something of yourself. In fact more than something."

"Well, I guess I did. I'm a lawyer. I have a family law practice."

"Family law, huh? I guess that makes sense, all you been through." Marcia smiled again, momentarily lifting the mask of age and decay. "Your daddy would be proud."

The waitress came, and they both studied the menus, holding them before their faces as though seeking respite from each other.

When the waitress left with their orders, Marcia asked, "How far along are you?"

"Four months."

"You married?"

Diane held up her ring finger.

Marcia smiled, bigger this time, revealing three missing teeth. "Is he a good man?" she asked.

"He is a good man. Tell me about my father."

"What do you want to know?"

"Anything. Everything. Now that I'm pregnant, family, whatever I have left, means more to me than ever."

"That's a tall order," Marcia said, rummaging through her pocketbook and pulling out a battered cigarette that she began to twirl in her fingers. "I'm still trying to kick the habit. When I get nervous, if I can't smoke one, it helps anyway to just hold one."

The waitress brought their small bowls of wonton soup and both women retreated from the moment by lifting their spoons.

Marcia had dropped her cigarette onto the table and after her third spoonful of soup, placed the spoon on her napkin and said, "Even when he was a child, Sammy acted like he'd been born into the wrong family. We lived over in Barry Farms. Back in those days, in the thirties and forties, it was a nice place. People had whole families. Daddies were around. People had jobs. Wasn't always much, but it was honest work. You could even leave your door open at night. Mama cleaned government office buildings. Back then, even the black college girls did domestic work, cleaned offices to get extra money. That was the easiest work for a black woman to get then. Sometimes the only work she could get. Our daddy was a junk dealer. I bet you don't even know what that is."

Marcia laughed, no doubt pleased by the thought that she knew something Diane most likely did not. "He'd collect old stuff people had thrown out, fix it up, repair it, or polish it so it looked like new and then ride around different neighborhoods selling it off a truck. Our mother couldn't read, and our daddy sold junk, and that shamed Sammy. Don't look surprised. Back in those days it wasn't so unusual to find black folk who maybe could add and subtract a little bit, but who couldn't even read a book their second grader brought home from school. The rest of us, me, Tyrone, and Tyler, we were satisfied with the life we lived, and thought in some ways we were lucky."

Marcia paused and indifferently placed her spoon in the bowl of soup, stirring the liquid and gazing into the bowl as though inside she saw the story she was telling beginning to unfold. "Sammy was always reading something—the black newspapers, old books, and magazines that Daddy brought home. He'd ask Daddy why he sold junk. Ask Mama why she couldn't read. And it was like he asked the question just so he could look at 'em with a cold look in his eyes. Daddy told him that junk put food in his belly. But Mama, something in her just shrank up whenever Sammy asked her why she couldn't read."

Marcia leaned back in the booth and looked at Diane unflinchingly and said, "He thought he was smarter than everybody in the family and because he thought he was smarter he thought he was better. He left us a long time before he left us. Mama and Daddy used to say they just wanted to live long enough to see us graduate from high school. Well Sammy didn't even tell nobody and he got hisself accepted into a small Negro college in North Carolina. He left and never really looked back." Curling her lips in distaste, Marcia said, "He'd write now and then. We had relatives in the town where the school was but they never saw him either. He'd come home for Christmas talking about his classes. I wanted to see my brother, but it was like a professor had come home instead. In his senior year, Sammy got a girl who went to the school pregnant, told her he was gonna marry her, and then just left."

"So he was always an outsider?"

"I guess that's one way to put it. You asked me, you want me to go on?"

Before Diane could answer, their orders came: Diane's stir-fried vegetables and Marcia's General Tso's chicken.

Diving into the food, Marcia said between mouthfuls, "He come back to Washington and worked over the post office. He had a college degree, but so did half the black men working with him. I heard some of 'em even had PhDs. That was in the days when the joke was, 'What did you call a Negro with a PhD?' And the answer was 'Nigger.' I'd run into him sometimes on the street and he would just complain about the black folks he worked with.

"Daddy died and then Mama died right after him, I think mostly 'cause she missed him. Sammy came to visit us whenever there was an emergency, mostly so he could make the rest of us feel like we were too stupid to know what to do. I was married to my first husband when Sammy brought Ella around and showed her off. He did all the talking, but all you had to do was look at her and you could see she'd fallen hard for Sammy. I ain't never had too much good to say 'bout my brother but I will say I'm sure he loved your mother. They'd been married about four years when it happened. Sammy called me middle of the night and said a man had broken into the apartment, tied him up, and made him watch him rape Ella and stole a bunch of their stuff."

With each new revelation, Diane lost more of her appetite. Now, she gave up any attempt to eat.

"You don't want that? Well, let me take it home," Marcia said.

"Sure."

"I went by to see them that night. The police had gone by the time I got there. If you looked at them, and looked in their eyes, it was like they had both been raped. All his life Sammy had wanted to be big, had wanted to be in control. That man busted in his apartment and *he* took control. Then Sammy got so he was over my house all the time. He'd sit on my sofa and just start crying. I saw a brother I'd never seen before. I wondered about your mama and told him he needed to go home and cry with his wife or at least let her cry on his shoulder and then he could cry on hers and they would be okay. He'd tell me he couldn't go home. He felt like he couldn't live in that apartment no more.

"About a year after it happened, I heard he and your mama had separated. Then he was gone. It was all too much for me. I lost a brother and that poor woman had been destroyed. When I heard about her getting run over, I swear to God I didn't know what to do. I felt too ashamed to come to the funeral. That man raped her, but then I think what Sammy did killed her long before them boys driving that car."

"Where is he now?"

"He comes to D.C. now and then, but he lives out in Las Vegas. Married some woman from Argentina."

"Does he ever ask about me?"

"Honey, I wish I could say he did. Back when your aunt called and told me Ronald died, I let him know about that. I was sure that he'd call you then. No, honey, in all these years he ain't never asked about you or your brother."

Diane left the meeting with Marcia making a promise to stay in touch, a promise that she knew she would not keep. Outside, the wind was still strong as the two women parted.

"You didn't ask me for his phone number and address but I wrote it down for you," Marcia said hesitantly, offering a slip of paper. Diane looked at the paper, still reeling from the story her aunt had shared. As the wind whipped up bitter gusts and pedestrians bustled against them, the two women stood as though frozen. When Marcia had entered the restaurant two hours earlier, Diane had not imagined the power she possessed. Now, Marcia reached for Diane's hand, pressed the slip of paper into her trembling palm, and closed Diane's fingers around it. Then Marcia lifted the collar of her red leather jacket, turned away, and walked toward the corner.

Diane hailed a taxi. During the ride home she settled in the backseat and instinctively rubbed her abdomen. "I did this for you," she whispered and then wondered, *But what have I done?*

Samuel Garrison came back to D.C. over the years but he had never asked about his son or daughter. She rolled down the window. The wind remained as furious as it had been all afternoon. She longed for its bruising touch on her skin, longed for it to lift what she now knew on its wings and take it unto heaven. They would have been so easy to find. She hadn't known where he was. Told herself that she didn't want to know.

Gone had become a destination, an actual place with dimensions. Over the years in her imagination, Samuel Garrison lived in New York, in Canada, or Chicago, and always there was some insurmountable obstacle that kept him away from them. Now the truth sealed her off from forgiveness. If she undertook the task of forgiving, her father would have to stand in a long line.

Gregory came home that evening and found Diane in the nursery, placing baby blankets and clothing in the four-drawer mahogany chest they had found at an estate sale in Arlington. They had compromised on the color of the room, settling on pale blue walls dotted with pink clouds on the ceiling and the wall where the crib sat, overflowing with gifts from the baby shower Paula had hosted a week ago.

"I'm sorry I went to see her. There's such a thing as knowing too much," Diane said, closing the drawer.

"What did she tell you?"

"That he always thought he was better than the rest of his family. That he walked out on a girl he got pregnant. And that in all these years, he's come back to Washington and he never even tried to find us."

Diane sank into a cushioned chair beside the crib. She closed her eyes and took a deep breath.

"Are you okay?"

She took a slip of paper out of her jacket pocket and held it up as though offering it to Gregory. "She gave me his address and phone number."

"Isn't that what you wanted?"

"Not after what she told me."

Diane crumpled the paper, and Gregory bent on his knees before her, pried open her fist, and snatched it out of her palm.

"I won't let you do that," he said, rising from the floor, his voice final as he slid the paper into his pants pocket. "You wanted to talk to your aunt and you wanted her to give you a perfect father. A father you knew you didn't have. We just buried my dad last year and I'm not going to let you cut yourself off from yours."

Her face was hidden behind her palms, and when her hands slid slowly down her cheeks Gregory saw the tears. "I hate him."

"Of course you do. And you love him."

"I never want to see him."

Gregory pulled a hassock before Diane, sat down, and clasped her fingers. "I'm disappointed in you."

"In me?" She sobbed, befuddled, and sniffled, her face now a glistening mask.

"Yes, you're bigger than that. Bigger than him. At least hear his side."

"He never asked about us. He never tried to find us. I wanted to give our child a grandfather, not a monster."

"There had to have been a reason. A reason for what he did. A reason for what he didn't do."

"How can you take the side of a man you don't know?"

"Because I don't know him. And neither do you. This isn't over and for now that paper belongs to me."

"He's a coward who turned his back on one family after another. Why would I want to reach out to him?"

"You don't get to choose your parents."

"Sometimes, Gregory, sometimes, maybe you do."

Chapter Nine

2011

The past is never dead. It's not even past. Gregory didn't remember who had said that. He'd tried to, but he didn't, or couldn't. And he was sick of searching the Internet for all the things he used to know. If the past is never dead and not even past, then their three decades together would outsmart the forces aligned against him. Against them. Massive, mercurial, but precise, the thing that had upturned his life wouldn't win. But it still felt like it had crossed the finish line, like it was already smiling, holding the trophy aloft.

He and Diane had been together all these years. Together through his battle with cancer. Together through the diabetes he now had. A warm-up? A trial run for this? *Together.* Not until Diane had he known the real meaning of the word. Marriage wasn't a contract. It was a bond of caring. Caring. Another word she had made him know, deep, inside and out. All those words that had joined them, made them: Wife. Husband. Ally. Friend. He was afraid one day he would forget them, too. They weren't afraid to talk about anything. But this? She, the litigator, the judge. He the designer, the builder. He hadn't figured out how to draw a blueprint for this. He still remembered reading his father's poetry, about broken bodies he struggled to heal, about life and death, and what those he saved and those he could not bequeathed him. Those poems had given his father something, added dimension to what appeared to be a full-to-the-brim life. Now *he* was using words, writing to himself what he did not want anyone else to hear or know.

FEBRUARY 10, 2011

I keep getting lost when I'm driving. Forgetting where I'm going. Arriving somewhere and not knowing where I am. So far, I've managed to keep it from Diane, from Mercer. But these days I'm always running late. Running behind. Running to catch up to where I'm supposed to be. I don't know what is happening to me. I should want to know. I do want to know. But if I find out I am afraid of the cost I will pay for that knowledge. Losing my company. Everything I've worked to build. Shattered.

MARCH 3, 2011

I don't feel the earth is assured anymore beneath my feet. This must've been how my father felt. I cared for him. I pitied him. I loved him. But I never asked how he felt, how it felt.

APRIL 16, 2011

I have two jobs now. The second being the work of masking this thing. Extending my business card to people I think I know but don't recognize. I'll offhandedly extend my card saying with as much casualness as I can muster, "Give me all your information; I think I lost it." If I'm lucky, they have a business card. If I'm not, I'll say, as I extend the back of my card, "Oh and write down everything, to make sure I spell your name correctly."

JUNE 20, 2011

There are two of me. Which one is real? I'll go days where I'm fine. Living the way I used to, not thinking about my thoughts, not wondering if around the corner of the next moment, I'll run into myself as a sham and a fake. Days when I'm fine. But the memory loss always come back. It comes back to take a little more than last time.

JULY, 2, 2011

Writing about it makes it better. Writing to whomever I am writing to, suddenly, I am not alone. But the writing makes it real.

———— ⊙◦⊙ ————

So this is how it begins, Gregory thought. Forgetting over and over. All day long. Forgetting and then remembering, and because you suddenly remembered, convincing yourself that the forgetting was a lapse, a series of lapses, not your soon-to-be-permanent mental state.

He and Mercer were reviewing plans for a retail and condominium complex, sitting elbow to elbow at Gregory's cluttered desk. He sat listening to Mercer talking about the cost overruns and constant calls from the owners, staring at the squares on the whiteprint, the lines, the boxes, the squares that he knew, yes, he knew were rooms, doors, light fixtures, stairs, skylights, windows, floors. He knew that even though there were moments, sitting beside his partner, when he had no idea what he was looking at, what the lines meant. This in and out, this feeling of being insubstantial, a breathing question mark, had his armpits drenched in sweat.

"When we go to the meeting, you talk about the changes in the design. I'll cover the new costs, okay?" Mercer asked, looking at him.

"Where is the meeting again?"

"What'd you mean? Where we always meet, in their offices."

"I've been swamped with emails, distracted. Where is it again?" He asked this with a nonchalance he was certain Mercer heard as utterly false.

"Mount Vernon Square," Mercer snapped, his brows clenched in concern. "Across the street from First Congregational Church. Don't tell me you need the address. Damn, Gregory, we've been going there once a week for the last six months."

"Gimme a break, I've got a lot on my mind."

"Well, clear some of that shit out of your brain, so you can think. And remember the meeting's at four p.m. I'll meet you there."

When Mercer left his office, Gregory pulled out his cell phone and searched for First Congregational Church on the phone's GPS. The map of the city popped up, and he could suddenly read and understand these lines. He saw Mount Vernon Square on the screen. Then he searched the pile of what looked like rubble on his desk and somehow found amid it a card with the address of the company. Finding the address stalled his fear. He now knew the name of the company. He knew the address. But as he recalled the landscape of the city, when he said out loud, "Mount Vernon Square," when he whispered, "Mount Vernon Square," there was nothing. His mind was hollow and bereft. Empty.

Gregory fingered the blueprint, a design done on crisp white paper, the kind he had been looking at all his life. His office wall cases were stacked with rows and rows of the paper, rolls and rolls of it, overflowing. All those lines and squares on the paper were now buildings where people worked, played, and lived. Those lines were the bread and butter of Caldwell & Tate, but there were days when the lines meant nothing.

How would he get through the meeting this afternoon?

He could still access his passion for talking about design, master all the jargon when needed, the language of his calling. He'd get through it, he'd muddle through. He hadn't blown a meeting yet. But the forgetting, the dislocation that plagued him, promised, he was sure, an awful day of reckoning. On that day, he would lose himself. On that day he would lose his thoughts. Would he lose Caldwell & Tate a contract?

Through the glass door to his office, Gregory watched Mercer heading toward the elevator. He saw the young designers they had hired in the last year—Martin Kim, Darren Jackson, Josh Watson—lounging in the kitchen over coffee. This was his company, his and Mercer's. *Mine to lose*, he thought, as he stealthily reached into a bottom drawer for a flask full of bourbon. With his head below his desk, he took a swig. The taste, so familiar, steeled him, erased the edge off of his terror. He returned the flask to the drawer and opened a pack of gum, cramming two sticks into his mouth.

Gregory leaned back in his high-back swivel office chair and closed his eyes. He hadn't designed anything in two years. After more than three decades together, he and Mercer now devoted their time to bringing in contracts and managing them. Looking for money to pay the staff. Slaying dragons. There had never been enough time to design, to feed his appetite for art and math. It got lost, so much of it, in the minutiae of keeping Caldwell & Tate afloat.

Odd things, things he knew by heart, he couldn't now recall. But he could somehow always remember the shame, the screwups. Last week at the Department of Regulatory Affairs solving a series of bureaucratic mix-ups on permits for the complex on Mount Vernon Square. When the site manager had no luck, Gregory himself had gone to the office.

He had walked up to the Plexiglas window when his number was called and the woman behind the window with a short blond haircut and light brown eyes began joking with him.

"How've you been?" she had asked, with a broad and inviting smile. "Been a couple of weeks since I've seen you down here. I met your daughter; she looks just like you. She's sharp. Your son still want to be a contractor?"

The steady, jocular stream of questions had assumed a relationship he had no knowledge of. He was certain he had never seen this woman before in his life. Yet she knew about Sean and that Lauren worked for his firm. And that would be like him, within ten minutes, to know her life history, to have shared his. But because he was polite and all-business in response to this onslaught, the woman had taken offense, making him stand before the Plexiglas window for forty-five minutes while she "researched" the problem in a back area where he could see her at work, leisurely and begrudgingly, stopping to chat with coworkers, nailing him to an unseen crucifix every few minutes with a bruised and bitter stare.

Gregory opened his eyes and saw Lauren in the outer office, her arms filled with blueprints as she headed upstairs. Next year she would take the licensing exam. She would be one of only three other female African American architects in the city. Smart, ambitious, focused. His twin.

She witnessed his days, his increasing mistakes. He explained them with a shrug and an excuse of a sleepless night, but Lauren had seen the flask in his desk and said nothing, out of love. She had slipped him a bottle of Visine for his red-rimmed eyes and interjected in meetings when she heard the faltering of his voice and sensed the flight of his memory. From bulwark to burden, that was the trajectory Gregory feared he was on, all that was left for him to bequeath his daughter.

Had his father given him this illness? He carried his father's awful journey within him. First there was the forgetting, the confusion, the day he had accused Gregory bitterly, shouting, spittle hitting Gregory's cheeks, of stealing his wallet. And the skeptical, long, and untrusting look that preceded the first time his father asked him, "Tell me, again, whose boy are you?"

"Dad, it's me. I'm your son, Gregory," he'd tell him.

Gregory's own muddy emotions had sunk him down into a soup of despair, until he learned that just telling his father his name momentarily cleared the gloaming fog choking his father's mind—for a half hour, fifteen minutes, until he asked him again: "Tell me whose boy are you?"

The dementia made a victim of his mother, too. Did she and his father make love during all that? Ever jointly revisit a past that was coherent and beloved for them both? He'd witnessed her stoic care of his father, knew the love was still there, but just like David and Bruce, Gregory never asked how she bore his father's day-by-day vanishing act. He never asked because he could not fathom how he would handle it if Margaret told him the truth.

Gregory had seen close up who and what he feared he could become.

A decade ago, cancer had been harder to fight, harder to beat than he had ever been able to tell anyone. He'd had a team of talented doctors, the love of his family, and the will to live, but his body never recovered from the brutal efficiency and side effects of the chemotherapy and radiation.

The cancer, Hodgkin's lymphoma, went into remission after ten months of treatment. He'd been in remission ever since. He had told Diane everything he could, but there was no way to describe the pain of cancer, how it depleted and deformed every ounce of fight and resilience, how it felt some days as if he were being devoured. After he was "cured," he developed diabetes. He had it under control, but still it was a new, invasive, and unsettling element of his body and health.

But he'd made it, kicked cancer's butt. Had even told friends that it had been a blessing because it reminded him how lucky he was to be alive, how gratified he had been by the outpouring of love and concern and support for him and Diane from colleagues and friends.

Cancer had quenched any dread he had of death, but this loss of memory, its stubbornness, its resilience, if it was what he feared . . . he could not even name his trepidation.

Gregory sat in the cafeteria of Washington Hospital Center waiting for his brother Bruce, a general practitioner. He had left the office early. As he stood outside the offices of Caldwell & Tate, he realized he would have to pretend he was a tourist and ask a stranger on the street how to get to Mount Vernon Square, a ten-minute drive from their offices. On his way to Washington Hospital Center, he'd gone out of his way and found the Mount Vernon Square office and thankfully it all came back to him. All the meetings with the investment company. All of it. A comforting tidal wave that baptized him in confidence.

He was facing the entrance so Bruce would see him. He was ravenous and had already filled his tray with a turkey sandwich, potato salad, a large cup of coffee, and a slice of apple pie. He'd need the energy for the meeting. He felt more in control, less fragile when he'd had a good meal.

Gregory gazed at the doctors and visitors wolfing down lasagna, soup, salad, and throwing their heads back to drain cans of soda, bottles of water. Which of them, he wondered, was there waiting for someone to die? Which of the doctors had a patient for whom they could do no more?

Gregory saw Bruce enter the cafeteria, look around, and nod to him. He then headed to the food court. His brother was at least thirty pounds overweight and had just stopped smoking a year ago. His black hair was thinning rapidly, leaving strands of sheer white covering his balding pate. Bruce arrived at the table with a cup of lentil soup and a vegetarian casserole on his tray.

"I'm finally taking my own advice," he said, pointing to his meal.

"About time," Gregory chided. "How's Aaron?"

"Coming home from rehab next week. It's costing us a small fortune."

"What do they say, third time's the charm?"

"Hell, it better be. My son is killing my retirement fund." Cutting into the casserole with a plastic fork, Bruce said, "Fucking drugs. Why would a kid like Aaron, with all his advantages, need to take drugs?"

"It's an equal opportunity curse. Diane says 80 percent of the cases she hears are rooted in drug abuse."

"So what's up?" Bruce asked, his eyes weary and indifferent, contradicting the intent of the question. Bruce could never wait for the end of a story, was nearly allergic to eye contact, a doctor with the world's worst bedside manner. Gregory watched his brother stuff the vegetable casserole into his mouth, studying his plate, avoiding Gregory's querulous stare.

Gregory wished then that David were alive. Their brother David had died three years ago in a small plane crash, returning home from a medical convention in Philadelphia. That's who he would have rather gone to with these questions. David might have given him some hope. But Bruce would have to do.

"Do I seem different?"

"What do you mean?" Bruce looked up, apparently finally interested. "You don't seem different to me," he concluded with a shrug.

"Do you see forgetfulness in your patients much?"

"What?"

"Symptoms of dementia, Alzheimer's."

"Why do you ask?" Now his gaze was riveted to Gregory's face, those brown eyes taking stock of him with a new intensity.

"I wonder if I'm getting what Dad had. I can't remember things. Addresses and people."

"I haven't seen any changes in you."

Of course not, Gregory thought silently, bitterly. *We're brothers who see each other four or five times a year.*

"I wonder if I have Alzheimer's. Dad had it. Dementia. That means it's in our DNA. My kids, your kids."

"But we don't know that's what you're experiencing." He paused. "Alzheimer's is a bitch. We can't screen for early symptoms. Even if we could, there are no treatments that make a significant difference. Patients come to us for answers and there is nothing we can do. What medications there are relieve some of the symptoms but can't stop the progression of the disease.

Alzheimer's erases all our education and training. It renders the hundreds of thousands of dollars we spent on becoming doctors useless. We hate Alzheimer's more than cancer. David used to say, 'Cancer fights fair compared to Alzheimer's.' And African Americans? We've got a 50 to 70 percent greater risk of developing it than anybody else, because of our higher rates of diabetes, high blood pressure, and high cholesterol."

Gregory laughed uneasily, looking around to avoid the resignation—*or was it defeat?*—he heard in his brother's voice. He looked anywhere but at the man who had just spoken those words.

"Still, I can give you the name of a specialist if you're concerned. Shit, man, Alzheimer's. Dad also had that stroke, diabetes, and high blood pressure. How's your health?"

"Fine. Diane and I are in the gym regularly. My diabetes is under control. I bought some software online to help my memory, but Bruce, I'm scared. I haven't said anything to Diane, but she notices all this and I don't know what to say."

"Yet you still drink?"

"Sociably."

Bruce shook his head dismissively.

"And you're still a pompous ass. Look I came to you—"

"For answers and for encouragement, I know, but you just asked me about a disease that won't allow me to offer you any of that. Bullshitting you would be worse than dashing your hopes. But you may be overreacting, Greg. You're still young. Hell, we both are. Haven't you heard sixty-five is the new forty?"

In response, Gregory stood up, reached for both their trays, and took them to the conveyor belt. He sat down again as Bruce leaned forward across the table, preparing to say more. Thrusting an armistice into the bloody campaign of truth his brother had waged, Gregory asked, "Do you remember the summer Dad took us to Mississippi?"

"Hell, yeah." Bruce's smile broke open his face. "The summer I decided to be a doctor."

"You mean the summer you almost got killed and not by the KKK?" Gregory laughed. "That night the three of us snuck off to that black juke joint on the edge of town."

Bruce blushed, his eyes lighting up in merriment. "Yeah, and I almost got cut by some crazy nigger named Blade for dancing with his woman. A fact I didn't know till he came out of the bathroom and saw us slow-dragging in the middle of the floor. Damn, she was all over me."

"Yeah, and Blade was about to be all over you, too."

The laughter bubbled up, an oasis between them.

"You got off lucky with just that black eye," Gregory teased.

"Till we got home and Dad was waiting on the porch for us with Reverend Reagan and his shotgun for emphasis." Bruce shook his head.

"Freedom Summer made you a doctor and me an architect, looking at the shacks those sharecroppers lived in."

The mellow satisfaction of the laughter settled like a mist as the two men rose at the same moment.

Instead of saying good-bye, Gregory told his brother, "All we are is memories, Bruce. That's all we are. Even more than flesh and blood."

Just before the four p.m. meeting, Gregory sat in his car in the hospital parking garage, as cars slowly passed by looking for an open space. He sat cradled by memories that felt on loan, battered and suspect.

Gregory watched several cars slowly drive past, drivers shooting him impatient sign language and looks that asked, *You pulling out?*

No, I'm not, he mouthed. His brother, the doctor had just told him there was no hope for what he feared was imminent. He sat in his car soaked through his skin with sweat and drowning in an unfaithful and mocking memory.

When they met in 1978, Mercer was driving a Crown Victoria, a whale of a car that pushed everything else off the road, back when everybody was switching to Japanese cars. Mercer's tape deck was full of Buddy Guy, James Brown, and Lou Rawls, who he had declared were actually priests walking among the savages on Earth. It was them, those men, Mercer swore who were the real holy trinity.

How many thousands of hours had they spent together, plotting, planning, conspiring to build a company that would leave a footprint in the city? Mercer, like a brother. Gregory felt him in the car with him.

And Diane was everywhere with him, all the time. Diane, who he had wanted so badly when he laid eyes on her. Gregory had dated what Mercer like to call "the United Nations" by the time he met Diane and had passed into that zone where a man is ready to make his next step with a woman beside him. The time when he prays at night that luck will wipe his slate clean and that he will recognize the woman when she appears. Caldwell & Tate was five years old and the small contracts, one after the other, had begun to widen their network, had gotten people who mattered talking about them. When he saw Diane at the party that night, he'd seen a woman without whom he could go no further. Yet there had come a time when he'd wondered where all that love had gone.

She had been a judge for a year when they stood facing off in the living room—this time, Diane accusing him of failing her and their children.

"The one thing that matters to me most, family, that's what

you make a mockery of. I might as well be a single mother. When will you look around and see the family you've left behind? Is there a finish line for this race you're running?"

"Actually no, hell no. I have to go out there. Mercer and I have to go out there and slay a dragon—a fuckin' dragon— every day. You've got families in trouble lined up, filling your courtroom. You'll never run out of a job to do. We've got a payroll that we magically have to meet. If we don't have a dozen contracts signed off on or ready to be signed off on, we're screwed. And you wonder why I leave here at six a.m. and fall through the door at midnight. Nothing we do can crack that damned glass ceiling. We can't be more than a boutique black firm no matter how good our designs. Diane, you say I should be with you and the kids more, but if I'm not out there scratching and clawing, hustling, I can't come home to you at all. Not empty-handed."

Without their determination, they never could have gotten some of the deals they landed. Caldwell & Tate was always competing against big white firms with track records of building half a dozen huge projects in any given year. There was too much money, too much ego and prestige bound up in the major projects for many black firms to ever be considered. They were always paying what Mercer called "the black tax."

Mercer reveled in recounting a presentation in the conference room and imitating the reaction of the corporate stakeholders. He would lean forward, narrow his eyes, and lance one of the designers with a look of withering disdain and ask, "Nigger, what makes you think you can handle a project worth this much money?"

Of course they had all laughed, for such raw, naked racism would never be expressed. Most often it came wrapped in condescension or paternalisms that could still land a bruising knock-out punch. The more he'd proved, the more he'd had to prove. How many ways could he tell Diane that?

But now there was nothing left to prove. That night on the Beltway had changed it all.

"Look, Gregory, we've got to face it. Something's wrong. Maybe you should give some of your duties to the other designers. We've got a company to run, employees to pay. Too much is at stake," Mercer had told him that afternoon.

Who was this man, ordering him around, he had wondered in astonishment. Mercer, schooling *him* on the company that was *his* idea. Gregory had looked at his friend's smooth, unlined face, the tailored gray shirt and crimson silk tie. Not a wrinkle or ruffle in Mercer's demeanor. So smooth, not unraveling like him.

"Lauren will handle the City Center visit tomorrow evening. I can't risk you taking the lead on that," Mercer had said. Gregory was expected to accept this conclusion.

Marshaling a calmness he did not feel, Gregory said, "Let me go with her. One last time. One last client. I promise I won't say anything, I'll let her do all the talking."

"This is a no-win, don't you understand? If you say nothing, don't answer questions, they'll wonder why."

"You can't just throw me out. Take the company, my work, away like this."

"Gregory, you can't remember a damn thing anymore. You're always lost or late. Throw you out? We've both got the devil at our back. I'm listening to myself saying all this to you. This is breaking my heart."

Mercer had stood before him talking about a broken heart when all Gregory saw was a man aging like some gleaming, hardy wood. Not being chipped away, eaten from the inside like him.

Before he'd slipped away from the conversation, for that was how he thought of *it,* he'd said to himself, *The hell with Mercer. The hell with them all.*

The next evening, he was on the Beltway, headed to the City Center meeting in Silver Spring, Maryland. He would get there ahead of Lauren, remind them that he wasn't dead yet. He'd popped in a CD, Donny Hathaway's "Valdez in the Country," a soothing assurance that he would be all right. Music helped. It grounded and calmed him.

The Beltway was a tidal wave of cars. How many thousands, he wondered, were at this moment creeping along the cement girdle that wrapped like a snake around the DMV as it was called now—the District of Columbia, Maryland, and Virginia.

The music and his thoughts, like normal, like before, working together, seamless, automatic.

Then he had no idea where he was. He felt himself oozing, slipping, and sliding, down a hole he couldn't outrun or outthink. On the other side of the glass, a nation of automobiles and trucks and the occasional motorcycle. Headlights, with accusing, blistering eyes. His hand had frozen on the steering wheel. Was there an emergency? An act of terrorism? A trickle of wetness and then he was sitting in a puddle of his own urine, the smell of it hot, pungent, filling the small space with his disgrace. The huge green-and-white exits, where would they take him? If only he could stop and ask someone in one of the thousands of cars in front, in back, on his left, on his right.

He'd dared to blow his horn once, then twice, at a woman in a car on his right. She looked at him. Frantically, he waved at her, not to say hello but for help. She smiled then sped to cut off a car in front of her.

By the time he finally had the nerve, the will, to exit the

Beltway, he was in Pentagon City, swerving off the exit ramp. The lights of a gas station quenched his fright. Parking near the air pumps and car vacuums, he felt his spirit, something inside him that he could not name but could only thank God for, take hold of him and set him crawling up and out of the darkness.

He could breathe. Think. Remember.

At a Burger King up the road, he had pulled into the drive-through and ordered fries and a cheeseburger, parked on the lot and consumed the food as though it were both his last meal and his first. Half a mile up at a Dunkin Donuts drive-through, he ordered two cups of coffee, which he was certain would help him find his way home. The client would have to wait.

He staggered through the front door at ten p.m. Diane was away at a conference. Slumping on the sofa, he checked his cell phone and found a dozen messages from Lauren. There was only one thing to do.

In the basement, in the rear of the top drawer of his filing cabinet, behind yellowing papers and old photographs and documents, his hands found the bottle. He'd sworn he would never go back. Back then he had stopped on his own. Hadn't needed twelve steps. But if there was ever a night when he needed a drink . . .

This meeting with clients would be his last. He had finally agreed with Mercer, with Lauren that he would work from the office. Today, his last hurrah. He couldn't sit here any longer. As it was, he figured he'd just make the four p.m. meeting. At the first stoplight, he reached for his phone, punched in his GPS, and reminded himself where he was headed: Mount Vernon Square.

He entered to see Mercer and the investors gathered in the cavernous conference room around a horseshoe-shaped table studying blueprints. He caught Mercer's eye, winked, and gave him a thumbs-up. Mercer's wary, worried eyes gave him nothing back, so Gregory walked over to the sideboard and filled a cup with coffee from a silver urn before turning to the wide picture window that looked down on Mount Vernon Square.

Remember who you are, he thought. *Remember what you have done.*

They'd beaten the odds and left an indelible mark on the city and the region, even with the insane deadlines, the clients who paid late or pulled the plug on contracts, the weeks and sometimes months that staff salaries were late. They'd worked on monuments and office buildings in Washington, Fairfax County, and Silver Spring. A sports stadium in Prince George's County, shopping and recreation centers, and schools. His wall at home was filled with awards, and he had served a term as president of the American Institute of Architects.

Their signature project was a new library in downtown D.C., the nexus of historic buildings. The building had heralded the remaking of the city's architectural identity and demographics.

The library was airy and spacious, a confident and nearly playful glass tower in a city of squat buildings which, even in contemporary design, were still paying homage to Greece and Rome. The library bore the imprint of the best of their design-teams' skills, with Mercer and Gregory fine-tuning and adding defining touches. That was the last time he'd had fun, been excited about the work.

The library had altered the city's landscape in a way that inspired imitations. The building received rave reviews and went on to win awards, but when the congratulatory dust settled, white developers told Gregory—while shaking his hand in admiration—that they liked the design so much they had hired another firm, a white firm, to design a building just like it for them.

There was the glory of the library, and then in 2009, falling off the economic cliff along with everybody else. The depression they called a recession. Rolling up their sleeves to let go of designers they were as close to as family, getting lean and mean, determined to rise again. It had taken a few years, but they were back.

Soon after, Caldwell & Tate partnered with another firm to put in a bid to work on the planned Museum of African American History and Culture on the Mall. The memory of the months spent planning for that presentation still buoyed him. A building was a story etched into stone, so there was as much discussion about the philosophy and beliefs that would inspire the design as anything else. Movement. Evolution. Those words had been the foundation of the design. In the end, Caldwell & Tate and their partners made the short list, but they were not chosen.

The lead investor tapped Gregory on the shoulder and engaged him in a conversation that he heard on a distant loop, only remembering that this man, with his white-blond hair and football-player girth and neon, self-assured grin, merely required that Gregory answer "Yes" to every request. He and Mercer told him "Yes" and then did what the project needed, not what this asshole wanted. It had worked so far. But today they had been called on the carpet.

Mercer walked to the head of the table and launched into an overview of the project's first six months. Then he signaled for Gregory to come to the front.

Just go ahead. Go on, he thought, walking to the podium before a screen that would soon fill with a PowerPoint presentation. For several moments Gregory said nothing, just looked at the six men around the table. How could he make them fall in love with the project again, he wondered, despite the delays and cost overruns. He clicked on the first slide, an image of the finished project. Sleek, modern, but they would be keeping the brick walls and high ceilings of the original building, preserving what had made it unique.

Finally he told them what he, in his heart, believed: "This building will make anyone who lives in it glad to come home."

Chapter Ten

JANUARY 3, 2012

We've never argued about anything like we're arguing about this. Diane says I'm in denial. That my pride endangers me. Twice I skipped, just didn't show up for doctor's appointments. "Don't you want to at least know what's happening?" she keeps asking. There's too much at stake. Too much to lose. But even this denial, this resistance. It's not me. I know it isn't. But neither is the other person inside me. Or is that really me now?

Gregory touched Juliette Beamer's ass. Standing behind her at the water cooler as she leaned over to fill her cup with hot water, Gregory touched her backside. First his fingers brushed the silky floral cloth of the dress he had been admiring all morning. Then his fingers tensed and grabbed her, feeling the easy give of flesh beneath his fingers. Her scream bludgeoned him into wakefulness from what felt like the grip of a hallucination.

Juliette abruptly turned around. Then he saw the disgust and fear in her eyes.

"You touched me. Gregory, why would you do that?" she shouted.

"I—I didn't."

"Yes, you did."

Afternoons when he was bushed and needed a break, it was the image of Juliette's wide, sensuous face framed by a neat, tight cap of reddish brown curls that he'd dive into. But he had never crossed the line. Had never even thought to. Juliette had worked with Caldwell & Tate for fifteen years, had started as secretary and was now senior administrative manager.

Gregory shrank beneath the outraged gleam of Juliette's eyes where he saw the depth of his trespass and the breadth of her pain.

"It wasn't me, I mean, it wasn't me, it was . . ."

"Who, Gregory, who? There's only two of us here, and I didn't turn around and grab my own ass." Juliette's anger swelled her with a fierce righteousness as she stood her ground, her face thrust into Gregory's so close that he could not see, sense, or feel anything else.

"I swear, Juliette, I'd never do something like that. It wasn't me."

"What's going on?" Lauren asked coming down the stairs from the second level. Everyone else was out to lunch.

Juliette stood now gazing at Gregory, shaking her head. Befuddled pity had overtaken her anger. "Your father," she said, the words a damning indictment.

"I'm sorry, I didn't mean . . . If you say I did, but I, I didn't know . . ." Gregory stammered, sweating, pinned between the curiosity of his daughter and the loathing of the woman who was the linchpin of his company.

"Lauren, your father touched me inappropriately. I don't know what's going on, but something's wrong. Maybe you should take him home."

As they stood at the water cooler watching Juliette stalk away, Lauren hugged her father and led him into his office, whispering, "What happened? What happened?"

Gregory slumped into his chair. He felt whipped, near tears. "I don't know. Why would she lie? Maybe I did what she said."

"Don't worry about that now, Dad. You're probably just hungry, tired maybe. Let's go get something to eat." Lauren comforted him. "Let's go get some air, you'll be fine."

"What if Juliette tells Mercer?"

"I'll talk to her, tell her that you haven't been feeling well. She knows you, knows how out of character this is."

"What if she tells Mercer?"

"Dad, come on, calm down. Let's go get something to eat."

That evening he couldn't tell Diane that he had touched Juliette. But who was he kidding? His need to keep secrets had made everything a lie, confusion. He had spent the first few minutes home pensive and brooding, and now he was complaining about a designer he and Mercer had hired several months earlier.

"We got punked," he said, while cutting the roast chicken breast. "His recommendations were great. He works well with his team, and his portfolio was one of the best we'd seen in years. Now, it's like some other person comes in to work every day. Just yesterday I told . . ." He chewed the sliver of chicken, stopped, swallowed, and reached for his glass of water.

"I said to . . ." he began again, placing his knife and fork noisily on his plate.

"Who did you tell, Gregory? Was it Mercer?"

"Yes, yes, of course. Who else? Who else would it be? We interviewed him together. I remember that. Who else would I be talking about?" he asked irritably, pushing away from the table and heading to the kitchen. "Don't say anything. Please don't say a damned word," he sneered, leaning against the kitchen counter, watching Diane as she rose to stand in the entrance to the kitchen.

"You don't get to say that to me."

"I'm tired, that's all."

"Gregory . . ."

"We're past deadline on the school in Landover."

"Gregory . . ."

"I forgot my best friend's name."

An hour later Diane moved close to Gregory beneath the bedspread and turned the plasma television to a jazz channel. The voice of Abbey Lincoln oozed into the room.

"Gregory, how does it feel?" she asked. "When the memories leave you? When you can't bring them forth?"

How could he create for her the sensation of the past, of all that he knew, was sure he knew, evaporating like steam, like thoughts turning to ash? When he tried to turn his mind into a hand, a fist that could retain the words and thoughts? Only to find that too often, he was not fast enough.

"I look at my driver's license twenty, thirty times a day to remember who I am, what my face looks like. I can't stand to drive anymore. What if I get lost, or go over the speed limit and get stopped, get arrested all because I can't answer a cop's questions?"

He can't tell her that he has imagined a way out if it is what he fears and what he dreads. Would he even be able to do it? He might start the process and in the midst of it have no idea how to finish. He could never say the word to Diane. He couldn't be that selfish.

Diane turned on her side and moved closer to him, closing her eyes, lying against his chest. Gregory clutched her arm and thought about how he had—yes, he had—touched Juliette, *touched* her. Even now, in this moment he remembered the feel of her strong hips beneath the silky softness of her dress, and how he had wondered at the color of her slip, her panties. He trembled, fearful and shamed that he had done that. He lay beside his wife remembering that moment, when so many other things he wanted to call forth were now gone. No, he couldn't tell Diane. What she had seen was more than enough. He couldn't tell her everything.

He reached for the remote and punched in a channel for classical music.

"Mercer," Gregory said, whispering his friend's name over the sound of the Brahms symphony. "Mercer," he declared, vowing never to forget it again.

He heard Diane's gentle breathing as she slept beside him. The Brahms symphony couldn't block the shame that warmed him. Gregory held tightly to Diane, both solid and fleshy beside him. His agitation woke her. She yawned and then her fingers rested on his penis, gently probing, fondling. Her tongue rimmed his earlobe. His hand pushed her gown up.

"I'll never forget how to do this," he murmured, words which fell warm and true against Diane's neck.

"I love you, Gregory."

"I'll never forget that either," he said as his fingers parted her thighs.

—∞∞∞—

"I'm not begging. I'm not pleading. Not anymore. Bruce gave me the name of a neurologist and we have an appointment on Tuesday."

Diane made the announcement, a stern satisfaction in her voice as she poured Gregory a cup of coffee. He tried to block out the words as he sipped his coffee—black with a touch of sugar—its warmth filling him with a salutatory sense of healing.

Sunday morning and they had finished breakfast. Sections of the *Washington Post* and the *New York Times* were scattered between their plates. A member of Congress was being interviewed on *Face the Nation*, which filled the TV screen in the living room. Outside it was raining.

He didn't want to resist. He didn't want to fight. Not anymore. Not about this. This thing had encroached on every part of his life. There was no hiding, no possibility of subterfuge. One morning Diane had come into the bathroom and seen him shaving with his toothbrush. The next day she woke up to find a gallon of ice cream melted in the microwave. He had put it there because he thought it was the freezer.

He knew it made no sense, his fear of a diagnosis. But he also knew it made perfect sense. The news that awaited him, and he knew it was bad, would obliterate his identity and gradually make everything, from drinking this cup of coffee, to loving this headstrong, determined woman, meaningless. And that would be his cross to bear alone.

"What if I refuse?"

"Gregory, you aren't a child. Stop talking like a three-year-old." The impatience in her voice stung him, stung him as though he *were* a three-year-old. All of them now, Mercer, Diane, his children, eyeing him like he was an alien or a broken object they couldn't decide whether to repair or throw away.

"We know something's wrong," she insisted.

"Nobody—*nobody*—knows how much is wrong as well as I do," he shouted.

"How can you stand this . . . *not knowing?* This isn't you."

"How do you know what's me anymore? This is me now."

Diane plunged into a bristling quietude, an absence, he thought, of even the sound of her breathing, a pulling back of her presence and energy as she looked out the kitchen window at the rain. *Over three decades together and now this,* he thought. There was no name for this betrayal. Her face had melted with age into a soft, certain beauty that reflected what she now possessed inside. She refused to dye her hair, and the gray and white strands framed a face of vulnerable, shimmering strength.

"You're not alone," Diane said, turning to face Gregory.

"You can't be there for all of it. Not inside my mind."

"I won't let you do this to yourself. To me or our family."

"So it's about you?"

"It's about all of us. Maybe you are afraid to know. But we all deserve to."

Dr. Lance Ogden had been a neurologist for forty years. In the initial visit, during which Gregory and Diane shared the changes in Gregory over the past year and a half and discussed his general health, he was compassionate and accessible. Today, Diane and Gregory sat facing him across his desk as he casually reviewed Gregory's test results.

"The MRI didn't reveal any strokes or tumors. It was perfectly normal. But the PET scan results are a different story."

PET scan, Gregory thought; the name sounded so innocuous and harmless. The procedure was an imaging test of his brain using a radioactive substance called a tracer to look for signs of disease and injury. It revealed how well or how poorly his brain was working. That's what Dr. Ogden had told them. He'd taken the test in a room down the hall, sat before a computer and was asked questions. He'd been so nervous he could barely think. He was being analyzed, judged; how could he possibly do anything but fail? If he couldn't think of an answer or took too long to respond, or couldn't remember something that had flashed on the screen a few seconds or minutes earlier, all that counted against him. Against him and his brain.

"Mr. Tate, are you listening?" Dr. Ogden asked gently. Gregory stared at the tiny brown spots on the doctor's balding head, his drooping yet oddly alert eyes, and wondered how he could stand telling people bad news all day long.

"Yes, of course," Gregory said, squeezing Diane's hand.

"The results of the PET scan reveal significant decline in your cognitive and logical thinking."

"Logical? I'm forgetting things, not going crazy."

"Gregory, please let him finish," Diane said.

"Mr. Tate, this is an objective measurement of what you have been experiencing. And in your initial visit, when I asked you dates and places and tested you for recall in our conversation, your performance was haphazard."

"Haphazard?"

"When I look at the MRI results, which revealed nothing abnormal, the PET scan results, which do, and factor in your accounts, this tells me that you likely have early-onset Alzheimer's disease."

Gregory felt himself upright, sitting beside his wife holding her hand, and simultaneously choking, drowning. All with his eyes wide open.

"What do you mean *likely*?" Diane asked.

Dr. Ogden paused and leaned back in his chair. He swiped the top of his bald head as though brushing back strands of hair. "Actually, the only method of definitively diagnosing Alzheimer's is with an autopsy or biopsy. It's a clinical diagnosis. It's too early to see on an MRI."

"My father had it," Gregory said mostly to himself, but loud enough to be heard. "It wasn't called Alzheimer's then. I think they called it old age or dementia."

"Neither dementia or Alzheimer's are a natural part of aging. As its prevalence has increased, many think of it as result of living longer, but it's not normal."

"Early-onset, what does that mean?" Diane asked.

"It's not strictly a disease of the elderly. I have worked with patients as young as fifty who have it."

"I'm sixty-five," Gregory said.

"It's still early-onset."

"Well, at least now we know," Diane whispered. She turned and faced Gregory, enfolding him in an embrace that enclosed them in a world of their own making. They sat breathing in the sanctity and solemnity of the moment.

"Do you two need time alone?" Dr. Ogden asked.

"No, no," Diane said, releasing Gregory. "We've got work to do. Tell us what's next."

"I want to put Mr. Tate on Aricept. It's not a cure, but it will help with the symptoms and slow their progression. You are diabetic, but seem to have that under control. You aren't overweight and your cholesterol is good."

"Why, Dr. Ogden, why?" Gregory asked. "Because of my father?"

"Not necessarily. Some people in the field argue that it is heredity; others think members of the same family can develop it for different reasons. Telling you I don't know why is almost as difficult as telling you that you have Alzheimer's."

"How long do I have?"

"You don't need to try to answer that, Dr. Ogden," Diane cut in.

"Mr. Tate, I want you to continue all the healthy things you've been doing, eating right, exercise. I don't advise alcohol. It's also important that you keep up your social networks. Engage in work as much as you can. Spend time with friends. Practice a hobby. We want to preserve every neuron and synapse possible."

Friends. Gregory thought of how isolated he and Diane had become, how friends and acquaintances had begun to drift away, embarrassed by something he had said or done or just by their being healthy and strong, not knowing what to say.

"How long have I had it?"

"Generally, the disease can take years before symptoms are apparent. It could have begun developing a decade ago. I don't have a patient for another half hour. If you want to sit here for a while, you can," Dr. Ogden said, rising from his chair. "Zoe will have the prescription for you at the front desk and will make an appointment for another visit in six months."

They both watched him leave, Gregory thought, as though he was exiting the scene of a crime he had stumbled upon.

The image of him touching Juliette rose up like the sparks of a flame. If he could do that, if he could think about her what he had thought, what else could he do? Turning to Diane, he whispered, "If I ever hurt you, I want you to do what's best for you. I don't want to be a burden."

"Gregory, I'll never—"

"Don't make any promises," he said, his fingers gently pressed against her lips. "The treachery of this disease will make liars of us both."

───∞───

They walked to the parking lot of Washington Hospital Center still holding hands, as they had been holding on to one another since entering the physician's office.

"We have work to do."

Sliding her key into the ignition, Diane repeated the words to herself. That was how she had managed to talk back to the diagnosis they had received. But now she did not want to go home. She was parched for the sound of laughter, a sighting, however brief, of joy. Surely they could not lose that. They had to fight for it. They had to find it. Somewhere in the city on this sweltering July afternoon.

"I want an ice cream cone," she declared, pursing her lips and braving a smile, casting it upon the still waters of her husband's face. "What about you?"

"Why not?"

They drove to Georgetown, parked in a lot, and entered their favorite upscale ice cream boutique. She could not speak for Gregory, but reading the blackboard, which listed thirty different flavors, Diane savored the return of childlike anticipation that had her mouth watering.

"Let's try a flavor we've never had before," she told Gregory.

"Yes, your honor." He winked at Diane, a minuscule action that after what they now knew she accepted as a miracle.

Gregory ordered a double scoop of banana split and Diane, Oreo cookie. Busily, greedily licking their cones, they left the store and walked into the rays of a broad-shouldered sun. They crossed the street and sat in the park facing the waters of the Potomac River. For nearly an hour, they sat watching tourists board the boat that would take them on a ride across the river to the islands on the other side, children squealing in surprise and delight as they were drenched in water beneath the waterfall in the center of the park, and cyclists, lean and strong, whizzing past them.

"You asked Dr. Ogden how long you have. It's not over yet. I'm not through loving you. *That's* how long we have."

"Let's go home," he said. "I want to be alone with my wife."

———— ∞ ————

At midnight, in the dark, Gregory said, "I want to say it. I want to tell them."

"Are you sure?"

"It's important for me to try." This was the first night she would hear him weep, without restraint. It would not be the last.

———— ∞ ————

Two days later, the family convened in their living room. Margaret, accompanied by Bruce, Lauren, Sean, and Mercer, all entered the house and hugged Gregory. None had asked what the family meeting was about.

"We have something to tell you," Diane had told each of them during the call.

Margaret settled in their midst, still feared a little by all them. She sat in the high-backed, royal blue taffeta-upholstered chair she had given Gregory and Diane as a housewarming gift when they moved into this house. Over the years, Diane had come to think that Margaret had purchased the chair for herself. She could not recall a time when the family was gathered in this room that Margaret had not sat in the chair, which made whoever sat in it resemble a monarch. Her salmon-colored, cowl neck blouse revealed a swath of Margaret's wrinkled neckline, and her auburn hair was pulled back in her signature bun, now thinner and marbled with swaths of gray. She gazed at her family with a face that was lightly rouged and largely unlined.

Gregory leaned forward and released his grip on Diane's hand. He looked at each one of them, lingering on their faces, faces Diane now knew one day he would not recognize.

"Diane and I went to see a neurologist, and I have Alzheimer's." Gregory exhaled a hollow, despairing breath, as if exhausted by the declaration, which he had offered as a kind of confession. He looked at his hands and when he lifted his eyes he told them, "One day I won't know who any of you are. I'm sorry."

"Are they sure?" Sean asked.

Diane was relieved when Bruce, sitting on a hassock beside Margaret, began to explain all that their internist and Dr. Ogden had told them about Gregory's illness.

"So he has to die in order for them to know if it was really Alzheimer's?" Sean shouted, storming into the kitchen where they heard the refrigerator door open, cabinet doors slamming. "Bullshit, bullshit!" The hoarse screams came from the kitchen, along with the sound of Sean's shoes scraping the floor.

Mercer shifted uncomfortably from his perch near the mantel. "You can come to the office as long as you want, Gregory."

"For what?" Gregory asked, looking up at his friend in surprise.

"I want to apologize," Diane said. "We suspected . . . we know you all have known there was something terribly wrong. We couldn't figure out how to face it."

"I hoped that if this showed up again in our family it would take me, not any of my sons," Margaret offered wistfully. "What can I do, Diane, how can we help? Was there something that we could have done earlier? My goodness, one day he called me and asked to speak to Ramsey. I didn't know what to say, but when I heard that tremor in his voice—the one I heard sometimes when Ramsey asked for the impossible or inquired about things he should have known—I told him that his father had gone out of town for a few days. What was I to do? Bruce, you told me he came to you and asked for help. Why didn't you do more? Wasn't there something you could've done for your brother?"

"They went to see the specialist I referred them to," Bruce said defensively.

"Listen to all of you, talking about him as if he isn't even here," Lauren shouted. "Mom said there's medications Dad can take. He's agreed to participate in a study that Hopkins is conducting. Isn't that right, Dad?"

"When did I say that? Study my brain? Why, there's nothing wrong with me." Gregory stood up and threw his arms open in supplication and reassurance. "It's the drug companies. They want to get us all doped up, that's all. Sure, I forget sometimes. But I'm not sick. Ask me anything," he shouted, bounding over to Margaret, his face bright with a terrifying lucidness. "I know you, you're my mother. I know today's date. I know my phone number. I know who you all are, you're my family."

When Sean reentered the room, Gregory looked at him

pleadingly. "Tell them, David. Tell them there's nothing wrong with me."

⎯⎯∞⎯⎯

The next day, Gregory was lucid and clear-eyed when he came into the office. He eased into the ergonomic chair that faced Lauren and said, "I wanted us to talk before I lose everything. While I can tell you what I want you to know about the business, about other things, too."

"Dad, there's no need. You've been a great teacher."

"It may be their building but it's your vision," he said ignoring her words. "Never work for anyone who doesn't respect you. We've had clients who thought our job was to just draw lines on paper. We're hired for our ability to give the client what they didn't know they wanted until we designed it. They can fire us, but we can also fire them."

Lauren watched her father look out the glass wall in her office at the designers at work, waiting for him to turn back to her, the moment between them feeling so tender, she dare not touch it.

"While I still have a mind, I get to say what's on it."

Lauren walked to the other side of her desk and fell onto her knees and held her father's hands. "Daddy, please don't go."

"Honey, that's the one thing we all gotta do. And we don't get to say how."

Chapter Eleven

February 2013

Diane was in community court—an effort by the city to place judges in the neighborhoods where lifestyle and life skills issues festered, creating breeding grounds for the most malignant forms of neglect. Parents who had dropped out of school in the tenth grade and now considered school to be optional for their children. Parents who had grown up hungry and now served Fritos and a Coke for breakfast. Parents who had never been to the dentist and couldn't make or keep a doctor's appointment for their child. This was how it started and ended in everything from teen pregnancy to murder.

Jacinda Reed was not sending her two daughters to school and she sat facing Diane across a conference table in a small room located in a recreation center on Minnesota Avenue, a room rank with the odor of cheap government carpeting and the nondescript furnishings to match. The weave that haphazardly crowned the woman's head was matted and lint-filled. A dark space behind the her lower lip that signaled a missing tooth enticed Diane's gaze each time Jacinda parted her lips and reflexively brought her hand to her mouth, too late to hide the sorrowful gap. Diane smiled at Jacinda to quell the judgment roiling in her mind, judgment that she had trained herself to keep at bay but that was becoming as unmanageable as an untrained pet.

In Jacinda's eyes, there was the dullness. This was where the seeds of the story often lay, Diane knew. Often, in women, the light had been extinguished by a loved one, or there was a steely, icy glare—evidence of a conscience frozen, compassion unknown. When she saw either gaze, Diane knew that all manner of neglect and abuse was possible. What chilled her was when she saw either gaze in the eyes of both parent and child. Looking in Jacinda's eyes, she saw the slack, glittering evidence of drugs and knew that the woman was high or coming down from a high. In Jacinda Reed's case file, there were reports on her throughout the foster care system and her later arrest for prostitution. But Jacinda, buzzed and unkempt, had initiated this current process and asked for help after receiving a warning from her daughters' school.

Nora Tolliver, Jacinda's social worker, red-haired and matronly, sat beside Jacinda, her fleshy arms resting on several files pertaining to this case.

"Ms. Reed, your daughters have missed thirty-five days of school since the beginning of the school year. You've been working with your social worker, Ms. Tolliver, on strategies to address this situation but she's told me you haven't been cooperative."

"How can I be cooperative? I'm on welfare, Judge Tate, your honor."

"Do you realize how much your daughters have missed in *thirty-five days* of absences? I will give you credit for contacting social services before they contacted you, but we're here today because you've been inconsistent in responding to the assistance of Ms. Tolliver."

"I'm on welfare, and by the time I get my check, pay the rent, buy food, and pay the other bills, it's hard for me to wash our clothes at the Laundromat, and I can't send them to school in dirty uniforms. I sure ain't gonna do that and have people thinking they come from a dirty home." Jacinda spoke confidently and sat up straight, her eyes now raging with defiance.

Diane slid a legal pad across the table and told Jacinda to write down all her monthly bills. As she watched her labor over the figures and the spelling of words like *electricity* and *Laundromat*, Diane wondered if Jacinda was even functionally literate despite, according to her case file, having graduated from Cardozo High School. Graduates of the city's school often read at a ninth-grade level. Over a third of the city's black population was classified as functionally illiterate. She once had a client who signed a legal document with an *x*.

"Judge Tate, your honor, like I told Ms. Tolliver, a load of clothes costs a dollar and a half to wash and seventy-five cents to dry. On what I get in my check I have to choose sometimes between clean clothes and a meal on the table. Guess which one wins?"

Diane vetted the list of expenses three times, each time coaxing fuller disclosure out of Jacinda. Finally, the grubby sheet of paper that now served as a binding contract designed to alter Jacinda's expenditures and behavior was completed. Jacinda Reed was followed by two other cases.

Two hours later, as Diane drove to the superior court, she thought of the cases awaiting her. She'd been appointed to the family court in the early nineties, when D.C. was a graveyard. Back then the number of murders in the city annually averaged four to five hundred. The city was gripped by years of bloodlettings fueled by the epidemic of crack cocaine, but the deeper root was the dark legacy of generations of neglect and indifference for people and neighborhoods that no one cared about until there was an election.

The emotional toll of working in the family court was often harrowing and so, twice, Diane had rotated out to serve three-year stints on the bench in civil court. But she had always felt her mission was on the bench in the family court. The families—mothers, fathers, and children—pulled her back again and again to a docket whose challenges and misery were often more raw and dramatic than those in criminal court.

Diane thought the Carl H. Moutrie Courthouse was an ugly building. It squatted like a giant gray lunch box in the center of Judiciary Square, the city's nexus of local and federal law and order. The FBI's Washington field office and the US Tax Court were among the buildings that occupied the six-block area. The National Gallery of Art and its spectacular east wing, guarded by the iconic sculpture of Henry Moore, was three blocks away. Each weekday, long lines of people snaked out the glass doors of the superior court, headed inside to get married, mediate a dispute, file for a divorce, seek child support, testify in a trial, or serve on a jury.

"It's a building where people go to find justice, only to find that it looks like a stockade," she'd often said to Gregory.

He'd explained that the superior court building was a classic representation of federal and judicial buildings designed in the 1930s and 1940s, which emphasized architectural stoicism, a style challenged in the city's more recent designs.

"Granted it's an expression of its time, but I would think you'd want the public's first sight of a structure to be an invitation, not a threat," Diane had said.

"Architecture is used to send all kinds of subtle and overt

messages," he'd said. "Some people might argue that a court-house *should* instill trepidation."

When Diane got to her office, she looked out her window and thought of how, more and more, she preferred the chaos of her work to the slow dismemberment of her life at home. As a judge, she had a reputation of being strict but caring, and she prided herself on her ability to listen to everything a person said—and sometimes could not say.

On this day, however, she shuddered at the thought that she would have to see Jacinda Reed again next week, and felt her temples throb at the thought of the cases she would have to hear after lunch. Gregory's illness had accelerated a burnout that had been seeping into the lifeblood of her work. The insubordinate reality of her own life had Diane wishing for a judge of her own. A judge who would set her free. Her courtroom had become a hard-edged refuge from which she longed to flee, and she had begun to think about early retirement.

Diane heard a knock on her door. Her assistant, Rudolph, reminded her of the family treatment court graduation cere-mony taking place in half an hour.

In the conference room, decorated with balloons hanging from the ceiling and vases filled with plastic flowers on the tables laden with food, she hugged the judges she had not seen in a while and gossiped with them about pending cases. She thanked the stakeholders from the private and city agencies in attend-ance.

All of them in different ways had shepherded the women of the program through a grueling and strict process of therapy, drug counseling, job training, and parenting classes. Each woman had lived for six months in a residential treatment facil-ity and earned the right to be reunited with her children by suc-cessfully completing the program. Unprepared for the rigors of the program, each year, nearly a third of the class found it easier to allow their children to remain in foster care or give up their parental rights than break the drug habit.

The room hushed as the six women walked to the front to sit near the podium. Kirk Franklin's gospel anthem, "Imagine Me," filled the room from a boom box in a corner. Each woman had charged the beaches on their own private D-Day in the past year and a half. Now each woman was clean. Each woman was sober. Walking down the aisle, they looked startlingly innocent, staring straight ahead, concentrating on a perfect march to the stage. Each woman carried a white rose.

Diane opened the program and realized that her thoughts had diverted from the welcome offered by the chief judge of the superior court and the remarks of the presiding judge of the family court. And then she heard her name and walked to the podium. Diane gazed at the family and friends filling the rows of aluminum folding chairs. This ceremony always made her emotional, and she gazed around the room to settle herself and to take in the full measure of what was about to take place.

"We call them ladies," Diane said, turning to look at the six women. "When we first meet them in our courtrooms, they have lost their children and all that makes a good life, yet beneath that often frightened—and sometimes belligerent—demeanor, they are ladies. *Ladies* is an old-fashioned term that we don't use much anymore, but we use it in the family court as a way of showing respect, because too often in their lives, these ladies were not accorded respect. They didn't respect themselves, their children, or the gift of life. But now they do. They have followed the sometimes tough-love rules laid down by me and my fellow family court judges, and when they've fallen down, they've picked themselves up.

"These graduates are all *first* ladies. First ladies to

themselves and their families and the children with whom they are now reunited. They are ready for the inevitable challenges of living a clean and sober life. They know they're not alone. If they get scared or confused, they've got a friend in the alumni circle of the family treatment court and in their caseworkers. These ladies are now shaping a life they may have once thought they didn't deserve. I call that a happy ending.

"These ladies have taught me how to be a judge, and how to keep the bar of my expectations high while at the same time keeping my heart open. The most underrated and yet important characteristic of the law is mercy. My fellow judges and I, we are gratified that they have fulfilled the requirements of the family treatment court. I congratulate you, my ladies."

After the ceremony, Diane posed for pictures with several graduates as they held their certificates. She met fathers and mothers, beaming and grateful at the sight of their daughters' resurrection. Rahema Elliot, chubby with eyes as bright and happy as those of the eight-year-old daughter whose hand she held, told Diane, "I'm gonna be honest with you, Judge Tate, Judge Bigelow told me if I didn't get my act together she was gonna send me to your court. When she told me that, I stopped playing around and got serious."

"You leave my judge alone," Jenee Kelly, said, bustling into the group surrounding Diane. "That was some tough love, Judge, but you always made me feel like I could make it."

This, I will miss, Diane thought, leaving the conference room and heading back to her office. *This, I will miss.*

Diane returned to her office and began attempting to bring order to the chaos on her desk. Overwhelmed and bristling with fatigue, she stacked files and assessed the significance of various forms and letters, deciding what to trash and what to keep. Another full day, a day of emotion, the frustration of community court, the joy of watching the women graduate. She twirled her desk chair around to face the wide picture window from which she could see not only Judiciary Square but the sky. How many times, she wondered, had she sat in this office simply gazing at clouds and finding in that act solace and hope? The five o'clock October sky was still studded with a few highlights of the day but showed signs of the impending evening.

Since Gregory had been formally diagnosed with Alzheimer's, Lauren picked him up in the morning and drove him to Caldwell & Tate. Having taken his medication, he could sit in his office much of the day, filing through the company's archives and records for a project Lauren had initiated. Caldwell & Tate's papers, some of its blueprints and digital files were to be donated to the D.C. Historical Society. A man who was losing his memory was in charge of compiling the history of the company.

Lauren had told Diane that most days Gregory managed well, and the younger designers still sought him out for advice. Either she or Mercer would take him to a nearby café for lunch or order something and eat with him in his office. She told Diane, "Mom, he remembers everything about the company, things even Mercer had forgotten."

He remembered all that, Diane thought but did not say, because the past was where he was headed. The past was his destination. The past was where he would end up. The past, an island offering no escape. Sometimes, she thought, maybe that was best. Who would want to have to face, sip from the cup of the present he endured and the future that lay in wait? Gregory had a dreadful disease, but all this—going into the office, giving him his own "job"—spared his pride, gave his life meaning, for as long as that was possible.

Diane turned from the window, stood up, and stretched, literally shaking off the hold of these thoughts. Tonight Bruce would come to the house after Lauren dropped Gregory off at home. Diane had finally said yes to Paula's invitation for an evening out.

∞

"Can you believe the old geezer wanted to *get with this*, as the young folks say?" Paula smirked. "And on the first date!"

Diane was sitting with Paula in the basement of Westminster Church having a plate of fried fish, coleslaw, and greens. Diane savored the sound of her own laughter since it had become so rare and nearly unfamiliar. Paula was driving her to tears as she recounted her latest date with a retired engineer she had met online.

Paula reached across the table and handed her a napkin, which Diane used to wipe the moisture brimming in her eyes. "Hell, I didn't even do that during the heyday of the sexual revolution. And that picture he sent me online had to have been thirty years old."

"Stop, just stop!" Diane chided her as she put her hand on her chest to still the effervescent beating of her happy heart.

The Friday night jazz program at the church had been an easy and cheap date for Diane and Gregory for years. For five dollars, they'd heard jazz played by some of the city's best musicians and bought soul food dinners. Mixed in with a crowd of retirees and seniors and the occasional college students or tourist, they'd hear a jazz standard by Ellington or Miles Davis, or a local singer belt out her version of a classic by Sarah Vaughan or Billie Holliday. The church was the citadel of old-school, straight-ahead jazz, and Gregory had enjoyed the music and the mingling. He and Diane never failed to find friends or associates also in attendance.

Diane hadn't been to a concert at the church in several years but she found that nothing had changed. Paula had been coaxing her for weeks to join her for a night out—"A movie, dinner ... something!"

Paula waved to a woman at a nearby table and bounded over to talk with her. Diane watched and thought about how far Paula had come, how far they had come together. Paula had stood beside her when she and Gregory got married and was godmother to Lauren and Sean. During Gregory's battle with cancer, Paula had given Diane a key to her house and told her she could use her guest room as a refuge any time she needed to, night or day.

Initially Diane had thought the idea generous but unnecessary, but the gift had quickly unlocked her need for solitude, silence, and self-care when she had grown weary of questions from friends and family about Gregory. The key opened the door to a room of olive green and a bed that cradled Diane as she'd closed her eyes for what she thought would be a quick nap only to find herself waking hours later. Sometimes Paula would sit on a recliner in the corner and watch her sleep. In the guest room, Diane's loneliness and unexpressed anger could live and breathe, uncensored and unjudged.

When Paula returned from talking with her friend, she said, "If you hadn't agreed to come tonight, I was gonna drag you out of that house."

"Thank you," Diane murmured, still warm from the onslaught of laughter.

She buttered a slice of cornbread and looked around the basement at the nearby tables. Men and women, not past their prime but seemingly entrenched in it, some heads bobbing, some fingers snapping to the beat of "The A Train" performed by a quartet upstairs in the sanctuary. A large screen on the wall showed the group playing.

"I feel like a widow. I don't mean to compare my experience in any way to what you went through after George passed," Diane said.

"You mean after George *died*. My husband died five years ago. He didn't pass, he didn't make his transition, he died. I get so tired of hearing all these useless euphemisms for a perfectly natural part of life, and you know I don't expect such imprecision from *you*," she said. "Rant finished, but I know what you mean. You have to face it though. You're experiencing a lot of what I went through. It's just that I'm a widow and you aren't. I go on. But I still miss him."

Diane pushed her plate aside and reached for the slice of sweet potato pie in the center of the table. She grazed at the pie with the tines of the plastic fork, carving Gregory's name into the creamy texture.

She thought of the diary she had found yesterday when bringing order to Gregory's sock drawer. The leather journal about the size of a paperback book was a heartbreaking testimony to what he had borne, what he feared, what he had found no words to say to her. The first entry was dated three years ago. The last was in May of this year, his script jagged and nearly unreadable. It had taken her several minutes to make out the last words he'd written: *Of all the things I will miss most . . .*

Slumping onto the bed, Diane had sat stunned, reading the rough outline of her husband's journey into a place that he feared promised the end of everything. The loss of everyone he loved. Her feelings were tumultuous. She felt cheated, angry that he had kept so much from her. She'd read the pages awestruck that Gregory had found a place to tend the ever enlarging wound that his life had become. She wished he had confessed his fears but the more she read, Diane knew that he had withheld these thoughts because he loved her. He wasn't able to spare her the sight of his decline. He could, he must have felt, at least protect her from being torn asunder as he was, haunted by what he could not evict from his life or even explain.

Diane slowly, meditatively, finished the pie, took a sip of water, and then said, "You know, at night in bed, I lay beside Gregory and take all of him in. It seems to be claiming him so fast. On my really bad nights, when I kiss him good night, it feels like an internment."

"What about the support group?"

"I went a couple of times, but with my caseload there's often a conflict. Somehow, I figure I can always find my own way. Besides, Lauren, she's always there, and even Sean sometimes helps out. Bruce is with Gregory now. And your calls keep me sane."

"Take it one day at a time. After all this time, it's still the way George died that gets me. One minute he's standing at the foot of the bed putting on his pajamas and the next he's slumped on the floor, dying of a stroke. One minute I had a husband and the next I didn't. I was buried, too. Sometimes it still feels like I am. I'm digging myself out a bit more each day. But you sound like you're digging your way in."

"Of course. I can't help but remember his bout with cancer. Comforting Lauren and Sean, assuring them that no, Gregory was not going to die, and that his prognosis was good. The absence of intimacy between us for nine long months. But Paula, *this* is different. We're going to lose this fight. I've begun to think that we're called *boomers* because just as we hit our stride, just as life begins to make sense, it all blows up in our face. It all goes *boom*."

"That's just too much to think about on a girls' night out like this. Can we pass on that right now?"

Upstairs in the sanctuary, the quartet had been joined by a buxom, honey-colored singer. The space pulsed with the sound of hands slapping thighs, murmured voices singing along, and snapping fingers offering up a lazy, syncopated undertow.

During the intermission, when the audience stood and stretched, walked over to greet friends, or went back down to the basement for more food or drink, Diane noticed a man staring intently at her. He was then walking through the crowd over to her. He was tall with a gleaming shaved head, a neat moustache, and a palpable solidity. He was substantial, yet fit, and he wore his size lightly.

"I think we've met before," he said leaning on one of the folding chairs in the aisle.

"Really, where?" Diane responded.

"Your last name is Tate?"

"Yes."

"Is your husband an architect?"

After a pause that drew attention to itself, she finally said, "Yes, yes he is." She hoped this man did not hear the falsity in her voice and she tried to defeat it by looking him straight in the eyes. "He's the co-founder of Caldwell & Tate Architects."

"Yes, yes, that's him. A couple of years ago his company built a brand new high school over in Brentwood. I was the principal there before I retired. They did a great job. The only school with solar panels in the city, very green, environmentally friendly. Full of light and color. The kids and staff loved it. You came to the ribbon cutting. After the speeches and pictures, your husband was being interviewed and you told me you were a judge in the family court. You asked me about the number of students at the school in the adoption or foster care system. If I recall, we talked about that for a while before Mr. Tate came over. I got another chance to thank him and then he whisked you away." He extended his hand and said, "My name is Alan Rich."

"I do remember now," Diane said, hoping that they would hear at any moment the announcement of the beginning of the second half of the evening that would preempt any inquiries about Gregory.

"How is Mr. Tate?"

His bated and genuine interest in her forthcoming answer forced Diane to blurt out, "He's fine, just fine. Please excuse me, I've got to go to the ladies' room."

She made her way through the milling crowd, breathlessly pushed open the door to the ladies' restroom, and scrambled into a stall. She could handle the odd friend who didn't know or hadn't heard, but on this night, a night designed as an escape, a new quandary arose: How to inform those who knew Gregory only from his work? Of course, his fellow architects had heard that Gregory had retired or knew the truth, but what did she owe someone like Alan Rich? The thought of giving voice to either the truth or a lie struck her as punishment that she, Gregory, and even Alan Rich did not deserve.

───── ⚭ ─────

When Diane entered the house a few hours later, she found Bruce sitting on the sofa in the family room beside Gregory. Bruce had volunteered a week ago to stay with Gregory sometimes if she wanted to go out.

He stood up the moment she entered, tossing his head back and his eyes to the ceiling. "How do you do it? Handle him, I mean? He kept talking about some meeting that he and Mercer had with the mayor years ago and keeps telling the same story over and over."

Diane checked her desire to tell her brother-in-law to stop

talking about Gregory as though he wasn't present or as if he were deaf. "What've you two been doing?"

"Watching the History Channel," Bruce said reaching for his jacket and striding quickly toward the front door. Clutching the doorknob and avoiding Diane's gaze, he stammered, "We ate something, and he got to walking all over the house. I had to follow him to make sure he was okay. He took a nap and woke up as soon as I settled down for a rest of my own. He wanted a glass of water and then knocked it on the floor. In desperation, I hoped the television would calm him down. Diane, I had no idea."

"The symptoms seem to worsen in the evening and at night."

"My offer still stands, but I need time to kind of recover, you know."

Then, in a move that was both awkward and unexpected, Bruce leaned forward and kissed Diane on the cheek before hurrying through the door.

Diane locked the door, kicked off her shoes, and walked into the living room where she found Gregory staring at the television screen, watching the erection of the Brooklyn Bridge unfold. As she got closer she could hear him mumbling, his fingers drumming the arm of the sofa.

"When I finally got down to the district building Mercer was fuming," Gregory said. "Pacing up and down. Back and forth on the sidewalk in front of the building. I was late because I'd spent the night before tossing and turning and didn't get to sleep until five o'clock in the morning, and our meeting was at ten o'clock. Well, he starts to light into me and then I tell him to save it, and we rush up the stairs back into the building."

Gregory laughed loud, a hearty bellow, and clapped his hands. Suddenly aware of Diane's presence he turned to face her and, buoyed by her presence, he continued, "We cool our heels for another half hour, all the while going over the presentation. This is make or break for us. The chance to design the first office building in the U Street corridor since the riots. Our chance to make something rise from the ashes. When we get called into his office, he walks over to us like he's honored that we came. I'll never forget what he said: 'Come on in, brothers. Come on in.' Like me and Mercer grew up with him down there in Itta Bena, Mississippi, picking cotton. And he's got his staff, most of them black, all around him at the conference table. Waiting for us. Ready to do business. And he leans back in his mayor's chair and says, 'Sit on down. Y'all got a reputation that precedes you. A good one. Now tell me why y'all should get this contract. And make it easy for me to say yes.' And you know we did."

Diane had heard the story hundreds of times by now and she sat down beside Gregory and held his cheeks in her palms, looked into those still-magical gray-blue eyes and said, "Gregory, that's a wonderful story."

And when Gregory began again, saying, "When I finally got down to the district building . . ." Diane gently placed her head on his shoulder and said, "Yes dear, I know, that was one of the best days of your life."

Chapter Twelve

AUGUST 2013

This morning his wife hands him off like a package to Cecelia, who stays with him during the day. Diane cares for him but he cannot any longer care for her. And caring for her is the thing he wants never to forget. His wife kisses him good-bye and then it is Cecelia and him. She has brought the morning paper in and hands it to him.

"Here's your paper, Mr. Tate," she says, removing her jacket.

She goes into the kitchen and prepares a cup of coffee and they sit together at the kitchen table. Cecelia is a tiny thing: slender and small-boned, large eyed. He remembers that she told him she is twenty-one. He looks at the newspaper, reports from a world he is no longer a part of.

After they have finished their coffee, Cecelia sets a jar of coins on the table and pours out the pennies, dimes, quarters, and nickels. This is his favorite game. Gregory's fingers slide toward the coins, and he sorts them into piles. Across from him

Cecelia methodically stacks her coins as he quickly builds towers of quarters. He is playing with money but he remembers the thrill of winning and the feeling of being first.

"You're too fast for me, Mr Tate. Just too fast."

"You're too slow. I think you let me win. Don't let me win. I want to beat you fair and square." Gregory pouts.

"All right, but be careful what you ask for." Cecelia laughs. "How many of these to make a dollar?" she asks, placing a quarter in her palm and holding it up for Gregory to see.

"I think it's three."

"Almost, Mr. Tate, it's four. Four quarters to make a dollar."

"I was good at math. I needed it in my work. I don't know what happened," he says staring at Cecelia quizzically.

At lunch, Cecelia stands over Gregory and begins to cut his chicken into small pieces. The knife, the fork, held in her hands instead of his, the concentrated look on her face as she cuts the meat into small pieces, disturbs him. Anything sharp—knives, scissors—are hidden from him. These are the things he still knows. His hand moves quickly and abruptly pushes Cecelia's hands away. The sudden sound of the knife and fork dropping and clattering onto the kitchen floor cuts through the anguish.

"Don't," he demands. "Stop, I can do that." The words are meant to hurt her and salvage his pride but they accomplish nothing. Cecelia reaches onto the floor and retrieves the fork and knife.

"Mr. Tate, now why you wanna be mean like that when I'm here to help you?"

He watches her go to the sink and wash the fork, dry it with a paper towel and place it beside his plate. Head bowed, Gregory grabs the fork and stuffs his mouth with the rice and peas and chicken.

"I'm sorry," he mumbles as Cecelia sits down across the table from him.

"Mr. Tate, you don't have to apologize. I know you didn't mean it."

"But I did."

After lunch, Cecelia tells Gregory that Diane has asked her to pick up some things at the drugstore. Gregory looks outside and sees the sun shining, closes his eyes, and presses his face close to the living room's picture window, his cheeks bathed in the sun's rays.

"Mr. Tate, get your jacket now, and we'll be ready to go."

He opens the closet and pulls out a thick winter parka, gloves from the top shelf, and a wool scarf. When Cecelia comes into the living room and finds him dressed this way, ready to go, she smiles and says, "I don't think you need so much, you'll burn up."

Gregory stands his ground. "I'm ready to go." And when she approaches him to remove his coat, he sits down on the sofa stubbornly crossing his arms.

"All right, Mr. Tate, we can't go out until you're dressed properly. And look at you, you still wearing your house slippers." The sight of his feet melts his resistance, and he removes the heavy coat and scarf, removes his slippers and slides his feet into his shoes. He stands up and Cecelia stops him. "One more thing." She ties the laces.

Rising from her knees, Cecelia is suddenly gay and begins dancing around the room. She has earbuds in her ear and holds her iPod. She slips a bud into Gregory's ear and he hears "Don't Worry Bout a Thing" by Bob Marley. The song transports him to a room of red and blue lights, bathed in the smell of liquor and warm bodies. Fingers balled near his ears, he moves in time, in rhythm. Cecelia places the other bud in his ear and for how long he does not know, for how long he does not care . . . the party, the blue and red lights go on and on. He sees women held too tightly, hears men's gruff, easy laughter. He feels a slap on his back. He is unmired. His tears are for joy.

The song ends and Gregory tumbles back on to the couch and asks, "Where are you from, Cecelia?"

"You know I'm from Jamaica. You told me you've been there. I came here to join my mother. To study to be a nurse's aide. I came to America to take care of you."

"Yes, Jamaica, I've been there." Gregory removes the buds from his ears and hands them to Cecelia. "The water is so blue," Gregory says wistfully. He looks further off and says, haltingly, "Marley, Manley, and Garvey."

"Oh, you know your Jamaican history, Mr. Tate. I tell them all the time you know more than you let on."

At the drugstore, Gregory walks beside Cecelia as she takes products from the shelves. They walk to the pharmacy in the rear of the store and she stands in the line. It is there that Gregory sees Randall Cullen: the short, muscular body, the jet-black hair Gregory always wondered if Randall dyed. They are friends. He still knows what it means to be a friend. They spot each other at the same time, and Gregory calls, "Hey Randall," just to hear himself say what he is sure is the man's name.

Randall unfurls a smile that is the most beautiful thing Gregory has seen in months, a beacon that reminds him of good things.

"Hi, Greg. Hi, man, how are you?" Randall asks as he approaches Gregory standing in line beside Cecelia. He peers at

Gregory through those thick glasses as though searching vainly for signs of life.

Gregory marshals a confident smile and throws his arm around Randall's shoulder and pulls him aside, a few feet from Cecelia. Suddenly he does not want Randall to know that he is with her.

"You don't call me," Gregory says, waylaying the words, piercing his friend with an accusatory stare, moving in so close to him that he can hear Randall's breathing, see the pores on his face, smell the sweetish tinge of tobacco on his breath. "We can talk about the Middle East, those damned Republicans, the city council, like we used to."

Randall shakes his head. "Greg, we talked a month ago. When I got back from those six weeks in Athens. And then Diane invited me over for dinner. We had a good time."

"We did?"

"I brought you and Diane a vase and a small rug."

The hopeful lilt in his friend's voice stings Gregory as he realizes he must have again let someone else down, someone besides himself.

"I've checked on you and Diane regularly, but it's time for us to go to dinner again, okay?"

Gregory rallies with a smile and says, "Call me. Don't be afraid."

"Sure, sure. I will," Randall tells him. But Gregory hears the disappointment in his friend's voice and hates himself, hates that he cannot remember any of what Randall has told him, hates that this man who he still knows as a friend, is not a friend, but a liar.

"Who was that, Mr. Tate? A friend of yours?" Cecelia asks as she comes to Gregory's side holding a bag of prescriptions and they watch Randall walk away.

"I don't know."

———— ◦◦◦ ————

As Cecelia prepared to leave that night, she told Diane that Gregory had seen an old friend in the CVS. "I think I heard him say his name was Randall."

"Oh, Randall Cullen. Did he remember him?"

"Yes he seemed to. They talked for a while."

"How was he today?"

"Oh you know, Mrs. Tate, it was a good day and a bad day. He performed pretty well on the games we played. But when I told him to get ready to go to the store, he dressed for winter. He couldn't remember how to tie his shoes. But he told me that Marcus Garvey and Bob Marley and Michael Manley are all from Jamaica. And when I asked him if that man in the store was a friend, he didn't know."

They heard Gregory's steps hurrying toward them from the living room, heard him furiously shouting, "Why, I can tie my shoes. Do you think I'm a baby? Of course I tied my shoes. I dressed for winter because it is winter, just look outside." He strode over to the kitchen window and pointed to the still light summer sky. "She's lying, why is she lying? Why is she lying about me?"

Diane gave Cecelia an envelope with her pay and signaled for her to leave them alone. She stood in the middle of the kitchen holding her husband, flooded with remorse, withered by fatigue, craving his once strong arms to comfort her.

"Why did she lie? Make her tell the truth."

The weekend stretched out before Diane. Before, when she came home from work, she would change into comfortable clothing, sprawl on the bed or sofa and vegetate before deciding if she would cook or they would order in. Now there was a part two to all her days, a studious girding for the unexpected.

She had grown increasingly vulnerable, unsure, felt sometimes unsafe alone with Gregory. It has not happened yet, but she could snap, surrender to the growing urge that quietly summoned her to ignore Gregory's needs and tend, without guilt, without shame, to her needs, her desires.

In the kitchen, Diane retrieved a package of lasagna from the freezer and slid it into the oven. Gregory sat at the marble island behind her, and she risked leaving him alone to go upstairs and change clothes.

When Diane returned to the kitchen, she said, "Cecelia told me you saw Randall today."

"I did?" Gregory asked, clearly surprised, his face a map of bewilderment.

"That's what she said."

"Mercer and I have that meeting with the mayor in the morning, so wake me up early. I have to go to bed early tonight."

"I'll make sure I do. Bruce and your mother are going to lunch with us tomorrow."

"All right, but not until after that meeting."

Chapter Thirteen

AUGUST 2014

As the months passed, Diane discovered new forms of agitation, as new types of bewildering, nonsensical actions committed by Gregory crept into their lives.

One night, one of her dress pumps went missing. An empty hanger bore no trace of a sheer, silk white blouse. Sean's graduation photo was gone from its conspicuous space on the mantel above the fireplace. Her favorite umbrella. An autographed copy of *Song of Solomon* that she stood in line for half an hour for Toni Morrison to sign, all missing. For only a fleeting moment did she suspect Cecelia. Looking in the most unlikely places, she found her blouse stuffed behind the dryer; the photograph of them with Sean beneath the sofa cushion; *Song of Solomon* protruding from a plastic bag of trash, grease stained and half the pages torn out.

Now, she couldn't find the topaz and silver necklace and matching earrings she'd bought in New Mexico. All weekend she had searched the house, her fury rising.

"Gregory, I don't have much anymore. So little. Why can't you leave me at least some things that I cherish?"

Feverish with paranoia, she was convinced the actions were not random. Gregory's mind, she was sure, was brimming with malevolence. Stealing like this took cunning, planning, forethought. Diane stood before her husband, herself a kind of wreckage. She had not washed in two days, brushed her teeth, or changed clothes all weekend. All she wanted was to find the jewelry. All she wanted, in the midst of this, was to hold on to one little thing. Even if it was material, tied to vanity and pride. It was *her* little thing, and he had stolen it.

"Just tell me where you put them. I won't be angry. Gregory, this isn't a game. The necklace and earrings, where are they?"

Gregory stood, like a shabby edifice, unmoved in a winter sweater and corduroy pants he had somehow found although it was August and the house was sweltering because the air conditioning was faulty. His answer was to lope away from her nonchalantly, another thing she'd come to hate, casting one last look at her that promised he would never reveal what she wanted so desperately to know.

Talking to Gregory like this set her on edge, made her hypersensitive. *There is no past. No future. Only now, this eternal moment. Now* lived in the extreme, a neon present tense. Each word, whether from him or from her, a possible precipice.

She knew not to touch him from behind because if she did, the inability to see her, to prepare a response often set Gregory howling and running from her. But she grabbed his arm anyway, shouting, "What did you do with them?"

Pulling out of her grasp, Gregory clamped his hands over his ears and stomped in circles around the dining room table.

"I didn't do it. I didn't do it," he said, head bowed forward, hands squeezing his ears.

"You did and you know it."

"No. No."

Trailing him around the table, Diane heard her voice, careening, mad: "You did, you know you did."

The doorbell startled them, and she thought it must be the air conditioning repairman. But when she opened the door and saw Lauren instead, Diane covered her mouth with her hands and reached for her, holding her so tightly, Lauren nearly clawed her way out of her mother's arms. They stood in the portal while Gregory raged in the living room:

"No. No. It wasn't me."

———— ⸎ ————

Freed from her mother's afflicted embrace, Lauren led Diane back into the house.

"He took my topaz and silver necklace. He hid them and won't tell me where they are. He's taken everything. Everything I had. I can't even have one thing of my own," her mother announced, her voice bruised with complaint and outrage.

Lauren took a deep breath, quickly deciding to care for her mother first.

"Come on, you need to lay down, Mom," she said, leading her up the stairs.

"Will you make him tell you what he did with them? You know the topaz necklace and earring set I mean; you borrowed it last year."

"Yes, Mom, I know, I know," Lauren assured her, gently

guiding her mother to her bed. A bed that was unmade, stacked with clothes and a tray holding what looked like the remains of last night's dinner. Lauren removed the clothing and set the tray on the nightstand and sat on the side of the bed, rubbing her mother's shoulders. Weariness was a pall draining her mother's face.

"I can't believe it. Before you arrived I was chasing him around the living room, shouting at him, screaming in fact." Her mother stared at the ceiling, her eyes widened by disbelief.

"Mom, just rest now. Just rest for a while."

"How can I?" She grabbed Lauren's hand and said, "Go. Please check on your father. Make sure he's all right."

Lauren had packed an overnight bag and left it in the trunk of her car in case this turned into a long night's journey where she could not imagine leaving her mother alone with her father. Increasingly, she'd become referee between her parents as they sparred—one coherent, overwhelmed, and growing more and more bitter, the other locked in a netherworld.

"She's mean to me. Why won't she let me go? I have places to be," her father shouted as Lauren walked toward him downstairs.

"Did you hide Mom's jewelry, Dad?"

"No. No," he shouted and folded his arms across his chest as he furiously circled the sofa.

At that moment, Lauren heard a knock at the door.

"Hi. I just stopped by to see how everyone was," Sean said when she opened the door. He stood staring at Lauren with a sheepish grin, wiping his forehead with a handkerchief. "I was in the neighborhood."

"Well, halle-fuckin'-lujah!" Lauren fumed, suddenly near tears. She wanted to slam the door in Sean's face but instead turned away and walked back to her father.

"What's going on?" Sean asked innocently, entering the house with careful, measured footsteps. The sight of his father, arms folded, mumbling angrily and circling the sofa stopped him in the hallway.

"Come on in. He's your father. He won't hurt you."

"Is he always like this?"

"If you were around more, you'd know the answer to that question."

The innocent confusion on her brother's face, the perplexity she heard in his voice enraged her. As their father had fallen deeper into the grasp of the disease, she had watched Sean's unease in their father's presence blossom. He always had an excuse for why he couldn't visit or stop by to give her or Diane a break. And when he did come by, the sight of their father shocked him so that he seemed to be saying good-bye before he had finished saying hello.

She was shocked, too. There was no getting used to it. But for her, there was no other choice. This was her task to perform, one that was onerous and yet, she had come to think, sacred as well. She wanted to ask Sean if he loved their father at all. As angry as she was, she could never go that low.

"I came by to help. You're always saying I never pitch in, but what can I possibly do here?"

"Talk to him. Take him for a walk."

"Talk to him how?"

Closing the distance between them, Lauren said, "Brother, I have to figure that out every day."

"You always had a special bond with him. Your own language, your own code. You're cut out for this."

"He's *our* father," she screamed. "Our. Father. Mom's upstairs trying to rest. I'm going to leave now and let you figure out how to do your share."

She grabbed her bag and stormed out of the house. Not until Lauren was three blocks away, having ordered a pizza from a corner take-out restaurant, did it dawn on her what she had done. Nonetheless, she forced herself to sit at one of the plastic tables outside and slowly eat, willing herself to believe that when she returned to the house, Sean would have found a way.

❊

They all thought he avoided his father because he was irresponsible. He had been absent, but his father was not forgotten. Only Sean knew how it felt to look at his father now and see him as a mirror. Without language to bind them, without coherent thoughts, what was there to say? The disease had stripped Sean of the ease and comfort they had begun to rebuild after his father had visited him that day, which now seemed so long ago, when he first knew something was wrong.

"Come on. Let's watch TV," Sean said and slumped onto the sofa.

He heard his father padding toward him and sit down at the other end of the sofa. Sean picked up the remote control and saw that his mother had taped a list of the channels and corresponding numbers in large black letters on the back. Clearly this was meant to help his father, but he'd lost his memory and no matter how large the letters and numbers were, just as the shapes had once meant nothing to Sean because of his dyslexia, they probably meant little to his father now.

"Let's watch the Nationals, Dad. There's a game on, I think. You know the Nationals are your favorite team."

Gregory shook his head adamantly. "My team is the Orioles."

"But, the Nats are our hometown team."

Making a fist with his right hand and punching his left palm, like a boxer, Gregory insisted, "Orioles, always the Orioles for me."

"Okay, okay."

Sean flipped between channels as Gregory watched him quizzically and said, "The Orioles will beat the Redskins next time."

"You know, I think you're probably right."

Sean watched at his father at the other end of the sofa, staring raptly at the screen. What, he wondered, did he see through those still alert eyes? Within minutes, his father nodded into a deep slumber. Sean went upstairs to see Diane and found her asleep as well. Coming back down, he saw Lauren enter the house.

"I'll do better. I will," he told her.

"Sean, you have to. That's our father. I need your help. Mom needs your help."

"I'll be here. I'll do more." He had said the words before. This time he meant them.

Chapter Fourteen

OCTOBER 2014

The bookstore was packed for a reading from the memoir of a prominent veteran of the civil rights movement, Eunice Benjamin. Benjamin, who had gone on to a career as a journalist and photographer, regaled the crowd with her reading and anecdotes about well-known political and cultural figures who had been major players in the black activism of the late sixties and early seventies.

Gregory sat in the third row of the audience with Diane clutching his hand and Mercer's arm thrown protectively around the shoulders of his friend. Gregory's attention span had been growing shorter and shorter and Diane counted it a minor miracle that he had sat for nearly twenty minutes listening or appearing to listen to the speaker. She was determined not to exile Gregory from life, from other people. Maybe during tonight's reading he would hear a word, a phrase, a question, that would give him a moment of joy, spark a brain cell into resilience. Life. She didn't want to go into hiding. She wasn't ashamed of her husband or his disease.

The audience sat hushed and rapt as Eunice Benjamin read a passage describing her days canvassing the backwoods of Mississippi for blacks willing to attempt to register to vote. She had just read a riveting account of a midnight ride down a darkened Alabama road with a carful of SNCC workers being followed by the police when Gregory released Diane's hand and moved to stand up. Mercer quickly pulled him back into his seat and Gregory said loudly, breaking the spell Eunice Benjamin had cast over them, "Bathroom, I have to go." Heads turned and Diane answered the quizzical looks with a humble, forbearing half-smile. Mercer guided Gregory out of the row.

She watched Mercer lead Gregory through the maze of tables stacked with books, past the shelves marked by category and genre, over Oriental throw rugs, and to the downstairs restroom. She turned back to face Eunice Benjamin, rearranging her body, sitting staunch and straight-backed in the folding chair, trying, with her show of resolve and indifference, to erase Gregory's outburst.

When the question and answer period ended, Mercer and Diane stood watching Eunice sign books as the staff collected the folding chairs. Friends who had entered after they'd arrived, or who had not greeted them earlier warily assessed Gregory, as though he were an unruly toddler whose behavior they had heard rumors of.

"How are you, Gregory?" Sadika Grey asked. She leaned in to hug Gregory and clutched his hand. "Gregory, it's Sadika. Diane will have to bring you to my shop one day. You'd like that, wouldn't you?"

Sadika was a sculptor and jewelry designer. Gregory had often visited her gallery and boutique in Adams Morgan for a unique birthday or Mother's Day gift for Diane. Diane had never seen her in any attire that was not African in origin. Tonight, she was dressed in a dramatic Senegalese-inspired flowing dress called a *bouba* and a starched *galae* of matching cloth reigned on her head.

"How is he?" she asked Diane as her smile collapsed.

"As well as can be expected."

"I mean it, Diane. Bring him to the gallery one day. It would cheer him up."

Diane wanted to ask, *How do you know?* But wouldn't she be just as verbally incompetent and unsure if the roles were reversed and it was she clumsily trying to talk to a longtime friend who had this disease?

Otis Shepherd, a loan officer at the city's only African American–owned bank, spotted them. He first shook hands with Mercer and then easily launched into a conversation with Gregory.

"Man, we haven't done anything since that Wizards' game a couple of years ago. You know, the one where they actually beat the Cavaliers when LeBron was on the team?" Otis smiled broadly. In response, Gregory lifted his hand and pointed his index finger at Otis. Otis told Gregory jovially about his grandchildren and his recent retirement. The ease with which he spoke to Gregory, the way he held Gregory's furtive shaky glance and would not let it go, burst Diane's heart with gratitude.

When Otis stood up to go back to his seat, Diane hugged him and he patted her on the back whispering, "Call me and Miriam anytime, for anything you need."

At home, Gregory turned to Mercer and said, "In the morning. The office," and shuffled into his study.

Diane prepared two cups of tea.

"Whoever thought I'd be drinking goddamn herbal tea," Mercer said. "Remember back in the day when you could just eat any damn thing you wanted to, when eating wasn't something you needed a doctor's prescription to do, when food wasn't something you took pictures of in a restaurant and sent to friends on their phones?"

Diane laughed as they heard Gregory rustling through papers in the next room.

"Is he gonna be okay by himself?"

"For a while anyway."

"I still can't get used to it."

"There is no getting used to it."

"Scares me to death, Diane. I'll be retiring from the firm in a year or two. I want to hang around long enough to mentor Lauren and the new leadership team. But all this has me thinking about my legacy, about having had three wives and no children. Who'll care for me like you and Lauren care for Gregory?"

"Some days, Mercer, when I'm really brave, I ask myself what he's feeling. What he's thinking?"

"What can life be like for him now?"

"I can't convince myself that the life he's living, that he's trapped in, means nothing. That it's only emptiness and torture. Please, Mercer, I have to believe there's more than we can see. More than we can know. Maybe more than we need to know."

"Is he all gone?"

"I still see flashes of who he used to be sometimes. But I feel caught in a permanent state of grieving. I've suffered a loss. It's like a hurricane every day. I've lost my husband, and I still don't know what that will mean for me going forward. It can't go on much longer like this. It's too much. I came in from an evening meeting last week and found Lauren sitting in the dark right here where I'm sitting. In the dark crying. Gregory had trashed the study, and she had finally gotten him to sleep. She told me 'Mom, I can't do this. I love him, but I want my life back. I want the life you both prepared me to have. This isn't it.' What could I say? I want my life back, too? I've started investigating alternatives."

"You mean like one of those places . . ."

"Yes."

A heavy, solemn calm mushroomed between them. Sipping their tea, only the sound of Gregory in the room with his papers crackled the silence.

Then Diane said, "Mercer, I love that man. With everything the last couple of years have demanded of me and of him, I love him. I feel no relief thinking about putting him in an assisted living facility. I feel guilt. I feel remorse. I feel like I have failed. Gregory forced me to reconcile with a father I never wanted to forgive. He never believed I would remain as small and as afraid as, for a long time, I was comfortable being. I owe him too much. Especially for that."

1994

"Are you ready to make the call?"

The question was generous and long-suffering, asked regularly. It spoke to Diane of an unfulfilled promise Gregory assumed, perhaps imposed, but that she had never made. Asked quietly, without a hint of judgment, the inquiry was founded on his unshakable belief that one day Diane would reach out to her father. Gregory believed what she could not. He believed *for* her. His belief became an element in their marriage that she resented yet relied on to alter the DNA of her thinking. Each time he asked, she was consumed by shame and the fear that he would conclude that the mother of his children, the woman he had married, the woman he loved, was a coward. What else could he think when she reflexively reached out to him with an embrace, a hug, a kiss, as she whispered, "No, not yet." Gregory had his beliefs and she had hers. She was cynical, bitter, and terrified, subscribing to a relentless faith in the power of lies and secrets. She had found herself several times edging toward the brink of calling her father, but the thought of the length of the potential drop, or a bloodied fall, always propelled her back from the edge.

Margaret's heart attack, suffered when she was seventy-three, changed everything. Back then, Margaret was active in her sorority, was a member of the Mayor's Advisory Board for Senior Issues, and held fund-raisers to raise money for Dorothy Height's initiative to allow the National Council of Negro Women to purchase the building they were headquartered in on Pennsylvania Avenue. She served on the "Free D.C." committee to gain statehood for the city, and in previous years she had taken Lauren and Sean to Paris for two weeks. Three months before the heart attack, she had journeyed to South Africa on a trip organized by her church.

Diane had come to admire Margaret, was inspired by the way that she had created a life for herself in these later years of widowhood, a life that included an ongoing relationship with a gentleman she referred to as "my old, new boyfriend," whom she had dated before she met Ramsey and who was also then a widower.

The heart attack, which Margaret felt the first signs of while sitting in the pew at Metropolitan AME one Sunday morning, was significant, but not fatal. During the weeks of recuperation, when Margaret stayed with them, Diane thought more and more about mortality and aging and wondered about her father. The distance and brittle stance of indifference that Diane had perfected cracked.

One evening as they cleaned up the kitchen after dinner, Gregory said to Diane, "Thank God I've said everything I needed to say."

"What do you mean?" Diane asked, pausing as she placed cutlery and plates in the dishwasher.

"She dodged a bullet. She's always possessed an air of invincibility, but my mother, like everyone else, is a mere mortal."

"Of course," Diane said.

Gregory stopped wiping the stove and said, "Diane, if you make me, I will ask the question every day for as long as we are together, for as long as we have. When are you going to make the call?"

⸺⸽⸻

Before she picked up the phone to call her father, before she ventured across the country to see him, she had to give her children what she had denied them, a grandfather and the truth. All these years, Diane had told her children what she had been told: "He walked away. He didn't love us anymore. I don't know why."

The truth would be more layered, tender, and raw than the hard-edged artifact she had been offered. Lauren and Sean were teenagers. And this would be the first time she had spoken to them at length about their maternal grandfather. Sitting beside Gregory on the sofa, enduring the quizzical, skeptical gaze of her adolescent children, who more and more seemed refugees from her love, who took every chance to brusquely struggle literally and figuratively out of her grasp, Diane, after days of imagining this moment, found herself speechless. It was Gregory who fueled the revelation, who found words she could not as he sat clutching Diane's hand, looking squarely and fearlessly into the faces of their children. "Your mother has something to tell you."

"Are you sick?" Sean asked, suddenly attentive and alarmed.

She wanted to say, *Yes, I have been sick. Sick with grief most of my life and now I want to get well.* There was nothing to say but everything, and so she used all the words she had sought to protect them from—rape, burglary, abandonment, and what she knew must be her father's shame, what she admitted was her own desire to punish.

"Why are you telling us this now?" Lauren asked, thrusting it all back at Diane.

"You have a grandfather that you need to know. I have a father I need to forgive. It's time."

Sean rose and Diane prepared herself to watch him leave the room, but he sat down on the sofa beside her and buried his head in her shoulder. "When can we meet him, Mom?"

The children were in bed and Gregory sat in a chair near the bed watching her make the call.

Now she was walking in the shoes of all the parents and children whose lives she mandated and adjudicated from the bench. Reconciliation, empathy, forgiveness—she routinely prescribed them for others. Now she felt their weight, how they loomed so large and unapproachable, how humbling and confusing it was to feel the sheer burden of words that demanded so much.

She dialed the Las Vegas number and he answered. *So this is all it took*, she thought, *all these years.* The sound of her father's voice, surprisingly soft and thin, halted her breath.

"Hello, can I speak to Samuel Garrison?"

"This is Samuel Garrison. Who is this?"

"This is Diane. Your daughter."

Whimpers, cast up from a place beyond imagining racked her father's throat. A convulsion he did not try to halt. Diane steeled herself against the sound of her father's shattered voice as he said, "I was ashamed. I never forgave myself. For what I did to your mother, you, and Ronald. It just got easier to stay away."

"Marcia gave me your number. Years ago. I could never use it till now."

"She's told me all about you. How successful you are. Your family."

"You never reached out; you never looked for us." When planning the call, almost as an act of theater, she'd imagined hurling the charge at a climactic moment, but the accusation tunneled out swiftly, would not be delayed or denied.

Then before he could answer, both to wound him and to acknowledge the depth of her own sin, Diane said, "I should have called years ago. I could've."

"All things in time," he said.

Not all things, Diane thought but did not say. "We needed you. All of us. I was five years old when you walked away."

"I've had years to think of nothing else."

———— ✦ ————

In the calls that followed, she developed a friendship with this man, a stranger who reactivated a primal, unquenchable desire in her to be loved. Samuel told her that after he left Washington, he moved around for a couple of years, avoiding everyone he had left back in D.C. He'd finally settled in Las Vegas, played the casinos and got lucky. Won enough money to open a dry-cleaning business. After Ella's death, he had remarried.

"I didn't attend Ella's funeral because I felt like it was me who had in some way killed her. If I had come, I felt like I'd have to turn myself in for punishment. When I heard about Ronald, I didn't leave my house for a week."

Diane sent him pictures of Gregory, Sean, and Lauren, and he sent her photos of his wife. Gregory talked to him on the phone. The children had stilted conversations with the man who was their grandfather.

"Can I tell you something?" Samuel asked Diane during one call.

"Anything. Everything."

"I had nightmares for years after what he did to us. He had a gun and held it on me while he forced Ella to tie me up. Then he raped her. Your mother. My wife. I never got over it. She changed, too. I couldn't touch her, comfort her after that. I could see it in her eyes . . . she hated me for not saving her."

"Did you ever talk to anyone professionally about it? A counselor? A therapist?"

"No. I didn't even know how to do that. When I met Inez, she made me feel as whole as I figured I'd ever be."

Diane thought of the two years she'd spent in therapy, another suggestion Gregory had made, and how their marriage might not have survived without it.

Diane and Gregory made plans to visit her father when the children were out of school, but Samuel Garrison died six months after her first call.

Marcia delivered the news and her father's wife, Inez, called Diane a few hours later and told her that she had discovered Samuel's body in his house.

"We talked a couple of times a week and when I didn't hear from him and when he didn't answer the phone, I knew something was wrong. He'd been in the house two days before I discovered him," she said. She told Diane all the arrangements were being made; all she had to do was come to Las Vegas.

Numbness returned, but this was different, not the numbness of before: a shellac around her heart, a glaze of resistance. This was a membrane separating Diane from the world, riddled with cracks and slivers. She had not cried where tears could be seen, but inside, she was sodden.

Inez met her at the airport. She was a woman of medium height, olive complexion. Her hair was a long sheath of solid gray that reached her shoulders. She was dressed in white capri pants and a striped top. She stepped forward from the crowd and hugged Diane. Tensing in the woman's embrace, Diane realized that Inez was her stepmother.

They walked silently to the parking lot and Diane loaded her suitcase into the trunk of Inez's car. As they prepared to pull out of the garage, Diane asked, "So he died alone and you found him?"

"Unfortunately, yes. Do you want to go to your hotel?"

"If you don't mind, I'd like to go see my father's body."

On the way to the funeral home, Inez told Diane, "This is West Vegas. When we were married, your dad and I lived in North Vegas, but in a sense, this is where he always lived."

Diane looked around at the streets. There were small businesses, boarded-up buildings, a pall of neglect and decay.

"He used to own a dry cleaners over there on that corner. This was before we met. But he got robbed so many times he closed it. But he always came back here. Even after we moved to the suburbs. He got people involved in clean-up campaigns and helped pressure the city to build a recreation center. He'd be in the library during election season registering people to vote. This was where his heart was. He didn't have a lot of friends, but everybody knew and respected him."

In the funeral home, Inez introduced Diane to the owner, Blair Harris, a small wisp of a man in a three-piece suit, his hair slicked back from a protruding hairline.

"This is Sammy's daughter, Diane. She just flew in from Washington."

"The state or . . ."

"The capital city."

"Welcome to Vegas, and I'm sorry you had to come under these circumstances. The memorial service is later this evening," Mr. Harris told Diane as he began walking toward the room where she was sure her father's body lay in repose.

The solemn, austere feel of the funeral home brooded around Diane as she slowly walked toward the front of the room and saw the casket. This is what she had come to do. To see her father.

Samuel Garrison was a large man, his head shaved and gleaming. His fleshy face was studded by a moustache. The powder and embalming fluid cast a gray shadow over his face. This was the face of her father, dead. It was not, therefore, the face she had longed to see all her life. The face she had first seen in a picture just a few months ago. Her father was dead, and because she had not really known him in life, looking at him now, she did not know what to feel or what to think. She did not know what she saw on his face. They said that in the casket you saw the face that the person had earned, but you could only see that face if you knew the person. Then you could judge. She did not know her father. Not really. He was dressed in a blue suit and gray tie, his large hands folded atop his groin. Despite the sins of omission, her father's face was a mask of calm. This was the posed theatrical face of the dead: cared for, designed to quiet the qualms of those who would have to look upon the face one last time. Diane searched the face for the story of her father's love for her mother or what it meant to watch your wife's rape. Her father's eyes were sealed shut, so she could not look into them to see whatever had, in the end, remained in his heart.

Inez sat in the front row of folded chairs that would fill later in the evening.

Diane turned around and said, "I'm ready to go."

"Would you like to get something to eat?"

Diane thought of the hotel room and wanted to delay her arrival there as long as possible. "Sure. I would like that."

Inez drove out of West Vegas and stopped at a mall where they found an Italian restaurant.

"I thought I'd feel more," Diane said.

"Trust me, you will."

"Could you tell me something about him, anything? How long were you married?"

"We were still married."

"I mean . . ."

"I met Sammy at a bingo game. I'm a midwife and still practicing. I was always delivering babies, making families happy, and I wanted a family of my own. I had given up. I was almost forty when I met Sammy. I never thought I would find love. I don't know if that's what I found with Sammy, but it was enough. There isn't much of an Argentinian community out here; most of my friends are black. I had heard about him, this guy who a couple of years back won big at the casinos and owned a dry cleaners. I knew he had lost something that mattered to him and

I knew that I would have to wait before he told me what it was. He seemed like a good man, though. We were both lonely and thought before it was all over, before giving up, we'd give love, give marriage a try. It was that simple. We were serious, at least I was. He said he was an old man but he wanted to start over. I wanted to try to have a child. But he told me he had a family once and something bad happened and he didn't want to risk having a family again. I said if we couldn't have a child maybe we could adopt. He didn't want to.

"I was happy for a while. We were like a normal couple. He liked showing off our life. He said I was enough. He had run all his life and he wanted to stop running. I didn't know what he meant until he told me everything. Everything about your mother, your brother, you. The terrible thing that happened. How he'd run away from all that, from you. I felt closer than ever to him because I finally knew what he'd been hiding. I felt so much love for him then. But the next day he felt ashamed for telling me. It's like he grew further and further away the more I knew him and the more I understood. I told him that one day he might see you again.

"After a while he stopped coming home at night, wouldn't tell me where he was, and so I left him. He had treated me bad, but after I left, he tried to make up. For a long time, I didn't speak to him or see him, then he called me one day and said he was tired and afraid of dying alone. Said if I couldn't be his wife, could I be his friend?"

"You said he didn't have many friends."

"People thought they knew Sammy, but they never did. People thought they were his friends but they weren't. But when you called, he was happier than I had ever seen him. He went to a lawyer and revised his will. Made the lawyer the executor of his estate, told him on his death, to sell the dry cleaners and divide whatever he got between me and you."

—— ∞ ——

The next day at the funeral, Diane sat beside Inez and listened to the young men her father had hired to work in his dry cleaners tell stories of his mentorship, the young men he'd coached on the basketball team at the rec center, who'd called him "Pop." One man who had promised Samuel Garrison when he got out of jail that he would never go back, didn't, he said, because Samuel let him work in his cleaners.

At the repast in Inez's neat bungalow, the old men and women came over to Diane and gave her hugs.

"Sammy never told me he had a daughter. He shouldn't've kept you a secret."

As the repast wound down, Diane sat alone in a gazebo in Inez's backyard and that is where she finally cried.

She stayed an extra day in Las Vegas, remained in the place her father had called home. She lay in bed in her room the morning after the funeral meditating on the hypotheses, the lies, the secrets, the conjecture, and the final truth her father had told her. Samuel Garrison fled to Las Vegas, away from the scene of the crime committed against him and his wife, two thousand miles from all of it, left behind like scattered debris. Miles and miles, and he never looked back. Or so she'd thought, but he'd been looking back every day. Looking back when he hid it all from Inez, from the people in West Vegas who thought they knew him. And after he had revealed it, he'd had to hide it all once again—hide it or die. All those people he helped, were they stand-ins for her mother, for Ronald, for her? In the end, he didn't want to be alone but died alone in his bed and in his house anyway.

Before she left, Diane walked the Strip, garish, overwhelming, a Disneyland for adults. She went into the casinos, saw the machines where her father had hit it big enough to be written about in the newspapers, the sprawling rooms where he came weekly, up until the day before he died, still looking for luck. He must've thought luck was a form of forgiveness. When he won, he must have been able, for a moment, to put it all to rest. Before leaving for the airport she called Gregory.

"So, who was he? Who was Samuel Garrison?" he asked.

"He was my father."

Mercer smiled in appreciation when she finished. "I thought I knew everything there was to know about y'all."

Mercer had sat listening to the story Diane told, his eyes never leaving her face. Gregory had walked quietly into the room and sat on a hassock, oblivious to the fact that Diane was honoring him with piety and tenderness. "Even friends keep some secrets."

Mercer reached for Gregory's hand and shook it. "You did good, buddy, you did real good by this woman here. Do you know that?"

Gregory smiled broadly, his eyes aglow looking at Mercer. He shook Mercer's hand vigorously up and down, until Mercer had to place his palm on their hands to quell the movements.

"And that's the man that I'm now planning to put away somewhere, Mercer," Diane said. "He did that for me."

Chapter Fifteen

MARCH 2015

The moment Diane opened the door to her study, Gregory pushed her aside, his face a mask of unreasoning fury. Her frightened gasp was swallowed up by the barrage of his hands grabbing her, his fists thudding and leaden, random yet precise.

Help me, thundered in her mind yet lay yoked, denied an exit by her throat.

If I hurt you . . . If I hurt you . . . Diane remembered as she sank to the floor, feeling her cheeks begin to swell.

Gregory, now spent, breathless and leaning against her desk, shouted, "My memories? Where are they? I want them back."

"Help, help me," Diane called, hoping Lauren was still downstairs. She burst in the room a moment later.

"Daddy, Daddy, stop, please stop," Lauren said, hugging Gregory, before carefully, almost gently, leading him from the room.

Diane rose from the floor, crawled to her office chair, and hauled her body upright.

"I made him lie down in the bedroom," Lauren said, entering the room again and firmly closing the door. "Are you all right? Did he hurt you?"

"Yes." That was the only word she could say.

"My memories, where are they?" he had asked, demanded.

It had been weeks since Gregory had spoken a full, declarative sentence. More and more, he broke through the simmering silence with a grab, push, or pull to express physically what he could not verbally. He would stand behind her and pinch her arm or bump into her on purpose. This, his doctor told Diane, was an expression of frustration and a language all its own. Yet periodically, coherence returned full blast.

"Are you okay?" Lauren asked again.

"No, Lauren, I'm not."

The bathroom mirror reflected the tender blush of a bruise beginning to form under her right eye, and Diane wondered how she would explain it at work.

Nightfall invited Gregory to rise from bed and roam the house, pacing from room to room. Their house, normally placid, slumbering at night, was now restless and alive. It was during these weeks that Diane allowed herself to wonder how long she, how long *they*, could live like this. Gregory had hit her. Given her a black eye. The lock and chain she'd installed on the bedroom door offered a fragile illusion of safety. They were both incarcerated in different prisons. He no longer knew her as his wife. She refused to accept that this man was not her husband, for if he was not her husband now, he never had been.

Days passed before Diane allowed herself to think and then speak the words. As caretaker, she was the closest and easiest target. The thought that they would not go on like this, that there would inevitably be an alternative, a separation, was never voiced. Speaking it to Lauren, to Sean, would turn her into stone.

"If I ever hurt you . . ." he had said. *Put me away.*

But back then, that was conjecture, hypothesis. Now, the *if* was real, and it rubbed her raw.

———— ⬯ ————

When Gregory gazed dismissively at the bowl of soup and pushed it onto the floor, Diane cracked as rudely, as instantly, as the ceramic. "Clean it up right now, you bastard. All that I've done and this is what I get."

Her pulse splashed bitterness into her bloodstream. Tears blazed down her cheeks. The sound of the profane words filled her with an edgy pride.

"Look at me," she screamed, marching around the table to face Gregory. Then it was as though her arm was not her arm, but she felt it rising, felt the full force of the slap trickling up, then the feel of Gregory's stubble against her fingers, the ripple of the slap in her fingertips. The slap that turned his face away. The slap that brought him to tears.

The tears no longer moved her, and she didn't care if he struck back. Maybe it would be better if they fought it out, she thought, fought it out . . . till the end . . . whenever that might be.

The slap transported her into an unfamiliar, virgin zone of new misery and guilt. She had slapped her demented, mentally confused husband. Yet the slap was the most intimate act between them in years because of the passion it unleashed in them both.

With an orgasmic radiance, the slap tingled in her fingers, pulsed throughout her body. She sank into the chair and watched as more tears filled Gregory's eyes, his stunned, bright, and knowing eyes. He knew that he had been slapped, hurt, and abused. There were more tears trickling down his cheeks than she had seen him shed since this all began. She sat stony, hardened, and too brittle to cry. Too ashamed to cry. Too stubborn in this moment even to lean forward and kiss the red and tender spot where her anguish left damning evidence. Gregory, wobbly and quietly weeping, pushed himself up with his hand on the edge of the kitchen table and walked away.

He could walk away from her. Find a hiding place where he would be safe from his crazed wife. But she could not walk away from him.

Could not grab her purse and keys. Could not go.

She could not, she could never leave him alone.

Diane cleaned up the broken bowl and wiped up the soup from the floor, then stood at the counter and finally released her furtive tears. Through that veil, she looked at her hand, her fingers, and began furiously washing them. Drying them, she stifled a final sob and went to find her husband wherever he was in the house.

There was only one person who she could tell what she had done. Later that evening, when Gregory had sunk into a deep and abiding sleep, she called Paula.

"How do I find grace in this?"

"You're both walled off against each other. The only thing I can suggest, Diane, is that you climb over that wall. You're the only one who can. Maybe grace is on the other side."

Diane was now a family court judge who had been both a victim and a perpetrator of domestic violence. An officer of the court who could be arrested. Gregory's blows, her act of violence, each had pushed them across lines never before crossed. Made the unthinkable easy, even necessary. If Gregory could punch her, she could slap him. Husband and wife teetered on and then plunged over tipping points both dangerous and seductive. Seductive, because on the other side of the slippery demarcation lay the promise of relief, unreasoning, but entirely deserved.

Despite what Diane thought she had decided, the prospect of placing Gregory in a memory care unit in an assisted living facility remained so toxic she thought of it as a kind of radiation that she could only approach timidly and with care. Weeks passed during which Diane shared her decision only with Paula, whom she asked to help her find suitable facilities to visit and assess. Octavia Sanders, the social worker who facilitated the support group she irregularly attended, guided Diane through the maze of the new world she was entering. She gave Diane a stack of booklets and brochures that Diane and Paula spent an afternoon looking through while Bruce and his son Aaron took Gregory out for a ride and to a steakhouse.

Diane and Paula sat at Paula's dining room table, passing the colorful booklets between them.

"Listen to the names," Paula said, "Lighthouse. Morningside House. Golden Pond. Heartlands. They sound like synonyms for heaven."

"I had no idea that a whole industry had sprung up to care for every aspect of growing old. Caregivers relief, life management, someone to come to your house and pay your bills when you can't do it anymore."

"There but for the grace of God, my sister."

Week after week, she and Paula toured the upscale, attractive, and inviting facilities. Facilities that were beautifully decorated, colorful, serene, where everything about the décor and the atmosphere, and the competence of the directors they talked to, promised calm in the midst of a family's storm. Home away from home.

Paula had a friend whose mother was a resident of Somersby and who recommended it, so they toured Somersby's memory care unit, guided by a certified nursing assistant. What they saw were mostly black men and women who had been middle-class professionals—airline pilots, lawyers, social workers. They looked healthy and prosperous, like life had been good to them—until now. When they looked closer, they saw the tall pecan-colored woman pacing the halls and hovering around the exit, her eyes as large as saucers, distant and suspicious; the man leaving his room in a business suit, newspaper folded under his arm, umbrella in hand, carrying a briefcase; and the woman sitting in a rocking chair, holding a doll in her arms in an ironclad embrace.

———— ❧ ————

The decision, in the end, was Diane's alone to make. There would be no family meeting. She would just tell them—Sean, Lauren, Mercer, and Bruce—what she had decided and she would do it on the phone to avoid a scene. But Diane knew that she had to tell Margaret in person.

In Margaret's apartment Diane watched her water a four-foot-tall philodendron she had named Oprah. Through the window, Diane could see the spires of the National Cathedral. Margaret valued her independence and had refused to move in with Bruce or into a senior citizens' retirement community. A half-finished crossword puzzle from the day's paper lay folded on the table beside Margaret's laptop computer. A CD of classical standards played in the background.

Margaret placed the plastic watering container in the sink and then joined Diane in the living room. In gray velour pants and a black sweater, Margaret possessed the air of a dowager:

her gray hair in a style that was braided, complicated, and regal; massive hoop earrings dangling from her ears; various rings on her fingers; and her reddened lips full and plump.

"I know why you've come to see me, Diane. Lauren called and told me."

"I wanted to tell you in person."

"You have to think about yourself," Margaret said, reaching for a crystal bowl of nuts on the table beside her. "Believe me, my dear, no one else will." Margaret gently scooped a handful of the nuts, offered some to Diane, who politely declined. "I was fifty-five when Ramsey died. Fifty-five," she said as though she did not believe it. "We were supposed to be entering our golden years."

"How did you cope, Margaret?"

"You were there for the last of it. You saw what I went through."

"Yes, but I look back and remember now that I never asked you how you were doing, how you were holding up."

"If you had asked me, I'm not sure I would have known what to say or how to say it. But there was someone." Margaret took a tissue from the box on the coffee table and wiped her hands.

"Someone?"

"Yes, a friend. A former colleague from Howard."

"Was it meaningful?" Diane asked, choosing the word specifically for the multitude of definitions it possessed.

"Very much so." Margaret smiled proudly. "He was a wonderful man. I needed someone who wasn't family. Someone who wouldn't ask me anything but would listen to what I said or even what I didn't say. My husband was wasting away before my eyes. That man and I spent precious time together. No matter what kind of day it was, he helped me carry it, he helped me bear it."

"So you were . . . friends?"

"And after a while we were much more. He made it possible for me to have the strength to love Ramsey the way he needed and not be angry because there was so little he could give me. You look surprised."

"It's not every day that a woman hears her mother-in-law say she had an affair."

"I don't think of it as an affair now and I didn't then. My son is gone. The husband you once had isn't there anymore. He's not coming back to us. If you feel it's time to place him in one of those homes, do it. I trust you, and I know you'll find the very best one you can."

"Back when all this first started, the day we got the formal diagnosis, he told me that as we went through this together, to do what I felt was best, and especially if he ever hurt me. But back then, that's the kind of thing I would expect him to say."

"Diane, he meant it. I know he did. He loved you too much not to."

Chapter Sixteen

SEPTEMBER 15, 2015

The broad-limbed, sheltering trees were cloaked in early autumn dusk. Small mountains of leaves coated the sidewalks and lawns. The streetlights felt more eerie than illuminating as Diane sat in her car, hesitating to enter her house.

Across the street, she watched Tim and Sandy Neilson heading toward her, arm in arm, walking their golden retriever, Sonny. Tim and Sandy were among the first on the street willing to talk to Diane about the changes they noticed in Gregory, and Sandy, a justice department lawyer, had told Diane that her own mother suffered from dementia.

Wind rattled and blustered, swirling the piles of leaves, and she knew she had to go inside. When she opened the front door, she stepped into a pile of mail that had been slipped through the door drop and stooped to retrieve it from the floor. She tossed her briefcase and cashmere coat onto the sofa and turned on all the lights. Then she went upstairs to the bedroom and changed into a pair of fleece pants and a turtleneck.

In the good times, dinners had often been casual, just the two of them: Gregory entering the house laden with bags from the Ethiopian place on Colorado Avenue. The bags of food on the counter. The smells humid, hot, fragrant, irresistible. That first look, that quick yet all-consuming gaze between them that affirmed he had come home. That look, so small and so much in it; *Hello,* his look said. *Welcome home,* she would beam at him. He often came home exhausted but wired, all of that at once.

Upstairs he would go, the heavy-yet-light footsteps. She would open the Styrofoam plates of food, a startling slash of more vivid color than she had seen all day: the split peas, a muted tender green; the lentils yellow as the sun; the tomatoes, tiny seeded hearts; peppers so hot their heat sprang forth. Above her, Gregory's feet padded across the bedroom floor as he removed the day's uniform, neatly, carefully hanging up the slacks, the jacket, tossing the shirt in the hamper.

Downstairs he would come, the steps lighter in slippered feet. The kitchen table now laden with food, the lamb and vegetables no longer in white Styrofoam cartons but on plates. Was this a night for paper plates, or had she lovingly spooned the meal onto fine china because they rarely used those dishes and they could make Tuesday night a celebration? There would be his beer, Sam Adams, and her glass of wine, chardonnay. They rarely said grace—*they were grace.* Eight, ten hours after walking out of the house, they had returned to it and to each other.

How was your day? The question might as well have been *Once upon a time,* for all that it inspired. The stories of that day would be told seeking sustenance, agreement, support—for it really was them against that stupid, bigoted, idiotic world.

But in the first week after Gregory's move to Somersby, Diane had slowly wriggled into the skin of an unalterably new life. She had given notice that in the spring she would retire from the family court, a decision a long time coming but that felt finally right. Howard University's law school had offered her a professorship that would begin in a year. A position that she had accepted. Howard University, where Ramsey Tate had attended medical school before heading the department of surgery at Freedman's Hospital, where Margaret had also attended before teaching social work for many years, and where Gregory had attended the school of architecture.

There was so much to look forward to, but the present she feared would never be past. There had been a call from Somersby about Gregory hitting one of the nursing assistants and his refusal to eat. These were common patterns of adjustment she was told, but she worried nonetheless about the decision she had made with so much guilt, anguish, and care. That call made it clear: her husband was institutionalized—no matter the charming name of the place or the lovely décor. She had left him in the care of strangers who she trusted would do for him only what was best.

On this night, after eating a quick, improvised meal of leftovers, Diane looked at the mail, mostly junk, bills, and an update about Medicare. She washed her plate and cutlery, and then went upstairs to her bedroom.

The day after Gregory had beaten her, she'd bought a chain lock and installed it on her bedroom door. It was a symbolic, second tier of defense in case Gregory dislodged the lock built into the doorknob. Diane stood in the doorway to her bedroom, quaking with memories of the fear she'd felt. If Gregory could hit her once, would he do it again? If he hit her again, what would she do to defend herself? The chain lock was modest and possibly inadequate, but both locks had withstood Gregory's occasional attempts to enter the bedroom at night.

Dismantling the lock was even easier and faster than

installing it. As her hands rubbed the rugged spot bearing the imprint of the lock that had defaced the door and her union with Gregory, Diane opened the door wide, its creaking a kind of song.

"Can I get you anything while you're waiting?" the server asked, breaking into Sean's thoughts.

"No, no, I'll wait. My sister's always late." He smiled then reached for his glass of water and took a sip.

He looked across the street and saw the city's main library branch. The ceiling-high windows of the restaurant showcased his father's signature building. Because of its electric exterior design and the exuberant play of light and weather on the five levels of glass windows that formed the basic structure, Sean had always thought of the building as a book cathedral. The way the building arched toward the sky lifted anyone observing it and elevated everything that took place within its walls. Inside, the colorful, carpeted floors and soothing, sky-blue walls were totally surprising, as were the plush, comfortable chairs, and wide, solemn, burnished wood tables that made the building flush with a composure that honored what libraries were for, foremost, the work of the mind. Whenever he drove or walked past the library, he was honored to be his father's son.

He had finally attended one of the support group sessions his mother had told him about. While Diane chose not to attend, she had nonetheless urged that he and Lauren go. Near the end, he had raised his hand and asked the social worker, Ms. Sanders, "How can I make my father remember me?"

"He hasn't forgotten you," she said. "But he doesn't know you as an adult. He doesn't recognize you, but I'll bet he knows your voice. Talk with him about the childhood you've left behind. When you visit him, bring a photo of yourself when you were much younger. Talk about yourself in the third person, point to the photo and tell him about the person in the picture using your name."

Now that he was making good on his promise to Lauren and spending more time with his father, they often pored over family photo albums. They sat together, his father relying on a shrinking vocabulary and a battered ability for recall. They had lost so much, Sean would think, watching his father's fingers trace the faces in the photos. But the communion created from the silences and puzzles and empty space the disease imposed managed to fill him with a sense of the life lived between them, and something very much like love planted its flag.

Sean looked away from the sight of the library and saw Lauren walking toward him.

"So sorry I'm late," she announced as she sauntered to the table.

Lauren looked both ready for business and feminine in a burgundy-colored suit and sheer black blouse. Her light brown dreadlocks were chin length and framed a face that Sean thought was quite lovely. This was the sister who had confessed to him one night in high school that she had always felt like an ugly duckling, as they sat parked in his car outside the house and shared a joint.

Lauren tossed a small, black leather handbag onto the chair between them, settled into her seat, and grabbed a menu, saying, "Let's order. I'm starved."

"Not starved enough to be on time."

"Truce, please?"

Sean signaled for their waitress, as thin and lacquered as a runway model, and they ordered. Lauren grabbed a slice of pita bread from the basket on the table.

"You look good," Sean said. "So carrying the weight of Caldwell & Tate hasn't brought you down?"

"Is that what you're waiting for?"

"Come on, you made your choice, and I made mine."

"You're talking to one of the three managing partners. They made me a partner not just because my last name is Tate, but because in the short time I've been with the firm, I earned that spot. Mercer lobbied for me and that helped, too."

"Mom told me. Congratulations."

"And you?"

"I've got my crew renovating a couple of houses across the river. Anacostia is the new frontier. I just wish Dad could see all this, what I'm doing. And understand it."

"You ought to take him to one of your projects one day. I keep telling you, Sean, it doesn't look like it, but he's still there."

His father *was* still there. One evening, Sean had asked his mother why he felt closer to his father now than he ever had. He confided that more than once he had looked into Gregory's distant, always disconcerting stare and whispered, "I love you, Dad." Why, he had asked his mother, did he feel able, emboldened to say that to a man who he was sure could not understand what he said, the words people spent their lives longing to hear.

"I don't know, Sean," she'd said. "Maybe it's because he is literally stripped to his core. There's nothing like pride or vanity or bitterness left for him. He's terribly, horribly free. And maybe, just maybe that opens up a region in our souls, too."

Their orders arrived, a dozen small plates of Greek, Lebanese, and Mediterranean food: hummus, eggplant, falafel, ground lamb, and more. Finding space on the table for all the plates was a feat that their waitress managed with skill and good humor.

They tackled the small plates before them as though their

hunger was more than physical, as though it resided in a dangerous place they had both inadvertently touched. The restaurant, all hardwood floors, open windows, and chrome, the size of a warehouse, was loud as an echo chamber.

"I told Mom I could move in for a while if she wanted me to until she gets used to being in the house alone. There've been a couple of burglaries on her street," Sean said. "I talked it over with Valerie and she'd understand."

"What did Mom say?"

"What do you think? 'I can handle it.'"

"I'm not surprised," Lauren said. Her cell phone rang and looking at the screen, Lauren said, "I'll call them later." She then looked at Sean.

"This has nothing to do with Mom, but I've always wanted to ask you, Sean. There's a test you can take to see if you might develop Alzheimer's. Would you take it?"

"I'd be afraid to know."

"Uncle Bruce says he counsels against it. Says the test isn't entirely reliable and there's no more you can do to fight it the day after you know you have the gene than the day before. And that it could affect your insurance, employment. What would I do with the information if it was bad? How would it affect the rest of my life?" Lauren asked, slumping back against her chair, fingering the rim of her water glass. "I mean, tell me, how do you even prepare for something like this?"

———— ◦◦◦◦ ————

This was the third test. Each time, the plus sign in the window of the plastic stick informed Lauren that she was pregnant. Plus sign. Positive. So why was she flooded with a foreboding that increased with each test? She and Gerald were good, they were happy together. Why was she so certain that this child, real and tangible in her imagination long before peeing on a plastic strip in her toilet, would change everything?

Lauren looked at the results again and then tossed the test into the trash can. She wiped herself, pulled up her panties, washed her hands, and went into her bedroom. Lying on her bed, she hugged herself, willed herself not to cry, and thought of her friends Whitney and Marla who had taken her to the club where she and Gerald met. Both had had abortions.

"The relief was a godsend," Marla had told Lauren. "I got a second chance to have the life I wanted."

Whitney had said, "I felt a lot of things—relief, but also regret that I had not anticipated, and guilt. But the relief, that never went away. The other emotions in time, they did."

Why was she thinking about abortions when, for her, that was not an option? No matter what Gerald said, she would have this baby. Their child.

Everything in her life until now had felt ordained by her genes, her talent, her father. Having this child was *her* first adult decision. She would mother her child with bold intentions. But how would that child be fathered? Her father had told her to have a life. Now life had her by the throat, and she inhaled its tingling and raw effervescence. She was afraid but she could breathe.

Lauren looked at the clock. It was Saturday night and she was meeting Gerald and some friends downtown in a new Spanish restaurant near Union Station. As she dressed, to calm herself, she thought about her and Gerald, about the things that made them a couple that Marla and Whitney both teasingly and convincingly said they envied.

The Sunday afternoon Redskins parties that she attended in the basement of his family's rambler in New Carrollton were raucous affairs where football became a blood sport among the seven Stone siblings and their girlfriends, wives, and children. Gerald's father, who worked for Pepco, was a Dallas Cowboys fan. His mother wanted the Redskins to change their name but said she'd support them win, lose, or draw.

Lauren didn't even like football, but on those Sundays, squeezed onto the leather sofa between Gerald and his mother, Nadine, she felt like she had another family. A family where no one was sick with a disease whose name she could not bear to speak.

Then there was the day Gerald had spent an afternoon with her as she drove to several Caldwell & Tate projects in the city, explaining, "I want to see what you do."

At a bar the previous week, they'd sat drinking and munching on exotic, artsy appetizers, all before going to see a review of comedians D. L. Hughley and George Lopez at the Warner Theater. His friend Lucian had leaned across the small table and asked, "So when are you two making it official?"

"Make what official?" Gerald had asked.

"What you got going on," he said, a broad conspiratorial grin beaming at Lauren and Gerald. "Y'all look like an ad for one of those dating services."

"We're doing just fine. Just fine." Gerald laughed, throwing a possessive arm around Lauren. "Don't give her any ideas."

Lauren had laughed nervously and wanted in that moment to remove Gerald's arm.

"We're *born* with those ideas," Lucian's girlfriend, Caitlin, had said.

"*We're* not." Gerald laughed again, too loudly, Lauren thought, as he leaned across the table and theatrically slapped palms with Lucian. Then to Lauren, he said, "We've arrived where we were headed. Smack dab in the middle of a comfort zone and it feels real good, right babe?"

Lauren had looked at Gerald and chose silence as an act of mild defiance. Her mother had told her once that silence and inaction were two of the most unrecognized power moves.

"Anyway," Gerald had said, looking slightly annoyed but clearly driven to shut down Lucian's jocular inquiry. "Okay, I'll speak for us both. We're just fine. In our comfort zone. With no surprises."

Now dressed, Lauren put on her silver earrings and looked in the mirror one last time. She liked what she saw.

Five hours later, after they had returned to her apartment, after she had tasted the pungent remnants of rum and Coke on his tongue as they kissed, after they laughed about the evening they had just shared, she told him.

He was silent. But the silence was not silent at all; instead it was a crackling electric heat groaning in the space between them. He was sitting, his legs spread, arms resting on his thighs. At the sound of her words, her declaration, what Lauren thought of as *their* truth, Gerald hung his head. She wasn't sure if he was avoiding her gaze in anger or defeat.

I'll touch him, Lauren thought. Her first thought now was to comfort Gerald. Comfort him as though he had been wounded. Hurt by what she had revealed.

"Aren't you on the pill?" He raised his head so she could see the disbelief, the mistrust, in his eyes. That question answered everything she had wondered. Closed every door she thought stood open between them.

"Yes, but nothing's foolproof. Even with the pill there's a five percent chance of pregnancy."

Gerald stood up, able, it seemed, only to place distance between them as he paced. She watched him pacing, the noisy silence threatening to engulf them again. She thought to apologize, to say "I'm sorry," but then wondered why she would lie.

"What do you want to do?" He had stopped pacing and stood still, asking her. The fact that she could not read the emotions on his face terrified her.

"I want to have it."

The admission forced him to sit down in a chair across from her. "I'm not ready to be a father."

"I'm ready to be a mother."

"So I guess that's all that matters?"

"This is a shock, Gerald, I know that, but we did this together."

"I guess we did."

He could not say he loved her. How was that possible, she wondered, when she felt *her* love like a contagion? When she walked through her life giddy but balanced, convinced that if need be, she could fly.

"I wish you could say you loved me. But loving our baby, I'll take that. Not as a consolation prize, but as the way it has to be."

"I just need some time."

"Time for what?" she shouted. "To fall in love with me by default? Because I'm carrying your child? What do I have to do?"

"Lauren, calm down. We've got a good thing. A great thing. We've got our whole lives."

"I don't feel that way, Gerald. I've got today. I've got now. Right now, *this* is my whole life."

"I'll be there for you and the baby. Don't make me a bad guy. I said I'd step up. I won't let you down." The words were an unconvincing whisper.

Lauren thought, but did not say, *But I want you to hold me up.*

"I don't know, I don't know," he stammered. "I feel trapped by this, all of a sudden. Out of nowhere."

"Nowhere? What have the last six months meant to you? So that's where we've been, nowhere? So then all this has meant nothing."

"Did I say that?"

"Yes, in a way you did. Yes, that's how I heard it."

"I care about you, Lauren, you know that."

"But you don't love me."

Gerald hid his face in his hands.

There was nothing left. No other way to stand up for her child. And so that's what Lauren did. She stood up slowly, unfurling her body with a methodical grace and calm. Standing before Gerald she offered him her hand.

"I love you, Gerald. I love our baby. Tonight, love me. Love us."

Their coupling was a storm, for Lauren an act of greed and hunger, for Gerald both surrender and retreat. Lauren cradled him beneath her heart, clinging to him. When she woke in the morning, groggy, unfulfilled, he was gone.

Lauren couldn't tell her mother that the house was falling apart. Not now, with everything she was dealing with. The leaking faucets in the bathroom, the chipping paint, the worn hardwood. This house no longer felt like her childhood home. They had both changed.

Sitting on the carpeted floor flipping through channels as her mother thumbed through a textbook she was considering using for her classes at Howard next year, Lauren asked, "What if I'm having the baby because we're losing Dad?"

"There are worse reasons for having a child," Diane said, closing the book.

"Mom, I haven't heard from Gerald in two weeks, not since the night I told him. He's not answering my texts or calls."

"Give him some time."

"I won't beg him to do the right thing."

"Lauren, you told me he said he'd do exactly that. It's just that your definitions of 'the right thing' are probably different at this point."

"I won't ask him for anything he doesn't want to give. I don't need him. I can do this alone if I have to." Rising from the floor, Lauren reached for her mother, burrowed into the shelter offered by her arms. "Am I wrong? To want this baby? Was I unfair to him?"

"Of course not. He's not wrong for needing some time to take all this in."

"Mom, are you lonely?"

"That's a word that has a lot of different meanings."

Lauren gently pulled out of her mother's embrace and asked, "What do you miss most about Dad? Since all this started I don't think I ever asked you that."

"Him seeing me. Knowing me. Understanding me. When I come home now, that's when it hits me. How much I've lost. I'd give anything, Lauren, to get that back. I miss your father. I miss our life. Very much."

Chapter Seventeen

SEPTEMBER 2015

He cannot sleep on nights like this one, so he slips out of the room they gave him and walks the long hallway. Walks until one of the women who wear the white pants and the blue tops and the white shoes, appears and takes his arm, her palm at his back, and steers him back to bed. This night, he has decided to trick them. Before, he would leave the room fully dressed, his shoes sliding against the floor's surface. That was how they found him.

But tonight, naked and noiseless, he creeps along the long hallway of rooms where the others must be sleeping, the darkness broken by night-lights plugged into the walls in the meeting room, the den, the TV room. His clothes lay in a forlorn pile at the foot of his bed, for he tore off the shirt, ripping the tiny buttons, hearing them pop into the air and then land with a soft thud on the floor. Stepping out of his pants and underwear, he left them stationed, waiting for the return of his legs to give them life.

He moves through this place naked, unhampered. Up the stairs, although there is no need to, he tiptoes, holding the ban-nister, relieved of the confusion within confusion that haunts him during the day, looking into the faces of the others. He grabs the steel knob and slowly opens the door. The lower floor is miles behind him. So he walks, his shoulders and head high. It is enough to softly trek these long, narrow hallways, so many more than in the house of the woman who brought him here. He turns a sharp left, a sharp right, and another hall awaits him. His destination is surely close. Nocturnal smells singe the air—sleep, tossing, turning, an odd moan, a cry like an infant from behind the doors he passes. These things possess an aroma unique to and brought forth by the day's end. His naked body even smells different at night, perfumed by the day just past, humming in his muscles, etched on his skin.

Down these corridors he moves, further with each step away from the women who are like nurses. As he runs down the halls naked, Wallis Peebles, who was the first of the other residents to speak to him and tell him her name the day he was brought here, opens her door, clutches the collar of her robe at her throat, and calls out, "Where are you going? Can I go with you?" Wallis rushes out of her room with a sheet to cover his body and helps the nurse blanket him, swaddle him in the sheet, then stands in the middle of the hallway waving good-bye, calling behind him, "Bon voyage," as the nurse leads him away.

In this place, where loneliness festers and desire is a haunting, unforgotten sign of life, Wallis Peebles knows that Gregory has been sent as an answer to her prayers. He bears himself as though in the other life, before this place, he had mastered his world.

If she had not tried, one too many times, to leave on her own, without her family knowing where she was headed, she would still be in her apartment in the senior citizens' complex. She knew where she wanted to go, told the taxi drivers to take her to Woodward and Lothrop, downtown on Eleventh and G Street. But they all said what her nephew Kevin told her, that Woodward and Lothrop, where she worked as a milliner for twenty years, was torn down years ago. All she wants to do is go to Woodies and see one of her hats in the window.

All her life she has loved hats. A woman became a lady, a queen, in a hat. Her success at Woodies inspired her to open her own shop with money borrowed from her sister and brother, a tiny place squeezed in between a tailor shop and a Chinese carry-out on T Street, not far from the Howard Theater. There she flourished for a while, but then when women started wearing short skirts, pants, and stopped wearing hats, only the Sunday church ladies came to her shop. So she had to go back to Woodies. But it was there that she became the lead designer and made hats for the rich white ladies who gave society parties in Georgetown and on Capitol Hill, the wives of congressmen and senators.

She retired, was living on Social Security and her savings. Then she began to yearn for who she used to be. She'd get up in the morning, and after her coffee, her bowl of oatmeal, orange juice, and her pills, she would spend an hour or more picking out just the right dress, shoes, and hat. Satisfied with the ensemble, she'd spray her neck and arms with a mist of Jean Naté and, giddy with a sense of purpose, lock the door behind her and go out looking for her life.

But the city had been turned upside down. Made her feel like she was Alice in Wonderland. Nothing was where it used to be. She never forgot her address. She always knew where she lived. She just had no idea where she was going. She'd ride the bus she thought was headed to Georgetown and ring the bell to disembark, and stand on a street in Brookland. Sometimes she left her apartment without her wallet. Twice, a stranger, finding her sobbing on a street corner, flagged down a police car. When the police officers escorted her into the lobby of her building she felt famous.

Her nephew Kevin took over her finances and her life and brought her here, he said, so she would be safe. So he would always know where she was.

Now, opening her eyes in her small room every morning, she sees the beautiful hats lining the shelves. Hats she had made. Hats born of her hands. Hats that were her assignment from God. More and more she cannot remember who she made the hats for. Every hat always had a story but the stories are beginning to fade.

She loves the Bible study with the cheerful blonde lady who always remembers everyone's name and asks them to fill in the missing word when she reads phrases from the Bible. Wallis can still recite the Lord's Prayer and the Ten Commandments. She has prayed all her life and her prayers became more fervent after no one wanted to buy her hats, and there seemed nothing left in this life or this world to do, except to wander. She still knows how to pray. And she knows God has answered her prayers because of this man who roams the halls naked at night, as though dropped from heaven.

————∞∞∞————

"I didn't eat when I came here at first either," Wallis says quietly to Gregory in the dining room. "But the food isn't bad." She gently pushes his plate closer to him. There is something in this movement that sparks a feeling in his stomach beyond hunger.

His plate is closer to him now. Although the people around him look healthy, he cannot be sure what the food will do to him. *I want to eat*, he thinks, looking into the sturdy face of the woman. He lifts a forkful of green beans into his mouth. The food does indeed taste good.

Gregory feels suddenly and deeply the hunger he has denied satisfying during the time he has been here, and before he knows it, his plate is empty. Wallis beams at him.

Fortified by the meal and this woman's smile, he announces "I can fix this place" and takes her hand. They rise from the table, and Wallis grips his arm, entwining her fingers through his. They walk down the hall to the library, the one place he has found peace. He opens the French doors and they walk to the bookcase where Gregory pulls a tube of paper from a space between the bookcase and the wall. He removes a rubber band from the papers and then slowly spreads them out on the long mahogany table in the center of the room.

Gregory feels Wallis lean closer, surveying the papers, her hands, her fingertips outlining the lines he knows that he had made. Lines that signify something bold and wondrous that he had once done. He hears Wallis whisper, "We both like beautiful things."

―⸎―

The receptionist was not at the front desk, so Diane took this solitary moment, which felt stolen and illicit, to breathe in deeply. Her closed lids nonetheless, sheltered the image of

Gregory's face, the last time she'd seen it over her shoulder as she ran from his room. She inhaled deeply, courageously opened her eyes, and walked past the elevator and punched in the code that admitted her to the memory care unit.

Once there, one of the nursing assistants told her that Gregory was not yet available for a visit. He was taking part in a memory stimulation exercise, but she could sit and watch. She walked down the hallway and found the residents gathered in a large, open room adjacent to a kitchen area. The fifteen residents sat in a circle as Lynette quizzed them gently about their careers before coming to Somersby. One woman sat stylish and alert, dressed in a tailored red power suit as though waiting to convene a board meeting; a dark-skinned woman who sat assessing those around her as though she was in imminent danger wore blue jeans and a T-shirt; a man sat next to her in a gray running suit, his lips moving in a private, rumbling conversation that evoked in him ripples of laughter, which he abandoned in order to tell Lynette that he had been an accountant for D.C.'s office of management and budget.

"I kept the books. I kept the money safe," he said proudly.

Gregory sat placid and expressionless.

"I was a teacher," said a slight woman whose formerly blonde hair was now a dull white. She clutched a cane that she wiggled beside her chair. "I taught history."

"Do you still teach history?" Lynette asked.

"I have a class when this meeting is over. We're studying the American Revolution."

The woman sitting beside Gregory radiated a nearly crackling energy. Her hair was a curly mass of gray, white, and brown. In a riotously colorful blouse, floor-length black skirt, and large dangling hoop earrings, she looked like she was dressed for

Halloween. The woman rocked back and forth in her chair, restless, shifting, impatiently awaiting the chance to talk.

"I was a milliner. I made and designed hats for Woodward and Lothrop," she announced, then pointed to a woman across the room "Ask Bonnie. I made her a hat last week. Didn't I, Bonnie?"

"I don't know," the woman replied irritably, waving the words away with a dismissive sweep of her hand.

Nonplussed, the woman sat back in her chair, turned to look at Gregory next to her. She smiled and patted his hand then before throwing her arm across his back and hugging him.

At least he has made a friend, Diane thought.

Lynette announced the end of the session and the residents drifted off down the hallway to their rooms. Diane nervously stood up and prepared to walk over to Gregory, straining to gather the flailing loose ends of her emotions.

The woman who had been sitting next to Gregory was now standing, hovering protectively over him. As Diane neared them, she extended her hand saying, "I'm Diane, Gregory's wife."

"I'm Wallis. He's my friend," she said with childish glee.

"Yes, I see. Hello, Gregory," Diane offered tentatively, flushed with discomfort.

"Hello."

Lynette approached them and led Wallis away. Diane could hear the woman muttering her resistance as she continually gazed back at Gregory over her shoulder. Diane sank into the chair that Wallis had occupied moments before and, now that she was closer, drank in the sight of her husband. Despite that now permanently indifferent, jittery gaze, there seemed to be more of him.

They walked down the hall to Gregory's room, Gregory

loping quickly ahead of her, out of reach. Diane longed to touch him, to hold his hand.

In his small room the request was simple: "Want to go home . . ."

"I can't, Gregory. This is the best place for you now. For a while anyway, until you get better."

Stalemated, they sat on the bed. Diane inquired about the food, the other residents, how he felt, all questions he left unanswered. Gone was the courage she had mustered. She was deflated, minuscule in the presence of this man, her husband to whom she was a mere visitor, someone making a foray into his world from a distant galaxy, a planet beyond his comprehension.

Gregory bounded from the bed and rifled through the papers on his desk. He returned to sit beside Diane and showed her a series of crude drawings of Somersby, the interior and the exterior. As he shuffled through the drawings he pointed to each one and told her, "I have to fix this place."

"You'll do a fine job. I know you will."

"I was an architect."

"Yes, you were. You were one of the best."

Gregory walked to the window and looked out at the courtyard, at a toddler playing in a thick carpet of leaves. The history teacher from his group, now bundled in a jacket, watched the child as a younger woman stood beside her.

Diane approached Gregory, stood beside him as he watched the scene.

He turned to look at her and said calmly, "You're Diane. Diane. That's your name."

Never had her name sounded so sacred. Months had passed since he had last spoken the word. *Diane*. Her name. Cradling his face in her hands, Diane kissed Gregory on the lips.

"Thank you," she said, whispering this, beating back the crushing rush of her heart. Stymying the rise of the one thing so hard to hold on to, hope. That he might say her name again. That he would remember her name. That he would never forget it.

"I was . . . I was . . ." he began.

"You were a father. You were my husband."

———— ✦ ————

A good visit was one in which Gregory talked, though usually the words were a mantra: "Go home . . . want to go home." Diane was the conversationalist, telling Gregory about her last months on the bench, Sean, Lauren, and gossip about friends Gregory no longer remembered. On weekends, Margaret, Bruce, Lauren, Sean, Valerie, and Cameron often joined Diane and Gregory at a restaurant or for walks. During a walk along the Mall, the weather chilly, brisk, Diane walked with Lauren behind Margaret and Gregory, Margaret's arm entwined in Gregory's, both of them walking slowly, as Margaret whispered stories in his ear of childhood exploits, stories of his father.

At Somersby, Wallis Peebles was Gregory's shadow, scurrying away from him when Diane neared or sometimes refusing to leave them alone, forcing Diane, in exasperation, to find one of the nursing assistants to lead her away. Diane would arrive to find Wallis and Gregory making crafts, hiking the hallways for exercise, or sitting together eating popcorn in the theater. Increasingly, upon Diane's arrival, Wallis's hostility grew. Wallis was a blast of rolled eyes and pursed lips. Once, she was certain that as Wallis stalked past her, she heard her whisper, "You, bitch."

Regardless, Diane befriended the certified nursing assistants.

There was Angela from Jamaica who had left a son and a daughter behind in Kingston, in the care of her mother, until she could get a visa to bring them to the US. Angela's Jamaican lilt soothed Diane, especially when she called her sometimes "my lovely," the nickname growing familiar as they grew closer. It was Angela who told Diane that Gregory wasn't drinking enough water and risked dehydration and a urinary tract infection, who revealed that in the first weeks of his residency at Somersby, Gregory had roamed the halls at night, attempting to punch codes into the security system. And it was Angela who said of Gregory and Wallis, "They're right good friends. It's good, you know, that they have friends."

Chapter Eighteen

NOVEMBER 2015

Diane stood in a virtual sea of food. The number of choices in the Whole Foods café was sumptuous and intimidating. A stand that held a dozen trays of different types of olives, another laden with cheeses from around the world. A fifteen-tray stand with familiar and exotic vegetables, fruits, toppings, and condiments for salad. She stood at the hot tray stand, trying to decide between deep-fried Brussels sprouts; stir-fried quinoa with shrimp; meat loaf; braised, locally grown beef floating in a bed of carrots, onions, and potatoes; herb-roasted chicken; and other dishes whose aromas tugged at her, making this one of the most difficult decisions in a day filled with hard choices. She had finally decided on the meat loaf and deep-fried Brussels sprouts when she felt someone's eyes, someone staring at her, as though she had been physically touched.

When she looked up, on the other side of the food stand stood Alan Rich.

"Hello, Mrs. Tate."

"Mr. Rich, I had no idea . . ."

"I've been staring at you for a while now. It was interesting to see a judge who couldn't make up her mind." His smile roused a tiny dimple she had not noticed when they'd met at Westminster Church. Had it been a year and a half or two years ago? However long it had been, Diane was flushed with unexpected pleasure at seeing him.

"Well, as you can see, I finally made my choice," she said, tipping her brown carton toward him.

"Me, I'm a quinoa man, myself," he said.

A tall, red-haired woman in a stylish hoodie and yoga pants reached over Alan to fill her carton with herb-roasted chicken, nudging him aside with a smooth yet definite shove.

"Okay, lady, the food's not going anywhere," he snapped. "This isn't Somalia."

"And this isn't your kitchen counter," she muttered.

Diane laughed and exchanged an amused glance with Alan, who moved away from the woman and came to the other side where Diane was standing.

"I was going to go home and eat," he said, "but would you like to join me upstairs? If you have the time, that is."

A torrential, freezing rain battered the streets outside. Between the rain and the wearying day she'd had on the bench, Diane had convinced herself not to go by Somersby on her way home. She'd pick up something to eat, shower, microwave her store-bought dinner, and eat in bed. That was the evening she'd had planned.

"Certainly."

"Great. Give me your carton and I'll pay for us both. I'll meet you upstairs in the dining area."

Diane saw Alan's dark, olive green trench coat stained by rain flow behind him as he hurried away toward the cashier.

Giddiness flooded her at the thought of sharing a meal with a man she did not know, but wanted to.

Alan found her wiping a table near a window that showcased the bleak sky outside. She had placed napkins and plastic cutlery for two facing one another. As Diane sat down, he said, "Hold on," and strode over to the watercooler and came back with two cups of filtered water.

As they opened their cartons and took the first bites of food, Alan asked, "How've you been? I haven't seen you, your friend, or your husband at the church. Naser Abadey turned it out last week. I sometimes go on Monday nights when it's blues night."

Diane took another deep breath, again summoning guidance from a faithful, clearly inexhaustible supply of courage. "Alan, my husband Gregory has Alzheimer's, and he's living in an assisted living facility's memory care unit. He's been there for about two months."

"Oh, I'm . . ."

"Please, Alan, please don't say 'I'm sorry.' I know you are. I assume you are. It can't be helped. That night at Westminster, I was still learning how to own it and not melt down, like saying it was an admission of guilt or a failure."

"My mother died of complications from Alzheimer's. Caring for her tore our family apart. I know you're tired of hearing it, but I'd still like to say, I'm sorry, and I want you to know that's neither a platitude nor pity."

Diane hoped that her smile expressed all the gratitude she felt for his words.

"So, you've been shopping," she said pointing to a bag from a chain bookstore.

"Yes, for my nephew's son. He asked for a couple of those

Diary of a Wimpy Kid books but I also got him an atlas and a dictionary."

"Do you have children?" Diane asked.

"No, and I'm divorced. Do you have grandchildren?"

"Not yet. My daughter is pregnant, though."

"Congratulations."

"It's complicated."

"Isn't everything? Hard day?"

"Yes and yes and no. Did you read or hear about that case last week where a woman high on PCP killed her boyfriend?"

Alan nodded.

"A real tragedy. She was a senior at the University of the District of Columbia. Had never used any drugs before, got in with a drug-using crowd, and the very first time she uses PCP, goes on a violent rampage and kills her boyfriend in front of her three-year-old son. Stabs him to death."

She paused and moved the Brussels sprouts around the carton, took a tiny bite of the meat loaf and a sip of water. Then she looked again into Alan's horrified gaze.

"She had worked hard to pull herself out of and away from a very dysfunctional family but now she's in jail facing murder charges and her son is under my watch in protective custody. He was placed with a foster family that we've had problems with in the past, so the child's lawyer and I were going back and forth today trying to find a more suitable home."

"The child has a lawyer?"

"A guardian ad litem—to protect his interests as he goes through the system."

"So mother and child both have lawyers?"

"Uh-huh. And she's probably lost that child for good. So it was a real hard day."

This was how it used to be with Gregory, she

thought—sifting through the remains of the day over a meal, the dinner table a confessional. Simply eating, an act that bound them always one to another. Her heart throbbed with regret. Then she stifled the onslaught of these overly familiar emotions and decided to look at Alan Rich. She wanted to be here, not back there where she could never be again. She silently commanded her thoughts to attention. *Look at this man. Really look at him. What do you see?* What she saw was the ease with which he occupied his body. The slightly chapped lips, the clipped moustache flecked with gray.

"Since I retired, I've been working with a nonprofit that mentors ex-offenders returning to the city after they've served their sentences. We work with them on everything: getting a degree, dress, tutoring, interviewing, and getting a job."

"So we're both in the trenches."

"Well, yours is a lot deeper than mine. You know, I play at Westminster sometimes. The piano. I've got a quartet I perform with now and then."

"That's wonderful. So you're a musician."

"Yeah, when I was younger I played in a local band. At one point, Motown was interested."

"Oh." Diane shivered with delight. "Why didn't you make a go of it?"

"I wasn't made for that life. The clubs were filled with inattentive, half-drunk audiences and rooms full of smoke. The other musicians were talented but too often just plain trifling. They'd miss rehearsals, let women problems interfere with gigs, and we never got paid what we were worth."

Having finished their meals, Diane and Alan lingered in the austere, nondescript dining room. A group of Ethiopian men sat huddled over their meals nearby, speaking their native tongue, their comradeship loud and jocular. As she watched

Alan stack their cartons and cutlery and take them to the trash container, she felt anointed.

Finally, Alan slid his business card across the table. "I enjoyed this, Diane. I don't know about you, but I can always use a friend. Will you call me?"

Diane searched her pocketbook for her own card and then handed it to Alan. "I'd be glad to do that."

When Alan took the card, he captured Diane's hand in his and held it encased in his palms. "That's good to know, very good to know."

✦

At home, preparing for bed, Diane reached in her drawer for her gown, a faded pink-and-white cotton nightdress she'd worn for the last four or five winters. Rummaging in the rear of the drawer, her hands found the cool, slippery material of a silk negligee she had not worn in years. The ivory-colored gown lay in her palms and she inhaled its musky scent then rubbed the sheer fabric against her cheeks.

First, it was memory; then touch was the next to go. The good-morning, good-bye, good-night kiss—over time, Gregory could only tolerate them impatiently before slipping from her grasp, turning from the aching and abandoned lips Diane offered. They lived bound by a chastity strictly enforced by the stranger residing in her husband's body. They had always loved with passion and imagination, but now she was consigned to a kind of sexual exile. When she pleasured herself at night, in the dark, lying beside Gregory as he snored sweetly as a child, or in the last year, while he trekked the hallways of the house outside the locked bedroom door, Diane had called forth the sight of Gregory's face, staring at her intently and exhausted as he hunched over her, their bodies bound by the slick thread of their joint release.

In the bathroom, after a shower, gazing at herself in the steam shrouded mirror, Diane said, "I'm a mess."

She opened the towel and let it drop to the bathroom floor. Her hair was uneven, unruly. It was time for a trim. Finally, in the last month, she had begun sleeping through the night again, but the circles under her eyes were evidence of the long parade of fitful nocturnal struggles. She had to get back to the gym. What had Alan Rich seen, looking at her?

Maybe she was a mess, but Diane allowed herself to recall the incendiary thoughts and feelings Alan had inspired. She had sat across from him one part the respectable, middle-aged judge, and one part a woman drawn physically to a man and striving mightily to hide it. She felt her thighs stained by a moist trickle of desire. Beneath her touch, the skin of her breasts was soft as a newborn's. She had buried, forgotten, and been stripped of so much. She whispered as her hand retrieved the towel, "Please, God, not this, too."

The coffee shop was chapel-quiet. Watching the people at other tables staring at phones and computer screens with the intensity of scientists in a lab breaking a genetic code, Diane thought how the coffeehouse had become a kind of church, and coffee itself, a sacrament.

A profusion of small wooden tables and matching chairs. A windowsill that was home to philodendrons desperate for watering. Exposed brick walls. Posters of an eternally young Bob Marley, his broad, toothy, ecstatic smile an invitation, and a debonair, white-haired Tony Bennett. Three bookshelves of poetry, self-help, and biographies of radical political activists beside the counter and cash register and makeshift kitchen—that was the décor.

This neighborhood off of the busy, traffic-clogged Rhode Island Avenue had been christened Bloomingdale. Communities that, in Diane's childhood, were known by a major street or thoroughfare now were designated by sprightly names conjuring up feelings and images of contentment.

Diane smiled when she saw Alan walk through the door and hold it for a young blonde entering behind him. She had called him three days after their dinner at Whole Foods and made a date to meet today, a week later. What, she wondered, was the etiquette for this? His buoyant, seductive energy inspired a surge of starkly sexual desire. Alan removed his sheepskin-lined hat as he walked toward her table and there was his bald shiny pate. He loosened the buttons on his sheepskin jacket, seeming eager to present himself, his full self to her. He sat down, easing into the small chair gracefully.

"It's good to see you again." He smiled jovially as he stuffed his leather gloves into his coat pocket. "You beat me to the punch. I wanted to call, but for all my forthrightness that evening, I was unsure of the etiquette, you know what I mean."

"I'm still unsure myself. We'll figure it out," Diane said with more confidence than she felt.

"What were you thinking about when I walked in?"

"I was thinking about the personality of the city now, how cookie-cutter it's become with the same mix of coffee shops, yoga studios, overpriced gourmet restaurants, and bakeries. Apparently, funkiness in the way we used to know it has been banned. When was the last time you saw a hog maw or a chitlin? Or a store that sold pickles or pickled pigs' feet in one of those big jars?"

"Don't tell me you eat that stuff. Nostalgia has its limits, you know. It's probably just as well, as my mama used to say, that back in the day we had no idea how toxic that stuff was."

"It kept generations of our people alive." Diane laughed.

"I know a hole-in-the-wall place off Columbia Road that's got the city's best sweet potato pie, the required amount of dirt and grime, a sister behind the counter wearing a hairnet, potatoes fried in two-week-old bacon grease, and in the summertime, they got no air conditioning. Wanna head over there now?"

"Oh, come on," Diane chided Alan.

"So in other words, you were sitting here waiting for me thinkin' *really* deep thoughts?"

Alan asked her what she wanted to drink and went to the counter and ordered two coffees.

Settling back at the table, Alan pried the plastic top off of his coffee. Diane reached for several packets of sugar and three plastic pods of creamer from the pile he had placed between them.

"So you like your coffee sweet? Or should I say, you like coffee with your cream?"

"Guilty on both counts. And you like yours black?"

"And strong."

In the midst of this back and forth, Diane realized that she was flirting. She was sporting a new haircut. Putting together a pink cashmere turtleneck sweater and black shawl draped over her shoulder with black earrings and matching necklace had consumed nearly an hour, as she searched not just for the right clothes to wear, but for a new persona to present to this man who she hoped would not be a stranger much longer.

"You know," Alan began, "Alzheimer's makes family of us all. When my mother had it, I was the only man in my support group, but I couldn't have cared for my mother without it."

"The assisted living option hasn't been a panacea, but it's given me back more of my life, and that's the main thing."

"With me, Alzheimer's affected my relationships with my sisters, who didn't inherit the compassion gene and who pushed off the major responsibility for our mother onto me. They say men aren't intuitive; that's a lie. My intuition was working overtime. But you know what got me through all the ugliness of the divorce? My mother. Visiting her in the home where everything had become so simple. I'd go to the home sometimes fuming because of an argument with Beverly and sit there with my mother answering her questions about friends of hers who had died years ago or listening to her telling me again about something she'd done before I was born. It was like therapy. My wife didn't love me anymore, and having to care about my mother kept me from becoming bitter."

"What drew you to work with ex-offenders?"

"Seeing so many of the young men who had either been in classes I taught or who attended schools where I was a principal end up behind bars. I wasn't able to stop the pipeline at its source so I figured maybe I could help at the end."

"I saw the same thing working as a public defender. That's why I turned to family law. Do you miss anything about the school system?"

"The kids mostly. There are still so many good, decent kids in the schools you never hear about. They get swallowed up by all the labels: inner-city, at-risk. Bush promised not to leave any student behind while Obama's got administrators racing to the top like crabs in a barrel."

"Are you hungry?" he asked when she was done with her coffee.

"Actually, yes."

They drove in separate cars to Chinatown and ate a leisurely dinner. When they parted, standing in front of Diane's car, Alan leaned in and enfolded Diane in an embrace pulsing with unspoken promises. Diane surrendered to Alan's touch, grateful for the possessiveness it contained. Closing her eyes, it was his face and his only that she saw rising to fill the shadowy vacant space.

Chapter Nineteen

NOVEMBER 2015

Sean's first visit to Somersby had confirmed all his fears. His father, a man who had helped shape the landscape of a city, was now confined to this place. It was as "nice" as his mother and Lauren had told him, but the quiet to Sean sounded like what waited for him in his grave. The residents all looked fine until you looked closely.

So, most days, he took his father out, anywhere: for a walk in a nearby park, for a slice of pie and cup of coffee at a diner in College Park. He'd joked with Valerie that although he didn't have to employ cunning, violence, or threats, each time he walked through the doors of Somersby with his father out into the world, he felt he was involved in a prison break.

Sean reached his father through stories. Stories, wasn't that all that conversation was? The stories he told his father were narratives peopled by his clients and his crew. Gregory had come to nod his head in what seemed, and felt to Sean, like understanding.

He had arrived early today to take his father to Ruth's Chris Steak House for dinner to celebrate his birthday. Valerie, Cameron, his mother, sister, and Mercer would meet them there. He tied his father's tie around his neck, a singularly confounding task that he recalled his father teaching him to do when he was twelve.

"We've got a few minutes, Dad," Sean said, sitting down. His dad's room made him feel claustrophobic, but here at least they had some privacy. "I finally did it. I let Archie go."

"Archie."

"You know, the guy I've been telling you about who I've depended on for so long but who's got a drinking problem?"

The blank stare no longer pained him, for he knew it did not necessarily signal incomprehension.

"It was the best thing to do but it was still hard, y'know. I don't know how you and Mercer did it. People look at the finished product and have no idea how much it cost in human terms to erect or renovate a building. Maybe they shouldn't know."

"I have to pay the staff," his father announced. Then he looked at Sean, his eyes narrowing in assessment and said, "I want to give you a raise."

"Dad, I told you, I don't need a raise and I'll take care of the payroll. You don't have to worry about that." Here he was in the present and also back in the terrifying roller-coaster past with his father. Pretending. Make-believe. Creating a now from the soil of a past his father hungered for and was deeply rooted in. More and more often when Sean visited, Gregory imagined that he was an employee of Caldwell & Tate. Sean had learned how to glide through his father's alternate reality, with only an occasional stumble.

"Riggs Bank," Gregory said, a bank that had closed its doors in the city years ago.

"Yes, I went there yesterday and made a deposit. Just like you told me to," Sean spoke the words of deceit calmly.

"Did you bring the receipt?" Gregory demanded skeptically.

"I sure did." Sean reached in his pocket and handed his father a deposit slip he had filled out earlier in the day, for this visit. This transaction had become a ritual between them. It did not matter that the deposit slip bore the name of his bank, Wells Fargo. His father imagined himself still at the helm of Caldwell & Tate, managing accounts, overseeing staff.

Gregory walked over to his desk drawer and placed the slip of paper in a small wooden box he had shown Sean the first day he visited him. "My money, in case I die. You know. My money," he had said placing his hand on Sean's shoulder. Sean had looked into the box and seen only a pile of tiny scraps of paper.

⸻ ◦◦◦ ⸻

"Go ahead and blow them out, Daddy. Go on."

Diane watched as Gregory warily assessed the two candles in the shape of a six and a nine lodged atop a coconut birthday cake. Overcoming his skepticism, Gregory leaned forward and expelled a half-hearted exhalation, then slumped back heavily against his chair.

The candles extinguished, Lauren began slicing the cake. Diane, Sean, Valerie, Cameron, and Mercer sat around the table in the private dining room at Somersby where they had come after an early dinner at the steak house, to celebrate Gregory's birthday.

Through the French doors that separated them from the

larger dining area, Diane saw some of the other residents watching the unfolding of this occasion. Fredrick Connor, a burly ex-fireman; the history teacher, Emma Bradley; and Trent Simpson, a small, wiry man who wore a patch over one eye as the result of a childhood accident, all waved at Diane through the doors. She waved back. Residents were informed of birthdays and Lynette had told Diane that earlier in the day, lunch had concluded with residents singing "Happy Birthday" to Gregory and eating slices of cake.

And there was Wallis, at a table with three other women, who sat in what seemed to Diane from this distance to be nervous, twittering awe of her. Wallis held forth with a monarch's confidence, her face an elastic, expressive mask.

"I brought you a gift," Lauren said, handing Gregory a box wrapped in glistening silver paper. Gregory simply placed the box on the table beside his untouched slice of cake, so Mercer said, "I'll open it for you."

"It's an electric shaver, Gregory," he said. "Old man, you're beginning to look like a caveman with that beard."

"When you want to shave, Daddy, that's what it's for."

Gregory nodded at the sight of a thick cardigan sweater that Sean lifted out of his gift box. There was a wool scarf from Mercer.

With more ceremony and seriousness than was required, Diane left her seat beside Mercer and sat down beside Gregory and slowly brought out of a large shopping bag a plush, tan leather briefcase.

Setting it on the table before Gregory, she said, "For a new set of dreams."

"Mom. That's beautiful." Lauren sighed, leaning in closer to admire the gift.

"You can use it for anything, Dad," Sean said.

"Don't leave it anywhere near me, man, or it's gone," Mercer joked heartily.

"Go on, open it," Diane urged him.

Gregory opened the snaps and reached inside. He retrieved several framed photographs. Diane moved closer to Gregory and the others stood behind them as she told the story of each picture: Gregory and Diane smiling into the camera from a table on a cruise to Bermuda. Diane and Gregory dwarfed by the pyramids of Giza on the trip he had longed for all his life. There was a photo of Lauren in hair rollers, wolfing down a slice of pizza at a birthday party sleepover when she turned sixteen. Sean shooting hoops in the backyard after his barbecue birthday party when he turned eighteen. Diane, chic and beaming, in a formal gown and Gregory in a tuxedo on the dance floor of the Grand Hyatt at the party Gregory had thrown for her fiftieth birthday. Gregory stared at the photo of Lauren, then pointed to Lauren, saying, "That's her."

"Yes, Daddy, that's me." Lauren giggled in delight.

"I saw a picture of the pyramids in school," Cameron said as he held the photo of the trip to Egypt in his hands before Valerie lead him back to his seat.

A gentle knock on the French doors interrupted them, and Diane looked up to see Wallis standing outside the door. She was dressed in a thick caftan as bold as a box of crayons and she was carrying a gift.

Lauren looked at her mother quizzically.

"Open the door, Lauren." Diane sighed.

But before Lauren could move, Wallis burst into the room.

"Hello," Wallis said cheerily, as though they had all been expecting her.

Wallis barreled toward Gregory, thrusting a gift into his hand. Gregory's eyes brightened and he smiled for the second time that evening and took the small box clumsily wrapped in silver paper. Blushing, he sat up in his chair, clearly revived.

Then Wallis hugged Gregory, her breasts stationed in his face, her hands and blazing red nails squeezing his head. Gregory lay against her sublime and relaxed. Releasing him, Wallis spotted an empty chair and dragged it beside Gregory, trying to squeeze between Diane and Gregory.

"Move, move," she ordered Diane, pushing her so hard she nearly fell onto the floor.

Cameron asked Valerie, "Who is that lady, Mommy?"

"That's enough, that's enough," Sean said, standing up. He shared a gaze with Mercer and both men approached Wallis, who, as they neared her jerked wildly in fright and turned around, her fists pummeling Sean's chest. The altercation and the noise brought Lynette running toward the room.

"Stop. Stop. Help," Wallis screamed.

Lynette expertly moved Sean and Mercer away from Wallis and led her out the door, soothing and comforting her. "Now Wallis, come on. It will be all right."

Diane was trembling. Enraged, confused, she felt assaulted, like the victim of a theft. Rare were the moments when they could replicate what it felt like to be a family again, when celebration was easy and heartfelt.

All evening, through dinner at the steak house and on the drive back to Somersby, she had been watchful, waiting, expecting disaster to derail her intricately planned evening. Would Gregory become suddenly disoriented in the restaurant and demand to leave? Would he stare in stoic, blank indifference at Cameron and reduce the boy to tears when he refused to or could not respond to the boy's frightened inquiries?

Neither had happened. And she had foolishly congratulated herself too soon, beaming when Gregory opened the briefcase, certain that her concerns this time were unjustified. This evening would be the special and love-filled gathering she had planned. Who was this woman, Wallis, to Gregory, she wondered. She didn't know but Gregory did, she was now certain of that. That woman, as lost as Gregory, had ripped out her heart. She had no idea how she would rise from her chair.

Sean now sat beside Gregory, his hand on his shoulder, whispering into his ear.

Mercer shook his head and said, "I wonder what *she* was like back in the day."

Summoning a composure from the scattered threads of her emotional tailspin, Diane turned to Lauren. "It's been a long night. I'm sure your father's tired."

Lauren and Sean gathered the paper plates and sodas. Mercer leaned over and kissed Diane on her cheek good-bye.

Diane helped Gregory stand up and they headed to his room, Diane carrying all the birthday gifts except the gift from Wallis, which Gregory clutched tightly under his arm. When they entered Gregory's room, Diane calmed herself by concentrating on placing the photographs in the briefcase carefully and strategically like sentries on Gregory's desk and bookshelf.

She had tried to ignore the woman, had convinced herself that she was a mere annoyance. Foolish. Vain. That's what she'd been. Seething with anger at herself, at Gregory, and at a woman she could not believe was a threat to her relationship with her husband, Diane crossed her arms against her chest to calm her rampaging nerves. "Gregory, why did Wallis give you a birthday gift? Is she your friend? Your special friend?"

"Wallis is my wife," he said adamantly, pushing her away for emphasis.

As nausea roiled in her stomach, Diane watched Gregory

place the boxes on his desk and sit so still on the bed that he seemed to be meditating.

"It's your birthday, and you're sixty-nine years old today," she whispered, determined that at least one thing between them would be true before she left.

Outside, the snowflakes resembled falling stars. Diane longed to float upward into the billowing darkness overhead. Sean reached for her as a spasm forced her to lean over a few feet from the car and expel the evening's hearty meal.

"What happened back there?" he shouted, rubbing her back while Lauren opened the trunk and retrieved a wad of paper towels that she thrust in her mother's hands.

Inside Sean's car, Diane sat in the passenger seat wiping her face and taking small sips from a bottle of water Lauren had given her.

"What happened?" Sean insisted.

"I asked him why Wallis gave him a gift. I asked him if she was his friend. He told me she was his wife."

"Mom, he doesn't know what he's saying," Lauren said, comforting her.

Diane looked at her children beneath the ceiling light Sean had turned on. She saw their faces mapped in concern and disbelief. Looking from Sean to Lauren and back again she asked, "How did we lose him? How did we lose him so completely, so fast?"

Wallis steps into a hallway that is as quiet as she imagines the beginning of time must have been and pads to Gregory's room.

His moan welcomes her as she unbuttons her nightgown and lets it fall to the floor in the room's patient, somber darkness. He cannot see her still tear-stained face. Wallis still seethes with the humiliation of being forced from the birthday party. She had never found a man worth her love. Now she has and they want to keep them apart. Sliding beneath the covers, beside Gregory, Wallis eases into his waiting arms as her sobs erupt like a howl. Gregory whispers "shh, shh" and holds her close, Wallis's body a bulwark in the night.

Chapter Twenty

DECEMBER 2015

Half a dozen prescriptions huddled around the lamp on the nightstand beside Alan's bed. He'd warned Diane away from his left knee, worn from years of running. She suffered from sporadic back pain only partially relieved by yoga and walking. Performing this dance, their bodies were aging, yet eager and sure-footed. Diane's kiss was fierce and anguished, all tongue, thrusting and impatient. Alan's longing was unvanquished and so the slick, moist, hide-and-seek of the first moments soon gave way to Diane mounting his solid fullness. The ecstatic shudder melted into a satisfaction sprung from the soil of tenderness, gratitude, and desire.

After, Diane lay swathed in the sheets resting on Alan's chest, washed up on the shore of him, stretching her arms around his girth. Gregory was all angles and length and muscle. Only the second man she'd had sex with in over thirty years, Alan was round and soft, his flesh sheer, grand invitation. Thirty years ago, she was sure he would not have moved her. Now he had consumed and resurrected her.

"Thank you," she whispered.

"You're more than welcome." Alan laughed, his chest rumbling in delight.

"I've wanted to do this for a long time," she told him.

"I've wanted to do this since that night at Westminster, but you were a married woman so I went home that evening and had a stiff drink and told myself such is life."

Their laughter mingled, glowing in the dark. Diane closed her eyes and listened to the sound of Alan's breathing and her own shallow, contented breaths. They both slipped into a sated slumber, shifting positions so that Diane lay on her side.

When they woke a half hour later, Alan turned on the halogen lamp on the nightstand. He kissed her earlobe, squeezed her, and told Diane, "You're still a married woman."

"Is this going to be too complicated for you?" she asked.

"It'll probably get complicated for us both. I kind of hope it does."

Alan released her and sat up, plumping the pillows behind him. Diane turned on her back, her head resting on his groin. She lay gazing at the bedroom walls where, like the walls in so many of the rooms of his house, Alan had hung moody, artistic black-and-white photographs of musicians. B. B. King sat in his dressing room cradling his guitar, Lucille, in his lap. Billy Strayhorn played a baby grand. Sarah Vaughn gripped a microphone in a close-up, her eyes closed, her face mapped with sweat as she sang on stage at the Apollo.

"Gregory told me that some woman at Somersby was his wife. In his mind and in the life that he's living, I've had to conclude that's the truth."

"What was he like before?"

"He wanted so much and felt he had a right to everything. He wanted all that and more for me and our children. He was brash, impatient, loyal."

"I like you. I more than like you," Alan said, "and I'd like to feel I knew where we were headed. Where we could go? I need to know that."

Need, such a small word that sprawled over everything they were or dreamed of. *Need*, the thing that defined them when they entered the world dependent on others for everything, and when they left the world hoping only to be let go with grace and acceptance. Didn't Gregory need someone, something he had found in Somersby with Wallis? Didn't she need what Alan was offering?

"One, we've been seeing each other for less than two months."

"You know that has nothing to do with what I'm talking about."

"And the kind of clarity you want evaporated for me four years ago."

"Wouldn't you like a new kind of clarity?"

"Alan, I can't just impose it. It has to rise from the muck and mire, from the chaos of everything. And it will. In time."

"Are we arguing or bickering?" he asked

"I guess we're being a couple."

"You still looking forward to stepping down from the bench, your honor?"

"Yes, and with less and less trepidation every day. In the early period of our battle with Alzheimer's I used to look forward to going to work, because there I was in charge, I set the rules. But as the disease progressed, I began to feel my work was a reflection of my other life, not an antidote to it."

"Whatever happened in that case a while back with the little boy whose mom was high on PCP and—"

"Her trial starts in a few weeks and we finally found him a stable foster home."

"Isn't that one for your team?"

"I just hope it's a win for that little boy."

The following night, plucking her earrings and watch from her jewelry box as she prepared to go to the Kennedy Center with Alan, for the first time Diane did not instinctively reach for her wedding band. Two gold bands melded together in a basket weave. She and Gregory had not wanted diamonds, supporting the growing international push to boycott diamonds from Apartheid South Africa, and they had wanted to use the money a diamond ring would cost for a down payment on a house. Gold bands had been enough.

When she finally removed it from its resting place in the velour-lined top drawer of the jewelry box, the ring seemed so minuscule. The gleam of the gold was dulled and bore nicks and scratches. It was now a perfect symbol of all they had weathered. She wore the ring now out of habit and because, as Alan had reminded her, she was still a married woman. But now the ring felt false. In all the ways that being a married woman, a wife counted, she was not. The ring represented her and Gregory, but she was the only one with memories of what it meant.

Her children, her family, her friends all asked her what she felt for Alan, where were they headed. Alan had reintroduced her to joy, but she was careening, falling toward and into a new version of herself. She was beginning to love herself all over, love herself anew. This love was a country to which she was ready to pledge allegiance.

There had not been a Christmas tree in the house in years. But the upheaval of this year, moving Gregory into Somersby, the fact that she had actual plans for her future, the bitter sweetness of it all increased Diane's longing for a tree.

Alan drove her to a pop-up Christmas tree stand next to a gas station on Georgia Avenue. The evening air was moist, cold, the lot fragrant with the scent of pine. The trees had been picked over, manhandled, for Diane had waited until December 23 to act on her desire. They searched through the limp, leftover trees, bundled in cord, and the few standing upright on display, and managed to find a fresh, hardy-limbed tree. Alan tied it to the top of his car and they went to a nearby big-box hardware store and bought lights. The rest of the evening was spent putting up the tree and decorating it. When Diane tossed the last handful of silver icicles onto the tree's branches, she burst into girlish laughter and for no reason hugged Alan.

She made grilled cheese sandwiches and a salad and they sat together for the rest of the evening assessing the tree and sharing stories of their own Christmases past.

And now, on Christmas Day, her family was all here for Christmas dinner. Alan was one of the hosts for a holiday dinner for the formerly imprisoned men that he mentored, a celebration at a northeast recreation center.

Bruce and his son Aaron, Sean, Gregory, and Cameron sat in the living room watching the football game and Diane was in the kitchen. Margaret sat at the table slicing tomatoes and cutting lettuce for a salad. Lauren, two months pregnant but still not showing much, smoothing a bed of marshmallows over the top of sweet potatoes, said, "The more things change the more they stay the same. Just look who's in the kitchen."

"Thank God." Margaret laughed. "The men would just be in the way."

Standing next to Diane, who was placing kale into a pot, Valerie brushed melted butter over a pan of rolls.

"You've been so good for Sean, Valerie. Please tell me he's been good for you."

"He has. Sean has grounded me. He's got his demons, but he's easy to love."

"For years, we thought we'd lost him."

"He feels terrible about that time. And he's mad at himself for those years. He's still trying to figure out how and why he let that happen."

"Maybe he'll never know, but asking at least proves my son has a conscience."

When Diane recalled this day, she would remember looking around the dinner table at Margaret beside Gregory, helping him eat; at Lauren, easy, comfortable with Cameron, her arm finding its way over his shoulder, again and again. Sean, proud and confident beside the woman he loved.

Chapter Twenty-one

Diane and Gregory had been together all day. Diane had picked Gregory up from Somersby to spend the day with her and all morning, she had enlisted his aid with small cleaning tasks around the house. She watched as he washed dishes, wiped the stove and counter. He helped her make the bed. Now, he stood at the kitchen counter stacking knives and forks.

After a lunch of tomato soup and chicken sandwiches, she helped Gregory into his jacket, slipped into hers, and they walked the length of their block. Back home, they napped. As Gregory slept, Diane watched a dribble of saliva stain his chin. There was no more desire. She no longer wore his ring. Another man was her lover. Alzheimer's had sacked and looted their relationship, stripped it to the bone, yet they were mated, soldered to one another beyond rings, ceremonies, and contracts.

Diane's mentor, William Larson, a respected judge, had died recently of a stroke. At Somersby last month, Trent Simpson had succumbed to a heart attack in his sleep. A friend of Alan's from high school died of diabetes-related complications. The son of a fellow judge hung himself in his garage after years of battling with clinical depression, and Randall Cullen, Gregory's longtime friend, had just died of prostate cancer.

Diane found herself suddenly entrenched in a season of relentless death and dying.

But more terrible than anything she had ever seen or known this closely, this intimately, was Gregory's suffering. According to his doctors, what she read, everything she knew and saw, Gregory was in stage three, or stage six, of Alzheimer's, depending on how the horror of the disease was calculated. He could live, declining in increments, for two years, a decade, or more.

And there was more suffering to come. His immune system would gasp for breath, impossible to retrieve. That mind, devious and cruel, would disrupt his body's desire to move, his yearning to eat. Lethal blood clots and infections sown by the steady shutdown would ultimately stop the intricate and elegant biological system from working. This was not just Gregory's fate to bear but hers to bear with him. A fate that could be distant and encroaching, drawing nearer every day. Her husband was dying. But no matter what, she would not turn away from the awful sight.

Later, Bruce came by to take Gregory back to Somersby and Diane sat with Margaret and Lauren in the living room, drinking lemonade, and watching a movie on television.

As a commercial came on, Lauren said, "Daddy won't know he's a grandfather."

"Oh, stop it," Margaret said. "I don't care what those doctors say. All the studies and research. Gregory will know he's a grandfather."

"How?"

"That's between God and Gregory. When he holds that child the first time, believe me he'll know."

"How are you and Gerald?" Diane asked.

"We're not dating anymore. It felt too weird to me. We're waiting to become parents. That's all I can say."

"Sounds to me like you're together in the way that matters most now," Diane said.

"I thought your generation didn't believe in marriage anyway," Margaret said.

"Grandma, you have to stop reading the Internet. I'm not 'my generation.' I'm me. Look at Sean and Valerie. They're engaged."

"Life is long, Lauren, and you have no idea how much of it still awaits you," Margaret said.

"In one of our talks right after he got the official diagnosis, Dad was rushing to tell me things, things he hadn't said and was afraid he wouldn't get to. He told me to have a life beyond my work."

"Well, dear, you now have a life, a real one." Diane laughed.

"And you aren't alone in it," Margaret said. "You aren't alone."

Sean had begun to "steal" afternoons like this one, to drive to Somersby and tell Gregory, "Come with me, Dad. Let's go for a ride."

This was a day of excessive, inordinate spring charm. The sky, flecked by speckles of sun lighting the mosaic of frothy blue and white, hovered confidently over the city. The playful winds and the hint of humidity promised a perpetual reign of days like this.

Gregory sat beside Sean in the front seat, stylish in a thick, heavy cardigan, the curls of his white hair peeking up at the edges of a Washington Nationals cap. Sean allowed him to play with the radio dial. When the sound of rap music with its jittery belligerence blared through the speakers, Gregory nodded in satisfaction and Sean laughed. Sitting with his father at Somersby or going over on Sundays to join Gregory as he watched football or basketball, Sean thought of the inadequacy of words, how they mangled meanings and were just as often roadblocks as they were passageways. At Somersby, he watched his father sit with Wallis in the sunroom, in the library, in the den. The two of them now flagrantly joined. Her chatter, endless, easy, soothed his father as much as it boggled Sean's mind.

Today, Sean wanted his father to see the city's frenzy of construction. The skyline was now permanently bejeweled by cranes; the equipment mammoth in strength could be humbled by a strong wind. The staid, mannerly city of Sean's youth was now brash and cocksure. New buildings arched upright and edgy. Downtown now had its own version of Park Avenue, lined with glitzy glass emporiums and temples to glamour.

Sean scanned his father periodically, ensuring that he hadn't unlocked the passenger side door or wiggled out of his seat belt or wet himself. Long, tender silences settled between them as they drove around the city. But he couldn't trust the silence. He hoped the cerebral backlog of memory didn't set his father on edge, agitate him, or fill his eyes with tears.

On the corner of Ninth and H Street N.W., Gregory looks up at the twelve-story building that has greedily taken possession of the width and length of the entire block. The cold efficiency and pompous grandeur of the structure makes him dizzy as he stares up at it. Why is the building here? Where is Doggett's rugged gravel and earth parking lot? Where is Security Bank? The sensation of bewilderment and waste descends. Emotions and thoughts that never find a solid place to land strangle him. In the grip of this terrible sense of loss and bereavement, he cannot tell this one beside him, the one who acts like his son and calls him *Dad*, although Gregory knows they are, in fact, the same age. He can never tell any of them—not the woman who calls him *Daddy* or the woman who was something important to him, which he feels deep inside but can no longer recall. He has learned how to deceive them as they came to him, diplomats from a region beyond reason or dreams. He won't ask the young man what happened to the bank, the parking lot, the liquor store. He sits wondering as he does every day how he will find Mercer, how Mercer will ever find him.

As they drove past a construction site on Massachusetts Avenue, Sean told Gregory, "Dad, a man fell into a hole there last week and died."

His father had always told him that the men and women who actually did the work that transformed his drawings into buildings worked fourteen- to sixteen-hour days. Stamina, strength, and courage was required, he said, and yet most people saw them in their hard hats, their jeans, and looked quickly past their sweat-drenched faces and grimy hands. The pedestrians who passed the construction sites, unaware that craftsmen and artists were at work, could not imagine the intelligence, delicacy, and precision of thought required to mount and work a crane, to work sixteen stories high, to check the wiring in a building with three hundred units.

The din of construction on the site of the National Museum of African American History and Culture on Fifteenth and Constitution Avenue drove Gregory to place his hands over his ears to block out the sounds that once he had loved because, as he had told Sean, it meant a building was being born. Circling the area teeming with tourists, Sean found a parking space a block away and he and Gregory sat in the shadow of the museum. Each story of the structure, designed like an inverted crown, leaned outward, the burnished grill and iron squares, protruding like molded sunbeams. Sean still preferred his father's design, which had arched boldly skyward.

"Dad, that building is where our history will be told. One day, I came here and watched them lower a Jim Crow train car, the whole thing, onto the lower level."

Gregory folded his arms at his chest and pointed to the structure. "I made that," he said proudly, narrowing his eyes in studied assessment. So the hundreds of hours Caldwell & Tate had spent on their design, their bid for one of the world's most prestigious architectural projects had not been forgotten. His father had gotten it all wrong but, in a manner that made Sean smile in satisfaction, he had gotten it right.

On days like this, Sean gave his father all he had. And he took all that his father was, a fractured husk of a man. Valerie had dared him to "love what was left" of his father. That's what he was trying to do.

When Sean parked in front of his parents' house, Gregory peered out the window and said, "Home," a lilt of indecision in his voice. Gregory stood for several moments leaning on the car and looking at the house.

Camille Baker, their next door neighbor, hurried down her

front stairs and exclaimed, "Why, Gregory, it's so good to see you. Diane told me where you are now. I'm so sorry I haven't had a chance to visit you. You look good, you look so well. I saw Diane leave a few hours ago. Sean, I'm so glad to see you are taking such good care of your father." This torrent of words drove Gregory to cling to Sean as though dodging an assault.

"Thanks, Camille. Let's go inside, Dad."

In his mother's bedroom, Sean placed a stack of his father's lightweight clothing in an overnight bag. Gregory inspected the bedroom with benign curiosity, then used the toilet. When Gregory came out of the bathroom, he wandered over to the bedroom door and stood, his hands rubbing the place that still bore evidence of the lock Diane had installed.

"I couldn't get in."

"She loved you, Dad. It wasn't you she was afraid of. It wasn't really you."

Today her husband would meet her lover.

Even as she so neatly thought of what was about to happen, Diane knew that this day was fraught with possibilities for closure and confusion. She never used the word *lover* when she talked about Alan. Yet in her mind, she played with the word. *Lover.* A word that was so much more generous and complicated than the sexual overtones it evoked. She felt beloved, respected, and cared for. The damning emotional isolation had been replaced by a personal revival.

Alan was in her life and an integral part of it. They had met each other's friends; she had attended his high school reunion in Paterson, New Jersey. He and Sean had attended a hockey game, and Paula, Lauren, Sean, Valerie, and Cameron had joined them for a birthday celebration dinner for Diane that Alan hosted at a Cuban restaurant in Silver Spring. They talked every day, and she regularly spent weekends at his house. She had met his neighbors, who smiled knowingly as they walked down the stairs some evenings toward Alan's car.

That this day would come, had to come, was an unspoken expectation rooted inevitably between them. She relied on Alan for advice, yet had long sequestered what they had from whatever was left with Gregory. This zone they had created was a fortress, but one that camouflaged a fragility she did not want to test. His mother had died of Alzheimer's-related complications. He had been to the hell, so her reports from her own purgatory were unnecessary. She had given Gregory so much, and the prospect of giving more loomed large and dark on her horizon. To invite Gregory into what she and Alan had felt like a betrayal of them both. Still, if Alan wanted her in his life, her husband would have to come with her.

Alan stepped through the door into the hallway and hugged Diane, who rested in his customarily extravagant embrace. Each meeting between them had the feel of a reunion, and Diane longed for a simpler greeting, one that signaled more confidence that what they had would last.

"Come on back to the kitchen. I made iced tea and I have some empanadas, those small meat pies. We can have a quick bite before we go."

Alan removed his jacket and cap and tossed them on the living room sofa and then wandered into Gregory's study, its walls covered with plaques, trophies, and framed newspaper articles about the buildings Caldwell & Tate had helped design and build.

"He was a real trailblazer. I'm intimidated whenever I come in this room." He laughed uneasily. This confession unsettled

Diane, and so she reached for Alan, slipping her arm through his and leading him back to the kitchen.

"What's all this?" he asked, pointing to a stack of textbooks.

"I'm choosing books for the courses I'll teach in the fall."

Alan stood thumbing through them. "You sound excited."

"I am."

"Thank you for inviting me along today. I've wanted to see Gregory again. Of course, not like this, but you know." He reached for the pitcher and filled a glass that Diane handed him.

Diane placed three empanadas each on small plates, one in front of her and one in front of Alan.

"Remember when I told you that Gregory thinks a woman at Somersby is his wife?

"Yes, I do."

"A week ago I discovered that it isn't just something in his head. She, this woman, she's having sex with Gregory."

"Well, good for him."

"Yes, it is," she said weakly

"You don't sound convinced."

"I am. I am." The declaration rushed out.

The evening Diane had discovered Wallis and Gregory in bed together remained an offensive jolt in her memory. As she'd approached Gregory's door she heard the muffled moans, deep and throaty and began walking faster, fearing that Gregory was in distress. Reaching for the doorknob, the other voice, a gritty murmur, morphed into a high-pitched, ecstatic squeal. Gently opening the door, she'd seen a woman's bare, fleshy back and the outline of the woman's broad hips, straddling the figure beneath her. Gregory's hands, grasping in the shadowy darkness, slithered around the woman's waist. She knew the woman was Wallis. A tremor of quiet laughter filled her throat at the sight and the idea of these two wayward, lost souls engaged in intercourse. The laughter was overtaken by a literal spasm of anger that brutally cleared her head.

Bristling with an outrage she could not fathom but only feel, Diane searched the quiet halls for Lynette or any of the other certified nursing assistants, determined to report what she had seen. But had she witnessed a crime? Calling Lynette, frantically searching the hallways, the den, and the TV room, she nearly knocked the woman down as she turned a corner.

"I heard your call, Mrs. Tate. What is it, did something happen? You look upset."

At the sight of Diane's face, Lynette placed a steadying hand on her shoulder and Diane heard herself stammer, "It's, it's nothing, Lynette, nothing at all." What could she say that was neither shameful nor demeaning to her sense of pride? Was she angry because she had found her husband having sex with another woman or was she angry because the man involved in that act was lost to her in all the ways that had once sealed their love?

"Are you sure?" Lynette had asked, clearly unconvinced.

"Yes, I'm sure."

In the parking lot, she had tried to catch her breath. How long had they been spending nights together? She told Paula, who had laughed and asked, "Aren't you relieved? In all the sadness of this thing, here at last, is something to be grateful for."

Now she told Alan: "I felt horrified, stunned, puzzled, a little bit of every imaginable emotion when I opened his door and found them making love."

"Come on, you call that making love? You make it sound like what we do. Remember, my mother had Alzheimer's. For them it's an act that's more biological than emotional."

Diane sat across from Alan chewing the empanada and suddenly had no appetite. "They're not animals."

"We're all animals."

"You know what I mean."

"Do I? Tell me about this woman."

While she had lost her appetite, Alan sat chewing on a meat pie, before reaching for another as he waited for her answer.

"Her name is Wallis. Wallis Peebles. She's seventy-eight years old but looks much younger. She used to be a milliner and she latched on to Gregory as soon as he arrived. She has more speech and abilities than Gregory. She cares for him."

"Gregory could be like a toy or a teddy bear to her. Do you think it registers with Gregory who he's having sex with? He no longer has any way of processing that."

"Stop. Stop." This clinical explanation that Alan clearly thought would comfort Diane instead reminded her of all that Gregory was not and all that he could no longer understand. "You don't need to remind me of all my husband's lost, of all he does and doesn't know."

"I'm just telling the truth. It's not the same as what we do, so don't say it is."

"Why are you being so hostile?" This was their first argument.

"I'm not hostile, I'm honest. What did you do when you saw them?"

"Ran. Ran because I didn't want to see it. But now I'm relieved. Alan, he may not know what love is anymore, or the multiple meanings of sexual experience, but I know it gives him something. Something he needs."

She had read that although Gregory forgot the visits from family and friends shortly after they occurred, if the visits had been positive, the good feeling they invoked could last and impact his immune system for hours. Each visit in some way extended his life. Was that a good thing? But what other choice was there? Did sex with Wallis Peebles bring Gregory satisfaction? Joy? Health?

"Are you jealous?" Alan asked.

"For a moment or two I was. It made no sense. I mean, of course there was the residual sense of—of . . ."

"'He's my man,' and 'Bitch, what the hell are you doing?'" Alan laughed cynically.

"Sort of."

"Well, he's in a different world. His world. Their world." Alan reached across the island and held her hand. "You have to accept that."

"I have. Alan, what do you think the last couple of years has been about? I've earned a PhD in accepting things I can't control."

"Have you?" The question sounded like an interrogation.

"Yes."

"Well, I think we'd better get going."

Diane knocked gently on the door before entering, a new practice since the night she found Wallis and Gregory together. Gregory was not asleep but lay resting on top of the quilt on his bed, staring at the ceiling. He barely stirred when they entered.

"Gregory, hello, dear," Diane said, leaning over to squeeze his hands as they lay folded on his chest.

Alan pushed a rocking chair near Diane and she sank into it while he brought over the desk chair beside her and sat down.

She was suddenly aware of the severe limits and artificiality of Gregory's life. As they'd entered the memory care unit, she'd explained to Alan the number of rooms on each floor and told him about the activities for the residents. Yet showing it to Alan, she thought how hermetic, small, and encased it seemed. Alan kept murmuring, "This is nice, very nice," but suddenly it all seemed meager. This was what was left of life for Gregory, and seeing it with Alan at her side filled Diane with a flash of guilt and shame.

Looking at her husband, whose eyes revealed no glimmer of recognition, Diane could hardly breathe. The three of them filled the room to capacity. How would she introduce Alan, she wondered. What would she say?

Alan reached for Gregory's limp, elastic hand and shook it.

"You don't remember me now, Mr. Tate, but your firm built a school I was principal of back in 2002. It was the most beautiful school I ever taught in. The students, the staff, we loved that building and we all worked harder because it was the kind of building that required us to do more and be more to reflect its refinement. I had a lot of respect for you back then, how you asked me and the teachers and the students what we wanted in the new school before you started designing it, how you made the building about us. I know I wanted some things you said were impractical and we went toe-to-toe, head-to-head sometimes, but you usually won in the end. And when I looked at the building and started working in it, I'm glad you did."

Gregory's eyes were a void that gave neither of them anything. He listened with a faux patience and then turned on his side, giving them both his back, curled in on himself, and drifted off to sleep.

In the hallway, Diane told Lynette that she was worried. "I looked in his drawers and closets and it seems some of his socks and shirts are missing."

With a look of chagrin, Lynette said, "We've had a problem with some items being washed and returned to the wrong resident. They can't always inform us of the mistake."

"But I labeled all his clothes, everything."

"I know, I'm sorry, Mrs. Tate."

At that moment a resident walked toward them wearing one of Gregory's sweatshirts.

"That for example, belongs to my husband."

"I'll try to get it back."

"Try?"

"The residents, as you know, are sometimes volatile and—"

"So Gregory's clothes just disappear and become the property of anyone else just like that?"

Alan held her shoulders and said, "Thank you. Come on, let's go, Diane. It's not the end of the world."

In the car she fumed. "For all the money I'm paying, you'd think they could at least keep track of his clothes."

"What's really wrong?" Alan asked.

"I feel so empty. I hadn't told him about us, about you. I didn't know how. I had hoped this visit would be one way to start that conversation. But even if I say the words, tell him about our relationship, what would it even mean?"

"Is this what you want for the rest of your life? Don't you want more?"

"I haven't thought that far ahead."

"Not even since we've been together?"

"Alan, it's only been a couple of months."

"Why do you always say that like weeks and months have anything to do with feelings?

You can go forward. You can always go forward."

"I'm here with you. I call this moving forward."

Chapter Twenty-two

June 2016

Forward, that was the only place to go, Diane often thought. Forward. There was no way to tell Gregory about Alan and so she no longer tried to. Whatever he shared with Wallis Peebles, that belonged to them. Apparently they were content in the universe they had created. In the months that had passed after Alan went with her to Somersby, she formally retired from the bench. She was moving on. There was no place else to go.

"Are you sure you're up for this?" Diane asked Lauren one day. "We can stay here if you want."

Lauren and Diane sat on the backyard deck. The garden Diane had tended and coaxed filled the yard, vivid and simmering with color and life. Lauren sat with her arms resting protectively on her abdomen. She'd cut her locks and now wore her hair in a close-cut, natural style that exposed a face Diane sometimes thought she had never seen before.

"I'm okay with the walking, Mom. Please, I wish everyone

would stop treating me like an invalid. What did enslaved women do? No one can believe I still come into the office. What else am I supposed to do? I gotta support my baby." Lauren giggled at her own insouciance.

"So have you and Gerald chosen a name?"

"If it's a girl, I like Simone, and if it's a boy, I want Daniel. Gerald says he's fine with that."

"Daniel, that's Gregory's middle name."

"That's why I chose it."

"I'm proud of you, Lauren."

"Mom, you know this wasn't the plan."

"You could have made a different choice."

"Not now. I couldn't imagine a different choice."

"And Gerald, he'll be a good father. That's all that matters now. You two aren't broken, you didn't fail at anything. You're just making a family. The way families, quiet as it's kept, have always been made."

"I still love him a little."

"Good, then you'll be able to one day forgive him for not being ready to be everything you felt you had to have. Do you want to go to the Museum of African Art first or Macy's?"

When the phone rang, Diane rose from the plush deck chair, regretting that even for this moment she had to leave this late morning sun, a sun that had not just warmed her but blossomed a fullness within her that she held fast to as she hurried inside to answer the phone. Leaning against the wall in the kitchen, already slightly annoyed, fearing that she would hear the voice of a Saturday morning telemarketer, Diane heard instead the voice of Leah Temple informing her that half an hour ago it was discovered that Gregory was missing. He had apparently left Somersby. The building had been thoroughly searched, and Gregory was gone.

Gone. The word landed, a rock from space, a sudden blow, a groin-tightening fright. There it was, despite her best efforts standing in her kitchen to erase it, slithering cold and wet.

Leah's voice was apologetic, straining to be clinical and composed as it narrated what could be an impending disaster. She summed up all the steps taken after it was discovered that Gregory was missing. All the rooms were checked. All the residents were taken from the building and the rooms checked again. Diane imagined a huddled mass of the elderly, some in wheelchairs, some on walkers in the parking lot, monitored and calmed by nursing assistants as everyone from Leah, to the receptionist and cooks, looked for Gregory again.

"Are you there, Mrs. Tate?"

"Where else would I be?"

"I know this is terribly upsetting for you. We've contacted the police, who've issued a Silver Alert."

Diane heard the echo of all the Silver Alerts she had seen on news reports about missing seniors. Grainy photographs of an elderly man or woman, the white hair, the face that looked like everyone's grandmother or grandfather.

And here she was now. In hell. She nearly gagged as her throat clogged and then constricted, her body urging her to release it all, what she had been told, what she knew, did not know, what she feared. To her amazement, she heard herself ask, "How could this happen?"

But she knew how it could happen, saw again herself in bathrobe and bare feet that early morning before the sun rose, chasing Gregory down their street, calling his name, willing him to stop, slow down, to hear her call. The human will can outwit even the most rigorous surveillance. But she had put Gregory in Somersby, convincing herself that this could never happen.

To forestall telling Lauren even for a few moments, driving

to Somersby, thoughts of suing the facility, of Gregory never being found, of Gregory found, Diane asked again, "How could this happen?"

—— ✺ ——

Diane couldn't drive fast enough and yet despised the idea of arriving. Maybe, she thought foolishly, crazily, grasping for a way out, a mistake had been made. By the time she and Lauren arrived, Gregory would have been found, somehow overlooked by the staff, not found in the two and possibly three checks of every room, every space in the building. All her training in the law codified for her the tangible, the real, the myriad of "realistic" possibilities, yet all her years in the law, her years as a judge, had taught her, too, that there was a higher law. The law of the unexpected, the miraculous. The law of the saving grace.

At every stoplight, she allowed herself to turn from the road ahead and scan the streets, crowded on this sumptuous summer morning with people. *Ordinary people*, she thought, not people like her who have, with one phone call, had their lives upended. People shopping, walking into and out of stores, waiting at bus stops, hailing taxis, clutching their children's hands as they steered them across the street. She was looking, too, scanning really for a sighting of Gregory. She caught sight of a gleam of white hair, a tall man in khaki pants, striding quickly, racing really, to catch an oncoming bus.

Diane nudged Lauren and shouted, "Is that him?"

"Mom, I saw that guy a minute ago. That's not Dad. He's not as tall as Dad, and he's darker. He was wearing sneakers. Dad never wears sneakers. He was wearing thick-rimmed glasses."

"He looked like him."

"Mom, trust me, it's not him."

Leah had told her that Gregory was dressed in khaki slacks and a light blue shirt and a baseball cap. So she was willing him, conjuring up the missing mate, seeing him in every tall, white-haired man. After the man who was not Gregory boarded the bus, after he rode away, out of reach, out of the possibility of questioning and further examination that might prove Lauren wrong, an ocean swelled between the two women, a stretch of emotional territory that separated them from the husband and the father neither would admit they already missed as if he had been declared gone for good.

Disappeared. Missing Person. Gregory had slowly descended into all those personas. Diane gratefully sank in to the silence that bound her to Lauren, finding in it a balm temporarily still-ing the eruption of fear.

Before leaving the house, she had quickly briefed Lauren on all that was being done, the Silver Alert sent out to radio and TV stations. Soon Gregory's picture would be on the news. Reverse 911 calls would go out to residents living in communities near Somersby, letting them know that an elderly person with Alzhei-mer's was missing and might be wandering in their neighbor-hood. It was Lauren who, sitting beside her in the car, Googled *wandering seniors with Alzheimer's* and told Diane that if not found within twenty-four hours, up to half of them could suffer serious injury or death.

"Most likely, we'll find him. We're near downtown Silver Spring. There are police cars everywhere and those police offic-ers have his picture." This was what Leah, harried and con-cerned, told them moments after Diane, Lauren, and Sean, who met them at Somersby, settled in her office.

Downtown Silver Spring, a phalanx of stores, restaurants, theaters, malls. Everyone hurrying by, everyone in their own world. Who would notice Gregory? What if he was mumbling? Got violent when a concerned person approached him? But wasn't that better than walking along the empty streets of the neighborhoods around downtown? Middle-aged homeowners inside, the few young children indoors playing video games? No one to see Gregory walking down their quiet streets.

"How could this happen? Where was the staff?" Diane asked, seething and so anguished she could barely remain seated.

"I wish I could say it isn't so, but no facility is fail-safe," Leah said with a shake of her head.

"What my mother wants to know," Sean said coldly, "is literally, how this could have happened."

"At this moment, I'm sorry to say we simply don't know. No one that we've talked to on the staff or among the residents saw him leave."

"I told you a few weeks after we brought Gregory here about finding one of the doors unlocked," Diane said.

"We took care of that, Mrs. Tate, and the person responsible had a poor security record and was fired."

"It seems some others need to be fired as well," Sean said.

"There will be a review and an investigation, I assure you of that."

"Why would he wander now? Did anything unusual happen?" Diane wondered aloud.

"I think it's because his friend Wallis was hospitalized for a lung infection yesterday. Since she was taken to the hospital, Gregory has been agitated."

"Does he know where she is?" Lauren asked hesitantly, "I mean *can* he know?"

"We explained that she had to go away, but that she was coming back."

"So he's looking for Wallis?"

"That's my best guess."

"We have to go look for him. We can't just sit here and wait. Your father is lost. He needs to be found."

---⊙≈⊙---

Two hours earlier, Sean watched his mother and Lauren walk away from Somersby, each searching for Gregory in different sections of the nearby residential neighborhoods. They would all keep in touch by cell phone.

Sean drove to the commercial area along Colesville Road, parked his car, and walked along the nexus of glass office buildings, looking through the wide windows at security guards inside pacing the deserted marble and chrome lobbies. Praying for a sighting, a vision of his father.

After a while, all the lobbies began to look the same with the same black security guard, and he had even searched the Metro station, purchasing a card, and going through the turnstiles, walking the length of the platform in both directions. He had entered the restaurants and shops along Georgia Avenue that had resisted upscale gentrification—the music store that sold R&B albums and CDs from the sixties, seventies, and eighties, the store that sold sheet music, the Korean nail salon, the comic book store. He even went into the fire station and told the men there to be on the lookout for his dad.

The heat, the frustration, the fear that this was all in vain—it wore him out. Now he sat at a Greek diner waiting for a gyro plate. He hadn't heard from his mother or Lauren and wondered where they were. He had texted them to update him, told them where he was and to meet him here. No news was supposed to be good news, but it wasn't in this case.

As the waiter brought his plate, his phone vibrated. It was

Diane: *Any luck?* He hated to think that was what they were depending on. Luck. He thanked the waiter and texted back, *Not yet.*

Lauren walked along the residential streets, searching for her father. The houses were shuttered against her, residents huddled inside their air-conditioned rooms. She had opened the gates and walked past the picket fences of several houses, knocking on doors where no one answered.

She'd try one more door. The neat, solid, two-story brick house beckoned her. Was it the sight of a bicycle resting on its side? The balls and Hula-hoop scattered around? Maybe it was her thirst, the heat penetrating the broad straw sun hat she wore, her blouse matted to her skin, the hunger taking root in her stomach. She was suddenly desperate to hear another voice, even if it was one telling her they had not seen her father.

An elderly woman answered the door, her olive-toned face framed by a hijab. Lauren saw the woman's thick black brows and burning brown eyes fill with unease in her presence, for she was a stranger.

So quickly, before the door closed, the words tumbled out: "I'm sorry to disturb you, but my father is an elderly man suffering from Alzheimer's and he's left his assisted-living facility. I wanted to know if you have seen him."

Lauren held up her cell phone and showed the woman a picture of Gregory. Then two young children, a brooding little girl in shorts and a pink shirt and a boy with an open, curious face, came up behind the woman, whose arms found their shoulders and brought them close to her body. Then a younger man came to the door, tall, with the same skin and eyes. The woman spoke to him in Arabic.

"Papa, she's looking for her father. Her father, he's lost," the boy said.

"Come in, come in," the boy's father said. "Sit, please." The words both an invitation and requirement as he gazed at her stomach.

Lauren sat eyeing the Koran on the glass coffee table, a news anchor speaking in Arabic on the TV and felt safe in the room with all the dark rich colors, gold and green and red. "This is my father, he's elderly. He has Alzheimer's. He's lost, and my family is looking for him."

The man studied the photo on Lauren's cell phone and then handed it back to her. "I have not seen this man. You have of course told the police?"

"Yes."

"Would you like something to drink, to rest for a bit?"

"Thank you."

When the man left the room, Lauren's sobs spilled forth. All day she had felt that to give into the tears might portend all she feared. Now she sat in a stranger's house weeping with a shattering abandon, not caring who heard or saw her display. When she could cry no more, she sat both renewed and overwhelmed by a fatigue she felt embedded in her bones. She couldn't stop looking. They had to find him.

The man padded quietly into the room. He placed a glass of water and a small plate of meat pies on the table. "Eat. Replenish yourself," he told Lauren with an authority both compassionate and firm. "Then you will join me and my family in prayer for your father's safe return."

———— ✺ ————

She always swallowed the big frog first. Working with families in crisis all these years and being the child of a family in crisis herself had taught Diane not to be afraid to enter the darkest space first and then circle back to the promise or even a flicker of light.

Fortified by the fact that the darkness had not yet swallowed her resolve, that in the darkness she still heard her heartbeat and the hum of her breathing, that in the darkness the world did not crumble beneath her feet, or if it did, she could pull herself out of the rubble, she had learned to make of the darkness a promise yet to unfold.

So, walking to the Greek café where Sean had texted her and Lauren to meet him, she moved with a stalwart heart that was already broken, a heart that she had repaired and mended because if the worst was yet to come, she would need a strong heart. She would be prepared for her heart to break over and over as it must.

She was too stunned for tears, for this was beyond all her fearful imaginings. In the novels she loved, the march of life was relentless, the shocks and surprises unfolded right up to the last page. If only her life were a text, one that she could let slip from her hands as she fell asleep reading in bed, the book shoved, harmless and inert beneath the sheets.

Their deepest fears for Gregory's safety had so far gone unspoken between the three of them. Now, she had been buffeted, tossed, her brain and senses and feelings scrambled.

The big frog was widowhood. She and Gregory had prided themselves on not being afraid to talk about death:

"If something happens . . ."

"If something happens to me before you . . ."

". . . this is what I want you to do . . ."

". . . this is where the important papers are stored . . ."

A therapist friend told her once that the process of grieving a spouse took an average of seven years. *Seven years*, Diane had wondered. Who had done the polling? What questions were asked? How could you tell when the grieving was done? She still grieved her mother, her brother, and the father she had not known. Had grieved them all her life.

Gregory had gone looking for the woman who had replaced her in his mind as his wife. But *she* was his wife, would be his wife beyond "till death do us part," for the parting was nothing more than a new beginning.

They had to find him. She had allowed herself the folly of thinking that there was some moving on because her husband was broken. There was no moving on, could be no moving on even as she lay in Alan's arms, laughed at his jokes, and beamed in the joy and comfort of his friends. She would be lodged in this space, the wide circumference of love that took in everything, all of them.

Gregory is engulfed by all the sounds in the world. Adrift in a roaring sea of dissonance.

Standing on the corner of Colesville Road a few feet from the entrance to a Ruby Tuesday, the crowd swoons around him. When he left Somersby, now two miles behind him, he strode the streets with a determined gait and one thing in mind—to find Wallis. Now, standing on this street, he feels only fear—agile, alert, freezing him in place.

He knows that there is only one person who can help him to find her. His best friend. His partner. Mercer. A headache nests at the base of his skull. Thankfully, it has not yet launched a full attack. But fear roils his stomach and several times it has taken all his strength to push back, push down against the terror that is a muscle poised to gush up and out from his insides.

So many people. Too many people. Immobilized in their midst, he has been bumped, cursed, and is near tears. But stubbornly, he decided that he would not drown. Not if he can find Wallis. Not if he can get to Mercer, who will help him find her. All these months, all this time, this is where he was headed anyway, to meet Mercer. Past and through the stop signs that have hijacked his mind. He just wants to get to 1213 U Street. Their office.

Out on the street, alone, hurrying away from Somersby before they realized he was gone, he was exultant, flush with courage. Courage he has longed to call forth. It was like taking baby steps: walking the first block away from Somersby, then the second block, and all the blocks that followed. Through the sea of cars, the sun, steady and hounding. He nearly tripped, for no reason that he could see, other than that suddenly, in these first moments of the freedom he had longed for, freedom overwhelmed him, freedom literally took his breath away. He stopped at each light, the memory of the place he was headed for blazing more brightly in his mind than even the flashing green and red lights telling him when to stop and when to go. He hurried across each street, for the cars were like animals he cannot trust. There was nothing around him that looks like what he knows, the one thing and the one place he remembers: 1213 U Street.

The voice of doubt huddles in his brain and he hears it throb with ridicule: *Where? Who?*

All that walking and here he is, forsaken, deserted on the corner of Colesville Road. How can he go farther? But he is a brash, eager young man who believes in himself, who has become an architect, designing buildings in the year of 1978, in the city of his birth, the nation's capital. He can do this. This remembrance, that he is more than the despair that now plagues his days and nights, activates his voice, and his first request for help.

The woman is walking fast toward him, her head slightly down, avoiding his gaze, clutching a shopping bag. He positions himself slightly in front of her and that movement makes her look up. She is startled.

Is she afraid? He marshals a steadiness in his voice that is pure make-believe. "Twelve thirteen U Street?"

He hears the sharp, quick intake of breath at the question. This close, she has to look at him. And he sees her full on. Asking her was not accidental. He assessed the quality and cut of her tan linen suit, the leather bag on her shoulder, and the colorful, designer shopping bags she carries. All that told him she would be the one to help him. He has chosen well, he thinks, for he has always been good with people, intuitive and knowing. Mercer signs the contracts, he seals the deal, ropes the client in. The woman is attractive, her skin flawless, her brown eyes curious and confident. If he was not looking for Wallis. If he didn't need to find Mercer . . . The train of thought, barreling down the tracks of his mind stops, as he understands the look on her face.

There is a pause as those wide eyes narrow skeptically and then she laughs. "That's a long way from here."

Her laughter relaxes him. But her look turns, despite the laugh, into a trap and she moves a few feet aside from the entrance to Ruby Tuesday and he follows her. Now they stand encased in their own bubble.

"Are you lost?" she asks, placing her hand on his arm. The question sounds sincere but does not calm him. He hopes she has not felt him flinch at her touch.

"Twelve thirteen U Street."

She is looking at him more closely now. Now he is being examined and he wishes for the return of the smile but knows he will probably not see it again.

"That's a long way from here," she tells him again. "That's in D.C. You could ride the Metro but you should probably take a taxi. Are you sure you're not lost?"

The concern on her face could prevent him from finding Wallis and Mercer.

"Wallis . . . Mercer will . . . I need to . . ." This explanation, so clear to him that it has taken all his remaining strength and belief in this adventure to say, seems only to confuse her. He spoke slowly, calmly, willing the upheaval inside to subside. But he sees the alarm on her face.

When the woman puts her shopping bags on the street beside her, reaches into her purse, takes out a square, pink object and puts it to her ear as she looks around, he knows it is over.

"Just a minute. I'll find a policemen who can help you." As she looks away from him, likely trying to spot a policeman right here and right now, he walks fast through the crowd, bumping into people, not pausing to say "Excuse me," when he side-swipes and nearly knocks down a woman eating an ice cream cone.

Walking fast, hearing the calls of the woman, breathless and terrified. The woman who wanted to call the police reminds him that he is not really free.

Whatever triumph he has felt in leaving Somersby is temporary and he knows it cannot last. Even if he finds Wallis. Even if he finds Mercer. A block away from the woman with the phone, he slumps onto a cement bench in front of a row of restaurants. He is hungry. He is thirsty. But now he is afraid to speak to anyone. For now he fears that they will all see in him what that woman saw. His hands fumble in his empty pockets. Sweat congeals in his armpits, warms his back and neck and mats his shirt to his skin. He smells the sweat and the terror inside it.

He has no money but he can still get a taxi to take him to the office. Mercer will pay for the cab when he gets there. He cannot allow himself to sink back into pity and despair. He cannot, because Wallis is waiting for him. She would want him to find her. So he stands up and walks to the corner of Georgia Avenue, past the windows of restaurants where he sees people eating and drinking, happy and laughing. Through those windows he sees a world he wants to live in. With Wallis and with Mercer.

On the corner he hails a taxi and once inside, he tells the driver, "Twelve thirteen U Street," and settles back into the seat, safe for the first time that day. Refreshed and soothed by the air-conditioning, Gregory relaxes, closes his eyes. He remembers waking up that morning and looking for Wallis. They always met at breakfast. At night, she came to him, though sometimes, he went to her. When he walked into the dining room this morning and did not see her sitting at "their" table, he asked where she was. Lynette told him Wallis was sick.

"Remember? I told you yesterday she had to go to see the doctor but that she would be back soon."

In Wallis's room he found her bed empty, unmade, as though she threw off the covers, walked into the night, and disappeared. As though there had never been any Wallis at all. The nursing assistants found him lying beneath the sheets on Wallis's bed and escorted him back to his room.

He struggled in their steely grasp and demanded, "Where is Wallis? Where is Wallis?"

"She'll be back soon. She had to go to see the doctor," they told him, but he did not trust them. Wherever they had taken her, Wallis was waiting for him. Expecting him. Just like Mercer.

He has thought often of how he and Wallis could escape, and when he met Wallis and knew he would not have to be alone when he left, he began to routinely linger near the exit of the memory care unit and watched staff members and visitors punch the pad on the wall. Their fingers, like a magic wand, unsealed the door. Fingers placed inside certain squares made freedom possible. He watched as though he was not watching. In time, he knew where to place his fingers.

One afternoon, in the deserted hallway, he risked a trial run, his fingers quivering as they raced over the face of the pad. Then he heard the click of the lock.

This morning, after they told him Wallis was hospitalized and made him leave her bed, he heard them say that she had been taken to Holy Cross Hospital. After he lay in his own bed, he dreamed of escape. Later, he entered the hallway and found it empty. Unseen, his fingers punched in the code and unlocked the door securing him in the memory care unit.

When the taxi stops, he does not know where he is and he tells the driver the address again. "Twelve thirteen U Street."

"Mister, this is the address."

Where, Gregory wonders, are the cranes looming over the dirt-filled, dug-up streets, nearly impossible to navigate as the city builds a subway system atop the decade-old ruinous decay left from the riots? The street is crowded with people. A CVS stands where his favorite bar is supposed to be. There are no empty, boarded-up storefronts but a profusion of shops large and small, new apartment buildings, people lined up in front of the box office of the Lincoln Theater, which is supposed to be shuttered.

"No, this isn't it."

"Look, mister, this is where you told me to bring you. I want my fare."

Ignoring the driver's belligerence, Gregory opens the door and stands before the place where his office should be, a building that is now a restaurant. The driver has gotten out of the taxi and is nearing him.

He enters the restaurant and knows he is lost. He has never seen this many white people on U Street. A young girl with pink hair and dressed all in black asks him if she can help him.

"Mercer," Gregory shouts and then he is stunned by the brusque grip of the driver on his back attempting to turn him around. When they are face-to-face, he punches the driver, collecting in his fists all his bewilderment and rage.

There is a scream and chairs scraping the floor and before he can turn around to look again at those happy, laughing people, living the life he wants to live with Wallis and Mercer, two men whose faces he cannot see are grabbing him and he is pleading, "Wallis . . . Mercer . . ."

─── ⸙ ───

The squad car pulled up to the entrance of Somersby just as darkness was falling, and two female police officers helped Gregory out of the backseat. After the altercation at the restaurant, Gregory was taken into custody and traced back to the Silver Alert and then Leah Temple was called. Bedraggled and sweat-soaked, Gregory shuffled past Diane, Sean, and Lauren, who stood, relieved, in the lobby.

"I know you all want to be with him, but let us check him out first, make sure there are no injuries, that his temperature and heart rate are okay," Leah says.

Half an hour later, Leah rejoined them and said they could see Gregory. Lauren rushed into the room and hugged Gregory, Sean fell to his knees and held Gregory's hands tightly.

Diane stood behind them, the impact of the day washing over her, blinking back tears at the sight of Gregory staring at them all with a distant, benevolent curiosity. Gregory wore clean clothes and his hair had been combed, yet Diane could see that his body was tense with the static of longing and dissatisfaction.

Sean tapped Diane on the shoulder and said, "It's been a long day, Mom. We'll leave you two alone."

Diane kissed Sean and Lauren good-bye then turned to Gregory. "You went to find Wallis, didn't you? And Mercer?"

Hearing those names, Gregory's eyes grew bright and he grabbed Diane's hand, pulling her onto the bed beside him. His adventure in the day's virulent sun had left his skin burnished with a sheen that countered the weathered, solemn gaze on his face.

The weight of the day, the force of the nine hours during which she had intermittently imagined and beaten back the worst possible outcomes, had chipped away at her strength. Even as her hands, like the fingers and palms of the blind, confirmed Gregory's face and body, his substantial, definite presence, Diane grieved. For the tight weave of the life they had once shared was now unalterably frayed and tattered. Never had she felt so close to Gregory as today, when scenes from their past constantly erupted, invading and skewing her thoughts. He had been brought back, returned, but not to her. Never again to her.

He had walked out of Somersby, strode through the front doors unaccompanied, back into the world looking for Wallis. All day, Diane had thought Gregory's absence had existed as an affront, a potential tragedy, a betrayal of her faith in the staff of Somersby, a wound. But this day had been about one simple desire: Gregory wanted to find Wallis. And this act, which Diane now considered more brave than foolhardy, confirmed that forward was her only destination. He had gone looking for Wallis. She had it in her power to reunite them.

As they drove to Holy Cross Hospital, Gregory sat mumbling, muttering to himself fragments of what sounded like the long remembered, recalled, savored, and hallowed conversation with the mayor on the day that Gregory and Mercer inked the deal for their first building for the city. At a desk in the lobby, the receptionist directed them to Wallis's room, and Gregory reached for Diane's hand as they walked down the hallway beneath the harsh fluorescent lights.

Wallis lay asleep in the room, whose medicinal, antiseptic smell was a presence all its own, as were the snores of the woman in the bed on the other side of the partition. At Somersby, Wallis reigned like an *enfant terrible*, but here, Diane saw her for what she was—a tiny, fragile, elderly woman. She was connected by tubes to machines purring as they provided oxygen, hydration, and life. Gregory leaned into Wallis, peering at her closely, his trembling hands smoothing the lightweight blanket beneath which she lay. There was nothing for Diane to say or do, save witness this, the fierceness of life.

A nurse bustled into the room and greeted them with a gracious smile. "Are you family?"

"Yes, yes we are. How is she doing?"

As the nurse checked the intravenous fluid drip, she said, "She's doing quite well. She should be able to go home soon."

Wallis opened her eyes, blinking groggily. When she turned from Gregory and saw Diane, they darkened with suspicion.

As the nurse pulled out a thermometer and softly asked Wallis how she felt, Diane, feeling more and more like an intruder said, "I have to go to the bathroom, I'll be right back." Instead, she stood outside the room leaning against the wall. Her cell phone rang and Lauren asked where she was.

"I'm with your father at Holy Cross Hospital. I brought him here to see Wallis."

"What?"

"I'll explain it to you tomorrow." She could not tell her daughter at this moment the strange, replenishing, liberating emotions she felt, so she said, "It's Wallis now that he needs, it's Wallis that he loves."

When she returned to the room, she found them both asleep—Gregory dozing as he clutched Wallis's hand. Waking Gregory gently, Diane told him that it was time to go, assuring him that if he wanted, she would bring him back to see Wallis tomorrow.

Back at Somersby, Diane helped Gregory undress and get into his pajamas and then she sat by his bed in the half-light and watched him fall asleep.

Walking toward the exit, Diane passed Wallis's room. She opened the door and turned on the light. Shelves of Styrofoam heads—white, dark brown—and frozen mannequin faces with bright red lips and thick black brows, exaggerated eyelashes, frightful in their blankness, gazed out into the limited horizon of the room.

Hats were everywhere, some on the heads of the mannequins, others on the shelves. There was a black silk, broad-brimmed hat with a veritable garden of white lilies and black feathers that arched several inches high; a red wool felt hat with a purple veil; a hat like the one made famous by Princess Diana, ivory straw with a large bow in the back; a hat bold and startling, made of two wide open funnels joined by a large black ribbon of bibbing.

Diane stood in the midst of forty years of the precise and artful work of Wallis's hands. For the first time, Diane wondered who Wallis had once been, how old was she when she made her first hat and knew that there was no going back. She stood in the small space, surrounded by all of Wallis' history and her yearnings, and was silent and shamed by the extravagant display of beauty she never would have imagined Wallis capable of.

Overcome, overwrought, flush with a fever-like fatigue, Diane remembered the day, months ago, when she and Wallis found themselves alone in the hallway outside Gregory's room:

"Leave him alone. He's my husband," Wallis had said. "I waited all these years for him and now he's come. Come *for me*. Come *to me*."

Chapter Twenty-three

JULY 2016

"So how is Master Daniel Burris Stone?" Alan asked as Diane lay next to him in bed.

"Still the world's best baby. Lauren says he sleeps through most nights."

"Congratulations, Grandma. How's the father taking it?"

"He comes over a couple of evenings a week after work to help out. He's in awe of his little boy and against all claims to the contrary, he was ready to be a father."

"All I know is, circumstances can *make* you ready. Have you decided about Somersby?"

"There's no sense moving Gregory anywhere else. The trauma of separating him from Wallis might induce a setback from which he'll never recover. I've formed a committee of resident relatives that Leah has agreed to meet with regularly about any concerns, from security to laundry."

A late-night talk show host was five minutes into his monologue on the plasma TV, and Diane yawned, stretched and sprawled, burrowing into Alan's side. There was the warmth of Alan's lips on her face and then the question.

"Where do you see us going, Diane? I want us to be together. I want—I need you to be my wife. You're my solid ground."

Staring at the ceiling, she said nothing as the question ballooned in the room, swelling like a bruise.

"My heart's on my sleeve," Alan said. "It's been there since the beginning of this. You had to know how I felt, how I feel. I know it's been less than a year, but—"

"Alan, I care for you deeply. But I could never divorce Gregory. I just couldn't do that."

"Even for a new life?"

"I have a new life."

"One of your own choosing."

"I chose you."

"You've chosen part of me."

"What do you want that I haven't given you?"

Alan reached over and turned on the halogen lamp on the night stand. In the muted, shadowy flush of light, Diane was prickly with exposure and pulled the blanket up to cover her chest.

"A life that belongs to us. I want to be your husband."

The word *husband* severed her heart, and Diane touched Alan's broad, trusting, open face.

Removing her hand, she said, "I can't give you that."

"I know it wouldn't be easy."

"That's not even an option for me. I'll never divorce Gregory. You're being unreasonable. Unreasonable and selfish. This is the life I have. I can't change it. I can't give you a do-over. I can't give you a happily ever after." The words charged into the still, small space between them. Words that were muscular, brutal, a bulwark that offered her shelter.

"I know of cases where spouses have divorced their mate who had Alzheimer's and . . ."

Sitting up on her elbow, she said, "Don't say it, Alan. Please don't tell me that lie. Maybe if I'd been miserable with Gregory or considering a divorce before the disease struck. And even then I'd feel I owed him some kind of guardianship. But I had a good marriage. I'm not living on memories. I'm not tied to the past. Even if Gregory dies before me, there will be no other husband for me. I know that now. I couldn't improve on what we had. I wouldn't even try. I can't be your wife."

"I want to give you a life, a real life."

"If this was any more real, I don't know what I'd do." Diane turned away from Alan and stared again at the ceiling. He slumped onto the bed and burrowed beneath the covers, turning his back to her.

Rising from the bed, she took refuge in the bathroom, locking the door behind her. If he'd known her at all, she thought, sitting on the rim of the bathtub, he would have known what he asked was impossible. Yet as she sat on the tub shivering with anger, Diane knew she was angry because she had considered a life without Gregory. A life free of Somersby, of Wallis, with memories of their marriage, memories of Alzheimer's just that, memories.

The affection she felt for Alan was deep, important. A kind of love, but not the kind he craved. Alan had resurrected her fluency in the art of affection and concern, it was acknowledged and received. That had been enough.

But now her anger was a blazing, blunt force. She, too, had imagined a life free of Alzheimer's. Only now did she allow herself to realize that she had not imagined a cure, a magic pill, a discovery to turn back the clock. She had only imagined and dreamed of an end. An end to Gregory's suffering and with it, the end of her suffering as well. She had been noble and brave and terrified and confused.

But she did not want to marry Alan. She would have to carve out some place that was her own, a place that nourished her even as she remained tied to Gregory but not tied down. She didn't want to marry Alan; she wanted to marry herself. His offer of love and devotion inspired her to fight even more, for this new, gestating self she had yet to meet. What *would* she do with the rest of her life?

Months ago, Diane had gone through all of Gregory's papers with Lauren and decided what to donate to Caldwell & Tate's archives and what they would keep. Looking through the stacks of photo albums had become a ritual of remembrance and gratitude. The photos captured a bountiful, blessed life, a life she had taken for granted. Her personal history was full to the brim—birthday parties, graduations, weddings, Thanksgiving dinners, awards ceremonies, Christmas mornings. And now a new album held photos of her grandson, Daniel Burris Stone, being breastfed while held by his mother, sleeping in his father's arms, sucking his tiny fingers in his mouth, held by Gregory, baptized at two months old.

One evening, Diane opened an album and on the first page saw the photos her father had mailed her a few weeks before his death. The photo of her parents on the day of their wedding: Her mother stunned, eyes bright. Her father solemn, wary, facing the camera but clutching Ella tightly around her waist. The photo of Diane sitting on her father's lap as all of them—her baby brother, her mother, and father—lay sprawled on a blanket in Meridian Hill Park.

She was the child of a family fractured by a crime and the loss and abandonment that consumed them in its wake, but the picture captured how her family had started, all the love and hope that had once formed the contours of their world. Her father had abandoned them. She had turned her back on her father.

But Gregory, she thought, turning to a page of photos of her, Gregory, Lauren, and Sean, watching fireworks, he had offered Diane another chance. Another way. He had stood firm, stood tall, always facing her and never looking away, his arms open wide.

―――∞∞∞―――

The search for a new home was a pilgrimage. Diane ventured into the gleaming condominiums and apartment buildings, each walk-through a solo flight.

She claimed her new home moments after stepping across the portal. Two months into evenings spent researching on the Internet, talking with a Realtor friend of Paula's, and spending hours forgoing her car and walking the streets of the refurbished, remade city, Diane found the building. A twelve-story tower on New York Avenue. Sleek teak cabinets and quartz countertops in the kitchen. The stone shower, the small, elegant chandelier in the dining room were all touches that she was sure Gregory would have liked. The floor-to-ceiling windows ushered sunlight into all the rooms and lifted her as she stood in the model two-bedroom. She had been unaware of how stifled and choked she felt at home until she stood in the top-floor unit. Each day she would look out into a skyscape that reflected the design of the life she now planned: open, free-form as clouds. She chose the top floor to conquer her fear of heights. That would be one more thing she would have to get over. Give up.

She had expected to feel some remorse, even regret as she began deciding what to donate and what to take with her to her new home. She had done this for Gregory and now she was doing it for herself. What was home and where was it?

When she examined the house closely and saw how it had aged—the sagging gutters, the water-stained ceilings in the basement, the decades-old bathroom fixtures, the cracks in the drywall—Diane decided what to do. The mortgage had been paid years ago. She would let Sean and Valerie live in the house, make repairs, pay the property taxes. It would be their wedding gift. She was moving out and moving on but Diane wanted the house to remain in the family.

"You looked surprised to see me," Diane said. "Did you write us off? Fire me without notice?"

She hadn't called Alan in almost two months, afraid to risk summary rejection over the phone. Instead, she'd shown up uninvited, without warning. Waited, parked outside his house for twenty minutes before approaching the front door and ringing the bell. Now they sat in his living room.

"I wasn't expecting this, that's all," he said.

She thought of the dance of their bodies moments ago when he'd chosen not to sit beside her on the sofa but in an armchair across the room. Silence froze them in place. They sat not looking at one another, as though the gaze they had once hungered for was now taboo.

Finally, Alan asked, "How've you been?"

"I moved out of the house into an apartment. A condo on New York Avenue. I'm having a housewarming party in a few weeks and I'd like you to come."

"So now we're supposed to just be friends? I asked you to marry me. You said no."

"I said no to marriage. I didn't say no to you."

"You're talking like a lawyer, like a judge, playing word games."

"I'm asking you to think not just about what you want and need but what I can give. It's not just about you, Alan. It's about me, too."

"I didn't call you because I figured we had said everything there was to say. I was all out of words."

That is exactly how I feel, she wanted to say but did not. "I'm glad you didn't call. I needed time to think, to collect myself."

As Diane spoke, Alan stood up and neared the sofa, leaning on the baby grand piano.

"I wanted to put those pieces back together," he said.

"Only I can do that."

"What do you want, Diane? Why did you come?"

"I can't be your wife, but I'm yours if you will have me."

Chapter Twenty-four

SEPTEMBER 2016

Sean and Valerie married in the chapel of the Metropolitan African Methodist Episcopal Church, where the funeral of abolitionist Fredrick Douglass was held. Where First Lady Eleanor Roosevelt and poet Paul Laurence Dunbar spoke from the pulpit. The site of the memorial for Ramsey Tate.

This was the Tate's family church.

Uncle Ray had walked Diane down the same aisle. Paula was her bridesmaid; Mercer, Gregory's best man.

She had faced Gregory, holding his hands, imagining flight even as she held on to his fingers tighter with that thought. Her mother's face had unfurled in her mind, and she vowed to have all the happiness Ella had been denied, all the happiness that had been stolen from her, all the happiness she had not lived long enough to reclaim. Her mother, whom she had never forgiven for denying her knowledge of her father, for being small, afraid, selfish, and protective of her secrets and lies. On that day of frightful exhilaration, holding Gregory's hands, that tiny stone of anger had lifted.

So lost in thoughts of her mother was Diane that she had to be asked twice, "Do you take this man to be your lawfully wedded husband?" Gregory's thumb wiping away her tears brought her back.

She'd whispered, "I do," and then shouted, "I do," as the congregation had broken into laughter.

Metropolitan AME was still not a large structure. But its red brick facade, white spires, steeples, and stained glass windows imbued it with the feel of a building both grand and welcoming. Its design was an architectural conversation that captured the aspirations both heavenly and earthly of the original founders of the denomination, and this, one of the city's oldest African American congregations.

When Diane and Gregory arrived, the pews were half-filled and people were filing in. Diane saw Valerie's mother and sisters. Valerie's uncle would walk her down the aisle. Cameron would be the ring bearer. Family and friends surrounded them; Gregory the nexus of hugs and kisses. He bore it and took it in. Margaret entered on Bruce's arm and her approach parted everyone. She reached for Gregory's hand and draped it over her arm as they entered the sanctuary. During the ceremony, Gregory was flanked by Margaret on one side and Diane on the other.

Sean and Lauren were baptized at the church. But the family's attendance had been sporadic and occasional. Despite the years of distance, whether it was due to Gregory's cancer, business troubles, or Alzheimer's, something occasionally brought Diane back—for the community, for the collective affirmation of faith in what she could not see and did not need proof of. The new, young pastor had visited them at home before Gregory went to Somersby and even now sometimes visited him there.

There had been so much she felt she could not bring here. Her anger. The day she slapped Gregory. Her wish for it all to end. Her longing for Alan. Everything she did at Somersby was sacred, an act of faith, but she loved this place. Her union had been sealed here. Once, she had feared Sean would never see a day like this, pledging to care for and love another. Diane smiled at the sight of Lauren rocking Daniel on her knees and rubbing his back. Beside her, Gregory snored lightly and she clutched his hand. Then Margaret nudged Diane in time for her to see Sean slipping the ring on Valerie's finger.

The office would have to do for now. The walls were bare and she would take her time decorating. The tapestry from Istanbul would probably fill the wall facing her desk.

Diane surveyed the wooden bookcase, most of the shelves bare. On the middle shelf, photos of Gregory were lined up: there was Gregory, beaming and triumphant, accepting an award from the Architectural Society of America for the Main Library. Mercer stood beside him as he held the statuette aloft for them both. Then there was a photo of him at Somersby, sitting on his bed, the window and shades behind him; the photo captured the absence, the vacancy clouding his eyes. The last photo was of all of them, before the beginning of the end, before Alzheimer's. She and Lauren sat on either side of Gregory on the sofa, their heads resting on his shoulders. Sean sat at Gregory's feet. On this bookshelf in her campus office, she would find her family each time she looked. Next week she would bring in photos from her weeklong trip to Aruba with Alan. The photos showed her dark and radiant on the sand, beneath the sun. The photos showed her laughing.

On the desk were copies of speeches and articles Diane had written over the years. As a family court judge, she had spoken at conferences, before civic and nonprofit groups, before foundations, before other judges and other lawyers. An invitation from the editor of a small press anthology of essays about new trends in family law had prompted Diane to go through her papers and speeches, to look back on her work, and to begin thinking on a topic to write about.

Her colleagues were a mix of legal scholars and practitioners who loved teaching the law as much as practicing it. A ruddy-faced professor of civil law had arranged a coffee date with Diane right after the first faculty meeting last week. The chair of the department had asked her to do an informal presentation at the monthly faculty brown bag lunch in November. A part-time adjunct, who was also a partner at one of the big K Street law firms, wanted Diane to contribute to his blog.

This was what she had begun to call the third half of her life. There had been the years with Gregory as they created a family, lived a life, then the arrival of Alzheimer's, massive, merciless leaving nothing untouched. And now there was this, all this, that she had taken on and all that she still looked forward to.

She sometimes wondered if the disease would afflict her. Paula had told her about an NIH trial study to test if the level of plaque in one's brain predisposed one to Alzheimer's. Paula had signed up, and Diane had signed up to be part of the study as well.

When she told Alan, he'd said, "You're braver than me. I'm old-school—I wouldn't want to know."

"Even though you saw what it did to your mother?"

"I can't think of any ways her life would have been different if she had known in advance. And some people might not be able to handle it. Think what they might do."

"Knowledge can be a powerful, liberating thing. I want to know. If the news is bad, yes, I might be so depressed there will be no way I can live each day I have left to the fullest or plan or prepare. But at least Alzheimer's wouldn't have the last word. I could say good-bye, still knowing what that word means. I could hear it from others and appreciate it more."

She would teach. She and Alan were going to Italy next summer. She would let herself love him. She would care for and love Gregory until he died. And she would love him after he was gone. Be a grandmother to Daniel and when Sean and Valerie started their family. Where was the fragility, the diminishment that was once the only promise for this phase of life? How could she have known it would be like this?

How did anyone ever know what they were capable of?

Looking at her watch, Diane gathered her briefcase and left her office. She took the elevator to the second floor and entered her classroom, a seminar with eighteen students. As she settled at the head of the conference table, she listened to the conversations now winding down and snippets of gossip. Diane smiled and handed out the reading for the next class meeting. After a discussion of the required reading for this week's class, she looked around the conference table at the faces of her students and said, "Tolstoy wrote that 'All happy families are alike. Each unhappy family is unhappy in its own way.' In my twenty-five years on the bench, seventeen of them in the family court system, my goal was to make it possible for children and adults to sustain happy families. I was never able to actually order, to mandate happiness. But I tried to."

As Diane stood up and began writing on the whiteboard,

she thought of her own happy-unhappy family. A family that included a woman more adept at loving her husband than she, a lover who regularly joined her when she visited her ailing husband. Her children, now adults, but who would always be her children. And there was this woman, older, more beautiful and loving than ever, who had stepped forth into the world. Stepped forth into the world in her name.

Acknowledgments

This is a novel that I never imagined I would write. Like all my most satisfying writing projects, this is one that I was literally "called" to write. While unprepared for the summons, I reported for duty because there was no other choice. My goal was not to write "about" Alzheimer's but to use Alzheimer's disease as a way to explore the way we live our lives, how we love, create families, survive, and endure. Every novel I have written has been about families in crisis journeying to redemption and love. There are many people to thank, who opened their worlds to me. The world of families with loved ones with Alzheimer's, caregivers engaged in honoring the needs of these absent but still present members of our communities, the world of architecture, contracting, and family law.

The secret weapon that all writers rely on is good editors. I was lucky to work with two exceptional editors, Krishan Trotman and Chelsey Emmelhainz. Both were sharp readers and both in different ways taught me how to shape and envision this book. I thank Carol Mann, my agent and good friend for over three decades. My husband Joe offered, as always, love and support and belief in me beyond measure. I also want to thank my dear friend and mentor Sidney Offit who, year after year, makes me feel so lucky to be his friend. John Bess, always there to help. Judges S. Pamela Gray, Tara Fentress, and Anita M. Josey-Herring. Marshall Purnell, the late Barbara Laurie, Edward Johnson, and Andre Banks for giving me new eyes with which to look at my city. Aminata Ipyana, Rosemary Allender, and Bettye Wages for close reading, wise insights, and an investment in making sure I got this story right. Loretta Bowers and Denise Love for sharing with me the details of their journey of supporting loved ones stricken with the disease. Cissy Stoner, Renay Blackwell, and Iracy Wooten for inviting me to "sit, be still, and know" as I spent time in a memory care unit, and for inviting me to read and discuss writing before one of my best audiences, men and women living with Alzheimer's. Sam Taylor and Walter Woodyard, Julie Daigle, thanks for your input and suggestions.

About the Author

Marita Golden is a veteran teacher of writing and an acclaimed, award-winning author of over a dozen works of fiction and nonfiction, many of which are taught in college and universities around the country. As a teacher of writing she has served as a member of the faculties of the MFA Graduate Creative Writing Programs at George Mason University, Virginia Commonwealth University, the Fairfield University low-residency MFA program, and as Distinguished Writer in Residence in the MA Creative Writing Program at Johns Hopkins University. She cofounded and serves as president emeritus of the Hurston/Wright Foundation.

Among her books are the novels *After* and *The Edge of Heaven* and the memoirs *Migrations of the Heart, Saving Our Sons*, and *Don't Play in the Sun: One Woman's Journey Through the Color Complex*. She compiled the collection of interviews *The Word: Black Writers Talk About the Transformative Power of Reading and Writing*. Her most recent book is *Living Out Loud: A*

Writer's Journey. She is the recipient of many awards including the Writers for Writers Award presented by Barnes & Noble and Poets and Writers, and the Fiction Award for her novel *After*, awarded by the Black Caucus of the American Library Association.

Visit Marita at www.maritagolden.com.

For a free copy of Marita's e-book *I Want to Write*, a helpful and inspiring guide to creating a productive writer's life, visit maritagolden.com/book-bonus.

Reading Group Guide for Marita Golden's
THE WIDE CIRCUMFERENCE OF LOVE

What do you do when your spouse of many years has Alzheimer's? What happens to your marriage, your family, your own sense of self as the disease robs your loved one of his or hers?

Marita Golden, the critically acclaimed author of over ten books as well as anthologies, took on those questions as she began the research for *The Wide Circumference of Love*. What she uncovered were both the hard numberws that will impact us all and the intuitive truths about what it means to love through this challenging disease. In the end, the novel is a meditation on love and an unflinching look at the ways in which identity, happiness, and the future are reforged in the wake of a single diagnosis.

This guide is meant to help your group navigate these dual aspects of Marita's work—the fiction and the nonfiction.

Questions to Help the Conversation:

How did you feel reading the opening chapter when Diane is getting ready to move her husband into the care facility? Were you shocked by her decision? Were you surprised by the author's description of his condition and his behavior? If so, why? How do you make that decision— what is the tipping point for when it is too much to manage alone?

Do you see Lauren's decision to take on her father's firm as really following her own passion or a way to get her father's approval? How does his illness shift her focus? How is his illness a problem for her finding her own vision in the business—or is that not an issue?

Sean's complicated relationship with his father is further compounded by his father's illness. What would you tell a son like Sean? What do you think he needs to resolve the outstanding issues he has had with his father? How are sons impacted differently than daughters when a father disappears because of illness?

How did Diane's past affect her decision to pursue the work she did, and her feelings about family? Was it a good idea for her to have reached out to her father's sister? How did learning about her mother's rape impact her? What do you think about Diane's decision to not find her father? Why do you think Gregory is disappointed with that decision?

Marita moves backwards and forwards in time to tell stories of Diane and Gregory's lives and courtship. What stories affected you the most?

One of the narrative techniques Marita uses is to let different characters tell the story—even within one chapter that perspective can shift. What did that do to your understanding of the characters? How did it change the way you read the book?

How did you react to being in Gregory's shoes when, in chapter nine, he begins to realize he's possibly inherited Alzheimer's, which killed his father, and experiencing that loss of memory from his point of view? Why does Gregory confide in his brother before Diane? What does this choice tell you about Gregory and his relationships?

How common do you think it is that patients at memory units fall in love? How did you feel when you read about Gregory's new love Wallis? Can there be a real betrayal in this situation? What do marriage vows mean in this situation? What did you think about Diane bringing Gregory to the hospital to see Wallis and wishing she had known who Wallis was before the illness struck?

Diane is very conflicted about her own developing relationship with Alan. What would you tell her about it if you were her friend? Is she right to reject his proposal? Do you know of any families who have had to accommodate a marriage that can't be broken because of an illness or a condition?

One of the many themes in the book is asking for help—who to go to, how to get help—from Diane's father who never got over the trauma, to Diane getting therapy, or Gregory's mother confiding in Diane when Diane most needed it. Do you avoid asking for help? Is it a generational issue when it comes to using therapists? Are there times when you think asking for help from a family member might be helpful? Does it take courage?

Marita's research led her to realize that African Americans are diagnosed two times as often with Alzheimer's as compared to other groups—and they are also only around 3 percent of the groups that are involved in testing or family research. What has led to this big gap? Why is Alzheimer's a silent disease in the Black community?

Marita also discovered that the leading researchers project that by the year 2050 African Americans will make up 40 percent of the total case load—that's a staggering number to come from one community. What kinds of measures should be taken? What part of the community is in a position to take a lead—churches, medical practices, fraternity and sorority groups or other community-based groups?

How do you think you would handle this kind of diagnosis—of someone you love or even yourself? How have you faced similar challenges? Are there ways you think Diane could have chosen differently? Should Gregory and Diane have had a more comprehensive plan to handle his transition? How do caretakers get the care they need not only for the afflicted but also for themselves?

Beyond the tragedy, Marita points to the ways in which love can still survive amidst all of the feelings of loss. She describes when she was researching the book she visited with patients, their families, and their caretakers and was struck by how blessed you can feel when you slow down and become part of the moment. What have been your experiences? What else and who else have you read about who has had this perspective? What other sources of uplift and comfort have you turned to or would recommend?

Resources Marita recommends:
Creating Moments of Joy by Joy Jolene Brackey—an inspirational read that will help reframe the experience so many caregivers and family member s feel.

Being My Mom's Mom by Loretta Anne Woodward Veney—one daughter's memoir that shares it all—beautifully.

Walter Mosley tackles the subject in fiction from another perspective in his novel *The Last Days of Ptolemy Grey*—he has his hero face a choice of having his memory back and then in three months death, or let the disease take its toll and live longer. In this Fresh Air interview, he talks about how his mother's dementia and her death informed his novel. http://www.npr.org/2010/12/06/131848211/mosley-s-last-days-restores-memory-but-at-a-cost

Alzheimer's Association has chapters all around the country, offering help for caregivers, advocacy, and events. On June 17, they sponsor The Longest Day in honor of all those who are suffering from this disease. https://www.alz.org/

UsAgainst Alzheimer's is one of the nation's leading advocacy group focusing not only on finding an Alzheimer's cure but on African American, Latino, and women's participation in clinical trials, advocacy, and research on Alzheimer's disease. https://www.usagainstalzheimers.org/

And Maria Shriver has started the Women's Alzheimer's Movement, with a June 4th Move for Minds event in eight cities in 2017! They also offer advice, support, and discuss prevention. http://thewomensalzheimersmovement.org/

Interviews with Marita you might find useful to check out:

Maria Shriver Facebook Live interview: https://www.facebook.com/MariaShriver/videos/10158566298500455/

Black Enterprise: http://www.blackenterprise.com/wide-circumference-love-alzheimers/

Washington Post Sunday Magazine article by Marita: http://www.washingtonpost.com/lifestyle/magazine/why-are-african-americans-so-much-more-likely-than-whites-to-develop-alzheimers/2017/05/31/9bfbcccc-3132-11e7-8674-437ddb6e813e_story.html?utm_term=.dd8396bdacd1

THE BOOK OF
TORMOD

A TEMPLAR'S APPRENTICE

KAT BLACK

SCHOLASTIC INC.
NEW YORK TORONTO LONDON AUCKLAND
SYDNEY MEXICO CITY NEW DELHI HONG KONG

For my brother
Billy

This book was originally published in hardcover by Scholastic Press in 2009.

ISBN 978-0-545-23411-5

12 11 10 9 8 7 6 5 4 3 2   10 11 12 13 14 15/0

Printed in the U.S.A.   40
First Scholastic paperback printing, April 2010

Book design by Christopher Stengel
Map by Kayley LeFaiver

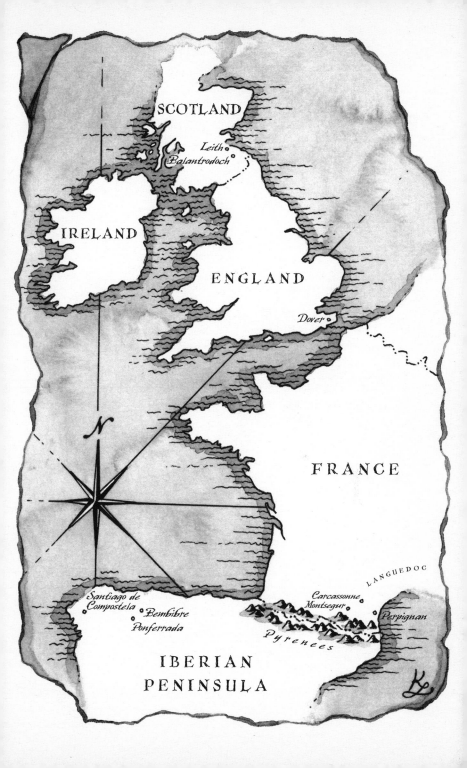

PART ONE

AN UNFORESEEN DUTY

It was the first of May in the year of Our Lord 1307....

The sun was sinking deep in the late spring sky. Its red and orange hues streaked the heavens with a strange and eerie light that made the dark of the woods shadowed and frightening. A creep of green moss covered the trunks of the trees, and old wet leaves covered the paths. It was not a night I wanted to be walking alone, but I had no choice in it.

Dung-heap cheater! The words pounded in my head. *I cannot believe that I took ye at yer word.* The breath of the forest whispered along my neck. The night air was changing, growing cold as the sun sank, but I was hot, inside and out.

Go get it, Tormod, he had said. *Can ye no' see that I'm busy, ye gomerel?*

My stomach twisted at the memory of my brother's tone and words. *Busy, aye! Busy making eyes at Bridie MacDonald,* I thought.

My hands were fisted tight and my face was hot. No doubt the freckles on my nose and cheeks were standing out, just as they had when Torquil ordered me to go for the box of tinder. Just as they had when Bridie had laughed and said, "Will ye just look a' him. His face is as red as his hair."

My hair was red. Not the soft auburn red of the burn as it washed over the rocks on its way to the sea, but more the ruddy orange of a freshly cut carrot.

I ran my fingers through the offending mess. Sweat from my jog had made the hairs stick out like the spikes of an urchin — a result of my mam's latest shearing. The lice had infested the household and she'd chopped the lot of us.

I was one of nine. Not the oldest or the youngest, not even the middle, I was thirteen, and seventh — the seventh son. The one who was never still, never quiet, never listening. I was different.

Someday I'll get out o' here, I thought angrily, and not for the first time. *They'll miss me an' be sorry!*

The wail of a bagpipe floated toward me from behind and I broke into a run. My breath quickened. *The festival.* Da would be furious if the lighting of the Beltane fire did not go off on time. And he'd not blame my brother Torquil. It would be me that felt the strap. My backside ached at the mere thought of it.

He'd not listen if I told him that Torquil had traded duties with me. He'd not care that I had done *all* of Torquil's hauling and stacking of the wood for the bonfire. No. All he would see was that I had delayed the festivities by not fulfilling my duties.

I stretched my stick limbs to make greater strides as I came in sight of the hut. As it was, I'd have to run the whole way back to the village to make it to the ceremony on time.

Our hut of stone and thatch was bigger than most of the dwellings spread across the hillsides. It had started out small but grew as the family did. I ran around the back and through the door closest to the animal stalls. The cows started and stomped at my arrival. "Be still, ye big hairy beasts. 'Tis just me, Tormod."

The hut was quiet. Our home was never truly free of people, and so the lack of sound was strange to me. The rest of the family was back in the village. Tonight was the celebration of Beltane, the beginning of true summer, a time for giving thanks. My brothers and sisters and I had joined with the families of the neighboring crofts to prepare. We had cleaned the square, even scrubbed down the enormous boulder in the middle, and cleared the old rushes from the kirk. The smell of the hay that had covered the dirt floors still filled my mouth and clung to my plaid.

The rush cart was filled with new straw and fresh flowers, and the celebration was ready to begin. It would start with the procession of the cart, led by Jordy MacFie, the village piper. Jordy had been waiting when I ran off.

The skirl of pipes sounded and my heart dropped. There was to be a feast, with storytelling and music, and a tremendous bonfire would burn straight through 'til morning. Well, that is if I ever made it back in time.

I, Tormod MacLeod, was to bring the box of tinder that would give spark to the great heap of wood I had helped stack for most of the day. Bringing the material that would start the fire was an honor, but not one I had planned on.

"Where is it?" I shouted. The box of tinder should have been on the shelf next to Mam's weaving. "Why is naught where 'tis supposed to be? Too many bairns," I grumbled. "Too many hands touching, and moving, and playing with things."

I was fair flying through the rooms of the hut like a squall, tossing aside everything in my path. I snatched up the twins' coverlet and the small tin box I was looking for bounced on their pallet. *What a relief.*

I was nearly to the door when the crunch of gravel beneath the heavy tread of a horse stopped me dead in my tracks.

"Da," I whispered. The lump in my throat threatened to steal my breath. I edged to the window, peeled back the oilcloth shutter, and peered outside.

AN UNEXPECTED VISITOR

"Come out, lad. I can see ye standing there."

My first look at the man brought a rack of shivers through me. He wore a black hooded cloak drawn close about him. And when he lifted his arm and called me forward, I saw a flash of silver glint beneath. I hesitated, frightened. Then a strong gust of wind blew back the cloak and beneath it I saw the white of vestments, a second cloak, and an armless tunic. The edge of a bright red cross glowed in the dim light.

I had never spoken to a Knight Templar before. My cousin Angus was in training as one of the Holy Brethren, but I didn't think he counted as yet. I moved quickly to the door and bolted outside, crossing the space between us.

"Aye, Sir Knight?" I gazed up at his looming form. Though I was considered a fair size for my age, I was still small next to him. My head didn't even come to his knees as he sat the enormous black horse of war.

"Where's yer father, lad?" His voice was soft and lilting, his brogue even more pronounced than mine. My mother was of the Highlands and my father of here in the Lowlands. We were a mix of dialect in my home.

"Gone to the village with the rest," I said.

"Everyone?" he asked. His fingers tightened on the horse's reins, making the animal balk.

"Why do ye need them? Is there something I can do?" I was eager to offer something of worth to the knight. I stared at him hard, taking in every detail of his presence. Even seated as he was, I could see that he was big. His shoulders were wide and his legs were long. His eyes were deep and dark, a brown so very brown they were nearly black. He had a thin beard that began beneath his nose and flowed long over his chin. Hidden as it was, I could not tell the color of his hair, but his beard was brown with silver shot through.

"Do ye know the way to Balantrodoch?" he asked.

I was so caught up in my inspection it took a moment for his question to sink in. "Aye. I do. 'Tis beyond the forest, just over three leagues from here." We all knew of the preceptory. It was the grounds of the main fort of the Knights Templar in this province.

He looked into my eyes a long moment, as if reaching deep into my soul to measure my worth. "I have a duty for ye, lad, one that is o' utmost importance."

I could barely contain my excitement.

"I need ye to deliver a message to the Abbot. Can ye read?"

The question seemed out of place in what he had been asking, but I answered nonetheless. "No, sir. We had a schoolmaster for a while, but he moved on and none has come since." I cringed with embarrassment. It was not unusual to be without the ability to read. There were no more than a few in the village who could. Still, it bothered me to be seen by the Templar as something less than what I might be.

The knight seemed relieved at the reply. He pulled from his side bag a rolled parchment. The seal in the wax was the crest of two knights on a single horse. He handed it over and a strange tremor passed through me at the contact. "Tell no one. Go quickly."

I was afraid then. The box of tinder cut into the palm of one hand and the parchment dented softly in my other. *They expect me a' the bonfire. Da will thrash me within an inch o' my life. Mam will worry.*

He motioned me on. "No one, lad," he repeated sternly.

A duty that is secret. Excitement rippled through me. *Someone else will run for the box of tinder. Probably Torquil.* With a grin I ran back into the hut and tossed the tin box onto the coverlet.

9

A DUTY REQUIRED

It was nearly dark. The wind had risen. I felt the strength of it — the last press of winter. It whipped through my tunic and breeks as I hurried. I was glad of my plaid, an enormous bolt of tartan cloth I had wrapped tight around me and pulled up over my head like a cloak.

I took the path behind our hut, up over the hills. It was rough country. The rocks were sharp. They dug into the thin soles of my boots, but I paid them no heed. I was my da's runner. I carried messages from one end of the village to the other, about the catch or the crew's arrival back on land. We were fishers. We had two boats and many nets.

The wood sat at the top of the hills. Its inky silhouette towered above me as I climbed, driving out the little bit of confidence I felt when the Templar had asked me to go. My backbone trembled. At the forest's edge I hesitated, but with little choice but to get on with it, I took a deep breath and plunged from bare light to none at all.

Inside the ring of trees, the wind stopped as if it had been snuffed out like the flame of a candle. I would have been glad of it, but the cold that remained was worse. The dark lay heavily on me like a shroud. The spot behind my knees trembled.

Cautiously I moved, focusing on the feel of my feet as they landed. Rocks and twigs, dirt and jutting roots clutched at my mind and soles. I paid great heed. The path through the wood was short, but I had never done the trek by night. It was unnerving. My heart leapt and started every few paces, and thoughts of the evil tales Torquil told of this place haunted me.

At nearly the half point, something rustled behind me. I turned and stared hard in the direction I had come. I could see nothing, but I *felt* it. Life stalked in that darkness.

My breath was loud in my ears. I tried to quiet it, to listen for what was there, moving fast to put distance between it and me. Suddenly my foot came down on a bit of unsteadiness. My body pitched forward with no way to stop, and the scroll fell free.

Sticks and rocks bit into me as I cast around, frantic. I had to find it.

A hazy danger lurked at the edges of my thoughts. Dry leaves crackled. I groped about wildly, searching until at last my fingers closed on the soft edge of the scroll.

Eyes tracked my movements. It was nearing. The tension in its limbs was coiled.

Starting up into a crouch, I peered through the endless darkness, fingers now seeking something I could use to defend myself.

But what I encountered in the last sweep was not what I had expected. Atop a cold mound of leaves, I felt the edge of another parchment.

Two scrolls! Two? I thought in shock. My breath rushed out in a burst.

A rustle sounded closer on my left.

My heart was near moving my ribs in its haste to beat. I rummaged through the leaves ready to bolt if I could do nothing else. Just then, my fingers closed over a palm-sized rock with sharp edges. I hefted it, as a small, glowing set of amber eyes met mine.

It was a boar, a female, a new mother. I was near her litter.

Go easy, Mother. I stared, willing her to feel that I was of no harm. Moments trickled by as we faced off. Then with a soft grunt, she turned and waddled away.

I was lucky. If she had chosen to charge, I might not have been able to outrace her. Though her tusks were not long, they were a danger.

I rose, legs trembling, now thinking on the two parchments tucked reverently against my chest. What might have happened had I not, by chance, come upon both? I was nearly faint to think on it.

My sense of direction was twisted. I let my mind drift, feeling the life of the wood flow through me. *Water behind. Mountain ahead.* I blinked then shivered. *Ahead.*

With great care I made my way through what was left of the forest. It seemed a lifetime before I came on a break in the trees, where faint light brightened the gloom. I stopped, finally able to breathe and examine the damage.

I brushed away most of the earth that clung to the outside of the sealed scroll. It seemed fine, just barely dented. The loose parchment was a bit worse. A smudge of dirt nearly obscured the first line, and the edge was crimped where my hand had closed on it.

I could not read, as I'd told the Templar, but looked on it nonetheless. Rough edges of land and waving lines of water were inked there, along with hills and a sketch that resembled trees. Placed over it all was a series of dots I guessed must be towns.

Off to the side a box was drawn, a close-up of a place from the land. Inside the box was a waterfall flowing down from a mountain surrounded by a forest. Lower, down in the corner was a small, strange silhouette. It was hard to make out in the dark, but I got the impression that it was a figure, shown from the back, with arms stretched up to the skies.

The map itself was old, the parchment thin and the edges crumbling. As I stared, a brisk wind set upon me and nearly lifted the fragile document from my fingers.

Carefully I rerolled the page and slid it back where it belonged. From the outside it looked no different. Praying the Abbot would be none the wiser, I took off at a jog. I'd lost time in the woods. I had to hurry.

The run was not the longest I'd ever done, but by far my fastest. The terrain flew by, as did the candle marks. I came on the preceptory during the night.

Balantrodoch was the largest and most important preceptory encampment of the Knights Templar in Scotia. I had seen it once. Torquil had hiked with me when I had begged him to come, but that was before he decided to hate me. It was painful to think on it. Torquil abandoned me, chose his friends, and left me with nothing but the dream of getting away.

I moved to the edge of the last rise. A long swath of dark stretched before me. *Balantrodoch*. It sat tucked into the sloping landscape as if it had been there forever. My breath came in gasps as I gazed in wonder at the many buildings I saw beyond its outer wall.

The greatest of these, and what stood out most, was the kirk — a grand church, fourfold bigger than the one in our village. It rose from the surrounding hillside, as if it had been chiseled by the hammer of God Himself. It stretched as high as four of our huts, one stacked on top of the other, its spire like a finger that pointed straight to the heavens.

Smaller buildings sat clustered around the kirk. These were built of stone and thatch, like our homes, but they were enormous in comparison. And surrounding the whole of the property stood a great barricade of oak. With sharpened tips jutting skyward, it kept out any who thought to trespass. Staring toward the preceptory, I was hit with a longing to step inside the walls and disappear forever, to be one of them, to fight and have respect.

My palm was moist where it gripped the scroll. I took a breath and plunged on. The path was long and winding. It gave the watchers up on the barricade time to see any who might dare approach. My skin crept with the thought.

I was in a hurry and yet, in those last steps that led me to the place I had always wished to be, I hesitated. The gates were forbidding. They towered above me like mountains.

"What business have ye at this late hour?" A guard scowled down at me. His voice was like sand scraping my ears raw, and I ducked my head.

"I've come with a message for the Abbot. A Knight Templar bade me bring it." I twitched beneath the weight of his stare.

"Leave it in the hollow o' the stump over there by the rocks." He gestured to my left. "A runner will fetch it shortly." His voice dismissed me, and I heard him call out the order to someone within.

"No!" I shouted, panicked at the thought I'd come all this way only to be turned back at the gates. "I canno'." The protest started out strong, but my voice cracked piteously. I ducked my face to cover my embarrassment. "My instructions from the knight were very clear. I must deliver it personally." *Not the truth, o' course, but better.* I looked up, and he stepped closer to the wall's edge. His expression made me step back a pace.

A man must never slouch or flinch from the scrutiny o' another. This gives proof that ye're upright and speak the truth. It was as if my da were standing beside me, the thought came so clearly to my mind. I stood straighter and met the guard's eyes, feeling a bit of guilt for using my da's trick when I was lying. "Ye're wasting time," I said. Inwardly I cringed, willing the man to believe my ruse.

He left me to wait. I trembled as the wind skittered across my skin, wrapping my arms tight around me. The parchments crinkled beneath my fingers. *What am I doing? I should be in the village, warm by the fire.*

The silence of the night was broken suddenly by the squeal and clank of gears and winch. Slowly the gigantic gate began to rise and all of my misgivings fled.

My legs quaked and my eyes grew dry, but I refused to blink and miss a single moment. Templar preceptories were closed to the outside world. They were secret and silent. What went on beyond their walls was a mystery.

A DREAM REALIZED

The gate rose by agonizing degrees. Sound crept toward me long before I could see inside. I strained to hear, moving slowly toward the growing opening. The scrape of metal on metal was loud.

Unfolding before me was a scene I had only ever prayed to behold. Knights! Knights by the dozen were sparring. The hard-packed dirt clouded beneath their feet. I could taste the earth on my tongue and smell the sweat from their bodies.

They were training in groups of two or three. All wore mail from foot to helm. Some wore the brilliant white tunic with the red cross of the Templar Order. Others wore black with the same cross of red. In one hand they held large leather shields, and in the other enormous Scottish broadswords. I watched, dumfounded, as they beat each other mercilessly. The clash of blades filled the night air, each strike pounding so strongly I felt the resonance in my chest. I moved close, desperate to see.

"Follow me."

I jumped. The rasping command of the guard, who until recently was above the gate, was now so close to my ear that I nearly cried out.

"The Abbot will see ye."

His words were slow to enter my crowded head.

"Move, lad, or orders or no ye'll feel the flat o' my blade."

I followed him readily. I'd been on the receiving end of a belt and that was bad enough. His sword would leave marks for a sennight.

The guard led me along an old and well-used dirt path. We passed a host of buildings. The shutters of one were wide to the night air. Inside a blacksmith pounded a slab of hot metal before a brightly glowing forge. The guard prodded me forward.

A weaver's shed was next. As the smell of the dyes leached out into the night, my nose and eyes burned and I hurried past. Men were grinding wheat for flour in the next hut. We only had flour near on once a year. *What Mam could do with that* . . .

We crossed an open courtyard and came at last to the doors of the great kirk I had spied from my earlier vantage. The guard motioned that I should go first and herded me up a dark stone stairwell. It twisted several times before ending at a small wooden door.

The guard reached over me and knocked heavily. He was large — strong and close in the dark space. I thought again of the flat of his blade and tried to edge away, but there was no room on the small landing. From inside I heard the voices of men.

"As ye can see, the man's no' here. I have heard naught from him in more than a fortnight. Feel free to search the premises, but I can assure ye, yer efforts will be for naught." The deep voice was calm but forceful.

There was a slight pause and I leaned closer. "I'll take you at your word, Frère Abbot."

Danger seemed to hang in the air. I shifted back knowing that it would not do to be caught listening.

"Come," said the Abbot.

I could not see a latch or handle in the space before me, and while I grappled, the guard pushed from behind. The weight of my body forced the door to swing inward on hinges that squealed. I darted a sharp look behind me for the rough treatment. The guard neither met my eye nor acknowledged anything amiss. I inched forward, as much to put space between us as to see who was inside.

There were two large men in dark riding cloaks. They looked to have traveled hard and fast. A layer of road dust coated their legs and boots. A monk clad in brown homespun linen sat at a desk across from them. His hair was cut in the tonsure, an odd-looking thing where the sides were trimmed short and the very top circle of his head was shaved bald. His beard was full-faced but cut close to the chin. He was small, I noticed, barely inches over me, and I was only five hands high. He was as thin as a reed as well.

Throughout my inspection they all ignored me. The two soldiers — if I was not mistaken that that's what they were — stood, one by the Abbot's desk, the other by the high window.

The Abbot inclined his head. "Excuse me for a moment, gentlemen. Aye, lad?"

I stepped forward. "A Knight Templar gave this to me."

His eyes flashed with surprise, and before I could give over the scroll, one of the soldiers whipped it out of my hand. And though the Abbot protested, he broke the wax.

"Here, ye have no business —"

The soldier ignored him completely. "So you've heard nothing from him, Abbot," the man said scathingly as he looked over the document. "We'll just take this as evidence of his duplicity."

The Abbot fumed. "Ye have no right to intercept a Templar missive."

"Where it concerns a Templar wanted by the crown, we have every right." He turned to me. "Where did you get this, boy?"

His eyes were fierce and frightening. "A knight gave it to me two days past. I come from Berwick. He bade me bring it to the Abbot."

The soldier's cold and steady gaze raked me from head to foot. "Two days past, you say. You've come a long way from home."

I nodded, praying he believe me. I knew not why I lied, but for some reason my mind latched on to the point that these men were hunting the knight I had spoken to, and I had just made a fatal blunder in not getting the message in secret to the Abbot.

The lead man advanced on the Abbot with menace. "He will be found and brought to justice."

The Abbot ignored the taunt, addressing instead the guard behind me. "See them to the stables then out of the gates." He said nothing more.

I stood quietly as the door swung shut behind the men. "I'm sorry, I . . ."

He raised a finger quickly to his lips. My heart beat faster as I waited for his signal to resume speaking. It didn't come until the echo of the footsteps moved all the way down the stairs.

"Ye're a MacLeod, are ye not?" the Abbot asked.

How could he possibly know that?

"The resemblance to yer cousin Angus is remark-able," he said.

O' course. I'd forgotten Angus. His training was here. The Abbot would surely know him. Angus and I shared the same brilliant red hair and hazel eyes. It was a relief to think that I might turn out looking like Angus when a man. "Aye. He's my da's —"

"Ye're not from Berwick. What is this about?" he said with impatience.

"Aye, sir. I am from Leith, in the other direction. The knight arrived a' the croft before nightfall an' bade me come here an' tell no one. An' I did, sir, until just now." I felt badly about that.

I could see in his eyes the truth that I had made a very bad mistake. Then, just as I would have apologized, the room began to waver. I bit down hard on my cheek, willing the oddness creeping over me to recede. Light burst behind my eyes. *No!* I thought, *not here, not now!* It was coming, and I was helpless. The world seemed to slow to a crawl, as a dark hillside rose before my eyes and the smell of the ocean filled my nose. The sound of a battle echoed in my ears and still blue eyes stared life-lessly into mine.

"Lad, are ye unwell?" the Abbot asked with concern.

All at once the vision dropped away. I was back with a racing heart and sweat trickling down my neck.

"The Templar is in danger. There will be an ambush on the trader road by the sea." I didn't explain how I knew and the Abbot didn't ask. "He must be warned." I started for the door then turned back. "It was my fault."

He looked at me, worry in his eyes.

"I recognized the road. It snakes out to the sea. If he left directly after seeing me an' travels on horseback, he would have to go around the hills. I can go over them an' reach him sooner." I could not believe the words coming out of my mouth. And yet, the vision was so sharp in my mind I was terrified.

"It's late. Ye're a child. It's too dangerous an' ye should be home." He pushed back his stool, stood, and began to pace. "An' yet, the soldiers will be watching. If I send a contingent out a' this time o' night, they will surely notice an' follow."

His eyes narrowed and he looked at me closely. "Ye know the way, well an' truly?" he asked.

"Aye, sir. I will reach him. Ye can rely on me."

He came to a decision then. Taking out a clean bit of parchment, he penned a message. "This missive must be delivered only into the hands o' the knight. 'Tis a matter o' life that I entrust to ye, lad. I will see that ye're rewarded for yer efforts."

But Da will already be furious, I thought. *Am I mad? The strapping will be bad.* And yet, the Abott's eyes were bright with encouragement. "I will do it, sir. But will ye assure the family that I am well?" They still expected me at the bonfire. This was no quick trip over the hillside. "Perhaps . . ." I hesitated.

"Aye?" he asked.

"Do ye think ye could see fit to sending my mam just a bit o' flour?"

"Aye, lad. O' course. It will be taken care o'. Here. Take this for yer own troubles. Be careful. Be swift." He dropped several coppers into my hand and stepped beyond the door, calling for a guard. I squeezed the coins, fretting. The guard popped his head in. "See that a pack is readied in the kitchens. Two days' fare," the Abbott said. The man disappeared quickly.

"Stop by the kitchen on yer way. 'Tis down those stairs an' through the corridor to yer left. Speak to no one. Not here. Not on the road. Go with haste, lad." He laid his hand upon my head and made the cross on my forehead. "Go with God."

RUN WITH THE WIND

What have I done? I left beneath the full dark of the night sky. I could scarcely believe the Abbot had agreed I should make the trip. An odd sense of moving in a dream hung over me. On the one hand I felt the urgent need to find and warn the knight. But I also felt guilt and worry that my family, by now, must be wondering what happened to me. It would take a while for a runner to reach the hut to tell of my errand, and even longer to find my family still at the festival in the village. Unless ... unless they were worried when I had not shown up and were, even now, hunting the woods looking for signs of my passage. "Please hurry," I whispered to the faceless messenger.

For my part, I ran from the moment I left the preceptory, sometimes fast, sometimes not quite as quickly. It depended on the terrain. Scotia, and in particular this stretch of land I traveled, was a maze of hills and vales. I knew them like I knew my own name. My direction remained true to my inner compass — and yet my spine tingled. Everyone knew that spirits walked abroad in the dark, waiting to ambush unwary souls and drag them off to the underworld. There were certain days of the year when that was more a possibility than others. Tonight was one of those nights.

Beltane. It was the time when the veil between the dead and the undead grew thin. Much as I would have liked to forget that bit of information, it hung around in my mind, popping out at every wavering shadow and rattle of branches. My fingers sketched the ward against evil as I ran: thumb, pointer, pinky, all pointed toward the earth.

Even more frightening, I heard a cry in the night. There was no mistaking it — wolves — a pack from the sound of it. Their howls rent the darkness with an eerie, inhuman wail. The Devil was hunting abroad.

I ran faster. Tales of evil, voracious man-wolves who traveled with the Devil were Torquil's favorite way to frighten me.

It was hard to figure from which direction they would come. Their cries echoed off the hillsides: first before me, then behind. Keeping to the flat, marshy wetlands, I bolted, staying low and silent on the moors between the hills.

The wind blew strong on my face. Ordinarily it would not have been long before the pack scented me, but the rains had been heavy for much of a fortnight. The rivers and small, trickling burns were swelled, and the ground was spongy beneath my feet. My boots were wet and I could not run very quickly, but I was glad of the earth's fullness. The deep mossy smell did much to cover my scent.

I traveled the bogs for more than a candle mark with a long, loping stride that was far from comfortable. When finally I cleared their uneven surface and hit flat-packed earth, I settled into a steady pace. It was good, not having to be constantly aware of my footing. My tread was light, my breathing regular. The sound of the wolf pack faded and my mind wandered.

I imagined the look on Torquil's face when he heard that I had been chosen as a Templar messenger. My mam would be fearful, knowing I was out unprotected in the night. I asked God to give her peace and also to make my da forget to beat me for delaying the Beltane festival.

Mostly, though, I thought about the map. It was of no place that was familiar to me. Though I knew nothing of the printed word, I was certain that the writing was scribed in a foreign tongue. It bore no resemblance to our native Gaelic. The landmarks on the map were strange, compelling shapes. I traced them with a finger in my mind as I ran, remembering them as if they were still strongly before me. The land's edge. The mountains. The waterfall.

It was the dead still of night when I came on the pass. I was up in the hills overlooking the beginning of the road that led out to the sea. There was no sign of the Templar, so I made my way down to an outcropping of rocks to settle in and wait.

I dug some dried beef from my pack and washed it down with water from the skin the Abbot had provided. In the pack was also some bread and cheese. We didn't get bread often at home. We ate mostly bannock cakes of oat and water. In moments I was full and sleepy. I'd only ever stayed up when helping bring in the sheep. It was late and I had been on the run for a good long time.

The rocks I sat on were cold, but I was far too tired to stand. Though my body shivered, I found myself drifting off every few moments. Each time I caught myself, I jerked awake with a start. I could not afford to miss the knight. When my body adjusted to the hard seat and it grew comfortable, I forced myself to stand and pace. When that was not enough, I entertained myself by redrawing the map, both in my mind and with a twig in the dirt at my feet.

I sat again finally, for in truth I couldn't keep upright. I dreamt then of a great flow of water crashing down over a mountain of rock.

The clop of horses echoed among the hills, and I woke suddenly.

A MESSAGE DELIVERED

I leapt to my feet. I couldn't see well. It might be the knight, but he was not alone. I opened my mouth as if to shout, but before I did the lead man slowed. I darted behind the rock as he turned his mount and scanned the hills. All at once his eyes fixed on me.

"Lad, come!" he called.

I hurried down the incline. "How did ye know to look for me? In the darkness how could ye see?" I sputtered. My breath came in short bursts.

"It matters not. How come ye to be here, little man?"

"Tormod!" I said with exasperation. "My name is Tormod. I bring word from the Abbot. There is an ambush set somewhere in the hills on the road to the sea." I handed him the scroll with the vision of what I'd seen fresh in my mind.

The Templar turned into the light of the moon, split the seal, and unraveled the parchment. He read the message rapidly; I saw his shock.

"The lad speaks true. The Abbot urges us to avoid the pass and seek the Archbishop Lambert at Dover Castle. Soldiers from France have been to the preceptory looking for us. They have taken the map." The Templar motioned his group toward a dense clump of trees by the side of the road. *The pass,* I thought. *Aye. 'Tis good that ye not go there.* I knew not when or precisely where the ambush would take place, but I was still certain the fight was coming.

The thought bothered me. I turned away, studying the men in his complement. There were five: the Templar, a soldier, two monks, and an old man.

"France. Could they be from the Pope?" asked one of the monks.

"Papal soldiers rarely set foot beyond the residence," said the soldier. "We have to assume others." He scanned the landscape. "The pass is the only way in and out o' these hills." He was, I estimated, about seventeen winters. He was tall, six hands for sure. His body was wiry, and not yet as muscular as the knights I had seen training, but he was on his way to becoming strong. His hair was a golden blond, and his eyes were bluish green. He wore the colors of a trainee: a black linen tunic with the cross of red, like my cousin Angus. He noticed my scrutiny and stared back, his eyes flicking over my thin form. It was a look I was used to.

"Aye, Seamus, 'tis the only road, but we dare no' use it." The knight had dismounted and signaled the others to do so as well. From a skin bag that had been hanging from his saddle he watered his horse. The sergeant, Seamus, checked the hooves of his own mount. I sat on a rock by the knight, puzzling over the conversation I had just heard. The rest of the company spread out, taking their rest nearby.

"Do we still try for the ship?" the monk nearest me asked. He was a small, round man with a red face and a nervous energy. He plucked at his robes and adjusted his seat several times before standing once again.

"Aye, Brother Callum. There is no' another due this way for many a day. We dare no' tarry," said the knight.

"Neither do we dare go through the pass an' put ourselves at risk," replied the second monk. He was a sharp contrast to the first. His voice was deep and seemed almost rusted, as if he used it infrequently. He was moderately sized, with a thin frame and the meek look of someone who preferred solitude to people. Still, he took some bannocks from his pack and offered them to me. I declined. I still had food in my pack that I had yet to investigate, but when he held out a skin of water I took it gratefully.

"There has to be another way through these hills," the Templar muttered, stroking the muzzle of his mount.

"We thank ye, child, for bringing the message," said the peaceful monk. "I am Andrus an' this is Douglas." The monk motioned to the old man beside him. He was wiry and withered, and yet he seemed strong and able. "Over there as ye heard is Callum, an' that is Seamus." He pointed to the other men in turn.

"I am Tormod," I said, nodding to the nearest.

"Ye traveled long. Ye must be tired," said the one called Andrus.

"I am well," I said. "I am my da's runner. I am used to delivering messages. I know these hills and the shortest routes for travel." Suddenly I knew I had the answer they sought.

"Sir Knight, I know a way," I said, climbing to my feet and moving to his side. "There are trails that wind up through the hills an' around the pass. I can lead ye. I'll not lie. 'Tis not an easy trek an' much o' it must be done afoot. The horses will have to be led. But it can be done."

Seamus protested. "Alex, what can he know? He's but a lad."

The mighty Templar's eyes assessed me then. "Aye. An' were it no' for this balach, we would have ridden to our deaths this very day."

The thought troubled me, almost as much as his calling me a lad. The vision, never far from my thoughts, loomed in my mind.

"Have any o' ye a better idea?" the Templar asked.

Seamus turned away. The others shook their heads no.

"Ye're sure o' this, little ma . . . Tormod?" He was not outwardly skeptical, but I could tell if there were another way he would consider it instead and this gave me pause.

Could I do it? "Aye. 'Tis the path o' the drovers. I have walked it many a time."

At his signal they gathered around and he told the plan. I watched the reactions on their faces. Most were receptive. Seamus was openly against it, but he was over-ruled by the Templar.

"Brother Callum, I must rely on ye to ride back and assure the Abbot the message was delivered successfully."

The Templar's eyes flickered over me, assessing. My stomach grew tight. "The rest o' us will go on as planned, with a bit o' a deviation that I pray will turn out right." He took the reins of his mount, and with a look around to make sure the others were ready, said, "Come, Tormod. Lead us."

THE PATH OF AVOIDANCE

We had to retrace a bit of the way I had come to them, but within the candle mark we had picked up the trail I remembered. It was a thin and winding track that wove up the slope and through the scrub. My da, the boys, and I had helped clear it over the past two autumns, helping our neighbors take their herd this way after losing several head to raiders in the pass.

I was awake, but the feeling of moving in a dream was strong. My eyes were gritty from lack of sleep, and my legs felt as if they didn't belong to me. The men spoke among themselves. The soft buzz of their conversation hummed in my ears. The Templar said little. He seemed content to walk with me, though his eyes never settled overlong on any one thing. His vigilance was constant. Had I to watch our trail ahead, the hills beside, and our back as well, I could not have managed it all. I had trouble enough making sure the track I sought in the moonlight was the correct one.

"Tell me, Tormod. How did the Abbot seem? Did he say any more to ye than what ye mentioned already?"

His voice took me by surprise. I glanced sharply up at him, scarcely believing not only that he would speak to me, but also that he would ask an opinion. "No. The soldiers were there with him when I arrived. The Abbot told them ye were not there and said if they didn't believe him, they could search the place. But . . ."

He looked at me expectantly. "Aye?" he asked.

"I knew they would not."

"Why?"

"He seemed powerful, my Lord Knight, as if it would somehow be a trespass they would regret." I knew I was not making a whole lot of sense.

"Powerful?" he asked.

"Aye." I said. "Not a' first, for the Abbot seemed small, ye know, but when he spoke, it was with such authority, I knew they, and I, would do anything he asked. Something strong seemed to come from the man.

I knew that if he commanded, I would obey. It's like with my da, but more so — though if ye should ever meet him, I'd ask ye not to mention that."

A small smile played about his mouth. I waited for him to speak more, but he went back to his silent ways.

We had walked a mark of the candle. My legs were beyond weary, and I felt as if I slept as I moved. And yet the night was barely begun. The others didn't seem bothered by the travel. Ahead was the highest peak we would have to cross. It was tough on the horses, and the men were busy both calming and coaxing them upward. I was trying to work up the courage to speak to the Templar without him speaking to me first.

I was leading the way and very nearly to the top of the heights when his arm reached out and snagged my plaid. "Stop here," he said softly. He motioned all of us to silence. To the one, each man dropped to a crouch as he, already low, scrambled silently to the cliff's edge and peered down into the blackness.

"What is it?" I whispered, appearing at his elbow uninvited.

His glare stopped my heart and stilled my tongue, and he yanked me from my crouch down flat onto my stomach.

Peering down, I didn't see them at first, but one chose that moment to dart from a clump of scrub. Men were scattered along the hillside behind clusters of rock, lying among patches of gorse. Their attention was focused on the path below.

"Do we attack?" I whispered tightly.

"No. Not unless we have no other choice. We do not shed blood lightly, Tormod," he whispered. Slowly he backed away from the ridge and signaled that I should do the same.

"They would have no second thoughts to killing ye," I mumbled.

He addressed me solemnly. "Death comes to all, but I do not hasten any toward it. We are outnumbered in man, strength, and arms. My mission is o' great importance. It canno' be abandoned for foolishness."

I nodded, chastened, and rose to a crouch, ready to make my way back down. Yet, as I stood I was suddenly hit by a wave of unsteadiness. It had been rough travel and I had risen too quickly. I felt myself lose balance and begin to fall. A shower of rock clattered along with me.

From beyond the rise, I heard them.

"Take cover!" the Templar cried.

The sound of men swarming over the hill overtook me, yet I could do nothing but tumble and slide down the rocky hillside. I hit my head and tore my hands trying to stop my descent and only slowed near the bottom. My head was pounding as I crawled behind a group of rocks. A trickle of blood ran down into my eye, and I rubbed it away trying to see what was happening.

The Templar and his men ranged on the slope above me. Brother Andrus and Douglas had moved behind trees and drawn their bows. The Templar and Seamus made a wall at the top of the hill, and for a moment there was no movement or sound but the clatter of stone and the war cry of the approaching men.

Turning back to back, the Templar and Seamus lifted their swords. Almost as one, their words rang clear. "*Non nobis, Domine.*"

And it began.

The first man came over the rise not expecting a frontal attack. The Templar swung mightily, and I gasped. The blade cut deep. The man staggered and went down with a scream that curdled my blood. The next man was right behind, another and still another. The scene was mad. I could barely follow the many things that were happening. Seamus had engaged two, and as they fell another came toward him bent on death. An arrow suddenly embedded itself in the attacker's shoulder and his sword merely glanced Seamus's mail. Brother Andrus was notching and firing arrows at a rate I could barely credit. And Douglas . . . Douglas I saw reached for an arrow only to find his quiver empty.

The blood in my veins turned to ice. I knew what was going to happen. With a sick lurch I stood, shouting to make him see and understand. "Douglas, get down!"

It was almost a dream, a horrible, revolting night-mare. *My vision.* I closed my eyes to shut it away. Yet the image remained before the brightness of my mind. I saw the sharp, black arrow pierce the fragile white throat. Blood, dark and crimson, surged around the shaft. I saw him stagger back, fall, and begin the roll downhill.

Something snapped deep inside me and I opened my eyes, my mind rearing away as I scrambled on my knees from my place of safety toward Douglas. "No," I cried. The blood from the wound on his neck trickled to the ground beneath his head. *I caused this to happen.*

My fingers began to throb unexpectedly. Heat washed over me, and the tingling feel of a legion of ants ran along a path inside me. I stared at the back of my open hand, uncomprehending, and the man beneath my fingers moved. His eyes fluttered, opened, and seized upon mine. I saw wonder in them, and then they drifted closed and his body became still. I slumped back on the rough, rocky ground and darkness took me.

GUILT AND REPARATION

"Tormod. Can ye hear me?"

The Templar's voice was far away, and I was so very

tired and heartsore that it took much to heed his call. He was persistent, however, far more than I could ignore. I opened my eyes a sliver and moaned at the shaft of pain the light brought to my head.

"Aye, lad. Stay awake. Look into my eyes."

I did, but it hurt like the very devil. "I'm sorry," I said. "I am so very sorry." I could not help the tears that leaked from the edges of my eyes, however much they mortified me. He thought their cause was the pain of my injury, but it was the dead, sightless eyes of Douglas haunting my mind.

" 'Tis over, Tormod. Ye've been hurt in yer fall, but naught is broken, I think. Can ye sit?"

"The others . . ."

He ferreted my meaning and then knew my thoughts well and truly. There was a terrible sadness in his eyes. "We are safe."

I understood the thing he didn't say. I knew that the old man had passed on, and yet still I had hoped. I turned my head, though the pain nearly broke me in two, and was sick in the dirt. A man was dead, because I had been careless. There was no getting around that.

"He was old, Tormod, an' lived a long, full life. It was the way he would have wanted to go. It was no' yer fault."

I could not meet his eyes. I would believe him in all, save that, for I knew better. I turned away only to see a pile of dead and bloodied bodies. I fought back the bile. I had wanted a conflict, to fight as a Templar. Yet it was nothing like I had envisioned.

"Come, Seamus, help me lift him."

Seamus came at the Templar's call, and I had the wish then that he had been the one to take the message to the Abbot. Seamus was angry and made it known.

Roughly he drew me to a sitting position. My world swayed as my head pulsed. The Templar interceded. "There are horses wandering below. Get them; we've lost two." His mouth was an angry line, and his voice was that of the superior, strong and not to be questioned. "We must no' delay, and Tormod canno' walk the rest o' the way while injured."

"He should go back," Seamus brooded. "We have no need o' a guide. The road is below, and we can pass unmolested. The balach should go home." Before he turned away, he raked a black gaze over me.

"Aye. His place is home," said the Templar. "But as we canno' afford the time to bring him, nor send him injured and alone on his way, he stays." His words raised my spirits a little.

Seamus spun around, his eyes wide with surprise. "Ye mean to take him with us?"

The Templar's strange assessing gaze was on me again. "At least as far as the coast. We can arrange an

escort to see him home. Go, Seamus. Do as I said."
Seamus turned away and disappeared over the hill.

As far as the coast. I was disappointed deep inside. I
had not really expected that I should become one of
them, but perhaps in a corner of my mind the possibility
had taken root. I stood on my own, though I teetered
with dizziness. "I am well enough."

The Templar caught me as I swayed. "Ye're strong
o' heart, Tormod, but yer body is injured. 'Tis nothing o' which to be ashamed. The enemy is gone for the
moment. We continue our journey through the pass
an' hope there are no others hunting us. 'Tis urgent we
move quickly or I'd give ye more time to recover. Can ye
ride, lad?"

"Aye. I'll not hold ye up." I tried to keep my head
still as I spoke though every movement sent sparks of
pain through me. At the corner of my vision, I saw the
rocks the men had gathered for the cairn of Douglas.
Tears filmed my eyes, and I blinked them away. It was
hard to swallow. Brother Andrus put his hand on my
back as he passed by.

"Ye will ride with me for now," said the Templar.
"There are four horses, two stronger than the rest.
Seamus and I will take turns carrying ye so as not to tire
the mounts unduly." I hoped we would reach the coast
quickly. Seamus had no use for me, and though I could

see that he would not disobey any direct command from the knight, nothing demanded that he be pleasant about dispatching his duty.

I sat and watched as the men piled the rocks over the body. I wanted to help them, but the pounding in my head made it difficult to move.

I looked at my hands. They were scratched and torn from my fall. I stretched and folded them, staring but not seeing. Then something about them struck a memory I had forgotten. I thought of the strange tingling that had gone through them. I thought of the heat and the last stirring of Douglas.

"He could help," Seamus grumbled as he added the last rock to the pile. His voice pulled me from my thoughts and I stood. A wave of nausea tilted through me, but I shook it off and approached the grave. The Templar began to pray and the others joined in. When they got to a part I knew, I added my voice. Seamus bristled. I could feel his anger crossing the space between us.

INJURY

We rode steadily, chasing the moon across the night sky. The wind had picked up as we moved through the pass, bringing with it the salty scent of the sea. Each foot forward of our mount was a penance I paid for the death I knew I had caused. And though it was much deserved, and I should have accepted it as my due, my traitorous, wretched mind prayed for the road's quick end.

It was a wonder that I was able to stay astride. It was much to the credit of the knight who held me before him. Even when it came time to switch me over to the sergeant, the Templar arranged to merely trade horses, sensing no doubt the other's feelings on it.

To my head's aching dismay, the knight kept a soft but running dialogue between us, urging my participation. "Tell me about yer life here, Tormod."

I shrugged, though regretted the movement as pain threatened to split my skull. "What is there to tell?" I said softly. "My life is naught but fishing an' family. Yer life is adventure with strange places an' amazing sights." I closed my eyes, preferring the darkness to the bright that hurt. I wanted and needed sleep, but he seemed determined to keep me from it.

"Adventure is a misleading thing, Tormod. It covers naught o' the pain an' guilt, uncertainty an' fear."

Fear, I thought, *how can one such as he be fearful o' anything?* The guilt I now knew firsthand, but I detected sadness in him as well. I began to tell him of the village, my family, and the celebration I had missed. He seemed to relax in the hearing.

43

"I kept ye from that," he said. "I ask yer pardon."

I twisted in surprise. It hurt something awful and I swayed. His big hand grasped the drape of plaid across my chest, and he hauled me upright. "Ye need ask nothing o' me. I've longed to be gone from there."

He remained quiet, perhaps assuming that I would explain my words, but I could not. How could I tell him that every day was a trial there, that I was looked on even in my own home as an oddity. I pushed aside the memory that haunted me.

"My mam will be worried," I said.

"The Abbot will assure them that ye're well."

I must have tensed for he read something in my manner.

"What?" His voice rumbled in my ear.

I was afraid to even voice my thoughts. "I was on my way to deliver the flint an' tinder for starting the Beltane bonfire when ye arrived. I didn't deliver the supplies. I just left. Do ye think that God will punish us if the Beltane ceremonies didn't start as planned?"

The livelihood of the whole village depended on the season's catch. If I had angered God, would He prevent a fruitful season?

He was quiet a moment, thinking on his reply. "God is not a vengeful being. Whether or not the Beltane fire was lit on time is not a reason He would punish a village. The catch will depend on the weather, the feeding cycles o' the fish, an' about a dozen other factors."

I was shocked to hear him speak so. Da was adamant on the doctrine that all of the ancient holy days be observed just so. But the Templar's words were confident. I wanted to believe him, even if it was just that I didn't want to worry over the possibility of one more bad thing happening because of me. I almost had more guilt and worry than I could deal with.

"Well, I'll be strapped for it either way." I said. It didn't worry me as much as it might. I didn't look forward to it, and it would hurt, but I would get over it within a day. To me, it was worth it to be here now. To have seen what I had and been a small part of their complement for even a short time.

"Will it be bad?" the Templar asked.

I cringed thinking on it.

"Not overmuch," I said. "But he reminded me twice today that I was responsible for the fire. I paid him no mind, because Torquil had agreed to do it."

"Why should ye be strapped then?" he asked.

"Because I trusted my brother," I said bitterly. "I traded a portion o' his duty hauling wood for running back to the croft to get the materials. He reneged on the arrangement."

"Ye will tell your da that happened?"

"I don't know. It was my responsibility. I should not have tried to trade it away in the first place. Mam gets worked up when there are punishments. An' she is with child."

"Yer mam is strong," the Templar said. "An' ye will set it to right with yer brother."

I didn't reply. There were times when I wondered if things would ever be set to right between Torquil and me.

"If ye would," I said softly. "Tell me where ye've been an' what ye've seen. I canno' talk anymore. I have not slept all night. My head aches something fierce."

"The ship is not long away. Sleep. I will keep ye upright. I don't believe yer head injury to be serious. 'Tis why I kept ye awake. To check it. We'll talk later."

I gave in, gratefully. And drifted into oblivion.

TAKEN

I came awake in bits and starts during the rest of the trek. The hills around us were deeply shadowed. The heather, a vibrant purple by day, was barely brighter than the rocks and road by moonlight.

On waking, the Templar passed me a strong drink from a skin. Its taste was odd, like berries, bark, and wood smoke. I didn't like it very much, but it seemed to make the blistering ache in my head go away. I must have slept again after drinking it, for I don't remember more of the trip.

I came to when I felt the horse beneath me stop and the Templar slide from his place. My head was thick and my mouth was rotted and dry. "Where are we?" I mumbled.

The Templar hissed for silence, and the strong grip he laid on my arm brought me awake fast. We were at the top of a rise, hidden by a copse of dense trees. Below was the sea. The rhythmic wash of waves beat in my blood and made the night seem alive and dangerous.

I knew to heed the Templar's warning this time. There was an urgency in his bearing I recognized. Quietly I slid from our mount, grabbing the saddle to steady myself. The Templar pulled up his cloak to cover his silver hood of mail and without a word slipped silently away. I watched, tense under the onslaught of a stiff breeze that whipped the hillside. His silhouette was dark, the black of his cloak nearly concealing him. He angled down toward the beach and I lost sight of him. Still staring down to the beach, I tied off our mount.

Seamus and Brother Andrus hung back in the shadow of the trees.

In the small harbor, an enormous ship rocked gently in the wash. It was a cog, a single-masted merchant ship, with curved outer planking at the sides of its hull. High on the single sail, the red Templar cross blazed in the moonlight. I had seen these ships in our harbor many times and watched as the cargo had been loaded and unloaded.

Two men stood sentinel on the small rocky beach. I had not seen them at first, for they carried no torches and blended with the darkness, but their voices carried over the wind.

The language was different than my own, a murmur that was nearly muffled by the surf. At my side the leaves stirred suddenly, and my heart lodged itself somewhere behind my tongue. The Templar moved past me to Seamus.

"Our ship has been taken," the Templar said softly.

"Who are they?" Seamus asked.

"More o' the same from the pass," said the Templar.

"What do they want?" I asked, though it earned me a dark look from Seamus.

The Templar answered plainly, "Apparently they want me."

"The odds are not in our favor, Alex," Seamus said. "There are two on the shore an' a' least one prowls the deck. We don't know if there are more below or if others were sent ashore to seek us out." His voice was filled with doubt, but I heard resignation as well. "We will take it back." It was not a question but a conclusion.

The Templar did not hesitate. "Aye. 'Tis our only hope. We must be gone from here."

"Aye," said the sergeant. "Ye have a plan?" My mind reeled trying to understand the conversation.

"Not much o' one, but better than none. I'll swim out from the east point. 'Tis not far from the prow. There is a rope that anchors the ship on that side. I will go up it."

I swallowed hard imagining such a maneuver.

"I'll need a diversion on the shore, something to draw the watch away from that side."

"I shall give ye one," said Seamus, reaching out. They clasped each other's forearms.

"May the Lord guide our steps with light," said the Templar.

"An' our faith remain true," replied Seamus.

The hair on my arms stood on end. The Templar turned away and started down the slope. I followed. My tread was not as silent as his was. He turned suddenly and motioned me back. I shook my head no. He glared and pointed back again, then turned and continued down the hill without another glance.

I hesitated, but for only a moment, then followed

him down the incline. He knew I was there, but refused to acknowledge my open disobedience. I moved as he moved, crouched when he crouched. I thought about the fall I had taken and the consequences of it and paid close attention to my footing. I would not — could not — repeat the incident and cause the Templar any more trouble.

When we reached the rocks by the jetty, he shed his cloak and vestments.

"Ye need someone at yer back," I murmured.

Though he was not speaking to me, I reached for his cloak. I could feel his annoyance. "I just mean to fold it for ye," I whispered meekly.

He was not happy with me, but let me take the garment as he took off his mail and dropped it beside his boots and sword. In tunic and breeks he moved toward the water.

"Would ye no' be faster in yer braies," I whispered. The smaller underclothes would be easier to swim in.

As he stepped into the water he said, "'Tis forbidden." I looked after him, puzzled. I must have been mistaken in my hearing. *Forbidden*, I thought, *to swim in yer braies in the ocean? How strange. Forbidden by whom? And why?* I could not ask as he was up to his waist by then.

The Templar was a good swimmer and the ocean

water was calm. I watched, breathing in time to the movement of his body as it dipped beneath the water. Then when I could bear the tension no more I turned away.

His clothes were piled on the rock beside me. I picked up his mantle. It was fine cloth, soft and tightly woven. Beneath were the hard links of iron that made up his mail. The loops rippled beneath my fingers, and when I lifted it, I was amazed at its heaviness and the way it was both hard and fluid at the same time. I lowered the mail to the rock to see what more was there. A glint of silver and flash of jewels made me gasp — a dagger! I wondered where he had kept it. The sheath had a cloth tie worked through its top. He must have had it tied to his arm.

In the half-light I lifted the knife, awed by its foreign beauty. The haft was silver and etched with many birds and animals. Their eyes were studded with glistening jewels that seemed to wink as I turned and admired them. The blade was not made in Scotia. I knew it came from the far-off, from the land of the Saracens.

Reverently I slid the knife from its sheath and rested the edge on the pad of my thumb. The quick jab of pain as the blade cut took me by surprise.

I looked up quickly. The Templar was nearly halfway to the ship. The knife glinted in my hand. My body tensed. He was unarmed.

UNARMED

I threw off my plaid, tunic, and breeks as fast as I could. *He was unarmed. Did he forget the knife?* The thought seemed to rattle inside my head. I stumbled down the dark and slippery rocks, determined to reach him in time. Barnacles tore at my feet, but I ignored them and hurried into the ocean.

The water was freezing. I clenched my teeth to still their chattering. My hands were instantly numb, and when I began to stroke, the knife was hard to hold.

I was a stronger swimmer than the knight, even with an aching head and sore body. The sea and I were long friends. I skimmed the waves and let the current do much to pull me out, but he'd reached the ship before I could catch him. There was no way to get his attention. His hands were on the anchor's rope. I stopped stroking and floated, lifting the knife above the water.

Suddenly, he turned and fixed a glare directly at me. Cold as I was, the eerie way he seemed to sense my presence made my shivering multiply tenfold. The scowl on his face, however, told me right off how angry he was that I had followed.

From the shore came the sound of an argument. It was Seamus. His words were overloud and quite unlike his usual serious tones. It sounded, I thought, like several of our crew when they've dipped overmuch into the ale.

"This is the ship I paid passage for, an' a good lot o' silvers it was, too," said Seamus. "They told me to be here a' the rise o' the moon, an' I am. Step aside an' let me by." His voice seemed to float across the water.

The silhouette of the Templar was black against the darkness of the ship's hull. Slowly he made his way, hand over hand, nearly silently up the rope. I watched him go over the rail and out of sight.

On the shore, Seamus was still arguing.

"What goes on there?" A strong, deep voice cut the night directly above me where the Templar had gone over. I held my breath.

"A drunkard," the man from on shore replied.

"Kill him," the one on deck commanded.

A clash of blades and muffled oaths crossed the water. Frantic, I glided toward the ship. Something was happening there as well.

What should I do? The whole of my body was trembling with cold and fear, but suddenly I decided. I stuck the knife between my teeth, reached for the rope, and began to climb.

It was more difficult than I had reckoned. The

Templar made it seem easy, but my body was wet and my arms ached beneath the strain. I tried to set my mind to other climbs, other times when I'd scaled the hut walls to reach the roof to do the thatching repairs. But never had the hut pitched beneath the roll of waves.

The sound of a scuffle grew loud as I neared the rail. My mouth was tight, holding the knife in my teeth, and my throat was dry. My legs shook and my arms burned as I pulled myself up and over, fearful that I would be seen, terrified that an assassin waited there to kill me.

The deck was black, but the silhouette of two men was clear. I scrambled behind a pile of sailcloth palming the knife as I went.

The Templar faced an opponent much larger than he. The man was enormous, and in his gigantic arms a broadsword gleamed. Yet neither man moved.

As I stared, I slowly became aware of a strange itch in the back of my mind, the movement of something behind my eyes and deep within my ears.

I shook my head to clear it, but the oddity remained. Then from my place I heard what I hadn't before — the soft sound of the Templar's voice.

"How did ye know I was here?"

His assailant's murmur was too low for me to catch.

"Where is the map taken from the Abbot?"

Again the other spoke, but I could make out nothing.

I moved closer. Listening hard. Nothing came to me. Frustrated, I leaned forward. Suddenly the mounded material I was leaning on began to slip. I couldn't stop myself; I pitched forward and the knife clattered loudly to the deck.

Immediately something seemed to snap and change around me. The attacker roared and swung his blade. The Templar dodged and spun, then, where moments before his hands had been empty, two palm-sized cross daggers glinted. Without pause he threw both — one to the heart, one between the eyes.

The attacker's sword wavered and a strange gurgle wheezed from his lips. I gasped. Shock and pain filled his eyes. Blood poured from his wounds, and yet I could not look away from him. The Templar quickly stepped aside and, as I watched, the man pitched forward.

All at once the night was still.

The Templar approached the dead man and removed his knives. Hurriedly he wiped them clean, then kneeling, he whispered a soft prayer, closed the man's eyes, lifted the body, and dropped him over the rail.

It was as if I felt the hungry waves reach up and accept their bounty.

"Are there others?" I whispered, unable to keep my eyes from the rail where the man had disappeared.

"Only on the beach." He moved past me, looking toward shore. The fight there was over. Seamus and Brother Andrus were in a small skin boat and nearly on us.

"Lower the rope for them. I must go below and see to the crew." As he turned away, he hesitated a moment, and then his soft voice filled the space between us. "Ye put yerself in harm's way, Tormod. If ye have no regard for yer own life, next time consider the lives o' others."

He was very angry with me. Without a backward glance, he went below.

I turned away and dropped the ladder. The swish as it hit the water reminded me of the sound the body made after it went over the rail. My stomach twisted suddenly, and I was horrified to feel what was left inside rush up. It nearly hit Seamus as he climbed from the coracle.

"Watch it, rat!" he hissed.

God's breath? What did I do? Sick with worry and confusion, I stumbled back from the rail and folded to the deck, wrapping my arms around my knees. The Templar came up from below, and I watched him as unobtrusively as I could. Seamus met him at the top of the ladder.

"Are either o' the two ashore alive?" the Templar asked.

"No," Seamus replied. "But they were from Philippe." He held out something small for the Templar's inspection.

"Aye. The brooch shows his crest. We must be gone from here now. There may be more on the way. Danger is high. We leave on the next tide, but we have a problem." I felt his eyes rest on me. "We don't have the luxury o' sending Tormod back."

Not go back? I thought. *Aye, please let me stay.*

"Not send him back?" Seamus was filled with amazement. "Ye must be mad. He's a disadvantage. We'll have to watch over him every moment. Why would ye do that?"

I looked daggers at Seamus but he didn't even notice.

The Templar was silent a moment before he spoke. It was with a tone I had not heard from him thus far. "I have seen it, Seamus. Our meeting was destined. There is a part this one will play."

Surprise rushed through me. *He'd seen it. . . . How? And, what could he mean? He was angry with me. I did things that were wrong. A part to play. What part?*

Seamus looked ready to disagree but held his tongue. The Templar stepped then to the rail and raised his face to the waning light of the moon. I read many things there — not the half of which frightened me terribly — but strongest was the sense of desperation, of a man seeking hope in the faintest of places.

In me? I dropped my head onto my arms, praying for the ship to leave, to hurry and take me into a new life of adventure.

PART TWO

CONFRONTATION

The splash of the waves against the ship was the only break in the silence of morning. A cold mist wafted across the deck. I was freezing and pulled the blanket someone had laid over me tighter. Bits and pieces of the night came back as I came fully awake. The memories seemed a part of some other life, not mine. So much had happened. My throat was dry and my body ached. And then out of nowhere a rush of excitement filled me. I was still here. The ship had sailed. I was with them!

But then, as if something warned me not to get too happy, his words came back. *If ye have no regard . . .* I pushed them away. *He said I had a part to play. I'll just have to make it up to him.* I smiled. For the first time in many days I had something to look forward to. *No one to order me about, no bairns, no sheep. No explanation needed for the things I could do or the things that happened when I was around.* My grin was wide. The Templar had been truly angry with me for disobeying him, but he hadn't sent me home. I would try very hard not to do anything foolhardy again.

The sun was well above the horizon. Water surrounded the ship. The air was sharp and cold. I shivered, drawing my knees close. My tunic, trews, plaid, and sporran lay in a pile at my elbow. The jeweled dagger lay atop them. I'd have to give it back. Quickly, I dressed, glad of the warmth, and went in search of the Templar.

At the door of the forecastle, I paused. Something stopped me from entering directly, perhaps the hushed tone of the voices inside.

"If they got to the Pope, could they no' have gotten to the Archbishop?" I heard Seamus ask.

"Aye. But we must take the chance. The Archbishop has to be told o' the treachery. De Nogaret must answer for his crimes. We're being hunted, an' Philippe's men have the map. We need an intermediary to go to Pope Clement," said the Templar. His voice had dropped to an urgent whisper. "The Archbishop will send someone."

" 'Tis too dangerous. Why do we not go straight to the Grand Master?"

"He has already left for a tour of the European preceptories. I dare not step on French soil without allies, Seamus." The Templar's voice was not to be questioned. "We go to the Archbishop as the Abbot instructed, an' rendezvous with Ahram by month's end in Spain, where we will seek out the Grand Master. He's due to see the

Spanish Templars in June. If we miss him an' he's gone on to France, Ahram will give us an armed escort there."

Neither said anything for a moment. I leaned closer to the door and the floorboard creaked. I bit down, holding my breath, when suddenly the door before me swung open, two hands grasped my plaid. Unceremoniously I was yanked inward to land with a crash on the planks at the Templar's feet. His sword was drawn and rested point down on my chest before I knew what had happened.

"What have ye heard? Who sent ye?" It was Seamus directing the interrogation.

"Nothing," I stammered, but it was an obvious lie.

"Come, Tormod, answer the question." The Templar's voice was calm. He didn't seem to be as alarmed to see me as did Seamus.

"I mean, my Lord Knight, I did hear ye, but it didn't make much sense. No one has sent me, save the Abbot. I don't know anything o' intrigue," I sputtered, shaking with the certainty that I was about to be killed.

The Templar removed the point of the sword and resheathed it. Then reaching down, he offered his hand to pull me to my feet. "I had hopes that ye would not be much drawn into the schemes of our making, but as I expected, fate has deemed otherwise."

I picked up the dagger that had fallen in the scuffle and moved to a large table covered with maps and instruments of sea travel. As casually as I could, I laid it there.

"Take it. Ye will need it someday," the Templar said.

Mine, I thought with awe. I picked it up quickly and slid it into my sporran before he changed his mind.

The Templar didn't continue the conversation nor did he speak more of what I'd heard.

"Where are we a' for manpower?" he asked.

Seamus replied, "The captain an' first mate were killed. All o' our crew remain."

"I can plot our course. We will alternate sailing the vessel," said the Templar.

"We must redivide the work load. Douglas's absence leaves us with a hole." Seamus said the last with a glare at me that set my face to burning.

Douglas, the old man whom in my recklessness I had killed. "I will take his place," I said, miserable and desperate to atone.

"You will never be half the man he was, rat," said Seamus.

The Templar motioned sharply at him. "Enough o' that."

Seamus had the grace to look chastised. "Fine, let him do the work, be our servant."

His servant! I spoke solely to the Templar. "I will do whatever ye need me to do. I can take the wheel as well.

I have done so for my da many times. Though this is a much larger ship an' I'd need some counsel at first."

"We'd be better off slitting his throat an' tossing him over the side," said Seamus. "He could be a spy."

"I'm not a spy!" I protested.

"No, ye're probably not. Ye stink a' it too badly to have stayed alive this long if ye were." With that he left.

I watched him go with relief. "He likes me little," I said, "an' I him less." I turned to the Templar, imploring. "I'm not a spy. I'm sorry. I didn't mean to listen."

"I think there are a lot o' things ye don't mean to do, Tormod, but ye do them nevertheless. Start thinking ahead. This is not a fireside tale. We are hunted. The price on our heads is redeemable whether we are alive or dead. One misstep by any of us, an' this will end. None of us can afford for this to end badly." He turned away.

This was more than I had heard him say in all the time that I had known him. It was a lot to take in. "I am sorry," I said meekly. "For everything. For falling an' alerting the enemy o' our presence. For causing the death o' Douglas . . ."

"Ye didn't —" he started.

I cut him off. "Aye. I did. An' I apologize for that. I didn't do it on purpose, but I take responsibility for the action."

He dipped his head in acknowledgment.

"But I'm not sorry I followed ye an' came aboard," I said doggedly. "I think that I was supposed to be there in that place at that time. I don't know why, but I'm sure o' it."

The speech was a bit self-important, but I was still stinging from his words. I looked down at my feet unable to face him and another remark I would not like.

"Aye. Ye're right. Ye're supposed to be here."

Whatever else he might have said, I did not hear for a strange chill riffled the air. His words reverberated within my head. I swayed with dizziness. Blood spilled over a cross. Red leaching onto a field of white. Metal on metal rang in my ears. Firelight danced on dark walls.

"Focus. Ground. Shield." Strange commands from the Templar pressed into my mind. I didn't know what he meant or what he wanted, and the vision continued to pound away at my mind.

Then suddenly it was as if a stiff breeze blew through my mind and I felt the vision slide slowly away. All at once I was back in the here and now.

The Templar was close before me, his face furrowed with lines of concern. I had not even known of his approach. "Hush ye now. It's gone," he said.

I stared at him long and hard, trying to reconcile the vision. I felt faint. My hands were fists of white gripping his vestment.

"Do the visions come to ye often?" he asked, sounding so earnest that I responded without thought. "Not very, but even that is more often than I'd like." My body shook. Twice now the visions had come to me in the presence of another. This strange seeing that had been with me from birth was changing somehow.

"Aye. The visions can seem a curse," he murmured. "Or a blessing. 'Tis all in what ye make o' it, Tormod. Tell me, why is it ye have no training in the basics of grounding?" he asked.

I had no idea what he was talking about. I had only shared a vision once, and I had great cause to wish I hadn't. Panic rose within me as my mind careened back to the memory I longed to forget. *The boat was capsized in the water. The father o' Torquil's friend Cormack floated facedown.* I had told Torquil of the vision and he told his friend. When the body was found, the whole of the village branded me a warlock. Torquil and I were never again as we once were.

I pushed it away, nearly forgetting in whose presence I now stood.

"What did ye see?"

I swore I would never again voice anything I had seen, but the Templar asked so plainly I was bound to answer. "I saw a broadsword waver, then blood on a cross." I didn't want to go on but felt I must. "I think I saw ye," I whispered.

He stopped me with an outstretched hand, his eyes commanding obedience. "'Tis not a tale to be shared."

"But ye don't know," I said, frustrated. "I feel ye must take heed. What I see *happens*." I needed him to believe me.

He pulled away and moved off several paces. "Aye. But what ye see is not the whole an' not always the truth o' the future." He didn't make a bit of sense and my face must have shown it.

"Think o' waters running swiftly in a stream. Drop a pebble an' ye change the path but a little. Drop a boulder an' ye have a diversion. 'Tis the same with lives an' futures. What ye saw may happen, but what I do between now an' then could very well change the outcome."

He reached down and picked up a large black cat that had wandered in and began scratching its neck and ears. The animal purred loudly and with much contentment. "I also think 'tis a very bad thing to know yer own future," he continued. "'Tis enough that I've heard what I have. I wish to speak o' it no more."

"You know o' the visions?" I said. "Do ye have them as well? I've never known another who does."

"Aye. I have the vision." He would have said more, but just then Brother Andrus came into the room. A sharp look from the Templar warned me to heed my tongue. I did, but inside I wanted to chase the monk away. I badly wanted to speak with the Templar. I was troubled. The visions had been coming to me for as long as I could remember. And in the whole of that time, each and every vision had come to pass just as they had been shown to me. Anxiously I moved around the central table, picking things up and putting them down again.

TEACHER

"Good morn to ye, Andrus." The Templar allowed the cat to jump from his arms then resumed his work with the charts.

"Good morn, Alexander. A strapping day. The air is clean and pure. It stimulates the soul." As I knew our conversation of earlier was not about to continue, I turned my attention to the newcomer.

"How is it that ye're different?" I asked the Templar. "The Brothers, as opposed to the Templars?" They seemed alike and yet not quite so.

"Andrus is a Cistercian monk. Our beliefs, as Templars, an' our religious practices are derived from theirs. The Templars are, however, a knightly version o' their order, the soldiers o' Christ. Both orders are sworn to poverty, chastity, an' obedience," the Templar said.

"Chastity?" It was not a word I knew.

"Aye. We are not allowed to marry or keep the company o' women."

All women, I wondered? It was not something I'd given thought to. Lasses, so far as I could see, were naught but an ache to the head anyway, but what about his mam? I didn't ask as he had continued.

"The Templar Order has a very specific set o' rules an' ordinances that are ours alone. But they are not to be shared with the uninitiated. Know only that we are a military order trained in all aspects o' warfare."

Now he was getting to it, I thought. "So ye use swords, bows, an' knives," I said. "An' train to joust an' fight mounted?"

"Aye. All of those things, but 'tis no' for tournament that we train. 'Tis to protect God's people."

"Aye. Ye defend those who choose to make the pilgrimage from the bandits on the roads." I knew that much from my cousin. "But ye do get to fight," I said, stabbing forward with an imaginary sword. Suddenly I remembered his daggers as they landed in the man's chest and brow. My gut heaved.

"Aye, we fight, but we give praise to God in equal

measure. We share many of the abbeys o' the Cistercian Brothers an' in return see to their safety."

Brother Andrus nodded and helped himself to a bannock. "It suits both, ye see."

The Templar continued. "Together we study mathematics an' astronomy, which is the patterns o' the stars an' sky. We map an' navigate the sea an' land." He gestured to the table. "These maps an' charts represent two hundred years o' travel."

I approached, interested. Da did all of the plotting, but it was to places he'd been scores of times. "Here is the first place we must travel." He pointed to a large mass of land on the map before him. "The land o' the Saxons. Ye've not been much beyond the villages?"

I shook my head no.

"Ye're far beyond your boundaries now," he said.

"How long did I sleep? How far have we traveled?" I asked, excited by the prospect of what I saw before me.

"It matters not. We've many days ahead. Ye've missed nothing."

From the moment we'd met, he had been serious and vigilant. Now, as I looked up to see him deep in a series of mathematical computations, he seemed at ease. He took pleasure from the work of divining our direction. That much was obvious.

"What o' the crew?" I asked. "Seamus said the captain an' first mate were killed. Do ye have enough men to operate a vessel as large as this?" The ship to me was enormous. It would take a crew of fifteen or more to see to the daily duties of sailing her.

"Aye. We lost two," he replied. "But we will make do."

I was quiet then, thinking of the faceless crew. I would know them, sooner or later. As the Templar said, we had a long distance yet to travel. I thought then of the trip, of being away from my home and my family. I'd wanted to get away for so long, but now that I had, I suddenly felt small and frightened. My fingers closed over the hourglass on the table. Its sleek shape seemed molded to my palm.

" 'Twas not long ago that the only way to gauge sea travel was by the glass in yer hand," the Templar said.

"Aye? I know naught o' gauging distances."

"I will take my leave now," said Brother Andrus with a smile, scooping up a bit of herring on the way. "When Brother Alexander has an eager ear, long lessons inevitably follow."

The Templar didn't acknowledge his remark. "The instruments that ye see here are o' a new breed o' navigation, Tormod. An' this"—he hefted the object aloft—"is the greatest o' all. 'Tis called an astrolabe."

It was beautiful in a way I was unaccustomed to. "'Tis old," I said, running my fingers along the timeworn brass.

"Aye. The Arabs have been using them for many years. This was a gift from a friend."

An Arab friend. I didn't know any Arabs or anyone who knew any for that matter.

He held the astrolabe by the small loop at its top. The strange instrument was a series of discs held through the center with a peg. The top layer was cut away and I could see the disks below.

"What do ye use it for?" I asked, lifting it. I turned it in the light spilling in from the window. It made strange patterns on the floor.

"Astrolabes can show us how the sky looks at a specific place an' a given time. If ye know where ye are, an' where ye want to go, then figuring out how long it might take to get there is simple."

The ideas he so easily proclaimed were enough to draw me readily into the discussion. We spent much of the morning at it. We spent much of the day at it.

I didn't hesitate in the asking of the many questions that came to mind. I sensed in him the mind of a teacher, one who would welcome the chance to share the knowledge he had accumulated. His passion for sea travel was strong. I took all he offered, absorbing everything I could.

A NEW BEGINNING

We met on deck at midday. The ship was moving along at a brisk clip. The winds were high and the weather was cool. Seamus was working the sail.

"Seamus. Take the wheel."

They switched positions. "Ye need to grasp the rudiments of sword work in battle," he said, advancing on me as if we had been in the middle of a conversation. "I'm sure ye know what 'tis like in theory, but let's see how ye'd fare in reality." He effortlessly flipped a sword to me on the outstretched blade of his own. It lifted off the deck like it was sailing on the wind. With no other choice, I reached out to catch it. Immediately my arms were dragged directly down to the deck and I tilted precariously. "Hah." His laugh was full of mirth.

"Right. We'll use something a bit lighter." He pulled a wooden practice blade and targe from the pile of equipment he'd had me bring up from the lower deck. I'd assumed it was for Seamus and himself. I was so very excited knowing now that it was for me.

"First then, stand straight, right foot advanced an' keep the center of yer body over yer left foot. Use yer shield for balance an' yer sword for defense." He stood behind me and fired off a rapid number of commands. I struggled to grasp them.

"We'll use this time to yer advantage, Tormod. As an idle mind is the devil's playground, sloth is an insult to God." With little warning he came at me. "Lift yer sword," he shouted, bearing down. I did, and my blade met his. The resounding crack echoed through my bones. "As I come from yer left, swing yer shield up an' take the blow. Aye. Get yer body beneath it an' solid up your legs."

Thwack. This time I felt it all the way down my backbone. I heard Seamus laugh and turned to see several of the crew had joined us on deck.

"Bring up yer sword to balance yer body as if it was swinging to and fro." I turned as he bid, and the flat of my practice blade met his. Instantly it skittered out of my hand, leaving my fingers stinging.

"Good. Still, ye have to keep ahold o' it." His words were encouraging, though his blows had little mercy. Again and again he had at me. For my part I stood and countered, working the various drills as well as I might. But it was far from the simple task it seemed. I had a great deal to learn. "We've got to work those muscles. Ye'll not have sword arms in a day, but this is the day to get them on their way."

Near on a candle mark later I collapsed onto the deck, winded, sweating, and aching in every part of my body. The Templar handed me a tankard of water. He was not even winded. "Enough?" he asked.

I hated to admit it. "Aye."

He clapped me on the shoulder. "Ye've done well for yer first day." Then turning, he called, "Seamus. Yer turn."

I struggled to make my burning muscles respond. I was sore from head to toe with welts in more places than I cared to admit, but I could hardly wait to see Seamus take his share of the beating, so I hurried.

"Watch an' learn," Seamus said as he moved away.

I made a mocking face behind his back and took the wheel.

The Templar and Seamus continued where I'd left off, but used real swords and shields. The onlookers who had watched me with interest but little comment swiftly came alive. Much as it bothered me, I had to admit that Seamus was good. His movements were smooth, unlike my jerking scramble to cover my tail hodgepodge. The Templar had moved from mentor to aggressor in moments. Together he and Seamus moved in a lethal, beautiful dance. The clash and slide of blade on blade, the clink of the flat, edge, and tip of the swords each had a different tone and volume. As

I watched them dodge and turn, spin to avoid confrontation, and add strength and power when there would be a direct hit, I was amazed. Would I one day fight that way?

As my body cooled and theirs grew more overheated, I became aware of an odd difference in the normal thrum of the world around me. The accelerated beat of their hearts, the feel of their blood pounded inside my head. I could almost read each of their moves and intentions at the same moment they had them. The sun came from behind a cloud, glinting on the Templar's sword, catching me straight in the eyes. I flinched and turned away, but the light followed.

The flame of a candle lit the space behind my closed eyes. The fragile edge of a parchment glowed and a word appeared where none had been.

Sound rushed back into my ears, and I had to grip the wheel to keep from falling. My tunic was soaked clear through, though it hadn't been quite that way when I'd finished sparring.

The Templar and Seamus had taken a break. Andrus appeared at my side with water. "Are ye well, Tormod?"

He urged me to drink as the Templar approached.

"Prayers begin shortly, Tormod. I suggest ye hurry or ye'll not have time to change."

My legs wobbled and I could barely lift my arms. *Prayers, again.* We'd done them twice already this morning. It was fair worse than Sunday at the kirk. But he hadn't asked me to join them. He expected it.

The kneeling was the worst, especially with a sore body. My lips spoke the words that I had known since near on birth, but my mind was far away. The more I thought of the recent vision, the more I was convinced the edge of the map I'd seen was the map I had carried, the map that had been taken from me at the abbey. But in the candle's flame a word appeared where none had been before. I had the exact shape of it strongly in my mind.

"Tormod." The Templar's voice cut into my musing and I realized that I had stopped reciting my prayer. I looked over sheepishly and, at his scowl, continued. It seemed like days before we finished. My knees were trembling as I struggled to stand.

"Come with me," the Templar said.

What did I do now? I followed him anxiously to the forecastle. He said nothing until we were alone. "We have to do something about the visions ye're having."

I'd not expected this topic.

"Ye had another at the wheel." I was amazed that he would recognize this.

"Aye," I said. "I saw the map."

"Was that all?" He took up an ewer from the sideboard, poured out some water, and offered me some. I took it gratefully and dropped to a stool by the table.

"I saw a flame that was held beneath the parchment an' a word was illuminated. I canno' tell ye what it was, for I know not how to decipher letters well, but I know the shape of it." I took up a quill and dipped it into the inkpot near by. "Can I?" I asked motioning to a bit of parchment he had been scratching on.

"Aye. Go on," he said.

I took my time, but drew the shape that I knew to be letters. He watched avidly. "July is what it means." He looked at me oddly then, his mind working behind his eyes. "Ye told me that ye could no' read, an' the Abbot said that the soldiers took the parchment from ye. How is it that ye remember a map that ye didn't see?"

I assured him quickly. "I canno' read, but on the way to the preceptory I dropped the scroll an' the map fell out."

He didn't say more on the matter, but I could tell that I wasn't entirely free of this subject. "We'll have to do something about this lack o' reading ability as well. Our journey will be a long one. There's no reason we shouldn't put the time to use."

Lovely, I thought, *prayer and schooling. Was this what I'd escaped for?*

"First we have to work on something that ye're in dire need o', some safeguards against the visions."

I was intrigued. I didn't know much about the visions except that they came to me and they always happened as I saw them. He pulled another stool over beside mine.

"Each use o' the power changes us in some way," he began. "If ye recall, ye're often physically weakened immediately after ye have a vision, an' sometimes ye have a difficult time pulling yerself away an' back."

"Aye." I had noticed the very same, but I didn't know there was anything to be done about it.

"I want ye to work on what I show ye now every day, three times each day. It has to come to ye automatically. There is so much more to the power than just visions. We will take it slowly, but in this I will no' tolerate slacking."

I was put off by that remark but hid the way it stung. I'd just have to show him that I was serious. The whole idea of there being more than the visions set my skin tingling. "What do I have to do?" I asked.

"Ye must learn three commands: focus, ground, an' shield. I will take ye through them one at a time, an' we will practice." He sat up tall and stared deeply into my eyes.

"The focus is here." It was suddenly as if my mind

cleared. Like all outside thoughts were stripped away. "Nothing but the task at hand, like a hawk diving down on its prey, I want ye to empty yer mind of all but the vision itself. Ye will notice small details ye would no' otherwise have taken in."

I recognized what he did, but I had no idea how to do it myself. "Give it time. Ye will see how."

I felt as if he had read my mind. It was a bit unnerving.

"Ground is this." All at once the power of the land around me swirled through my mind. The wind rushed. I felt it on my skin and heard the roar of it in my ears. The earth thrummed. It was as if the ground beneath the deck, deep beneath the waves, reverberated. "Let it roll around ye, Tormod."

I could do nothing but let it do as it would.

"Now see it. Feel it. Let it fill ye from yer head to yer toes." I didn't understand, but he nudged something and a rush of color and sound flowed up from my feet and straight out through the top of my head.

"Now shield," he said. "Push all the power out o' yer mind an' body an' let it settle a' the very edges o' yer skin from the inside out." He didn't exactly do it for me but helped. I reeled at the odd twisting-tugging going on inside me. Then there was peace.

"That's it, Tormod. Ye did well this first time. Ye're on watch in a quarter candle mark. Why don't ye get something to eat an' think on what I've shown ye."

He stood and left me staring off to the distance.

✠

It was late and I was finding it hard to sleep. Around me the crew slept. The smells and sounds they made brought the blackness alive. I had always been a bit of a coward about the dark. At home, I slept near the hearth where the fire always glowed.

Home was truly far away now. I was on a ship with strangers, journeying to a place I didn't know. The missing came on me fast, and I found my throat tight.

I thought of Mam and Da, wondering how they fared and if they had by now heard I had gone. And then each and every one of my brothers' and sisters' faces ran through my mind, and I had the quick realization that I might never see them again. It was as if the mere thought would break my heart in two. I pulled the coverlet up to my ears and burrowed down, feeling the tears well. Then, from out of the darkness came a sound. Soft and low, the purr was completely welcome.

"Here, Cassiopeia," I called, dropping my hand down toward the floor. I could not see her but felt the presence of the cat moments before a tiny tongue scratchily lapped my fingers. She leapt to my chest, and I curled my fingers in the soft fur of her neck. Sleep came a short while later.

✠

I marked the wall next to my hammock with a scraper Seamus gave me to clear the cracks in the decking. Fifteen days at sea. It seemed longer.

There was a strange sameness to life on the ship. We rose early and did our assigned duties; we prayed constantly and trained nonstop. I received lessons in reading, writing, and astronomy, and I learned to focus, ground, and shield.

Odd. I had thought that getting away would mean that I'd never have to do things that people demanded of me again. I was wrong.

If it was not the Templar, which I didn't mind at all, it was Seamus, heaping every horrible task aboard on my back. I looked at my hands. They were callused and cracked, and my legs were killing me.

Still worse, I was having trouble sleeping. My duties on watch tonight meant I had to rest during the daylight. I'd not gotten used to it.

"Tormod, I told ye to help even out the ballast before ye bedded down. O' course ye didn't." Seamus's voice cut across the dim quiet of the hold. "Get to it. Ye've duties to attend."

I gritted my teeth and swung my feet to the deck. Seamus was an unending source of misery. No matter what I did, it was not good enough. No matter how I tried, it was not what he would have. He harassed me nonstop.

"Move it, Tormod."

I wanted to beat the man bloody. I swear it. Every day during my prayers I asked God to strike him repeatedly with all of the plagues. But to no avail. I was not going to get the sleep I needed. Grumbling, I heaved to my feet.

From the stairs I heard coughing. One burst followed by another, and then a hacking wad of spittle was heaved somewhere off to my left. Seamus cleared his throat and sent one last parting jab. "Ye'll have to take the wheel this afternoon. I'll take the night."

I crossed the dark hold, pleased. Perhaps God had heard me after all. Seamus was ill. I hoped that he was miserable.

As I came up from below, I saw one of the deckhands, Horace, at work. The sweat gleamed on his dark-skinned back, and his arms, the size of great tree trunks, flexed beneath their burden.

It was Horace's job to shift the enormous rocks we

used as ballast to keep the ship evenly weighted. The constant crash of the waves undid his work nearly as fast as he'd accomplished it.

The duty was, to my mind, terrible. The stuff had a stink about it that was most unnatural. He said the rocks had been dredged from the harbor where the privy pits emptied. Still, even with that, he was of a good temperament. When I'd asked how he could be content doing what he did, Horace had told me that it took him up from the depths of the dark hold and into the light of day.

I understood not wanting to be in the dark, but not how he could find peace and contentment redoing the same job day in and day out. He actually sang as he worked, songs I'd never heard the like of before.

"Greetings, Horace," I called as I approached. It was good to give warning, else the strong man might heft a rock in your direction. He looked up and smiled, his teeth bright in the dark of his face. The smile was always a surprise to me. He was quite fearsome without it.

"A beautiful day, is it not, Tormod?"

I looked up to the cold, chill sky. "If ye say 'tis, Horace. I've come to help."

"I'm near on done," he said. "Don't trouble yerself."

Geordie, another of the deckhands, called out, "I could use ye here, Tormod, if ye're free. This damn mist is making the tar unpredictable. 'Tis thickening before I can apply it."

I hurried to his side and took the tar bucket and began to stir the mixture. Geordie was a small, wiry man whose duty it was to tar and retar, caulk and recaulk the planks all over the ship. This ensured that the wood remained strong and the seawater stayed out.

"What say, Geordie? D'ye think we'll be seeing the sun again this season?"

Geordie was bent low, and I dropped to the deck beside him. He dipped his brush and expertly sealed the space between the boards. "I don't know as we'll ever see her again, lad. My bones are surely not liking this cold damp."

Across the deck, the Templar stood at the wheel. "We'll be making land before nightfall, Tormod. I've sent Seamus to his pallet. Ye will accompany me."

I couldn't believe my ears. He was taking me ashore and leaving Seamus behind.

The afternoon passed like the slow drip of Geordie's tar. Excitement bubbled within me, but I was fearful as well. I recalled the conversation between the Templar and Seamus when first we'd boarded. We were going to the Archbishop to tell him the map had been taken. The thought nearly made me ill, especially as I was responsible.

LAND HO!

The Templar was correct in his calculations. The day was gray. A fine mist painted the decking where I huddled, watching and waiting. Finally the call came.

"Land ho!" the Templar shouted. "Tormod, ring the bell."

I scrambled to my feet and tugged strongly on the bell we used to announce the candle marks of the day. Deckhands came quickly from below.

"Oars, hard to starboard," the Templar shouted.

The ocean was wild and unsettled. As we closed the distance to shore, the ship rocked, fighting the direction of the crew's oars. I felt the Templar behind me at the rail, watching the ominous darkness crest beneath the waves. The rocks were still far below the surface, but they bore watching. It would be awful to come all this way and tear open the hull on a jut of rock.

The Templar took the wheel and fought to keep us on course. The two-ton wooden ship bucked and lunged, riding each wave and crashing through the trough with such force I had to grip the rail to keep from being thrown across the slippery deck. At first it didn't appear as if we were making any headway, but then, gradually, we began to turn and inch our way past the rough water and rocks into the calmer surf of an inlet.

My first view of English soil was a bit disappointing. The beach looked much like the one I'd left, and the trees and land far too similar to be such a vast distance as we had traveled from my home.

There was a great deal to be done and I, as much as anyone aboard, was eager to set my feet once again on solid land. I was coiling the rope to the sail when the Templar called over to me. "Go below and get ready to leave."

The loud clang of the iron links rumbling across the winch made the deck tremble as I crossed it.

Within a candle mark we were ready to disembark. The mist had turned to a steady rain. I huddled within my plaid as a coracle was lowered down to the water. The Templar came up behind me. "Come. 'Tis time."

I feared this opportunity would never come. The rope ladder on the side of the ship was an easy feat. I was first into the boat, steadying myself as it rocked, and dropped quickly to sit. The Templar followed. We each took an oar and began to pull toward the rocky shore.

The wind picked up as we fought the waves, blowing spray into my face and down my neck. I ducked deeper into my plaid, pulling hard on the oars.

The boat was shallow and we were able to row in close. "I'll go first an' drag ye to the beach, so ye can jump to the sand." He bared his feet and rolled up his breeks to the knee. "No point in the both o' us freezing."

I was grateful. I was cold just being on the water. In the water would not be good at all. I grabbed his boots when the boat's hide scraped the sandy bottom and jumped ashore.

We dragged the boat up into the shadows of a copse of trees, and the Templar shrugged into his boots. A thin, curving track snaked through the dense woods. The rain dripped from the branches onto my head. I huddled waiting, wondering what lay ahead. And then we were off.

Beyond the trees, the visual similarity to home disappeared. A long, wide road stretched ahead, tamped solidly by those who had traveled and continued to traipse along its length. It was muddy and pocked with rain-filled ruts. I avoided them as best I could, but my boots were soaked in moments.

The town was surrounded by an enormous stone wall and appeared to have grown upward in a spiral toward the crest of a hill. Approaching the gates, I was stunned by its bulk. The wall seemed as tall as a mountain. "I've never seen anything like this," I said.

The Templar laughed, clapping me on the shoulder. "Aye. 'Tis awe-inspiring, but no more than the manor within. Let us not tarry. A warm room an' hot food await."

He shoved forward and I stumbled along staring gap-jawed. How such a feat as building it could have been accomplished, I could not imagine. It stretched above our heads and to our left and right beyond sight.

"The wall surrounds the whole o' the city," he said, nearly reading my thoughts. "There are towers built at regular intervals all around. An' there—he pointed upward—are walkways between that guards patrol. Look up as we enter."

I did as he suggested, though the rain drizzled in my eyes and down my chest. Amazed, I let out a hissing breath. A fearsome iron-studded gate hung suspended above our heads. If it were suddenly let loose, we would be skewered and crushed by the sharpened points of its base.

" 'Tis called a portcullis. 'Tis lowered at night or in case o' emergency when the city needs to be sealed off. There are two with a small passage between. Beyond the first ye'll see holes in the roof beams above. If an enemy makes it through the first gate, the second is dropped, an' hot oil or pitch is poured from above."

I shivered at the horrific image and moved quickly inside. The noise and smell hit me immediately, and a wave of travelers entering behind threatened to bring me to ground. Jostled and elbowed, I lost sight of the Templar. In a panic I spun around. A hand clamped my arm, and I was jerked roughly aside as a group who had come in behind us nearly plowed me down. "Stay with me, Tormod."

I didn't have a chance to argue as he tugged me along. A variety of shops lined the road's edge, and an open market was being held against one length of the great wall. We hurried through the rain, dodging the crowds that did business no matter the weather. I tried to absorb everything at a glance as I trailed. Merchants, with tarps staked and strung in a succession of low-hanging shelters, had arrayed their wares on wooden tables against the wall. There were vendors of fish and vegetables, booths of earthenware, jewelry, and weapons. Voices were raised in barter as customer and vendor argued over the best price. Bairns in wet homespun ran and played amid the booths as business went on around them. It was familiar to our trips to market. Chaos reigned, and yet it was life as usual for those involved.

"This way," he said, taking off along a road that snaked between two rows of shuttered houses. "Stay close and keep pace. We've a walk ahead to the manor and some o' these roads attract a rough sort o' traveler."

The smell in the alley made my throat close tight. I had often complained about the air belowdecks. Though open to the morning sky, this smelled worse, if that could be believed. Urine and refuse mingled beneath the onslaught of the rain and wafted up my nose, lingering in the folds of my plaid, which I held to my face. The Templar paid little attention to me as we walked, save to occasionally make sure I was still at his side. He seemed to withdraw deeply into himself, a condition I was getting to know fairly well. I didn't distract him with idle chatter.

I had no need, for I was engrossed in the new sights spread before and behind us. We traveled in a strange twisting that seemed to wind ever upward. I marveled that the Templar made his way unerringly, for there were a good many turns we took that I would have thought would wind back on themselves and end our journey. He had obviously been here before.

Below us the town spread like a tapestry woven with dark, vivid colors and sharp blackness. The higher we climbed, the more enthralled I became. The manor was on the very tip of the rise, and I craned my neck to see past the sheer walls of rock that surrounded it. When finally the road we traveled ended, we stood before a formidable gateway. There were two dark wooden doors at least six arm spans wide, crossed by bands of hammered iron.

The Templar used the hilt of his sword to gain attention from within. I felt the thump of his rap in my chest. Far above our heads on the stone walls a guard appeared. The Templar spoke. "I am Alexander Sinclair, Knight o' the Holy Temple o' Solomon. I was told Archbishop Lambert is within. I wish an audience."

AUDIENCE WITH AN ARCHBISHOP

My knees felt suddenly too weak to hold me upright. An Archbishop . . . the rank to me was as would have been the King. Though I knew this was the man who the Templar sought, it didn't hit me until this very moment that I might be in his company when it happened. The child of a fisherman in the presence of one most holy . . .

"Our great Lord was a fisherman, Tormod," the Templar said with amusement.

I shook my head in disbelief: again this reading of my thoughts. He had done it several times now, and it was unnerving.

He smiled. "Ye mumbled, Tormod. As ye do more often than even ye can recall."

It was a long wait. We huddled beneath the small overhang of the wall, avoiding the worst of the downpour. My plaid enveloped the whole of me, but I was far from warm. It had rained so much that the wet now penetrated the heavy wool, and I was chilled from the bones out. At times it crossed my mind that we might be turned away. The Templar kept his hand resting lightly on the haft of his sword, his body set in a rigid stance between the door and myself. Thoughts again pummeled my mind. *Could we be walking into an ambush?* Just then the great doors swung slowly inward. And my heart sank.

The doors didn't open to the main residence but to another winding, now cobbled, road. I suppressed a groan. Whatever was to come, I wished that it would finally come to pass, for I'd have given my right arm for a warm fire and a space out of the rain. We passed through a series of arches, outer buildings, and large open spaces. When finally we were shown to the grandest of them all, I realized we had reached the pinnacle of the heights. I stopped for the barest of moments and looked down, back from where we'd come.

Ours was the most wondrous of views. Below and all around us was a patchwork of color. At first glance I understood why I had been so drawn to the map. From my current height the whole of the land looked like one great parchment — as if the world had suddenly flattened. If I looked at any one particular area, I could quickly make out the individual rise and fall of the village in the distance. The trees were great billows of green and brown, and when I looked at the land as a whole, one thing blended into the next.

The Templar had already moved toward the manor, and I scrambled to keep from being left behind. All the while the image of the map, the one that haunted my memory from the first, stood sharply in my mind's eye.

The manor, as he called it, was no less than my idea of a castle — a great house of stone built into the rock of the hillside. It was several stories tall and stretched back and away so that I could not see where it actually ended. A servant dressed in robes of gray linen met us at the door and escorted us inside.

The entranceway was dark, and I craned my eyes to see in the dim space before me. The sconces on the walls held beeswax candles. They smelled pleasant but didn't throw off much light. The room, however, was a haven of warmth, and I reveled in the difference.

"I will take your outer garments and lay them by the fire," said the servant. "The Archbishop will see you momentarily. He is in conference. I will be back to escort you."

The Templar nodded and, as soon as the man was out of sight, moved furtively toward the entrance ahead, staying close to the wall as he peered beyond. I made a move to follow, but he forestalled me with an open hand. I moved instead to the wall closest. A group of paintings were set in frames on the walls — men in formal dress. I'd never seen images portrayed so realistically. *How incredible,* I thought, *to be able to capture a likeness that way.* I slid my fingers along a rounded cheek and across an ear and was surprised to find the surface rough and dry. My mind expected to feel the soft and wrinkled skin my eyes so clearly beheld.

"This way, Brother Knight. The Archbishop awaits you." The Templar started after the servant of the house, and I reluctantly left the paintings to follow. So dim was the corridor that I barely saw the men whose backs I followed. We were shown into an enormous room lit by a multitude of glowing, golden lights. Tapers, tallow candles, and the flames of lit straw rushes abounded, so much so that I had to blink several times to accustom myself to the brilliance.

The Archbishop was seated on a richly appointed chair facing the door through which we entered, and he rose as we were announced. He was large, with wide shoulders and a light olive complexion. His hair was white like his robes, a set of unornamented linen, and yet his bearing proclaimed his rank as a high official of the Church. I hung back, awed.

"Brother Alexander, God's hand has guided ye to me."

"Aye, it has, Yer Grace, an' we are humbled an' thankful o' it." He knelt before the Archbishop and kissed his ring. Then gaining his feet, he said, "I have troubling news nonetheless an' had hoped ye might counsel me in a few matters."

His gaze flicked to mine and back to the knight. "I am always yer servant, Alexander."

"My pardon, Yer Grace," said the Templar. "Allow me to introduce my apprentice, Tormod MacLeod. He is a rare lad an' will be a welcome addition to the Order." He turned to me. "Tormod, present yerself."

I nearly stumbled as I crossed the short space between us and sank to my knees to kiss the ring before me. *A Templar's apprentice? Could he possibly be serious?* I had dreamt half my life of the possibility. "Yer Grace." I spoke breathlessly. "'Tis an honor."

He turned to the Templar. "I would speak to ye privately a moment, Alexander. Help yerself, Tormod. There is food set out beyond that door. Break yer fast. We will no' be long."

I was nearly as glad of the excuse to absent myself from the piercing gaze of the Archbishop as I was happy to indulge in food that was hot and not salted or dried. I moved quickly across the room and through the door to give them their privacy.

The chamber I entered was richly appointed. Heavy, vividly embroidered tapestries lined the walls, and in a great hearth real coal burned. I stretched my hands to the warmth. Peat, the turf we used in my homeland, never burned as hotly as this.

On a long table were dishes upon dishes, platters of stuffed eel and pheasant, sweet onions and plums, puddings of rich reds and browns, and breads drizzled in honey and coated with almonds. Even on the highest feast days the family had never such an assortment at one time. *A Templar's apprentice,* I thought. *Could it really be true?*

As I ate and my body warmed, I became aware of a need that had been pressing in on me for much of our trip up the hill — something I had forgotten in the presence of the Most Holy Archbishop and the prospect of food. I had to make water. And at this moment it was a desperate urge.

I fidgeted, willing my unhappy bladder to cease its pressure, but my body was in no mood to take yet another of my mind's commands. At last I knew I had to find the garderobe or I'd make a fool of myself.

I crept into the chamber, quietly so that I would not intrude on the Templar and His Grace's discussion. If I could but slip by unheeded, I thought, perhaps the servant beyond would give me direction.

But as I skirted the edge of the chamber, my eyes turned toward the two at the dais. The Templar was down on one knee with his head bent low. The Archbishop stood before him, and in his outstretched hands was a small carving. It was an odd scene, to be sure, but something even stranger happened then. On my skin I felt the waft of a warm breeze — a breeze with no origin in an enclosed room. I stopped, perplexed, my eyes riveted to the scene before me.

Suddenly the darkness of the carving began to slowly change. It grew brighter and the wind blew stronger. The candle flames flickered in a way that made the room shimmer with light.

Without thought I dropped to one knee mirroring the position of the Templar. In moments the whole of the chamber was as bright as the pure light of day. I heard the Archbishop's voice from far away. His words were in a language of beauty unknown to me.

The golden glow of the room seemed to crowd around me, blotting out the form of the men, and sound rose in my ears. "Blasphemer! Heretic!" I felt the crowd around me, angry, pressing me forward against a barrier.

Up above, a platform hovered and the smell of burning wood curled in the air.

"Focus. Ground. Shield." The Templar snapped the words at me and I felt myself react. The force of the vision broke, but my eyes and mind were still filled by the scene. My body trembled.

The Templar was on his knees before me. "Shhh, leanabh." The Gaelic endearment felt like home, but I was far away. "'Tis gone. Ye are safe. Breathe deeply."

"A crowd was gathered. They were frightened. Four men were brought in in chains."

My words came haltingly, but I forced my impressions into the air of the chamber. "High above, a man shouted, 'Blasphemer! Heretic!'"

The Archbishop stepped down from the dais. I felt his eyes on me, staring as if I were a specimen in an alchemist's lab. "What more did ye see?"

"I don't know," I said. "Nothing. 'Twas images an' sounds, colors an' feelings." I struggled to explain how the visions came to me. My breath felt short, my chest tight. My head was swimming.

The Archbishop approached. The Templar and I stood. "To see what lies ahead is a frightening ghost." He spoke softly, almost as if he were riddling something out for himself. I wondered why he was not surprised at my vision state.

"I cannot stay with ye for I must ready to journey to Rome. Stay. Eat. Warden de Kendall's staff will see to your reprovisioning." His mind was elsewhere, already dismissing our presence.

"A moment, Yer Grace, if I might . . ." Their eyes turned toward me. My face burned. My body's persistent need still compelled me and I felt a sudden embarrassment. "A chamber pot?"

"Are you ill?" The Archbishop moved quickly to the sideboard and drew a pot from beneath.

"No, but if I don't hurry, I will be wet."

My words were so completely out of place that the Templar let burst a sharp laugh. Shaking his head, he said, "Beyond the door is a garderobe, Tormod." The bewildered smile that played about his lips distracted me from the worries that lingered in my mind.

HISTORY LESSON

I met up with the Templar a short time later in the same room I had begun to feast in earlier. Two chairs and a table had been set while I was away. I dropped down opposite, feeling tired and worried. The vision made me uneasy.

The Archbishop had arranged with the castle's keeper for fresh supplies to be readied while we ate. Two large packs lay on the flags at the Templar's feet.

"Templar Alexander?" I asked.

"Hmm," he murmured, distracted.

"Is this the Archbishop's residence?"

"What?" he said, pulling back from the path his thoughts had taken.

"This castle. Is it all for the Archbishop?"

He looked down the table as if seeing it for the first time. "No. The Archbishop is here on business to Rome. He is friends with the Lord Chancellor of Dover and so stays here when he visits." He finished his last bite. "We should be on our way. Are ye done?"

I nodded. Though I was hungry and the food abundant, I ate little. I could not seem to push the vision from my mind.

At full dark we set out once again. It was still raining and the sky was a lead gray, which seemed fitting as that was the way I felt.

"Tormod, I don't need to tell ye that ye must not speak o' the carving with any aboard, aye?" he said after we passed through the first archway.

"Aye," I replied. "But we're not aboard yet. What is this thing?"

He looked as if he would put me off, but nodded, as if to himself. "Stop here."

The temperature had dropped while we were inside. It was cold and I was uncomfortable. On a stone bench in an alcove against a high hedge we sat. His face was grave when he turned to me.

"We have to be careful, Tormod, now more than ever. I know no' what yer vision portends, but the fact that it has come to ye with the aid o' the carving makes me leery. These particulars *are* quite probably destined to happen."

"Everything I *see* happens," I mumbled. He ignored my words. "The carving," I prompted. "What is it?"

He was silent a moment. "I will start a' the beginning. I'm not certain that it is good for ye to know so much, but I don't seem to have a choice in it. Many o' my visions have included ye."

I was not surprised, since I'd heard him speak of it to Seamus, but to hear it again said directly to me in so plain a manner made me feel a bit off. I wondered if his visions involved blood and injury. A shiver ran through me and I tucked my hands beneath my plaid to still their shaking.

"Do ye recall what I told ye o' the origins o' the Order?" he asked.

"Aye," I said, remembering. Hugues de Payen, a knight of France, had joined the Crusade to liberate

God's Kingdom in Jerusalem. He arrived with high ideals only to be shocked at how poorly trained and ill equipped the men who had flocked to the Church's cause truly were. Those who fought fell quickly beneath the Muslim swords. Those who roamed the roads were easy prey to the bands of mercenaries.

Hugues had called to him eight strong knights, related by blood and marriage, and approached the King with a proposition. If the King would back them, these men would dedicate themselves to patrolling the roads and giving what protection they could to the pilgrims. They started out, nine men based out of the palace stables, a place said to be located atop the ancient Temple of Solomon. They'd named themselves the Poor Fellow Soldiers of Christ, but the world came to know them as the Knights of the Temple of Solomon or, more simply, the Knights Templar.

"What have the origins to do with the carving?" I asked.

"Tormod, Hugues de Payen was gifted, as ye an' I are gifted," he said.

"He had the vision sense?" He had not shared this with me. I leaned foward, determined not to miss a word.

"Aye. An' while sleeping in the stables, turned into a dormitory, he saw a storehouse built into the bedrock o' the original temple. He an' his men excavated —"

"An' they found the carving!" I burst in.

"Aye. Along with a library o' scrolls an' a host of gold, treasure, an' jewels."

My mouth dropped. *Treasure*. I knew what I thought was the history of the Knights, but I had never heard of a store of ancient treasure. The night seemed to grow darker as he spoke, the rain and clouds growing thicker. I remained quiet as he continued, fearing if I broke the spell, he would stop.

"The carving we named Baphomet, meaning wisdom, for in its presence all o' our kind, the gifted, experience an enhanced vision sense."

His eyes were steady and a great rush of excitement overtook me.

"Why do ye have it now?" I asked, impatiently. "What has it to do with the Archbishop?"

"What ye overheard on the ship that first day is part o' this," he said. "The Templars, as ye know, are the right hand o' the Pope. We've been that from the beginning. We answer only to the Holy Father — no sovereign, no acolyte, no one — an' in return the Holy Father relies on us for things he would ask o' no other."

I squirmed on the bench, desperate to know more.

"Three an' a half years ago a map came into the hands o' Pope Boniface. It had been found in a cave a' the edge o' the sea, sealed in a jar o' clay. In the right-hand corner was a drawing, an exact image o' the carving

I hold here." His hand curved around his sporran where the bulk rounded out its shape.

"Tormod, Pope Boniface an' his successor, Pope Benedict, as well as a few select members o' the Church, are part o' a secret upper-echelon sect o' the Templar Order."

"They're Templars?" I asked, incredulous.

"Not in the ordinary way. They took no vows, but are a part o' a group who oversee the greatest decisions concerning the Order," he said.

A secret sect of the Templars, and he trusted me with the knowledge. I could scarcely credit it.

"Pope Boniface immediately recognized the image o' the carving from the map an' sent it to the Order in Paris. But things in France were getting a bit tense, an' it was judged prudent to move both map an' carving to Scotland."

"Why? What was happening?"

"Pope Boniface clashed with King Philippe an' excommunicated him. The King retaliated by having the Pope kidnapped."

I was horrified. That anyone should think to kidnap a Pope was beyond my wildest imagining.

"The Templars rescued Pope Boniface, much to the anger o' the King, but it was too late. He was old an' the experience harsh. He died a month later."

"And then?"

"Benedict was next in line for the Papacy, but he was no' long in power."

"Why?"

"Philippe's man poisoned him. Can ye credit it? I had a vision, not five paces from the King a' court, while I was picking up tribute owed the Order. I saw Guillaume de Nogaret, the King's councillor, take the Papal ring from the Pope's dead finger." He shook his head.

"I've never killed a man in cold blood," he said. "But in this instance, I think that I should have."

I nearly reeled at his words. "Ye could not. Ye would not. 'Tis no' the way o' the Templar."

He didn't move or blink. "He has killed two o' the most holy an' powerful men in the world. Let us hope my inaction has no consequences for the future. I left him free to continue his reign o' recklessness, Tormod. Was that something a Templar should have done?"

I was suddenly colder than at any other time. It was as if a frigid wind whipped across my soul.

"Somehow Philippe knows about the map. He's tracked us from Paris to Scotland."

"That's when ye found me," I said.

"Aye. I saw ye in a vision, carrying the map to the Abbot in my stead."

"Ye gave it to me," I said. "An' I gave it up to those hunting ye."

The Templar nodded. "But why would the carving

107

have me entrust the map to ye, if only it was to be lost," he said almost to himself.

"If yer visions are like mine, then what ye see is the future. The carving is not directing; it is just relaying what is to happen." I was nearly mumbling to myself trying to figure it out.

"Unless . . . I was meant to carry it, so that I could later redraw it for ye. I can, ye know! I know its lines an' shapes like I know my homeland."

"Maps are no' simple things, Tormod. They must be precise an' accurate," he said. " 'Tis a good thought, but ye only could have seen it for a moment, an' that's not enough to redraw it." He stood, dismissing my offer.

"Listen to me. I know the map like 'tis still here afore me. I have oddness with things that I see. I remember. Even if I see something for only a moment, it stays."

He stared at me, weighing the possibility. "We will try it then. Stranger things exist in this world than a good memory. Particularly when it comes to the carving."

"I can do it." I said with confidence, getting to my feet and shaking off the rain that beaded on my plaid.

"Where do we go from here?" I asked.

"To the Grand Master. I still have the carving an' I need to get it to a safehold."

The idea seemed preposterous. "Is he not in France, where the soldiers who are seeking ye reside?"

"He's due to tour the Spanish preceptories before going on to Paris. We will seek him there, in Spain. I have allies who will help. Remember what I have said an' do not speak o' this to any."

A SECRET HELD

The moment we boarded, the Templar installed me at the table in the forecastle. With several parchments, a quill, and ink, I got to work though it was not as easy as I had originally imagined. It was one thing to see a map, a whole other to draw it. I had some trouble with the scale and proportion, but the shape of things came to me easily.

Several marks of the candle later, I got it right. The last bit was the most difficult: the strange series of dots scattered across the surface. I fussed over these the most. When I'd added the last, my eyes drifted down over what I'd drawn. Something was not quite right, I thought, tracing the map. Suddenly the candle flickered in a draft from the window. The memory of the vision I had came back to me. *Julio*. I added the word in the lower left-hand corner.

The Templar came in as I was sanding the ink on the final bit. He stood beside me and I held my breath waiting.

"Well, from what I can recall it looks right." He stared at it thoughtfully. "Julio. . . . Thank ye, Tormod. I'll take it from here."

I stood and wriggled my fingers, pleased. He had already moved into place and forgotten me. I wandered out of the forecastle, back toward the ladder to the hold. Seamus blocked the way. "Geordie needs ye aft, move on."

"But I've been working for —" My protest was cut off by his look.

"Now."

Plagues, God. Boils and famine would work. A few dozen locusts down his back and in his breeks. Feel free to drop them now.

The Templar worked closeted away for the next two days. Near noon on the third, I felt his shadow over me as I caulked the decking with Geordie.

"I need ye tonight, Tormod. We are going to shoot the moon. 'Tis time yer lessons resumed."

I squinted up at him. He seemed pensive, as if his mind were still far off in calculation. "Aye," I said.

"Geordie, can ye do without the lad? I'd like him to sleep a bit."

"Aye, Captain. 'Tis not as if the boards are goin' anywhere. Prevention, this is. Get ye gone, ye bilge rat." I smiled at Geordie's good-natured chafing. His names for me changed by the day.

"Ye need me an' ye know it, old man." I tossed a floppy straw hat to him. "Cover yer head before ye burn out what little mind ye've got."

The Templar cuffed me as I passed. "Respect for all, Tormod. A knight can be funny but not disrespectful o' an elder."

I ducked my head guiltily but caught Geordie's wink as I stowed my bucket. The Templar walked away.

"Bilge rat," Geordie said beneath his breath.

The night sky was black and the stars winked like fireflies. Not a cloud marred the view, not a wind crossed the bow. I stood at the wheel as I had for the last several candle marks. Tonight's lesson was how to shoot the moon. I looked forward to it. The astrolabe, our charts, quills, and ink lay on a plank set across two casks. We were to take our headings from the height of the moon from the horizon as it related to the position of several stars.

The door to the forecastle creaked behind me, and in the still blackness I saw the silhouette of the Templar silently cross the deck.

"Have the others gone below?" His question was nearly lost in the wash of the sea, and suddenly, for no reason I could fathom, the skin on the nape of my neck prickled.

"Aye. None have been about for more than a candle mark." I matched my tone to his, not knowing why, but sure that it was something I should do. He stepped into the moon's shimmer of light and I saw that he carried a small bundle in his hands. He glanced quickly about and laid his burden on the plank beside our equipment.

Recognizing the wrappings, I stepped back, uncertain and no little bit frightened.

"Prop the wheel an' come to me. Be quick about it, the moon is even now reaching its apex."

I looked up. The moon seemed full, but I had no experience to judge the absolute peak of the cycle. "What must we do?" I asked.

He unwrapped the carving. This close I could see what I was not able to before. It was made of hardwood, stained dark with age. It was a woman. She was on her knees, but sitting back on her heels. Her hands were lifted above her head, palms up, as if reaching, waiting.

The Templar moved behind the cask and crouched, looking at the carving. He shifted it several times, and it took me a moment to realize he was arranging the figure according to his sight of the moon. When the form was where he wanted it, he said, "Hand me the astrolabe."

"What are we doing?" I whispered, giving it to him.

"Following a vision," he said mysteriously.

I watched as he turned the astrolabe's back to us and then placed the instrument into the hands of the carving. "God's toes," I gasped. It was a perfect fit, as if one had been made for the other.

The warm rush of air and the tingling of a million pinpricks that I had felt before in the carving's presence flowed across my skin as the carving began to glow. Its brilliance lit the ebony of the night with a cascade of shimmering stars. And as I looked on these, lights began to lessen and spread out, their tiny reflections winking on the dark wooden planks at my feet.

"Here, Tormod. Hurry. Crouch an' tell me what ye see."

I moved to his side and took a sighting through the center of the astrolabe. My breath caught tight in my throat. The brilliant sparkles of light that radiated from the carving were exactly in position with the myriad of stars surrounding the moon. As I stared and the moon reached its fullest, the lights began to flicker, growing stronger and brighter, filling the space in my mind, turning to dots. Black on a page, atop an etching that shifted from lines of ink to the sharp clear edges of a real mountain. Valleys dipped in the folds that formed before me. Water careened over a ledge, the crash of it filling my ears.

Focus. Ground. Shield. Abruptly, the world shifted and I swayed. The carving before me turned black once again.

"Are ye all right, lad?" His words came to me from far away, but his hand on my arm felt solid.

"I am well." I murmured, the vision still strong within me.

"What did ye see?"

"The stars mark the map. They're laid over it."

He smiled and nodded. "I had a suspicion," he said and crouched. I watched, waiting.

"Did ye have a vision?" I asked breathlessly.

"No," he said. "I see only stars."

"But why would ye have me look first? Why did it only work for me?"

"I don't know, but I dreamt last night o' ye doing just this," he said. "The carving is once again providing the key."

"Ye speak in riddles. The key to what?"

"Finding what's been left for us to find," he said.

"Back to the wheel, now. We'll have to shoot the moon another night."

✠

The Templar spent much of the next few days closeted away with his maps and charts. Whenever I stopped by the forecastle between shifts or just during the quiet of afternoon, he was elbow deep in mathematical formulas that he scratched on every available surface.

In midmorning of the fourth day, I was at loose ends. I had finished the Matins prayers and stood at the aft part of the ship with nothing to do. The weather was downright eerie, the sky a deep and forbidding gray. The rain and wind had died off during the night, but the air was still and cold. I huddled in my plaid by the rail staring at the ominous deep green of the ocean. Barely a ripple marred the surface, and the sail hung slack.

Seamus had the wheel. I watched him across the length of the deck. His face was pinched; something worried him. Unease slid through me. "Tormod, get Alexander."

He almost never addressed me directly without some kind of a venomous jab. So I was surprised. I shot him a sideways look, but did as he bid. I bolted to the forecastle and popped my head inside. "Seamus needs ye."

The Templar looked up. His eyes were tired, red-rimmed and bleary. "Aye." He laid aside the maps and quill and followed me outside, scanning the ship, sail, and sky as he moved. "What is it?" he asked Seamus.

I felt it then, or rather I didn't feel it and knew.

"There's no wind. Not a stirring since last night." His voice was grim. Wind didn't mean much to a fishing vessel, but on a ship this size, it was nearly essential to travel. The Templar moved to Seamus's side and took the wheel, peering anxiously ahead.

"We should be all right for a while. We have enough provisions. The barrels o' ale from the Archbishop, an' the food is plenteous."

For some reason I felt the Templar's words were not as confident as they might be. "How fare the water barrels?"

"Two o' the eight are contaminated," said Seamus. "We have enough for a normal journey, but I don't know."

A white sail billowed in the forefront of my mind. Wind whispered in my ears.

"It will be enough," I said, lurching back to the present.

"It will be enough," the Templar echoed, striding across the deck and back to his maps.

Day passed into night, then again into day. Everyone took their turn at the oars, moving us slowly across the calm water. I was as jumpy as a kitten. It was my prophecy that the wind would come. Part of me knew it would — everything I saw *happened*. But it was not an easy wait.

Seamus was even more affected than I. The longer we were forced to slowly crawl our way across the expanse of blue, the edgier he became. He took to prowling the perimeter of the ship in unending sweeps, constantly eyeing the horizon. But nothing he did changed the course of our placid wake. The Templar watched for the wind's change with no less impatience, yet he at least appeared calmly accepting of the situation.

I was above deck, off in a shadowed corner, casting my net when Seamus's voice reached me.

"Alex, we canno' go on like this. We must alter our course an' go back the way we've come." His outburst was loud, even in my ears a challenge.

"Our course is Spain." The Templar's voice was low but his authority carried.

Seamus paced away and back, agitated. "I have a very bad feeling."

"I canno' heed ye this time, Seamus. Yer visions are not specific enough; the power comes to ye sketchily. It could mean anything. We must continue. We will lose too much time going back. Unless ye've seen something more specific than what we spoke o', we continue on."

Seamus paled, and a slight tremor wracked his body. "No. I've seen nothing more."

The Templar turned away, but I could see that he was bothered. "It will be all right, Seamus," he said, slowly pacing before the rail. His mind was working, puzzling out the bits and pieces he had already encountered.

Seamus swallowed hard. He looked my way and his usual animosity appeared, then he turned back to the bleak horizon. "This damn stillness is killing me," he said. "Mark my words, Alex, something bad is about to happen, an' if we go on, we are powerless to stop it."

The Templar did not turn back, but I knew from the sudden tension in his posture that the words had reached something inside him. The small hairs on my arms prickled as he turned his eyes to my darkened corner and, for no reason I could justify, I felt suddenly frightened.

"Things are changing. I can feel it." The knight's words were meant for me. "We go on as we are, windless or not, and put in to Santiago."

Seamus sighed with a depressed sort of acceptance. "As ye will it, Uncle."

WINDS OF CHANGE

By nightfall the ship was back under a steady breeze and tensions aboard began to turn as well. That is, everyone's mood improved but Seamus's. The man literally vibrated with anger, and it was all the worse when he was near me.

Reason or no, things between us remained balanced on the edge of a blade. While the others returned to their tasks, the Templar bade me continue to fish, ending for a time my duties with the deckhands. This appeared to chafe Seamus all the more. Truth be told, I would have caulked the entire hold or rowed for days rather than spend time on deck with that man, for fishing gave him even more opportunity to cause havoc in my world. Nothing pleased him. Not my skills, nor the catch, nor the way I handled the wheel. Not even my scrubbing of the privy was good enough for the sergeant. I dreaded his presence around me.

The pale gray dawn brought with it a tiding of things to change. The wind whipped briskly across the deck as I dropped the first of our nets, letting the line slowly drift out and down. It was heavy and slick in my hands. I felt the bite of it in my fingers and the weight of it in my arms. Balance was a fine line I trod. I tipped over the rail, and the blood rushed to my head as I slowly lowered the bulk of the net seaward, making sure it fell evenly and didn't tangle.

The water was rough, crashing against the hull and rushing up in a spray that wet my arms as I dangled. The waves surged and dropped away, surged and dropped away. On one deep dip of the ship, as I was letting out the last of the net, I was surprised by the feel of someone behind me. I twisted to see what was going on. I saw and felt him at the same time.

Seamus's fingers closed over my shin. I didn't stop to ask questions, but kicked out and caught him square in the chest. It all happened so fast. He staggered back and cursed. I saw the rope tangle and tried to right myself, but the sea tugged the net out of my fingers. Then Seamus was yanked over the side.

What possessed me then I'll never know, for in truth I hated the man, but the moment he went over I grabbed my fishing knife, tossed aside my plaid, and dove in.

The water hit me with a crush, nearly tearing the knife from my grip. It was colder than the first ice of winter, and though my eyes stung, I searched for him in the blackness. In moments my ears were ringing and the pressure in my chest grew unbearable. He was deep and struggling. The rope was wrapped tight and grew more tangled by the moment.

I swam toward him to try and loose the rope, but he fought me off. The burning need for air made my head pound, but I ignored it and made a lunge for him.

This time I got close enough, for by now Seamus had stopped struggling. With the breath heaving in my chest, I sawed until the rope frayed and broke. With Seamus limp in my arms, I kicked for my life.

The surface glistened above, taunting me. His heavy, awkward body shoved me deep each time I reached for it, struggling to get Seamus's face and my own above the waves. The undertow was strong, fighting to suck me below, churning water into my open, gasping mouth. My body was exhausted and not working as it should.

"Tormod!" The Templar's voice floated over the roar of the sea and hope grew where none had been. I swam in circles, looking and listening, but the waves were coming from all directions, confusing me. A great crest broke over me and the force of it wrenched Seamus from my grasp. I began to choke on water that rushed down my throat. My chest was exploding as I fought again for the surface, and when at last I broke through, I knew that I'd lost him.

STARLIGHT

I ducked beneath the waves again and again, stroking though the dark, desperate to find Seamus. The water was so cold I couldn't tell if my arms or legs were moving. Somehow the direction I thought was the surface never seemed to be right. Blackness was all around me. The only heat I felt was the burn in my chest. I thought I was going to die.

Suddenly the darkness broke, and a glow of brilliant light filled the ocean's depths. I swam as if in a dream. No — as if in a vision. Before my eyes a thousand embers glowed. One by one the lights winked off and on, calling me forward.

With the breath so tight in my chest, every heave turning me inside out, I followed the trail of starlight. And as I passed each glowing point, my need for air lessened and my body warmed.

An eternity later I broke through the waves, gasping for air, determined to float. I heard them then, the Templar foremost in the shouting, and long moments later, I was hauled aboard.

"Tormod, lad, come back."

The Templar's soft voice called to me through a haze of mist. I heard him, but I could not speak or seem to come fully awake.

I drifted and dreamt. Though I don't know how long I stayed in that strange and silent place, I knew full well the waking.

Pain seared into my dreaming and I jerked to. The chamber was dark and frightening. The black wrapped around me and squeezed the air from my body.

"Lay still, Tormod. I'll get Alexander. He wanted to be told the moment ye woke." Seamus's voice startled me.

My eyes darted around the room, frantic. Nothing looked familiar. "Where am I? What's wrong with me?"

"Ye're in my quarters. Be calm." He moved quickly toward the door but didn't pass through it right away. He stood instead as if he could not move on. Suddenly he pounded the wall. "Why? Why would ye do it? I gave ye no reason to play savior."

I struggled to remember, to understand his words. The feel of the icy water closed in on me. "The water. We were in the water," I said raggedly. "I could no' find ye." It was all so bleary in my mind. I remembered the dark and cold and shook with the thought of it.

He hunched by the door, brooding. "I would not have done it for ye." He seemed embarrassed by what he'd said, but it made little sense to my mind. I didn't reply. I could not. Fear choked the words in my throat. *It hurts. My leg . . . the burn.*

"If there was something I could do or undo, I would."

I struggled to sit, and the pain ripped through my body. I howled with it.

He moved quickly across the room. "No, lie down. Ye'll tear the stitches." He pushed me flat, and I'd not the energy again to rise. *Stitches.*

Seamus left me then, in the dark that seemed to smother me. It felt like a candle mark, though probably only moments passed before the Templar opened the door. A blur of fur streaked past him and leapt onto the pallet. My leg throbbed beneath the cat's weight. "Cass, get off him," he said, shooing the animal away. Cassiopeia jumped from the bedding but stayed at my pallet's side. I could hear her purr in the darkness. It was comforting, and yet I squeezed my eyes shut. I wished to never open them and know the truth I would hear. "Tormod, I am truly glad that ye've finally awakened."

"What's happened? I know there's something. Something bad."

I felt his hand on my shoulder, strong. I didn't feel strong. I was filled with a well of sorrow that had no end. His silence brought my tears brimming to the surface.

"Ye were long in the cold, lad. We barely were able to bring yer body temperature back to normal. I'm sorry. It was the freezing sickness. Ye're lucky to be alive. Ye've been lost to us for many a day."

"What?" I cried, embarrassed by the wobble in my voice and the tears in my eyes.

"Yer foot, lad. It was yer foot. Ye've lost two toes on yer left."

The dark seemed to deepen, chilling my soul. The tears I'd been pressing away escaped to rush down the sides of my face. *I was my da's runner.* The thought repeated over and over in my mind, louder with every pass. "No," I said. "No, no, no. It cannot be. Why? Why to me?"

"It's not that bad, Tormod." His words were harsh. "There are many that get by with far worse. We were able to save both o' yer feet. Ye have two strong legs. Ye will adjust. It will take some time. I'll not lie to ye, it will pain ye for a good long while."

His words barely cut the fog in my mind. I had done nothing to cause this, but it didn't feel that way.

I want to go home. I want my mam. I want to be left alone. I want my foot whole. I shouted at him deep in my mind but not aloud. His hand slid from my shoulder to my arm. I pulled away and huddled in the corner of my pallet. He hesitated and then left quietly. Cassiopeia leapt back onto the bedding and curled up near my head.

DARK BEYOND THE STORM

The Templar left me alone that night with a strong tea of willow bark to dull the pain. I didn't want to see him, and yet I did. I was angry . . . at everyone and everything — at Seamus, at God. *I prayed to Ye nine times a day. How could Ye do this to me? Why?* I railed. *I saved him. I should have been rewarded. Why have Ye punished me instead?* It was bad, all of it. But what was worse was there was a small part of me screaming that the Templar knew it was going to happen. He had the vision sense. I could not help but wonder if he had seen it days ago. I was confused. I had never been able to change the future — what I *saw,* happened — but what if he could, and he didn't?

I slept to escape all that had happened. My dreams were terrible. I ran in them, not happily with the wind at my back as I once would have, but jerkily, and forever chased by something or someone pounding heavily behind me. I woke several times in the night, the last when the Templar came to check on me, but I was not yet ready to face him.

A full day and night passed before I had the strength and courage to peel back the dressing. The sight of my bloody foot made me retch into the chamber pot by my bedding.

"Go easy, leanabh." I knew that he had entered, for the draft from the open door made the light of the candle flicker. As the last of the heaves and tremors passed, I leaned spent against the pallet's edge and took the cool scrap of linen he offered to wipe my face.

"It looks bad, aye, but it will heal well. Ye've got to be vigilant about cleaning the site, though. I've seen such before. Ye need to make sure that the wasting does no' progress further."

My empty stomach heaved yet again.

"I'm sorry, lad. I forget that my words might fall harshly on yer ears."

"No. I . . . 'tis all right." Though I tried to suppress it, my voice shook. I swallowed hard, willing myself to be strong. "Who has seen to me?"

His gaze met mine. "Seamus didn't leave yer side until ye woke. And even now, he'll let no other prepare the water and herbs."

Anger tore through me at the name and the thought

of my mangled foot. "He need not bother. He had no use for me. I want no part o' his guilt."

The Templar didn't even raise an eyebrow and his voice remained calm. "I'll arrange for one o' the others," he said. "Tormod, what ye did back there was nothing short o' heroic. He would surely have died had ye not thought quickly and acted as ye did."

It would have been better for me if I had not done as I had, my mind shouted. *If I had to do it again, I would not.*

"Ye do yerself a disservice, Tormod. Ye did as was right. Ye've a good heart." He spoke again as if he could read my mind. I had not the faith in myself that he placed upon me.

I could not bear to meet his eyes, to see the disappointment that would surely be there. I just wanted to be left alone. My foot was throbbing, and my mind was a blur. He stood. "Lay yer head, lad. Get some rest. We've time to talk o' it later."

I did as he bid. I could do nothing else.

Horace brought the supplies for my wound care. The big man moved surprisingly quietly for the giant he was. I watched him wordlessly.

"Master Tormod, did I wake you?"

"No, Horace. I'm sorry I was added to yer duties," I said quietly.

He laughed his great barrel laugh. "An' ye're so much worse than shifting ballast."

I wanted to laugh, but I didn't have the energy. "How do I do it? Clean the wound, I mean?" Talking seemed to push away the threat of tears that came on every time I thought of what I'd lost, or what I would have to face.

"Seawater boiled with garlic bulbs and leaves o' witch hazel. Ye clean it like this." He was gentle, another surprise. "Do this for as long as ye need, but when ye feel able, soak the whole o' it."

As he spoke, he carefully showed me how to clean the wound that someone had stitched with rough black thread. The pain was so heady that I could barely hear him. My ears hummed and black crept up behind my eyes. I had no notion that my tears were running freely until I heard my own hiccupping breath and felt the dampness on the blankets. It was embarrassing.

"It will be all right, Tormod. Cry if ye need to." Fiery jags raced through the whole of my leg. I focused on the back of his neck and saw the thin white scars I'd never seen before. It was a shock. I ran one finger over the closest and he flinched.

The lash came down with savage brutality. Pain

rippled, close and hot, not within me, but an echo of a memory that still contained it.

Focus. Ground. Shield. I was back in seconds, my body trembling. Horace thought it was from the pain. Maybe it was, but I knew this pain was nothing compared to the one he had endured.

The chamber was dark and it was late, but I was restless. The air shifted, and I closed my eyes to just a slit. Someone came to change the water. His bulk was not Horace. Fury washed through me. Seamus.

Silent, he stood by me. I wanted to move, to yell, to smash his face, but I couldn't. The coverlet had fallen to the floor, and I held my breath as he lifted it and laid it back on top of me. The weight was painful, but I could not afford to wince. It seemed forever before he left.

I sat up shakily, pushed aside the bedding, and carefully began to remove the dressing. It was stiff with dried blood and the sight of it was as nauseating as the last time I'd looked, but the Templar's warning made me press on.

Wasting no time on a dry wash, I inched the whole of it slowly into the bucket. The pain was heady; my body shook with it. Several moments passed before I was able to draw a breath without feeling the need to retch.

Cassiopeia came in through the open door and

began nosing around the bucket. Absently I reached down and rubbed her neck. The light of my candle sent out flickering bits of gold that illuminated a small area of my berth. I could see into the bucket. The blood had mixed with the solution and the water had turned a dark and murky red.

I could not bear to touch it yet, so I let the water do what it would. The scarlet depths of the bucket called out to me and I slipped inside.

Old and blistered feet cried out for relief. A clumsy bag pressed into back and sides. A familiar heat wafted through the thin material. The crash of a waterfall played in my ears. A myriad of sparkling lights danced before my eyes.

Focus. Ground. Shield. As I lurched back to the present, my foot burned like the devil. I lifted it from the bucket, swaying in my seat, recovering from the vision. My breath was shallow, and the room faded in and out for many moments. Cassiopeia sat on my coverlet eyeing me as though I were an oddity.

This vision was unusual. Somehow important, I knew. I blotted the wound with the edge of my plaid, barely noting the clean pink skin and dark stitches. I had to tell the Templar what I'd seen.

Replacing the old bandage with a new one, I chanced putting weight on the foot. The pain was heady and so instead I hobbled to the wall and on one foot crossed the room. The deck was empty save for the Templar, and when he saw me, he propped the wheel and hurried to my side.

"Are ye mad? Ye'll tear the stitches and have to start the healing all over again." He helped me down onto a pile of sailcloth. The short journey had robbed me of all strength and much breath. "I've had another vision.

"It was an old man. Someone from the past." The Templar's silence urged me on. "I think he may have carried the carving. I felt the heat and saw the light. 'Twas in flashes, like always, but an echo o' his thoughts was tied to the images as well. He had a responsibility, and was determined to see it through."

"Can ye recall the setting?" the Templar asked. "What was 'round him?"

I closed my eyes. I was beyond tired, and my foot was throbbing. The lap of the sea was comforting. It came to me then. "A waterfall." Sleep was calling out to me. The Templar draped a length of canvas over me and left me to return to the wheel.

SEASICK

The days that followed passed slowly. The pain of my wound continued. At times the burning came from deep inside, like my bones were spewing flames. At other times it was like a distant ache, and it was then that I felt as if the toes were still there — like they had gone to sleep and were now waking with a rush of pinpricks.

I was on deck, sitting next to Geordie, chipping away at the board nearest. My foot began to ache and I stopped working, biting my lip. "Why does it do that?"

The Templar was at the wheel. "What?"

"Hurt like the toes are still there."

"The blood is circulating in a healthy manner, rushing to the area to provide healing. I would worry if it were not doing that."

As always, the things he knew were surprising. He was not at all old, but his experience and learning were endlessly vast.

"Ye don't have to push yerself this way, Tormod," he said.

"Aye, but I canno' sit idly by; the seasickness comes on."

My stomach rumbled but I ignored it. The prospect of food had little appeal. We had long since eaten anything fresh. All we had now was a store of dried and salted beef, with an odd turnip or old onion thrown in as a treat. And with the weather so often wet or misty, we could not even use the ceramic fire pit on deck to cook the fresh fish we caught. Some of the crew ate it raw, but the thought of it made me sick. I ate what

I could but not much more. I had no appetite for anything, really. Being with people, being alone, it was all the same.

We had been at sea for a very long while. The notches in the hold had grown and grown. The horizon line where the light of the sky met the dark of the water was the only visual break, and I spent much of my time staring in its direction.

And then there was the oddness of my nights. The dreams that I had on waking from the fever seemed to have unlocked something deep inside. Every night, from that first night on, I experienced a vision while I slept, a different place, a bit of life that was not my own. They came from all over, but they had something in common — the sparkling light and heat of the carving was there.

But now, many times, there also came an aspect I began to dread. The heat I associated with the tingling warmth became at times unbearable. It was as if my body was aflame, my skin scorched.

As I worked, chips of tar scattered before my blade. *Danger.* I sat up, confused. A thickness floated on the wind, like a sour scent. I inhaled it and cringed. The sky was no longer clear and blue, but dark and overcast. My foot ached, deep inside, as if the bones were swollen. My body was tight and my mouth was uncommonly dry.

We were nearing the harbor. Several ships were anchored there ahead of us. I leaned over the rail to see. Dread rose up inside me the closer we came.

I moved toward the Templar. "Something is wrong," I said. "I feel it."

<hr />

"Seamus, take us wide. Horace, drop the sail." As the Templar called directions to the men below, I walked the deck keeping the ships ahead in sight. The wind whipped past me, billowing my plaid. I watched as it crossed the water, building peaks of white. My sight lifted just as the closest vessel's pennant unfurled. The image of golden lillies floated on a field of blue.

"Tormod, get back."

I ducked and scuttled to his side.

"The markings are Philippe's. We move no closer." The Templar's voice was urgent. Beneath my feet the ship pulled as Seamus corrected course.

"Follow the coast an' put in to the cove two miles on," said the Templar.

A shiver raced through me. Perhaps they had not seen us.

"We go ashore within a candle mark," he said to me. "Be ready." As he spoke, a sharp bristle of irritation crossed Seamus's face.

"I need ye here," the Templar said. "I want a careful

135

watch on the ship. No one leaves, and none enter until we arrive back. I do not intend to be long. If anyone asks why we are here, it is to take on wine from the Santa Marissima Vineyards." He didn't take his eyes off the French ship until we rounded the coast. "Seamus," he said, approaching the wheel, "if anything goes wrong an' we don't return, get a message to the Archbishop."

"Have ye seen something?" Seamus asked.

His body grew still, his eyes fading, distant, reaching for something. "It is like water, a' times as clear as day, and a' others like a murky stream."

I knew not what he meant, but thoughts of the men hunting us were more troubling to me.

The cove was small and shallow. We anchored with no fanfare or issue. The sail was lashed and the lines coiled the moment we tied off. I scrambled to my berth and dressed my foot. Much of the trip had been spent without any covering but a bandage. To go ashore, I needed something sturdier. The thought of jamming my boot over the linen bandage made me cringe, but I got on with it nonetheless. The soft hide stretched as I forced in my foot. It was tight and uncomfortable at first, but I waited it out and the ache seemed to lessen.

Cassiopeia twined around my legs. "I canno' take ye with me, Cass. I don't know what is going to happen." Deep in my body I felt hollow. "Be good, an' I'll bring ye something from shore." The words did not ring true. I could very well never see her again. I reached down to stroke her head and saw that my hand trembled.

When I emerged, the Templar turned and dropped his eyes toward my feet. "Can ye walk in those?"

"Aye. I'll not hold ye back," I said with as much confidence as I could muster.

He smiled faintly. "Ye've said as much before, an' ye didn't. We will take it, as we must."

"Perhaps he should stay behind, Alex." Seamus was at the wheel. I knew by his voice that he was not saying it because he was angry, but still his suggestion got under my skin.

The Templar forestalled my retort. "He is needed. We will get on."

Seamus said nothing and went below. Horace stood at the rail with Geordie, watching as we maneuvered the rope ladder to the lowered coracle. It was a difficult climb for me. I could barely feel the rope beneath the padding in my boot, and I slipped and got tangled up in my rush to get down. Then as my feet touched the boat, I overcorrected my balance and the coracle tilted dangerously. The Templar merely shifted his weight and righted us before we took on any water. "Go slowly, lad. We need to make haste, but not a' the peril o' a dunking."

The trip to shore was quick and yet I seemed to have

no end of difficulty. I had not reckoned actually getting onto the shore. There were far too many rocks to take the boat in close, so we needed to get out in water that was knee-high. To keep my injured foot and boot dry the Templar insisted on carrying me ashore. I thought of Seamus, Geordie, and Horace, and my cheeks burned. Though the distance was short, I felt as if every eye on the ship was trained on me.

"That was hard for ye, lad, eh?"

I blew out a breath and shook my head. "Aye. I didn't like it a bit."

IMPULSIVE GESTURES

The air was cold and damp, swirling around me in gusts I could not avoid. I wrapped my plaid tighter, willing warmth into my body. I thought of the ship we had seen, and there seemed nothing in the world that could warm me again. The Templar took the lead, saying little as we walked. I felt unsettled in a way that I was fast becoming accustomed to.

"We make for Santiago de Compostela," said the Templar. He drew his cloak up over his head and pulled it low over his eyes. I did the same with my plaid. " 'Tis the shrine of the Holy Way. I dare not take the main road. Stay close an' keep yer wits. We may have to move quickly. 'Tis a bit of a walk. Tell me if ye have trouble with yer foot."

I nodded.

Our pace was moderate. Though the Templar's legs were longer, and I was able to keep up, my foot throbbed beneath the wrapping. It was difficult not to limp, but I forced myself to do it, to stand straight and endure. I could feel the Templar's tension and I didn't want to distract him. We walked for at least two marks of the candle, across great swaths of land filled with hills and valleys. Brush and bramble covered much of the ground, catching my legs and tripping me as we walked. Without the sun I had no way to accurately gauge time, but when my stomach set to grumbling, I judged it past our evening meal. We were deep in a strangely fragranced forest by then.

I was hard put to keep the quiet he had set. I needed the reassurance of his voice. "What is that smell? 'Tis not like any o' the forest a' home," I said. The Templar grunted, as if he had not quite heard what I asked.

"I said, the scent here. Do ye know what it is?"

I thought he was going to ignore the question. His

back was as tight as a strung bow, and his eyes peered intently ahead as he walked.

" 'Tis the leaf o' the myrtle," he said quietly. " 'Tis said to have soothing properties. The scent calms the mind an' refreshes the soul."

I went quiet again, hoping against hope that what he had said was true. If there was one thing I craved at that moment, it was peace of mind. I was sick with the thought of the men hunting us.

Traveling a rough path through the forest, we avoided the main road for a time. When there was no other choice, we chanced walking where we could be seen; but as people came within hearing, we darted to the side until they passed. Many of those on the road were in far worse shape than I with my bandaged foot. Their clothes were ragged, and their bodies were gaunt. Their smell, though, was by far the worst thing about them. It was so strong at times, even from our place of concealment, that I covered my nose and mouth with the edge of my plaid and still I felt the constant need to gag.

The Templar spoke when we were once again alone. Perhaps he noticed that I needed a distraction. I jumped at the crackle of leaves and, more than once while I was looking behind, trod on his heels.

"Santiago de Compostela is the final destination o'

a holy pilgrimage an' one o' the greatest sites o' adoration in the world."

"Aye?"

"The story goes that James, one o' Jesus's first four Apostles, was beheaded by the king Herodes, who forbade the Apostle a proper burial. The Disciples smuggled the body out o' Jerusalem, loaded it into a skin boat, an' launched it on the sea.

"Wind an' the guiding hands o' the angels, they say, carried the boat safely here to Compostela. An' the people brought the body to the local queen, Lupa, who 'tis said had a vision that instructed her to give the Apostle a proper burial. She had him laid out in a great marble sarcophagus in the crypt where we head."

I nearly trampled him when he stooped and picked up something small and white from the path. He grunted and recovered his balance quickly. "A little room, Tormod."

"I'm sorry," I mumbled, moving away.

"Scallop shells," he said, looking at the bit he had picked up, "became the symbol o' the skin boat wherein the Apostles laid the body an' now represent this Pilgrimage."

I looked around. Shells littered the path we had just come upon. "They carry them with them?"

"Aye, pinned to their hats or carried in their goods."

Up ahead, the noise of a group of people alarmed me. We had not seen any for quite some time and it was loud to my ears. "Here," he said. "Come this way."

A queue of pilgrims lined up before the doors of the kirk. The Templar led me to the side, and we followed a rough trail to the back stone wall. The land was uneven. Rocks and briars blocked our path and caught our clothes as we made our way.

"Where are we go —"

He swept his arm wide, flattening me against the wall of the kirk. My breath was halting as we listened and waited. I kept my peace but wanted to shriek. Slowly, carefully, he inched the door open and silently moved inside. I followed.

We were in a room, separate from the main kirk. The chamber was completely black and as silent as a tomb. We stood in absolute stillness as the moments ticked by, one by one, until at last I could bear it no longer. "Shall I light a taper?"

My whisper was like a shout in the darkness. His hand shot out and clamped over my mouth. A quick scratch was followed by a burst of light. I shielded my eyes.

Illuminated by the flame, not three hand spans from my face, was a sight that chilled me to the marrow. We were not alone. The Templar had known it all along.

Dark eyes met mine, and they seemed to glow with an inhuman shine.

FRIEND OR FOE

The man was a terrifying sight. He was swathed in many dark and flowing robes, from his veiled head to his sandaled feet. The skin of his face was a deep brown, as if the sun had shone on him for years and toasted him crisply. His fingers were long and thin, and flowed gracefully as he touched his forehead, then chest in greeting. "Salaam, my brother. It is good to see you yet alive."

The Templar breathed out heavily, and I felt the release of tension from his body. He took his hand from my mouth with barely leashed violence. "Tormod, there are times when ye tempt my sword an' my peace o' mind mightily."

I was shaken. I'd done it again. I'd done something stupid, something dangerous, and made him angry.

"Ahram," said the Templar, grasping forearms with the man. "Ye don't know how glad I am to find *ye* here an' no' another." His glance passed over me, and I ducked my head and moved away from them both.

"We have had a watch set for many a night in hopes of your arrival," said the other. His voice had a melodic ring.

"What news have ye?" asked the Templar.

"Mercenaries scout the bays seeking a Knight Templar traveling from the north. They are most persistent in their inquiry. You cannot linger here."

My head snapped up at his words. *Mercenaries? Hired killers?*

"Tell me all," he said quietly.

"They landed two days past, and small parties have been going out at regular intervals. They've men positioned all along the road, and one contingent has moved on inland." His hand found and rested on the haft of his sword, perhaps out of habit. I stepped back a pace in case there was another reason, but he paid me no heed. "I sent men to follow the ones who went on and have not heard back from them yet."

"What direction did they take?"

"East."

The Templar's mouth was tight and furrows stood on either side. He moved to a table near the back wall and lit several tapers. I stood beyond the edge of the light, watching the stranger and wondering at the easy relationship between the two. I had always thought that Arab and Christian hated one another. Clearly these two didn't.

The Templar drew a rolled parchment from beneath his vestments and placed it on the table.

"Tormod, come here." I crossed the space slowly, looking down on what he held. It was the map I'd drawn, but set in a much larger tract of land.

The Templar spread the parchment and bade me hold two corners. He held the others and began tracing a path with his finger. "We must travel here," he said.

The dark man moved closer into the light to look, and I sucked in a breath. A series of strange runes were inscribed in the skin of his cheek. He felt my stare and turned to me. I was startled by the near total blackness of his eyes.

A white mantle stirred. The sound of battling swords cut the air. Black eyes flashed as blood splashed dark runes.

Focus. Ground. Shield. I barely remembered the commands, so strong was the vision. As it winked out, I wavered, backing away from the man, my eyes still locked with his. He said nothing, turning to the map.

"Tormod, the map," reminded the Templar. My eyes beseeched him, but either he didn't notice or chose not to act on it. I reached out once again and held the edges, carefully avoiding contact with the Arab. I needed to tell the Templar he could not trust the man at our side, but I could say nothing.

"We have reasoned that these markings here are stars that are set in the sky as it appears over this land. They will appear clearly during the July moon. Using those calculations, I place the map's destination here — beyond the mountains, deep in the Languedoc. Have you been in this region?" he asked.

"I have not. It is not a place that would welcome our kind," said the Arab.

"Ye should be welcome in all lands," said the Templar.

The Arab dipped his head in acknowledgment. "The ports are patrolled," he said. "You will best be served moving across the land."

The Templar stared, thinking. "Aye, perhaps," he replied. "We must move quickly, an' those seeking us must be diverted. I'll send my men on ahead by sea. If chased, they should be safe enough without my presence. The enemy seeks a Knight Templar an' entourage. Seamus does not wear the white as yet. I would ask that ye take yer men to the ship an' tell Seamus the plan. We will move on as pilgrims. Keep watch for us at Ponferrada. We travel the Holy Road."

"May Allah watch over you, Alexander. You seem to have more enemies than friends these days."

"I'll be pleased to have His protection."

The Arab left, with a cursory glance that passed over me. I was glad of it. We stayed only long enough to

reroll the map and douse the candles. A storm was building. The air fairly crackled with energy.

"We go on alone, Tormod. How fares yer foot?" he
asked, climbing the bank of dirt behind the kirk.

It ached, but I was too caught up in my worries to
dwell on it. "I'm well," I said. At the top of the slope, we
quickly angled east over a meadow of tall grass. Night
had fallen while we were inside. The damp from the rain
seeped into my boots and in moments it was fair uncomfortable, but I said nothing.

"Ye're excessively quiet," he said after a while. "Let
it go. Ye need not obsess about it every time I snap at ye,
Tormod." His voice was peevish.

"No, I'm not. Speaking out when I did was a stupid
thing to do, an' I will try not to do it again, but that's
not it." I suddenly felt unsure about telling him what
really bothered me.

"Ye had another vision, while we were inside," he
guessed.

He had recognized the signs. "Aye. An' I feel that I
must tell ye, though I know ye don't want me to."

He said nothing.

"Beware the man with the runes," I said. "Danger
an' pain surround him."

"In this ye're mistaken. Ahram is like my brother. I
would trust him with my life."

"Then ye throw yer life away!"

I cringed expecting another reprimand, but instead he said, "Good to see ye returning to yerself, Tormod. I thought ye had lost yer spark with yer toes. But that is enough."

It was said with a quiet authority. I shut my mouth then. We walked for a moment in awkward silence. I asked, as much out of curiosity as out of the need to get back on a solid keel with him, "Will they find us?"

"I'll do my best to protect ye, Tormod. I pledge that on my life."

It was not a guarantee, but I felt all the better for it.

REST AHEAD

We worked our way across the land in near silence and constant watchfulness. Keeping far from the main paths, we skirted the villages when we came on them. The Templar's pace was quick, and I struggled to stay abreast, or at the very least, right behind him. My foot burned with the unaccustomed exertion, but I didn't complain. I had no idea where we were headed, but it was clear that we needed to arrive, wherever it was, in great haste. It took all the willpower in me, but I didn't initiate conversation. He was troubled, and though I would have liked to think I could help, I knew that I could not.

It was late when he broke the silence. "The Order has safe houses scattered throughout the Continent. We will make for one I know. 'Tis just beyond a league from here. Can ye bear it? We dare not stop. They are close. The carving is glowing in the depth o' my sporran. I can feel the heat. There is danger."

I craned my neck around, sure that they must be waiting behind the next bush. The constant ache of my foot until then was not so tremendous that I could not put it out of my mind, yet the moment he mentioned it, the pain seemed to come on doubly. "I am well enough," I said, gritting my teeth as I stumbled over a snarl of roots at my feet.

He looked on my pinched face with doubt. We had been traveling through a thinly forested area. Around us now were many stripling trees. He took his sword from its hilt and hacked at one of the dry limbs. "We will clean it properly later, but for now use this to support some o' yer weight. 'Tis not much, but the best I can offer at the moment."

It was awkward and no help at first, but after a while I was better at making the stick and leg move in unison. It didn't, however, take away the pain. I felt more

149

tired and weak as the night progressed. The moon remained behind a dark scud of cloud, and I stumbled often.

"Rest is not long away." His voice was harsh, and I felt ashamed for my weakness, as if I had failed the faith he entrusted in me.

"Ye mistake my mood. Ye're recently arisen from the sickbed and ye cannot be expected to travel this way. Yet ye must."

I wanted to keep on, to live up to his expectations, but I was having trouble keeping the ground before my eyes steady. We moved deeper into the forest. The trees grew dense, and in the darkness my eyes and legs were uncertain.

The moon slid from its place in the clouds just as we came on a croft set near the base of a steep grade. It was so like home that for a moment I slowed.

I could well imagine that off to the side in a paddock were sheep and a goat. And in the morning a rooster would strut with great purpose across the rocky lane that led to an old stone hut.

The Templar read my mood. He said nothing of it, but nodded to me.

At the crude wooden door, he knocked a strange pattern. An old woman peered out with pale and wary eyes, seeking his features within the hood.

I was surprised when he pushed back the cowl. He had been so careful during our travels. The woman started visibly and quickly sketched the sign of the cross. Then, with a rapid-fire burst of speech in a language I didn't understand, she took both his hands in hers.

"Aye, Marta. It is truly myself." He laughed; his smile was warm and wide. I found myself smiling as well.

We were quickly drawn inside and I was directed to a mat before a central fire. I stumbled to it, scarcely keeping my eyes open. The woman drew a bowl of stew from the heavy pot hanging from the ridgepole. The smell of the soup, and the scent of the wood burning beneath, again struck in me such a longing for home that my eyes teared. I ate quickly, swallowing over the lump in my throat, and finally lay down. The buzz of their conversation lulled me, and I gave in readily to sleep.

The Templar woke me before the sun began its ascent into the morning sky. "Our presence here will not go unnoticed. We dare not stay 'til nightfall." It was a small phrase, but it brought me awake, though I felt I had just gone to sleep.

"I thought it was safe. They'll look here?" I mumbled.

"Aye, but perhaps not for a while."

I rubbed my eyes, pushing aside the sleep that still tried to claim me. Sitting up slowly, I looked around, barely remembering the room.

"Here. These will give ye a start." He set a platter of lush blue-black fruit between us.

"What are they?"

"These are grapes, Tormod. Marta has a large vineyard behind the hut. She and her family harvest the fruit an' make wines an' juice from them. They supply the priories of France an' Spain."

"Would that not take more than a small single family?"

He smiled. "Aye. But Marta's family is not small. Her husband, God rest his soul, began a partnership with the Templars. Marta runs it now with the help o' her sons. Many o' our knights, sergeants, an' apprentices work for a time in the vineyard an' winery. Do ye recall the fields o' vines we have been passing through?"

I nodded.

"Did ye feel a shift in the life o' the land?"

I had noticed the change. We had moved from waving plains of wheat to lush and verdant fields of tangled vines.

"Aye. The life's beat is deeper. 'Tis like a different resonance strummed beneath my feet an' in the air."

"Aye. The land is ancient. All o' this is Marta's. There are hundreds o' acres o' vines an' a small town just beyond the hills to our west. Marta lives out here in her modest hut out o' preference, with one or two o' the men looking in on her."

"So how do ye know each other?" I asked.

"I apprenticed here for a time," he said, stretching his feet out in front of him.

It pleased me to imagine the Templar toiling among the vines, an image even more fitting than that of him in full battle regalia. The more I knew of him and of the Templars, the more conflicted my picture of them became. Nothing was as black-and-white as I had thought. I was slowly beginning to understand the Order through him, and the more I knew about them, the more I wanted to know.

"Did ye rest at all?" I asked unable to restrain the yawn that stretched my words.

"I did," he said.

I didn't truly believe him.

"Here, change into these." For the first time I noticed that he was wearing the plain brown serge robe of a peasant. He had given me one as well. "We will travel out in the open with a group returning from the pilgrimage. They are staying a' the main house by the winery an' leave shortly."

Rested by the night's respite, I shrugged into the

foreign clothes. My robe was old and a bit large, but its well-worn surface felt soft on my skin, and the drape was less heavy than my plaid. I felt silly in the old straw hat, but the Templar insisted it would be valuable both as a disguise and as a way to keep the heat off. To complete my look, he draped my neck with a beaded crucifix of wood.

"Take off yer boot an' clean the wound in the bucket outside. Then wrap this around before ye put it back on." He handed me a bundle of soft fur, the hide of a rabbit.

Outside, the morning air was chill and damp. There was a well down behind the house, from which I drew a bucket of cold water. Sitting on the ground, I set to it.

The hide of my boot had stretched with the extra padding and it slipped off easily, but the interior of the linen was dry and stuck. My stitches had not fared well. Some had torn and bled. The skin around them was red and irritated, and it burned now that the bindings were off. Quickly, before I lost my nerve, I poured water over the injury. Pain flooded my mind with waves of heat.

The Templar came out moments later. "Here, this ought to help as well." He had stripped the bark from a strong limb. A much sturdier stick, already dried, hardened, and more than likely used before, leaned against the well. I stuffed my plaid into a sack of supplies and adjusted my robes to match his, keeping my sporran beneath.

He seemed fully ready to leave. "We will travel weaponless?" I asked.

"Not entirely," he replied. "I will have knives, an' ye, yer dagger, an' o' course my sword still sits in its place." He shifted the straw hat to reveal the hilt. The rest lay hidden beneath his robe. "Still, it would no' be easy to get to this way, so . . ." He pulled his staff apart and a thin wicked blade gleamed in the half-light.

"God's breath!" I was astounded. "Where can I get one o' those?"

The Templar laughed. "There are times when ye're much older than yer years, an' others when I am reminded o' the lad from the village."

"Where did ye get that?" I asked, looking at my own staff to see if it had a hidden blade as well. *Nothing.*

"I made it long ago, when I was here, working." His eyes had a far-off look, as if he were remembering that other time.

Marta had laid aside some food to take with us on the journey and brought it out to us in a linen sack. I was beginning to feel the stirrings of excitement over our covert travel, a definite shift from my nerves of the night before.

I had finished washing, and my foot was packed in the soft fur. My boot slid back on snugly. When I looked up, I realized that the Templar's eyes had gone wide and unfocused. Almost immediately he snapped to.

"Tormod, come. We must leave. A band o' soldiers is traveling this way. They approach from the south and will be here within a candle mark. We cannot wait for the rest o' the pilgrims. The carving feels as if it will burn a hole in my sporran. We must be away, now."

The Templar spoke rapid Spanish and Marta came out of the hut, looking off down the road warily. The Templar rolled his vestments into his sack, and with a wave we were off. The ground was rough and rocky, and my foot was tired from our forced travel of the night. Still, I hurried.

As we gained the slope into the woods, a nasty chill trickled along my spine and I looked down. At the very edge of the snaking road that led to Marta's, I saw the faint outline of men approaching.

"Into the trees," the Templar said, hurrying me. "They canno' see us, but we take no chances. Do no' stop or slow to look back again."

I hurried behind him.

We traveled many leagues. Even as the sun slid from the sky once more, we continued. I was glad of the rest taken at Marta's, for even after we broke for food, we didn't make camp but continued our forced pace.

"How could they have found us so quickly?" I asked, hurrying after the Templar.

"I don't know." The answer was short and didn't brook an invitation for more. It was as if he'd sunk deep into himself, as if I was not there at all.

When at last we broke for sleep, I am fairly certain that only I laid my head. The Templar sat with his back to a sturdy rock. His broad sword lay across his knees, and though he didn't kneel or close his eyes, I heard the steady drone of his prayers.

ATTACK

A woman's cloak lay tattered on the ground. Frightened eyes plead for mercy. Cries rent my ears.

"Tormod. Wake up. It's just a dream."

I was awake, but the vision would not leave me. "Get away! Stop! She knows nothing!" I shouted.

"Focus. Ground. Shield. Push it aside. Listen." The Templar's voice was in my ears, in my mind, and yet I could do nothing to heed him.

"Leave her alone! Stop!" A blade glinted red. Her scream and mine were one.

A strange, cold thickness washed over me, enveloping my mind. I latched on to it and let it separate me from the darkness. The vision faded. But its memory lived on. Tears trickled down my cheeks.

"Shhh, leanabh. Hush ye now. Embrace the stillness. Feel the cold." I realized I was in the clearing, beneath the trees, huddled against him. My tears would not stop. Beyond my mind, I heard his instruction again. *Reach, Tormod. Distance yourself.*

I understood then and embraced the peace he was projecting. In moments I was still. My eyes dried and awkwardly I pulled away. "I'm sorry."

He left me to deal with the embarrassment of my tears, tending the fire, then bringing me a skin of water.

"Do ye want to tell me?" he finally asked quietly.

My head hurt and my heart ached. The words were slow coming, and when they came, it felt like someone else was speaking them. "Marta is dead. They killed her after we left."

His face paled and his body hunched in pain.

"I should not have gone there. I brought them down on her. She was an innocent," he said. His anguish was painful to watch.

I knew not what made me speak. I had no experience in anything of this sort, save the words my da might have uttered in the same situation to me. "Ye did what ye thought best. Ye didn't kill Marta. Those men did. It was not yer fault."

"It is," he insisted. "They will stop at nothing." All of his usual light dimmed. He looked weary and sad beyond my experience. "An' then it will end."

He moved to a nearby tree and laid his hand to the bark. "The heartbeat o' the living land will thrum no more."

His intensity was frightening.

"The communion we share with all o' the earth an' its creatures is a gift beyond measure, an' yet 'tis something foreign an' strange to those whose touch is blind. In ignorance they will destroy us. We canno' allow the nongifted to possess the carving. I have seen it."

My skin grew cold. "What do ye mean?"

"Ye have the vision o' what is to come, Tormod. I have a gift that shows me not only what is an' what will be, but also what might be. My vision is split. The Order has not seen another with a gift o' this kind."

"So 'tis as ye were telling me before. Sometimes the truth o' the future can change. Ye've seen it?"

"Aye," he replied. "One future shows the carving broken an' the land's power gone still an' silent. There are no gifted in that vision, Tormod."

It was as if I had been struck. Only recently had I learned of this Brotherhood. To know that it might be on the verge of elimination, to never again feel the life that ebbed and flowed through the land — the thought was devastating.

"What o' the other future?" I asked.

"The same world, rich in the power as never before, with a new breed o' Guardian an' a legacy that goes on. Generations will birth new generations o' gifted who will serve an' protect the life o' the land. The carving gave me both o' those visions. I believe that 'tis up to ye an' I to influence one outcome or the other. We are the pebbles — or boulders — that have been thrown into the stream."

He was exhausted, his eyes were red-rimmed and his body slumped. "Try an' get some more sleep, Tormod. We're up again with the dawn."

"I canno' sleep. Ye need it more. Let me take the watch. Ye canno' go on without rest."

I could tell he was torn, but he knew I was right in this. He sighed and took a last glance around our shelter. "Aye. Don't let me sleep more than three marks o' the candle. We must travel by night long before the sun rises."

It pleased me to know that he trusted in me enough to sleep. I took out my dagger and fisted it tightly. The vision of those men and what they had done to Marta was still strong before my mind's eye. And though I was prepared to take this watch, nothing could stop me from jumping at every sound that broke the night's stillness. They were out there looking for us.

I spoke truly. There was no danger of my falling asleep on a watch with thoughts of our pursuers racing through my mind. I hadn't prayed in a long while, but needed it tonight. My prayers were not what others might think appropriate, but I didn't care. I spoke direct and made no apologies.

Lord, how could Ye let that happen to her? Why are Ye letting this happen to any o' us? I shivered with revulsion as thoughts of what happened to Marta returned. It was so brutal, the violence of it beyond imagining. She was a small old woman. *Why?*

Mine was not much of a prayer, but it was all I had. I was torn up inside — about Marta, my damaged foot, the constant need to run. The Lord had not saved any of us. Maybe there was no Lord out there at all, just the power of the land and whatever held it constant. Such a thought would have Da on me with a strap. Nonetheless, the troubling thought stayed with me all night.

I was tired when the moon began its descent. The sounds of the night — the creak of the woods and the song of the insects — were making it worse. I woke the Templar with a quiet hand. He sat up right away; he had been awake.

He knelt and began the Matins, the Morning Prayer. I yawned and dropped beside him, adding my voice to his knowing he expected it.

Shortly thereafter we set out. We ate as we walked, a handful of dried beef and cheese, washed down with water from the skin we shared.

"We will make for Pamplona," said the Templar. "Following the pilgrim route through the mountains. We must break the pattern o' what is expected. They'd not think we'd travel out in the open, an' so that is the way we will take."

My legs were tired but growing stronger each day we walked. My foot seemed to ache less, though perhaps I had just grown used to the feeling. The Templar remained quiet, deep in his own thoughts, leaving me to obsess about the men hunting us.

We traveled the land as the cold of the night hung low over the hills and valleys. And as the sun began to rise, we crested a hill that overlooked a wide dirt road.

"That is it, Tormod, the Holy Road," the Templar said.

It didn't look all that holy to me. It seemed just a road, but nonetheless I followed its snaking path with my eyes. Even as early as it was, there were travelers out and about. A thin trickle of peasants — men, women, and children alike — walked the road.

The Templar watched for movement at the road's edges and, seeing none of the hunters, deemed it time we move on down the slope. As the pilgrims grew near, we ambled from our place and trailed their group. We spoke to no one; the Templar drew his hat low and I did the same.

None of the travelers seemed to mind our joining their group. It was the way of the road. Others added to the queue as the day progressed, and eventually we were in the middle of the pack and no longer at its end.

The heat that rose with the sun was stifling, especially beneath the dark robe. Sweat dripped down my back and neck in a nasty stream. I would have given anything to throw off the peasant robe and hat and bare my skin to the air. But we could not take the chance of discovery.

There were times during the trek when the road before me wavered, but the Templar seemed to know just when to ply me with water and dried meat so that I remained upright. It was a long and difficult journey. The land was one big series of hills that dipped and climbed at steep intervals. I didn't complain, though, even when the breaks came not as often as I'd hoped.

We traveled a week in their company without mishap. By then, I almost was able to forget that we were hunted. And this was nearly our undoing.

We stopped for a rest by the side of the road. I could feel the life of a small stream beyond the trees and with a skin in hand set out for it. Water trickled softly over the rocks. I bent and splashed some on my face, washing the grime of the road down my neck.

Hide. The thought echoed urgently in my mind. I spun, waiting for the attack. There was nothing, yet I crouched and made my way to the trees' edge to peer beyond.

Two men had approached, soldiers caked in the dust of the road. I searched for the Templar. He was not with the group. Reaching, I sensed him by a tree opposite the pilgrims.

An old man I had shared some of my dried beef with pointed off down the road away from the direction we had come.

The soldier leaned in threateningly. "Down the road," the words of the old man came to me as he gestured again. A burst of impatience brushed the edges of my mind. I turned toward its direction and gasped as the second soldier grabbed a child. The family had only joined us the night before. The father held the mother as she strained to go to the boy. "We know nothing!" he shouted. The soldier's blade glinted in the sun as it came to rest against the small, unprotected neck of the boy. I could hear the boy's blood pulsing in my head.

"Let him go." The Templar stepped from the safety of the trees, his hands held high in surrender. "Ye have no need o' a child. Release him, now."

A strange hum floated on the air, a high-pitched whine that hovered just at the edges of my hearing. It brushed my skin with an odd heat that made my legs weak and the inside of my head itch. The soldier holding the knife seemed unable to make a decision — until the blade against the boy's neck dropped away. *Run.* The command snapped inside my mind and that of the boy, who scrambled to the safety of his father's arms.

"*Que faites-vous?*" The first soldier shouted angrily.

"*Que?*" The second shook his head, as if he were coming out of a daze.

"*Rapidement, obtenez-le!*" cried the first. Both men charged the Templar, and I rose from my crouch ready to help. The Templar moved quickly. His upraised hands knocked away his hat, dipped over his head to the hilt of the sword, and drew in a motion that I barely marked. The first man to reach him caught the swipe of the blade deep in the crease of his neck. Blood spurted bright, and the child began to scream. The second soldier followed, drawing his sword on the run, and he and the Templar engaged. Metal on metal screeched in the still, hot air as the Templar parried and swung. The soldier's advance slowed. In moments he'd lost ground. The group of travelers scattered with cries of fear.

The soldier might have been adept in his company, but the Templar was far superior in one-on-one combat. As the man struggled, the Templar's blade descended like a strike of lightning, sliding inside his guard, sinking deep in the soldier's chest.

With a sharp cry of surprise the soldier dropped to his knees, grasping at the wound as the blood flowed from his body. Then, all at once, he fell sideways and moved no more.

The Templar approached and made the sign of the cross over both men. "Tormod," he called. "Come quickly. There will be others."

The boy's father helped us drag the heavy bodies behind some rough scrub. My legs were shaking, making it hard to move them. My robe was damp with blood. "What will we do?" I asked breathlessly.

He spoke not a word but moved quickly along the road past the pilgrims. I trailed after. None of the travelers moved to follow us, and in moments we were out of sight. When we rounded a curve, the Templar left the road. I followed. Our plans had changed.

We hiked for a long time at a quick pace. My body

was tired, but there was nothing for it but to move on. Those who sought us were close behind.

The sun slipped low in the sky, but the air remained still and stifling. I wanted to keep silent, to let him lead us and think out whatever had drawn him into himself, but there came a point when I could hold back no longer.

"How did ye do it?"

He knew what I asked. " 'Tis simple, for one o' our kind," he said, raising his arms and turning his palms down as he spoke. "It only works small miracles — just a bit o' shifting o' the natural forces. 'Tis not something ye should ever rely on, but it helps in a bind." His stride remained strong, but he made room beside him on the path we'd been traveling single file. "What did ye see?" he asked, the teacher in him surfacing again.

"The first man hesitated."

"Aye. Good. Notice the small things. He was hesitant, afraid before I'd done anything."

I realized that he spoke true. The one he had approached looked leery and frightened. He was young, perhaps not long in his post.

The Templar went on. "It only worked in the moment o' surprise. It would not have done much on more than one, particularly if they were bent on coming down on us."

"But how?" I pressed.

"Hmm, how to describe it?" he mused. "Ye can sense the life o' the land, aye?"

I nodded.

"Well try an' see it in yer mind's eye. Imagine it lifting right up out o' the earth an' filling the air. Then with yer mind whisper it into the form ye need."

"What form? I don't know what ye mean."

"Well, if ye want to delay someone from acting, ye whisper a screen o' uncertainty. Ye project fear an' hesitation. It will only work if the person ye're whispering it on feels that way to start. Our gift plays on emotion — yers, an' theirs."

"And if ye just don't want them to see ye?"

"Then ye whisper a bit o' preoccupation. Ye turn their minds to something that would consume them."

"Can I do it?" I asked.

"Aye. With practice. If ever we're not on the run again, we'll work on it together."

A VISITOR

Travel for the next few days was tense but uneventful. That is if you think uneventful covers walking across leagues of land with little stop or rest, with a fear that makes you start and jump every few minutes. But, compared to what it might have been, our journey was blessedly peaceful.

And then it all shifted. On the banks of the River Sil — with the bloodred sun shimmering rays of unending heat down on us, and the water, a cool and murky brown — our quiet came to an end. I stumbled to the edge, dipping my hands and soaking my face. My body felt oddly tight, as if a string that stretched from my feet to my eyes had been wound to snapping. I shook my head to clear the haziness creeping over me.

A sea of blue-and-gold pennants snapped in the wind. Rows of silver helm gleamed.

Focus. Ground. Shield. I came to with a lurch to find the Templar stooped beside me, the carving out and awash in a gleaming light.

"Danger awaits at Ponferrada," I said.

"Ahram is seeking us," he said nearly at the same time.

"But . . ."

He said nothing, just stood and continued on through the cover of high grass that grew along the bank of the river. I followed with a lump in my throat. The carving had glowed. I saw the armies. Why would he still go there?

It was the first time I had any doubt about a decision

of the Templar. It made me feel badly, like I was breaking a trust of some kind. I kept quiet, letting him lead the way, allowing the ache of my foot to occupy the best part of my mind.

We came in sight of the walls at sundown and camped in a thicket below the road. "Sleep while ye can, Tormod," he said. "I will wait for Ahram; then we'll go on to the preceptory."

Thoughts of Ahram didn't make me feel better, nor did the idea that we would go to Ponferrada when clearly we could not. I fished my plaid from the sack, needing its comfort and warmth, and by an old stump I hunkered down. I must have slept then, for I awoke to a heart beating painfully. The darkness around me was absolute. I listened for the animals native to the woods, but it was unusually quiet, not the chirp of a cicada, not the cry of an owl.

A snap of underbrush brought me to my feet, my dagger extended. I nearly embedded it in the back of the Templar before realizing he was standing in front of me with his sword held at the ready.

"Peace, Alexander." The voice was strong and I recognized it immediately.

"Ahram," the Templar said with relief, his sword dropping to his side. "What has happened?"

RESPITE

"Your ship has been taken. Your sergeant and a monk have been detained, but this is not the place to speak. Ponferrada is overrun with the armies of King Philippe."

The Templar seemed surprised. I was shocked by his reaction. He had held the carving. I assumed that he'd had the same vision as mine.

He scrubbed fiercely at his beard, then his scalp. "Think. Why is it that I canno' think?"

I don't know why it struck me then, but I suddenly knew without a doubt what was ailing him. The carving. When I handled it on the ship, it drew strength and energy from me. He'd carried it constantly, and I had seen his drawn look many a night as I was drowsily moving toward sleep. If I had been drained by just a few of the visions, and he was receiving them day and night, how much more affected was he? I resolved to speak of it at the first opportunity.

In the darkness I could barely see, but I keenly felt the lifeblood of men behind the Arab leader. Two, clearly guards by their solid flank of him, waited silently as he spoke. I noticed what I hadn't in our previous encounter. His English was fluent, if slightly accented.

"Come, let us be away from here."

Ahram and his men led the way. The night was black as pitch, but they moved with unerring accuracy. I was, for my part, so bone-weary that it was all I could do to put one foot ahead of the other and pray for our travel's end.

The hum of the Templar and Ahram's steady conversation played at the edge of my hearing. My foot throbbed. Rest was sparse today. I could do little more than concentrate on keeping my legs strong beneath me. And yet even that was more than I could manage.

I do not know what it was that caused me to stumble, probably nothing more than the drag of my foot, but suddenly, I was on my face in the dirt and the others had to quickly adjust their stride to keep from tromping on me. What was worse, I could not seem to rise.

The Templar was beside me at once. "Tormod, are ye all right?"

"Aye." I wanted to get up then, I truly did, but there seemed no path between my mind and my body.

"Ahram," he said. "Help me."

Between them I was somehow righted, but when I tried to shift my weight to the leg, I crumpled again.

"Why did ye not tell me it was this bad," said the Templar. I felt like a bairn being taken to task and straightened, trying to ignore the fiery jags shooting through me.

"I'm fine. I just canno' seem to get my legs to work. Give me a moment an' I'll be all right."

"No. Ye can go no farther," he said, scanning the area for danger.

"But ye canno' afford to stop," I protested. "Ye have to go on. Leave me here. I'll rest a bit an' catch up to ye."

He looked at me as if I'd grown several heads and could not tell which one was speaking. "Are ye daft? There's no way ye would ever find yer way alone."

I could not have felt worse, or at least that's what I thought at the time, but I was wrong. Staring at the face of the Templar, I realized that I was exceedingly hot. And the dark seemed to close in on me quickly. I shook my head, but it did me no good. The ground was coming up to meet me, and I could do nothing about it.

A few moments later I woke, with my body folded like a potato sack over the shoulder of one of the Arab men. My ribs felt like they'd been beaten, and my back was stretched. "Stop!" I cried. "Put me down!" My face was aflame and my nose full of the spicy smell of his body.

"We canno' do it, Tormod. We have to get ye to the next preceptory. Ye need a healer. The injury is weeping and red. If we don't care for it soon, it will not go well for ye."

"I can walk," I insisted. " 'Tis true. Just let me show ye."

He moved close and said, "I'm sorry, Tormod. Ye're far from the safety o' home. I have to protect ye the best way I know."

I heard and felt his exhaustion and I held my tongue, wishing that I had never complained, never been a burden to this man already so taxed. I vowed that I would be better, do more to help, and cause him no worries.

It was hard, I tell you. Mine was not an easy transport. Even though my foot didn't hurt as much, hanging the way I was made my head feel light. I was lucky that the distance was not as much as it might have been. But better still, not long after the first man traded me to the second, I asked if I could not sit at his back with my legs and arms wrapped around.

It was strange. Though the man bore no resemblance to my da, I had a quick flash thought of doing just this, riding his back when I was a bairn. My throat quickened and my eyes filmed. As luck would have it, we came on the preceptory just when I most needed saving from my thoughts of the past.

It seemed less a preceptory than a fair-sized croft. I

slid my legs from their cramped position around the waist of the man carrying me, and the sudden drag forced him to let me down. I rued the decision straight off, as hot jabs of pain rippled through my foot. Slowly I limped to the Templar's side. He quickly put his arm around my waist to support me. "Just a bit more. I know ye can make it."

As we passed through the last of the trees, I had never felt so keenly that I'd come home. The face of the guard was not familiar, but the strong red cross on the white of his vestments brought a relief that had been long away.

We straggled up the road bedraggled and so dead on our feet that the last few steps were a pure trial. "Can ye stand?" the Templar asked of me.

"Aye," I said, and fought through the sudden wash of disorientation caused by my effort. The Templar approached the guard at the door of the manor house and spoke several words, some of which I recognized as his name.

A tall, broad-shouldered, older knight crossed the courtyard before us, eyeing our party with ill-concealed wariness. He had a strong profile and sharp gray eyes that seemed to miss nothing. Though he didn't speak, I felt power issue from him, as if he glowed with something vital, something unearthly, holy even. I could do nothing but gawk.

The Templar stepped forward. "Grand Master." His relief was obvious. "I feared never to cross yer path. There is much we must discuss." The man greeted the Templar, clasping forearms. "Well met, Alexander. I am ever your servant." His voice was like thunder before the rain. Deep, rumbling, purposeful.

There was something in their position, mayhap the posture or the light.

A rush of sound rose in my ears, the furor of a crowd bent on destruction. Against the purple of an evening sky, the billow of white robes glimmered. The red glow of a spark kindled dark wood. Smoke lifted and curled. And gray eyes flashed with anger and conviction.

I crumpled to the ground, as an all-encompassing blackness took me beyond the night, beyond the preceptory, and beyond the pain, to a peace that filled my entire being.

ABANDONED

A horrid smell filled my mouth and nose. I twisted away, trying to breathe, but it followed me wherever I moved. I shoved at it, fighting to keep from retching up whatever remained in my stomach.

"Here, here, lad. I mean ye no harm. I just need ye to wake."

I woke, but the vision that had caused me to reel hung before my mind's eye. "The Templar, Alexander, where is he? I need to see him straightaway!"

"A fellow Scot, are ye?" the healer crouched before me exclaimed. "Well, whatever ye need to speak o' will have to bide, lad. He's closed up with the Grand Master. I don't expect ye'll hear from him again tonight. And still, there is this wound we must be tending."

My insides felt a jumble. I had fainted, and the Templar had left me. Just gone off about his business as if I didn't count, or he didn't care. I had a lump the size of a stone in my throat.

"Be ye all right, lad?" The voice of the man was not familiar, but his brogue was. And this settled me a bit. I looked around for the first time. I lay on a pallet of thick straw in a room that smelled strongly of herbs. It was dim, lit only by a small oil lamp set far from me. A small man dressed in the brown linen of a monk had his back to me, and before I could reckon what he was about, he peeled the boot, and rabbit skin I had cushioned it with, clear off my foot.

"Yow, that hurts like the devil! What are ye about, man?" I tried to jerk my foot away from him.

"I know it hurts, lad. I'll be gentle with ye in just a moment, but it has to come off. Ye need tending. 'Tis raw an' swollen from yer travel." His voice had a rough lilt to it, and I responded to his authority. It was clear he was a healer, if not from his manner, then from his place of trade. I was in a stillroom. I'd seen one before in our village. All about me hung herbs and plants drying in the warmth of the room. Lined up tidily on a large, plain table were jars of various sizes, sifting screens, a mortar and pestle, and a variety of clear vials with odd-colored liquids in them.

"Bless the good Lord's bones!" he exclaimed. "Ye've sorely tended this bit. There's a story here, to be sure. An' ye but a lad, traveling far afield on foot." He spoke quickly and so much so that I would have been hard-pressed to get a word in edgewise, but I was not of a mind to speak of my journey.

"There now," he said. "That's the last o' it. Let's take a look at that foot, then." He moved to the other side of me, and I saw his face for the first time. It was a good face, strong and caring. Carefully he prodded and turned me, so as best to see by the light in the room. It took much not to flinch, but oddly enough no pain did I feel with his efforts. Instead I felt a very strange tingling from my ankle, down my foot, and into the area that was most damaged.

I looked up into his face then and gasped. His eyes were not focused. They were in the vague far-off place I knew when I was in the visions. Without knowing how or why, I let myself drift in the same manner, not looking at the man, but seeing what it was he saw. I was shocked by it.

Just as I recognized the flow of sap in a tree, I saw in my mind's eye the inner workings of my body. I saw and felt the rush of the energy he directed deep into the wound. I was astounded. Though I could not credit the fact, it was plain that he was healing the bit where my toes used to be.

His work took no more than a few moments, and I felt myself shift back into my own world as my other sense drifted away. He cleaned the area with some soap that smelled much like the plants that surrounded us. " 'Tis a miracle," I whispered reverently.

"Aye," he said, not bothering to deny what he had been doing. "A gift given by God, not o' myself, ye know. I *see* that ye have the abilities."

"I have the vision," I said. Save the Templar, it was the first time I'd spoken to any about it.

"Aye. Ye have that, too. But ye also have the healing. 'Tis just beneath the surface, waiting for ye to learn how to use it." He cleaned away the bandages and the matted rabbit fur and straightened up his work area.

"I felt ye watching with yer other senses. Ye need only to be trained or to experiment. In time yer healing powers will be as strong as mine."

I didn't know what to say. *A healing gift? Mine?*

"I know from yer words that ye come o' Scotia, but I cannot place the accent. I am from Arbroath, myself."

I was reminded that I must watch my words. Still, he was obviously one of us. "I am from the fishing village o' Leith. Tormod MacLeod is my name. My mam is o' the Highlands and my da o' the Lowlands. 'Tis why I speak oddly."

"There's no oddly about it," he said. "'Tis a Scot ye are, and pleased I am to hear again the lilt o' my home. I am Bertrand Beaton. Tell me, lad, what brings ye so far from home in such a state?"

"I am to be an apprentice. I travel now with a knight o' the Order toward the land o' the most holy." Not the truth, but I couldn't readily tell him more. He patted my knee. "'Tis fine, lad. 'Tis none o' my affair. Just curiosity."

I let out a breath of relief and changed the subject. "How do ye know how to heal that way?"

He moved to the table to finish grinding herbs he had obviously been working at before I arrived. "Much o' it just came to me as a child. I was forever out on the shores, mending the sea creatures that washed up with an injury. We lived a ways from the rest of the world, ye know. My da was a fisher and so was I. The village was a good day's travel away." He dusted off the pestle, poured the ground leaves into a vial, and corked it.

"Then, one day, a Knight Templar appeared at our croft. He spoke to my da about me joining the Order. I didn't know then that there were others with the ability I had. Many I met later, through my training." He cleaned the work bowl and stowed it away beneath the table, then brushed his hands together and looked around his workroom. "The rest is history. I was brought to Balantrodoch and my training began. I have been all over the world and healed many o' our brethren since then. I am here now. Who knows where tomorrow, but 'tis a good life. To know that I'm doing what I love an' making whatever contribution I might is gratifying."

I wriggled my remaining toes and tested my weight on the foot. It felt so good in comparison that I did a bit of a reel. He watched with a smile.

"I do miss the shores o' home, though. I miss my ocean, my family. I hope to return someday." It was a melancholy thought, and I could relate to it well.

"I miss home as well," I said quietly. My eyes met his, and again I was surprised to see that his gaze had drifted wide. "Ye have much ahead o' ye, Tormod

MacLeod. If ye should find yourself in need, come to me, laddie. I will help in any way I can."

I didn't know what to say. It didn't matter, for just then a runner from the Grand Master arrived. "You're to come with me," said the boy. He wore the black tunic of a trainee.

A VISION WRITTEN

The room I was shown to was simple. It held but two beds, a stool, and a small writing table. Quills, parchment, and an ink bottle lay on the table, and a thick candle sputtered, giving light to the room. I was beyond tired, but when I finally lay down, I could not sleep. I had much to think on.

I knew that the writing supplies had not been laid out for me, but I moved toward them nonetheless, as if drawn. In truth I missed my shipboard studies. I dropped onto the stool and carefully began to form my letters. At first they were random, a set of practice exercises, but then, as I warmed to it, my thoughts began to slowly appear on the page. If I could not speak it aloud to any, I could at least put down on the parchment what I had seen in the vision. It was all very rough. I'd never attempted something like this.

The candle had burned down a long way when the Templar at last arrived. He moved to my side and looked over my shoulder to see what I was about. "Once stirred, the need to express yerself is a difficult thing to deny, eh?" His voice trailed off as he realized what I'd written.

"This is a part of the vision ye have already seen?" he asked.

"Aye. It begins the same, but things add to it and it becomes stronger the more I have it."

"Ye're sure it was the Grand Master?" His eyes were dark with worry.

I nodded, going back over my words, in my mind and with my eyes. I could read and write. It was such an oddity, but more it was a way to make it all real, to give credence to what was happening, and to what I'd seen.

He took the parchment and read it once more, then held it up to the flame of the candle. I watched in fascination as the flame caught and curled a bright orange. "Have a care about what ye write, Tormod, at least until this is over. I'll have to speak to him at once, but how do ye tell a man there is a possibility that he will burn alive?" He shivered.

He made to leave but I stopped him. "Ye said it could be changed," I said.

"Let us hope so, Tormod."

"Templar Alexander, carrying the carving is taking a toll on ye, is it not?"

He stood by the door, his body hunched with the knowledge of what he had to tell the Grand Master. "Aye, ye know it rightly. 'Twas not so in the beginning, but as the visions continued, and we moved across the land, 'twas as if 'tis a full-time trial."

"I felt that way on the ship when I used it to *see*. But, as I've not held it directly for a bit, I'm stronger. How would ye feel were I to carry it a bit o' the way for ye?" I didn't want to seem impertinent. It was truly a powerful talisman, and it was his to carry, and yet he was so very tired.

He ran his hand over his face and stretched. At my words he looked over at me, considering. "Aye. I think that I'll take ye up on the offer. The carving is not something that would ever harm us. I feel that strongly. But sometimes the visions it shows, and the strength it takes to see them, are a bit overwhelming. We'll leave it be for tonight, for here. With what I've just heard from the Grand Master, I'd like to see if aught comes o' my dreams. More is happening than we knew."

His words didn't bode well for us. "What?"

"Pope Clement has of late been in conference with King Philippe. They were friends as boys. There are rumors that the Papacy is moving from Rome to France."

"What?" I exclaimed. "That is just . . ."

His gaze was far away. "Disturbing."

"What do we now?"

"We follow the map and find out what lies a' its end." He stretched and yawned. "How is the wound?" he asked. "Are ye fit to travel?"

It hit me then, that I had not told my other news. "I am healed," I said proudly, and with an awe that had not diminished. "Did ye know that some o' the gifted have the talent and are able to do that?"

I took off my boot and he came over to examine my foot. The toes were still missing, but the site of the incision was completely healed, as if years had passed, not weeks.

"I had heard tales but never witnessed it firsthand. That is truly wondrous. Ye're blessed, Tormod, to have been touched by the miracle."

"Aye. And what's stranger still is that I have the possibility to heal within." I said this last, expecting disbelief. After all, I really didn't credit it myself.

He raised his eyebrows in surprise. "Aye? What a boon that would be. We cannot stay and look into yer training, but when we return, we shall see to it."

A cold shadow drifted across my mind. A strange part of me felt that he should have said *if* we return, but I left that unsaid.

We knelt for the Compline, and though I was still very angry with the Lord, I took comfort in it. Way in the back of my mind I asked Him to make it so, to let us return, together to live out this tale. I wasn't sure I believed that He was listening, but it was important to ask.

I didn't see the Templar for the remainder of the night. He left for another audience with the Grand Master, and I took to my pallet and didn't stir until morning.

✠

Ahram and his men met us in the courtyard of the manor house. The Grand Master had arranged that we would have horses. I was glad of the fact that we would no longer be walking, but nervous, too, as I'd barely sat a horse a dozen or so times in my life. Still, I was given a good, sweet-natured mount, and we seemed to have an instant accord. I promised her quietly that if she would be good to me, I would surely be good to her.

The Grand Master met us in the courtyard before we took our leave of the preceptory. I was surprised when he came and stood directly before me. "We all must bear a cross, son. Let not what you have seen be yours. I have been warned. It is all that you can do. I go willingly to do the duty of Our Lord. There is a great duty that is yours, a destiny to fulfill. God grant you success, Tormod MacLeod." I trembled as he made the cross on my forehead, afraid to speak and yet . . . "It can be changed, My Lord. If only the right pebble is tossed into the stream."

He smiled. "Then Godspeed your voyage, Tormod. I pray you make a splash like none has ever seen."

✠

We set out in better shape and spirit than in a long while. The Grand Master was aware of our goals and was sending an armed contingent of knights to parlay for Seamus's and Andrus's release.

I had taken the carving from the Templar with all due reverence, and it now sat hidden in the sporran at my waist. The sun was high and hot by the barest hours of morning, so we broke for a time beneath the trees and rested.

It was scorching, even in the shade, and so with little to do I roamed, looking for signs of life at the base of the trees and in the clumps of weeds in the roots.

"Hah, I've got ye," I said, closing my hand around a brown and black gecko. He skittered and turned in my palm, looking for a way out. With none to be found, he settled into my hand. I sat beneath a tree watching his stillness. He was like stone in the way that he didn't move for long stints of time. Even when I nudged him, he refused to play my game. His eyes were a deep, dark brown. I stared at them as I ran my fingers down his soft back, mesmerized as the hilt of an old knife appeared in my mind's eye, fingers curved tight, curls of wood drifting to the ground. The drape of a robe emerges from the pale block. A strong swirl of power surrounds the carver.

Heat at my middle drew me from the vision. My hands rested on the precious bulk of the carving. I returned the gecko to his freedom and rose to find the Templar.

He was sparring with Ahram, though it was hot as Hades. Sweat beaded on my neck and trickled down my back. I could scarcely credit that they had the stamina to take it on, but such was the regimen of the knights. The Templar would no more miss his practice than he would skip the prayers that he did so many times a day.

Ahram was stripped to the waist. His dark skin stretched tight over well-defined muscles. The Templar fought in breeks and tunic. I had forgotten the odd injunction that he was not allowed to bare his skin before others. Such an odd rule.

The Arab's ability impressed me. He fought with a long, thin, curved sword called a scimitar, and he was, I was surprised to see, a true match for the Templar. I held my breath the whole time they sparred. The vision of the Templar being wounded was close and uncomfortable. Luckily nothing came to pass.

When they finally broke, I approached. "Templar Alexander, could I speak with ye for a moment?" I had grown a little more comfortable with Ahram as the morning and our travel progressed, but still was not sure how much I could safely share in his presence.

Ahram inclined his head, touched his forehead, then chest, as a salute, and went off in search of the stream.

I led the Templar away, off into the trees to tell of what had transpired.

"Truly interesting," said the Templar. "Ye don't know who it was? Were there any other clues ye might find if ye think on it?"

"Not that I can recall," I said. "But I will tell ye if I remember aught else. I have the image o' it, here," I gestured to my head. He nodded, and we went back to eat with the others.

I stooped beside a pile of kindling the Arabs had gathered. The men who traveled with Ahram had names that were new to my tongue. Bakir was a tall, very dark-skinned Basque who said little. The other man, Fakih, was shorter, but wide and strongly built.

Bakir had just returned with a brace of hare he laid on a bed of leaves. He'd skinned them before returning to camp and was cleaning sticks to use as skewers.

"Can I help?" I asked using hand gestures as well as words. We spoke different languages, but we'd begun to improvise.

Bakir motioned to the stream at our back. Fakih watched me with intelligent eyes. I'd seen all three Arab men washing by the river's edge before eating a short time past. I plunged my hands into the water, deep into the sand of the riverbank. The fine grit swished beneath my fingers, and I washed as I'd seen them do.

The Arabs were fastidious people. They'd washed more today than I had in a month. They even went so far as cleaning their fingers before they ate. It made me think on my own appearance and scent.

Late in the afternoon we began again and, save a quick break for each of us to relieve ourselves, we rode straight through the evening. It became the norm after that first day. Though my legs and tailbone were sore from the exertion and I nearly slept astride, I became accustomed to the pace. We were crossing the countryside at a rate that could never be matched on foot. And I was getting fairly good at convincing my mount to listen.

The Templar resumed putting forth questions about the patterns in the sky. Ahram, I noticed, paid close attention to our conversations, asked his own questions, and provided some of the answers I could not. I found, during these travels, that it was becoming increasingly difficult to reckon the man, who the Templar had obvious fondness for, with the killer I had seen in my vision. He seemed to accept me readily enough, though his quiet intensity unnerved me. Of the men tracking us, we had no indication, until we entered a village on the outskirts of Bembibre.

It was the smell that warned us.

THE MESSAGE

The waft of charred thatch and the strange smell of something roasting met us halfway up the lane. We saw the farmhouse, or what was left of it.

Partial walls of stone were all that remained standing, and a small blackened tuft of thatch hung at a sharp angle near the hut's entrance. I felt the old man's grief pulse in the wind before the others noticed. He stood so still and silent that he was hard to make out in the growing dark of evening. The Templar noticed my look and turned. The closer we came, the more I could see. Before him lay a freshly mounded grave. An old sword had been thrust in the ground beside.

I slid from my horse, grasping the reins as my legs nearly buckled. The Templar had no such problem and approached ahead of the rest.

"Go away," the man murmured as we came closer. "Leave a man to his grief."

"We have no argument with ye, sir, nor wish to disturb yer mourning," said the Templar. He approached with his hands wide, showing no weapon or threat.

"Like the others," he said. "I thank you, no."

"What others?" asked the Templar. "Truly, we mean ye no harm."

The man looked at us with lost, frightened, but very angry eyes. "My son is gone. Gone! Do you hear me! My home is in ashes. There is nothing here for you." He rose and drew the sword from the ground beside him. I took a step back, out of the way, and my head began to buzz.

Large blue eyes stared with fright. The tines of a pitchfork gleamed in the blaze of a torch. The crackle of fire played in my ears. Smoke filled my nose.

Focus. Ground. Shield. I blinked, trembling.

"Be at peace, old man," said the Templar. "I can see yer pain. I know yer loss. We will trouble ye no further."

I could feel a strange ripple in the air as he spoke, as if the life beat of the land had become the gentle lap of the sea. The man's eyes seemed to dim and lose the fire of his anger. The sword dipped toward the ground.

I felt the Templar's power, and I reached as he had described to me. I added to his sway, keeping the man quiet and docile.

"How many, and how long ago?" the Templar asked. I watched and listened to the way he used the power. The old man's eyes filled with tears and he sat heavily back down. "Fifteen or more soldiers rode in two days past. They wore the colors of France."

"What business does the French king have on Spanish soil?" asked the Templar, though we knew well already.

"They seek travelers." His red-rimmed eyes narrowed and turned my way. "A Knight Templar and a young boy."

I sucked in my breath, helpless to the quiver that gripped my spine. They knew of me.

"What happened?" The Templar approached the man and knelt at the end of the grave.

"He was my son," the man said quietly. "No man should bury his son." His grief was overwhelming. It made me want to drop down beside him and beg his forgiveness. I was stunned suddenly by a thought that robbed my chest of breath. *How would my da feel if this adventure should turn out in like? It was a mistake,* I thought, *to come here — a horrible, terrible mistake.* I must have made a noise or my face gave me away for the Templar looked up. There was sadness in his eyes as he turned away and began to pray. I knew what to do without even thinking on it, and I embraced it as I hadn't before. The ground was hard beneath my knees as I dropped beside the two men and joined the prayers for the soul of the boy who had died in my stead.

Finally, it was done. We stood, lost in the quiet of the moment as crickets and cicadas filled the night air with their song.

"Come away with us," the Templar said quietly. "There is nothing for ye here."

"My home is here," the man replied. And nothing we could say would sway him from his course.

In the end we moved on, but it was with the promise that we would send men to help him rebuild when we reached the next contact house along the way. I looked back over my shoulder twice as we left. The old man stood where we had left him, with a trail of tears flowing down his weathered cheeks.

We ate beneath the stars that night. The men seemed much as they had been of late. Perhaps they were used to seeing people burned out and mourning, but I was not. When I took my rest, safely beside the Templar, I could not stem the series of images that played again and again in my mind. It was worse when finally I closed my eyes. The images were freed to grow, and fear surrounded me.

I saw them in order, as if they were slowed. First, Douglas, as the arrow pierced his throat, falling forever beyond my reach; then Marta, in terror, being flung from one soldier to another, her dress in tatters, her body cut and bleeding. I saw the old man then, and then the son we had been too late to help. I saw the fear in the son's eyes.

And then came the worst. Flames surrounded the wood, licking the pitch. Smoke spiraled up past a white robe, singeing the red of the cross. I saw the face of the Grand Master, white and filmed with a layer of sweat and dust. I saw the movement of his lips. I felt the cadence of his prayer.

The image of the carving came to me in a bright white light. A woman smiled. Her eyes of deep amber held mine. The vision faded before I even had time to focus, ground, and shield. I woke with the woman fresh in my mind — her image, not as a carving, but as flesh and bone.

I must have stirred or made some sound to alert him, for his eyes were on mine a short distance away in the dark. "What did ye see?" The Templar's voice was a quiet question that didn't travel beyond my hearing.

"I saw a woman, the model for the carving."

He said no more and just closed his eyes. I rolled to my back and stayed awake for a long while, staring at the stars.

THE PATH TAKEN

We rose early and wasted no time in clearing the camp of signs that we had been there. A renewed vigilance had once more taken hold. The soldiers were two days from us. It was vital that we move on and do it quickly. Our best hope lay in the belief that they were ahead of us, not behind.

The Templar was quiet, more watchful and rested than I had seen him in many days. As we made our way across the gradually changing landscape and up into the mountains, all of the men were in a state of alertness. Swords were palmed at the slightest sound, and no one initiated conversation beyond what was necessary.

The hills were rocky and travel difficult. What began as a gentle climb, a slope that crept forever upward toward the clouds, eventually became a steep grade. We led the horses and walked, sometimes singly, sometimes abreast. Footing was precarious.

The higher we climbed, the more excited by the view

I became. As we crested the rise, I sucked in a deep breath. Down below, a deep green valley lay on either side of the path. Up ahead, a thin track skirted the mountaintop.

"If we take the safer path down below, we are sure to run into the soldiers," the Templar said. "Ahram, ye've come this way before, how dangerous is it?"

"The winds are high at this time of the year. If there were another way, I'd not risk it," he said.

But we all knew we would risk it, for just this morning we had come across the evidence of a fire pit still warm from the night before. It could have been any traveler, but it had the feel of those hunting us.

"With care, and Allah on our side, we can only hope," said Ahram.

God, Allah, Jesus, or whatever Yer faithful name Ye, I thought, *if Ye would, please help us*. It was strange, but I didn't feel it was blasphemy to speak to the Lord in that manner. I knew now that there were many ways to worship the one God, and that there were many people doing it happily in all those ways.

We took nearly the whole of the night to make our way up the first steep grade, then down across the floor of the valley, and back again up the next monumental hill. And as if Mother Nature had planned it for me alone, we reached the pinnacle as the sun rose with coral fingers of light that banished the dark of an evening sky.

One by one we stepped out onto a path no wider than two men stretched lengthwise. The drop on either side seemed to careen down hundreds of rock-strewn ledges. The view was amazing. I felt as if I were on top of the world, looking down. Below me the land once again resembled the map I had seen.

"Have a care, Tormod. I dare not walk beside ye. Hold the reins tightly, and keep her head down."

We had tied a strip of linen across the eyes of our mounts, so that they would not spook and bolt. Even still, the horses twitched nervously, sensing the danger of the road before them. Ahram went first, tethered and followed closely by Fakih. I stepped out next with the Templar behind me. Bakir trailed.

Slowly we walked, leading the horses one behind the next as if it were any other narrow road at any other time. But as we neared the center, something suddenly began to change. The wind that had barely stirred the dust of the path rose in intensity. At first it was welcome for we were hot and sweat-filmed from our ascent; but when it began to blow in earnest, it stirred the birds that were below us.

I know now that I should have been holding the reins tightly, but a movement down below caught my attention and my mind wandered in its direction. It was a hawk winging slowly upward. As I watched, it caught the breeze and shot up, sweeping low over my head. I heard the flap of its wings and the scree of its cry and flinched.

My horse, already nervy, bumped against me and knocked her blind askew. I tightened my grip on the reins as the terrified creature began to back away from the edge it could see, crowding me toward the ledge it could not see. I tried to turn her, but the horse was too frightened and was heaving and shying.

"Tormod!" It happened so fast that I could not even formulate a plan. I heard the Templar's cry but could not make my mind grasp his meaning. He could not possibly want me to let go. I held the reins as the horse began to rear up and shifted my body to her side. The wind tore across the ridge. I felt the press of it against my body, pushing me. My balance was not what it should have been, and when the back legs of my mount slid off the road, the only thing I thought about was saving her, and so it was a complete shock when we both went over the side.

HELP FROM BEYOND

The bite of the rope seared like a brand, and in shock I let go of the reins. I hit the side of the cliff with such

199

force that the breath was knocked out of me. Horror filled my mind as I watched a slide of rock follow the screaming animal down the side of the mountain. Huddled against the cliff, I tried to push it out of my mind.

I heard the men above shouting and trying to calm the rest of the horses. My rope jerked, and I dropped a bit lower. "Brace yer feet, Tormod," the Templar cried.

But I could only stare at the rock face, holding the rope that was tightening more and more while I hung. All around the life beat of the land and air swirled furiously in my mind.

"Tormod, ye need to help us!" The fear in his voice cut through, jerking me from my own terror. I would not cause him more grief. I could not. I brought my legs up and scrabbled for a foothold, using my hands to ease the slack on the ever-tightening rope. Slowly as they pulled, I clawed my way upward. But my thoughts kept drifting far below with the animal that had been entrusted me.

Tormod, feel the rock. He spoke directly into my mind, distancing me from my sorrow and pain. I focused on the shape beneath my boots, reaching with my mind to find the niches my feet could not. But rock was different. Its life beat was slower, more difficult to decipher. The carving in my sporran burned at my middle as tears dropped from my cheeks and chin, falling to the earth far below. The task seemed impossible, but suddenly I felt the beat and I understood the shape and feel of the ledge. My feet found purchase that I could almost swear was not there before. Slowly I began to climb. It seemed like forever that I made my way upward, and even longer before I was hauled back onto the cliff. The Templar was the first to draw me to my feet. I felt him shaking as we grasped arms. "I thought we'd lost ye, Tormod." His eyes were dark and worried. "I've got things to do, an' I don't intend to do them without ye!"

For the remainder of the descent out of the mountains and into France, I didn't speak. I mourned the loss of my mount, a good, spirited horse whose only mistake was to be assigned to me.

THE CHANGE

"Ye've been quiet o' late, Tormod. I would share yer thoughts, if ye'd have it." I had moved away from the group after our midday repast. I sat on a deep rock sharpening the blade he had given me. No others were within hearing. He had made sure.

"I can feel the change," I said. "Something is building. There is tightness within me. My stomach, my bones. I know not what this feeling means. Best I can describe it is when Torquil an' I are readying for a brawl. There are no solid reasons, but I know that something will spark the flame an' by the day's end I will be on my back with his fists planted in my stomach."

He nodded, a slight smile lifting the corners of his mouth at my comparison. "I feel it as well. A discord is vibrating along the channels o' our power."

"The visions are coming more often," I said. "The carving is glowing dimly. 'Tis been this way since we came over the mountain. This land is dangerous. I feel the warning."

"We must travel day an' night for a while. Just to put some distance between them an' us. I feel the presence o' our seekers more clearly than before."

We didn't delay getting back on the road. The fire was stamped out and the ashes distributed so that none would see we had been in this place. The enemy was close.

How close we didn't realize until almost too late.

The sun had not yet risen. We had been traveling for much of the night and had crossed into France many marks of the candle before. Our destination was a deserted wayfarer's hut deep in the hills beyond Tarbes. We pushed our mounts and ourselves to make it, and I was very nearly asleep in the saddle. Fakih and Bakir were sharing a mount today. I had Fakih's mount and rode behind Ahram when suddenly a strange ripple of awareness shot along my spine.

Before I could alert anyone, the Templar's warning broke the stillness of the night. "Arm yerselves and make for the trees. Protect the lad a' all cost."

"Look to yerselves," I cried, drawing my dagger and kneeing my mount with fervor. I was no hero, but I refused to add yet another life in trade for my own. I raced for the darkness of the trees ahead.

I heard the clash of steel behind me. Close by my side I felt and heard the thunder of horses. A scream of pain split the air, and I wheeled the horse, terrified. The earth seemed to rumble beneath me as the overburdened mount of Fakih and Bakir went to ground. I pulled hard and circled wide, determined to help the men who were now on foot in combat.

"Ride for the trees, Tormod," the Templar commanded. "Now!"

He had never used that tone with me before, and every instinct in me wanted to obey. I started forward.

Ahead, I saw the darkness of the trees, their trunks spaced far enough apart that I would be able to enter at my rapid pace, but beyond its edges lay an eerie dark. I slowed the horse, chancing a glance behind. There were none following. I pulled up on the reins and wheeled my mount in a close circle. Ahram and his men were heavily engaged with a group of fighters. None wore French colors, and yet these men *felt* familiar. These were the same men who had been at Marta's.

An unholy anger came over me then, as I saw in my mind's eye what they had done to her. I kneed my mount back the way I'd come with only my dagger as a weapon. The Templar was before me, fighting his way toward Fakih and Bakir who fought valiantly on the ground. His broadsword cleft the air — the ring of its metal just one clang in the din of the skirmish going on all around. Ahram was engaged with two others.

The men on foot were helpless against mounted soldiers. They would be run down. As I watched, a man came at Bakir from behind. I threw my dagger, just as the Templar had taught me.

LIFE AND DEATH

With absolute accuracy my dagger caught the soldier moments before his swing came down on the unprotected back of Bakir. My blade landed square in the attacker's chest. I was shocked at the blood that spurted and could not force myself to retrieve my weapon. As the man reeled in the saddle, the Templar drove his horse at him and plucked my dagger free.

Wheeling in my direction, shouting with a fury that I could not ignore, he commanded, "Ride!"

I circled my mount once again and sprang for the trees, but not before I saw that Ahram had gotten himself between the soldiers and his men.

I entered at full speed. *Feel the trees,* the Templar commanded. His voice nearly shouted impressions inside me. In my mind I saw the aura of the trees.

I understood. Reaching, I felt for the lifeblood of the trees and fed the information directly into the legs of my mount. We flew then, unencumbered by lack of sight, with no one following our charge.

But no one could keep up the pace my mount had set. I rode for a good mark of the candle before I began to slow. The horse was frothing and my heart was beating furiously. The only sound in the forest was the birds, chirping as if nothing in the world could disturb their happiness.

I had left all of the men behind — the Templar, Ahram, Fakih, Bakir. I wanted to turn back, to help, to find out what had happened, but I knew that I needed to obey him, especially this once. I had the carving. If no one else survived, I must find a way to follow the map to discover what lay at its end.

As the sun began its quiet ascent and the darkness of the wood lifted, I found that I didn't have to focus my attention on directing the horse through the trees. I could see, as could my mount. It was then, when my attention was free, that the reality of what I had done crashed down on me.

I had killed a man. A stranger. I took a life.

I stopped the horse and stumbled toward a tree and was sick at its roots. I saw again the dagger as it flew from my hand. I saw the blood spurt and heard the man's scream. My breath rasped and I felt faint.

The Templar's horse pounded through the trees with dead accuracy. When he neared me, he vaulted from the mount, apparently not caring that the horse might run. He was in a rare fury. I found myself backing up against the tree.

"Tormod MacLeod, what in the seven hells did ye think ye were doing back there!"

I flinched from his roar. "I didn't mean —"

"O' course ye didn't mean! Ye never mean!" He was pacing and shouting. "I told ye to ride! Ride, an' no' turn an' throw the only weapon ye had on yer body. Now, I know well why yer da beat ye! Ye drove him to it!"

I could not take one moment more. "I did my best! I could no' leave a friend behind, just to save my own skin. I'm sorry, ye asked too much o' me!"

I could not believe what I had just done. Shocked by my own action, and afraid that he might tan the skin right off of me, I turned and ran like the devil himself was on my tail.

He took off right after. I should have been able to outrun him, but I had just vomited and he had anger on his side. He caught the back of my robe and yanked, and I flew off my feet. His impetus took us both to the ground where we lay heaving and crumpled.

"Tormod."

I tried to squirm to get away.

"Hold," he commanded. I shook, sure now that he would beat me. "I'm sorry."

I could not believe my ears. "What?" I gasped.

"I'm sorry ye had to go through that. 'Tis more than ye should bear."

I was horrified that he thought he needed to apologize to me. "No, I'm sorry. I knew that I had the carving. The most important thing was that I take it far from the conflict. It just happened so fast, an' I saw that man going for Bakir. An' I just could no' ride away." I buried my head beneath my arms, ashamed as tears filmed my eyes. "I killed a man. I can scarce believe it."

He rolled to his back in the brush. "To kill is never an easy task," he said. "Ye saved his life. Ye did what was right for a friend, and what's more, ye did what was right for a Templar. A Templar never runs from a confrontation, and he never leaves a man behind."

I should have felt pride in his words, but instead I felt hollow.

"Is it always this hard to bear?" I asked, tears choking my throat.

He nodded. "Each life taken is a toll on our own. I wish that I could tell ye otherwise or give ye a way to somehow make it acceptable. But that is something that must come from within. Ask for His forgiveness, for all life has come from the Maker."

I was silent a moment as we got to our feet and made our way back to the horses. They were peacefully grazing as if nothing had happened. "How are the others?" I asked. "Why are they not with ye?"

"They fare well, considering how many we took on. Fakih was cut. They are taking him to the closest village for tending. Ahram knows our path. If he can come, he will." We remounted and once again we were off on our own.

Near the height of midday we came across an abandoned wayfarer's hut tucked away in the midst of a deep wood. I was nearly overcome with heat and swaying in the saddle. My robe was stuck to me and my back was burning from the sun. We hobbled the horses in the shade by the hut and entered.

It was a small place, no more than a box of stone, with a mound of old straw, the remnants of a crude shelf that was used as a table, and several low benches. Inside was dim, and only slightly less hot.

"'Tis too hot to hunt and there's no stream about, so let's just rest. Chew some o' these." He offered a small pouch filled with oats and a skin of water. It tasted terrible, but filled the hole in my stomach.

"Where next?" I asked, working to mush the oats with a sip of the brackish water.

"We make for Montségur. 'Tis a castle preceptory o' the Knights Hospitaller," he said.

"I've heard the name Hospitaller, but I don't know much about them. Why do we go there?" I asked, tossing off the hat and robe, fishing out my plaid, and dropping down on it.

"They are a sect like ours," he said over a mouthful of oats. "But where our knights are pledged to fight for the pilgrim's safety in the Holy Land, these are pledged to help find cures for the ill, an' provide refuge an' shelter for the sick an' injured. They're no' much in the way o' fighters, though they've been named as such. We go there for time — to rest an' recover without fear. We travel by night from here on out."

It did not take long for sleep to take me.

The hut was black as pitch and frightening. My dreams were near — red flames danced before my eyes. Though I'd not slept long, I was afraid to get back to it. Nearby, the Templar's soft and even breath hissed. I was glad that he could find rest.

Focus. Ground. Shield. Though I was not in the grip of a vision, the exercise helped push away my sudden fear. Beyond the hut I heard the whisper of the trees and the sound of the insects that chirped in the night. Still, I knew I'd feel better if I could but have a bit of light.

The Templar stirred and rolled over in his sleep. I was careful not to wake him and slowly began crawling toward the door. Straw was sharp beneath my palms. And as I put forward a knee, it came down hard on something. I barely muffled the cry.

Rooting around, my fingers curled around the hilt of a blade. I knew, even in the dark, that it was my dagger and that the Templar had left it for me. The one I had killed with. It felt different in my palm, heavier than I remembered. I closed my eyes, but opened them just as quickly when the memory followed me there. Overwhelmed, I stood and made my way outside.

The night was lit by a great number of stars. I sat on a rock by the door frame staring down at the dagger in my hand. The jewels in the hilt appeared dark without the light to shine on them. I thought they were very like me. I didn't feel as if the light shone on me, now that I was a killer. I did as the Templar had told me and said a prayer to the Almighty to help me bear this burden. I didn't feel any better when I had finished.

The Templar awoke shortly thereafter. I heard him moving about while I fed the horses the same oats that we had eaten earlier. When they finished, I watered them with two of the skins poured out into an old tin bucket I found by the side of the hut. I could hear his prayers now, a murmur that passed through the stone wall beside me.

As he finished, I went back inside to get my things. It was too dark to reckon, but I could see his bundles on the table and the staff with the blade inside. I carried them outside. While I waited, I unsheathed the blade from the staff and went through what I remembered of the exercises he had taught me. When he came outside, I resheathed it quickly.

"Keep that from here on out," he said. "I didn't like that ye had only the one dagger when it came down to a skirmish."

"Aye?" I said. "For my own?" I could not believe that he would trust me with something so amazing.

"Let us be gone from here. They will not be long away."

I tossed him a skin of water and the bag of oats. "Imagine them as toasted honey cakes," I said. "It seems to help."

He nodded and took them with little enthusiasm.

I fisted a handful of oats and chewed them dry. My imagination didn't work this time, and I could barely get them down. I wondered if I would ever get used to the sparse fare we were living on. My stomach felt like it touched my backbone.

The horses appeared well, even with the short rest we'd given them. They were strong, healthy animals, and I was appreciative of their service. We rode in silence for much of the night hours.

A SECRET REVEALED

As we came in sight of the hills that led to the peak of Montségur, the hair on my arms stood up despite the heat of the day. Up ahead I could see the dark line of the castle, stark against a crimson sky. With the sun going down beyond it, the castle seemed afire.

We made the road to the gates by nightfall, pushing our mounts as far as we might without harm. The castle was perched on the very top of a jut of stone, its walls apparently unchanged by time.

"We will sleep safely here," the Templar said. "'Tis too far out o' the way for Philippe's men. The Hospitallers would not admit them. Within their walls no speech is allowed. Nor any outsiders. They will welcome us as brothers, but even if Philippe's men came an' insisted, they would not be admitted inside."

As we drew closer, the rise grew sharp, so we dismounted and walked the remaining distance to the main gate. The castle to me was a wonder. It was larger even than the Archbishop's residence and seemed completely impregnable.

A Hospitaller Brother met us at the gate, wariness in his eyes. The Templar exchanged a series of hand gestures that the Brother accepted, and we were led inside where we were relieved of our horses.

No one spoke as we were led to the main refectory for a meal with the rest of the knights. The head of their Order was in attendance, and so Templar Alexander sat at his side at the main table, while I sat below the dais at a long communal bench with the apprentices. I didn't mind. I was tired, and since no one was about to talk to me, I was able to sit, think, and eat. I was so relieved to be eating real food that it would not have mattered if I sat in a dung heap in the stables. A trencher of roast pheasant with heaping platters of vegetables filled me as I had not been filled in what felt like forever.

After the meal, we followed the knights and trainees to the main chapel for a silent Vespers prayer. It was good to feel part of a group such as this. They were like us, I thought. Like us. . . . This was the first time I had accepted readily that I was a part of the Templars. The thought pleased me.

Directly after prayers we were seen to our room. It was a sparse cell — two pallets with a tiny table between them — but it was very high up in the castle, and there was a window, though it had been shuttered to keep out any draft.

"Could we not open it a bit?" I asked. The room had been unused for a while, and it was stuffy from being closed. It had recently been dusted for our use and muskiness hung in the air.

"Aye. I don't see why not. I can just about reach." He strained upward and opened the window.

The night air was warm. "I bet ye can see forever from here," I said. "Would it be all right if I looked out?"

"Aye," he said, helping me drag the small table over beneath the window. "But be careful."

The view when I gained the table was wondrous. Outside, far below, the land sloped sharply. Rocks and scrub dotted a swath of deep green that stretched for miles. It was beautiful.

I turned back to descibe it for him, but didn't get that far. The carving began to glow at my waist, and I felt myself waver on the table.

Dark figures crouched by the window. A light bag passed hand to hand, then was tied to a waist. Moonlight illuminated a man. The view down from a staggering height made me reel.

The table tilted beneath my feet, and I felt myself falling.

"Tormod!"

The Templar caught me as I toppled to the floor. "Monks," I said, gasping. "Four escaped with something in a sack. There was fighting beyond."

"What was in the sack? Can ye describe it?"

"Small, about the size o' two o' my fists. 'Twas important." I met his eyes. "They were desperate to remove it before this castle fell."

He was quiet, thinking. "There is a legend that surrounds this place," he said. "Monks escaped during a siege o' this castle. 'Tis said they went down the wall with something worth dying for."

I stared out the window, thinking on what I'd seen.

We left after Lauds, greeting the rise of the sun with the Hospitallers in residence. Our horses were refreshed, well fed and watered. We were renewed as well. The head of the Order saw us to the gates and outside the castle. Only then did he speak.

"Your letters o' transport," he said, handing over a small scroll that the Templar tucked in his sporran. I knew from an earlier conversation that there were trade agreements long in place between the houses of Hospitaller and Templar. It was a form of checks and balances. The Templar had gone off earlier and signed a contract with the house. They provided us with coin and this letter of transport, which was passage for two aboard a Hospitaller ship, docked in the harbor down the coast. They would, in turn, receive payment from our house, the Templars, when next their transactions were due.

"Thank ye, Brother," said the Templar. "We are forever grateful o' yer hospitality."

He nodded and went back inside. As we rode away, I asked, "Do they do that for others? Lend money? Make travel arrangements?"

"Aye. The Templars originated the process. When a man goes on pilgrimage, instead o' risking his currency to brigands, he is able to deposit his gold with the preceptory closest his home. He receives from the preceptory a coded chit that he then can redeem on the opposite shore for his currency, minus the fare for his passage."

I thought it a brilliant scheme.

When we reached level land, I looked back on the castle, remembering the vision of the monks who had gone out the window and down the steep mountainside. The weight of the carving in my sporran seemed to multiply.

BY LAND OR SEA

We boarded the Hospitaller ship as the sun sank in the golden sky two days later. The ship lay at anchor in the harbor of the village of Perpignan and was set to sail before nightfall for Avignon, still several days away. The Templar went below to rest. Travel had been hard on him. He slept far less than I did, and now, secure for the moment, he gave in to the need.

I, however, could not stand being stuck inside the ship after so long living on the land. The crush of people belowdecks was intrusive, and my mind was still much occupied with thoughts of those hunting us.

I went up on deck, pleased at the way my body so quickly adjusted to the sway. I wandered, trying to stay out of the way of the men preparing for the ship's departure. It was strange not to have any duties, when the last time I'd sailed I'd had so many.

I watched the crewmen scramble up and down the ridgepole of the main mast like Seamus had done. Though I would never have credited it, I was a bit melancholy about his capture. The thought made me smile — when had I ever mourned the loss of Seamus's company?

But so much had happened. So much had changed. The petty squabbles we had didn't seem to bear much weight now.

I thought of my brother Torquil. The trivial wrongs that we fought over were even less important than the ones with Seamus. If I ever got a chance, I decided that I would make it up to him.

The wind swept the deck and the sails towering above billowed. A group of gulls flew and hovered looking for scraps of refuse that the sailors would occasionally dump over the side. Their cry split the air, and I squinted to see the sailors above as they moved with ease from one handhold to the next, tightening the ropes and checking the lines for frays.

"You, boy. Get above and check the sails from the crow's nest."

He had mistaken me for one of them, perhaps because I had changed out of my pilgrim garb into my old breeks, tunic, and boots. But I didn't hesitate. I approached the ridgepole and started up. It was not a difficult climb, but the winds were high and the ship was dipping ferociously in the waves. Several times I had to stop and readjust my foot. Without the missing toes, and with the loose boot, I had to compensate by squeezing my muscles and clenching my foot. Slowly I ascended and came in sight of the basket that surrounded the main mast. No wonder the man had sent me. It was small. And it was not nearly as solid and secure as I had anticipated. The platform of wicker, woven to an inner and outer steel frame, had steep sides, but was open in a space about as wide as I was across the chest. There were holes in the base, and more in the sides, so I carefully made my way around the weak bits, seeking the stronger, safer parts.

Far down below, the ocean rolled, glistening beneath the golden rays of the evening sun. Away, off in the distance lay only the vast ocean, and yet, staring back from whence we'd come, I saw the beauty of the mountains. I was entranced by the play of light across their crystal peaks.

Lathered horses pounded across a green field. Blue-and-gold banners snapped in the wind.

I came to with a force that made me reel and my foot slipped through one of the gaps in the wicker. I screamed, teetering back.

A COMING DANGER

I threw my arms wide and with a shock connected with the upper rib of the basket. Pain shot through me. My shoulder felt ripped from my body. Sweat pooled beneath my fingers. High above the ocean, I hung.

Cries of alarm came from below as a crowd gathered. "Go easy, lad. Hold tight. Help is coming."

It won't be soon enough. Fear was so close and tight in my chest I was sure I would faint. I swung my legs to the lower rim. They didn't connect. Desperate, I grabbed the ridgepole between my legs and clung with all my might. The ocean yawned far below. I felt the pull of it, as if I were being dragged downward. My arms and legs were trembling. I cast my mind out and away, seeking help. The wind was blowing mildly. Frantic, I tried to whisper it into shape. Then, suddenly, the carving flared with heat below my waist. With the heat came the wind, and I was able to move my legs up the mast feeling buffered, lifted by a strong and sudden gale.

Higher. Higher. Then just a bit more. At last, I felt the metal of the bottom rung beneath my legs. With near disbelief and a last burst of energy I leaned back and hoisted myself once more to safety.

The wind dropped off as suddenly as it had risen. Gulls swooped in arcs above. I shook so badly that I dared not move. When the first of the sailors reached my perch, it took me a moment to realize he was there.

"Boy. Give me your hand," he said. His eyes were blue, deep as the sky, and kind. It's strange that I should notice such things when I had very nearly dropped to my death, but there it is. I took his hand in mine and let him pull me upright.

"Good. Just come toward me and I'll see you down." He had me scoot back from the hole and turn so that my body faced the pole and my feet were squarely on the rungs. He was at my back with his legs spread wide to a second set of holds. "Now, easy as a babe's first steps, we'll just go down this together."

And we did. In no time at all I was once again on deck. My body was a mass of aches. The Templar was waiting.

"Is there ever a time when I'll not have to worry over

ye, Tormod?" His anger was justified but I had no mind for it.

"They're coming," I said. "We have to get off the ship."

His head jerked toward shore. "Quickly, go below. Get our things. We must be off before they sail."

I scrambled to do as he bid. We didn't have much. I took the staff, and the water skins, the bags of oats, my plaid, and the bundle of tied-up supplies that was his. The horses had already been boarded, and we could not wait to have them brought up; they would have to stay.

I met him on deck bare moments later, where he paid for a coracle that would take us ashore. We boarded as fast as we could. As the Templar rowed, the dread in my chest grew. We didn't wait until it was fully beached before we were out and running. We left the coracle bobbing in the wash.

The sand gave way beneath my feet. The loss of toes made my gait less smooth. We made it to the trees, breathing hard. I felt them. The carving was afire. They were close.

FROM BEYOND THE TREES

Just as I thought that maybe we were mistaken, I saw them. With banner unfurled, the first of the men broke through the far clump of trees. Following in his wake were the rest: a group of eight men, armed, and in full fighting force. They wheeled up on the shore watching the ship leave.

I held my breath as they regrouped and spoke to one another. Then, as one, they turned back the way they'd come. My heart beat a frantic tattoo.

"Come, before they realize we are not aboard," he said. "Hurry, Tormod, an' don't speak."

We moved, into and out of the shadows, silent and wary. There was no place safe. I knew it for truth.

Skirting the wood's edge, we paced the shore. The heat was high and the midges were thick. We followed no path but stepped over rocks and downed trees, making our way ever north. We came often to a place that was impassable and, when this happened, backtracked until we were clear.

I felt like my bones were strung on a harp. I imagined

the hunters around every bush and tree, and their eyes on me at each turn.

The Templar had sunk into himself, leaving me with only my terrified thoughts for company.

It was late in the night when we came to the wood's end, several leagues up the coast. I assumed that we would continue on across the road and into the field ahead, and so I nearly shrieked when the Templar put out his hand to stop my progress.

"Go softly here," he said quietly. "Just ahead is a safe house, a kirk where we will be among friends. Speak nothing o' our business, even if it appears all right to do so."

I nodded.

The kirk was a small stone hut set amid a tumble of bushes and trees. It didn't look at all like a kirk to me. It had no cross, no sacred well, nothing that marked it as a place of worship. Only the barest of paths led to it. I could see no light inside, not from beneath or around the door frame.

"I don't think anyone is a' home," I whispered.

"Hush," he said. "Not another word until I tell ye 'tis safe." The Templar was more wary than I'd ever seen him. He scanned the area and seemed to hesitate, something he had never in all our travels done. I would have spoken to him about it, but his hushed warning, and the fact that I always seemed to do the wrong thing in these situations, stilled my tongue.

On his signal, we set out across the clearing, crouching low and making little noise. He stood outside — stock-still, listening. It was then I thought of the carving. I had turned my sporran to the back, and it was buried beneath my plaid.

The Templar was still waiting to make up his mind, and I shifted the plaid and made to turn the whole thing around just as he knocked on the door. I could not see it, but suddenly I could feel its heat flaring.

BETRAYAL

The door of the kirk opened inward. It was difficult to see inside. Only the sullen glow of a small fire lit the gloom. As we passed beyond the frame, I kept close to the Templar, nearly treading on his heels.

I knew even before the door shut behind us that we had made a grave error in coming here. The carving at my back was burning. The Templar realized his mistake at the same time, for he shoved me back that he might draw his sword. A scratch of flint, then flare of light filled the dark before us as a rush torch suddenly flickered to life.

My heart dropped, and I drew a ragged breath. We were surrounded. Six or seven soldiers in the colors of blue and gold crowded the room, their swords drawn. There was nowhere to turn.

One of the soldiers dragged a man forward. His clothes were in tatters, his face badly bruised and swollen. He was barely able to stand. "Is this the man?" demanded the soldier, giving his ward a shake that made the man's hood slide back from his head.

I sucked in a breath, sick in my heart and soul. *No! It cannot be.*

"Is it? Answer me or you will not live to see the morning," he shouted, prodding the man with the hilt of his sword.

Seamus's head rolled back. I could see the spittle slide down his chin. "Aye," he whispered. "God save him, it is."

Betrayal.

I was mortified, but that was nothing compared to the emotion ripping through the Templar. I sensed the jump in tension and grabbed his sword arm, holding on tight.

"Alexander Sinclair, you are under arrest for the crimes of heresy and treason. As mandated by King Philippe of France, you are to lay down your sword."

I could almost see his mind calculating the odds of taking on every man in the room. In the end it was Seamus who decided him.

"Stop it, Alex. They will kill us all." His words were a whisper filled with the fear of knowledge. He knew what they were capable of; he had been in their hands for a long while.

With great effort, the Templar lowered his sword.

What filled me most with fear was the possible discovery of the carving. All I could think of was his vision, of the broken carving and the world falling into ruin. I tried not to draw attention to myself.

One of the soldiers looked my way nonetheless. *He is o' no consequence.* The Templar's push was as light as air. *Just an underling. Not worth yer notice.* The man's eyes moved on, dismissing me. I took a quick breath, shaken.

The Templar submitted without argument. I did the same.

Rough hands turned us about and quickly we were bound. The sharp cut of the frayed rope chafed my skin. I tried to make a fist with one hand so that later I might be able to slip the bonds, but the large hairy soldier who tied me thought my efforts a joke. He yanked the ropes even tighter, and I cried out. I could not feel my hands and my wrists burned like fire.

My captor jerked me forward by my ropes, and I

bit the inside of my cheek to keep back the scream. They dragged us outside. Though we didn't struggle, they seemed pleased to do whatever harm they might. I supposed that they must have been hunting us long.

Horses were brought from behind a hut across the field. They had taken no chances. The Templar spoke not at all, but when his eyes met mine, his impressions seemed to echo inside my head. *Safeguard it.*

A CHANCE

What I recall of the road was a long and grueling trek with none of the pleasantry that I'd shared with the Templar. The soldiers treated us as the criminals we were branded. Food came in the form of a hunk of moldy bread that I had to pick the weevils out of with my teeth. Drink was the last dregs of a watered wine that tasted sour and made my stomach heave. And yet it came infrequently, so I took and ate every bit that was offered. We stopped only twice during the days, when the soldiers needed to void. We were allowed to go at the same time, but it was difficult in that our hands were still bound before us. And they stood watch all the while.

They didn't pay me as much heed as they did the Templar. I was of no concern. I was just a boy. They had not searched my body and found the carving. His whisper had worked. For once being considered nothing played out in my favor. I listened to their words at night; I knew that they were frightened of him. A caged and cornered Templar was something to fear. We all knew the stories telling of the oath that in battle a Templar would never give up; he would fight unto death. Watching him, from my place, tied to the tree opposite, I knew that he was working it in his mind, looking for the opportunity, seeking the moment they would make a mistake.

We were a week into the travel, moving north and west by my calculation of the sun and the stars. The roads were harsh and untraveled, and my mind remained frozen and filled with fear. Seamus was tied to the horse that held the supplies. He was in rough shape. I could see the welts on his back, for the blood had seeped through his tunic.

I had branded him traitor, and yet what information they took from him was at a cost that, in all truth, I didn't think I, in his place, would not too have paid. He swayed in the saddle, and several times he fainted away completely. The soldiers treated him roughly when he slipped, twice, sideways. That was when they had tied him, with his face to the horse's mane, spread-eagle, his arms and legs tied round the animal's neck and girth.

The Templar watched him with worried eyes. I did as well. I didn't like Seamus, especially in light of my injury and the fact that he had led these men to us, but I didn't think either act was something he should die for.

Thoughts of the carving kept me on edge. At all costs it had to remain hidden, but this was proving difficult. The blaze of its heat flared beneath my plaid in the sporran at the base of my spine. What was it trying to tell me? The danger was already upon us. My thoughts drifted. I was hot and tired. My bonds were too tight. The skin beneath was raw and bleeding.

We were not allowed to speak to each other, but they could not in truth quiet us from saying our prayers unless they gagged us. It was not above them, but they didn't do it. And so each time I heard his soft murmur, as I did now, I added my voice just as quietly. This time the feel of a rise in the power floating on the air while we prayed surprised me.

I tried to look, without seeming to, over at the Templar. His eyes were turned in my direction, and yet even from where I sat I could tell he was in the trancelike state of the vision sense. I heard him then.

His voice was soft, playing at the very edges of my hearing. Though his prayers continued, and all there could hear him plainly, I could hear something else as well. I could hear him speak only to me.

Remember the ledge. Seek the life. Rope once a plant.

I thought to answer him, but he knew and forestalled me. *Don't speak.*

It was difficult to keep silent, but I held my tongue and concentrated on fraying the rope. The challenge was unique, different than feeling the sap running through the trees. The rope was something long dead. I had to reach far, and think on the hemp that was, to find even a whisper of its former life. But when I did, it was so clear that I wanted to shout for joy. I very nearly lost my place in the prayer but caught myself in time.

I could see and feel the inner life of the ropes, and I knew that I was doing just as the Templar asked. *Hold now,* he whispered.

As the prayer ended, I let the link I felt with the rope seep into the earth's memory, back from where it had come. The Templar's head rested on his chest. I had no doubt that holding the link with me while he worked on his ropes had been draining.

I was frightened. I didn't want to look at any of the guards, but I could not help myself. The closest one met my eyes, and I felt a hard slap from his hand. My head snapped back. I flinched with the shock of the pain. And yet, I would rather that reaction than the one he would have shown if he had noticed anything had transpired.

Night. I didn't know whether I wished it would arrive sooner or later.

The dark settled in around us. Sounds of the night filled the air. Most of the guards lay sleeping scattered around the perimeter, their weapons at their sides.

My hands were cold. I could feel nothing of the tips. It was as if they were dead. Gone, like my toes. It was a terrifying thought. I sat up straighter, pressing my back against the tree, feeling the bite of the bark and peering down through the dark toward my bound wrists. Memories filled my mind, dark whispers of waking to the pain and horror of my mangled foot. A small, frightened whimper escaped my mouth, and in a panic I yanked at my bonds.

And then, suddenly, I was free.

I sat for a moment of disbelief, trying to steady my breathing. I was thankful then of the dark, for it hid my face as feeling rushed into my hands, like a fire raging through my arms and on down my wrists. I was near to shrieking with it.

Easy, he whispered into my mind.

I looked across the way to where the Templar was tied. I could see nothing but the vague shape of him in the dark. *Seamus?*

The first time I tried to speak back felt as if my mind was coated in a thick layer of sheep's wool — my thoughts, my words had to fight their way past. *No movement.*

Staff?

Aye. One of the men had taken it from me when they arrested us.

My sword?

On your horse. It was slowly getting easier to form the words.

Take Seamus. Escape.

His words sent a chill up my spine. I thought for a long while about the moves he had taught me, and the conflict about to come. But no matter how much I thought on it, when it happened, I was not nearly as prepared as I had hoped.

The clearing was dark and quiet, save for the crickets chirping all around. My hands had long since regained their feeling; now they just shook with terror. I stayed awake, watching the moon, watching the Templar, waiting.

And then I heard him again.

Now. Ride. Don't look back.

I wanted to protest, but I knew it would do no good. He meant for us to escape, and he was going to do everything he could to make it happen.

I turned my knees to the side, and started up. It felt as if the noise I made was enough to wake the dead, but no one noticed. Crouching low, I slowly began edging my way from the cover of the tree.

The moon was high, but its light didn't shine on me. I was mindful to move as he had taught me, softly, without disturbing the ground cover. Twigs and rocks were thick beneath my feet, but I traveled over them with barely a whisper of sound.

My heart pounded so strongly I thought I would die long before I reached Seamus. But then scarcely before I could credit it, I was there. Quickly, I stooped to feel his chest. He moaned as I turned him from his side to his back and didn't open his eyes at all. "Shhh," I said.

They had not bothered to tie his hands. I could see why. He was burning with fever and was no real worry to them. So they thought, anyway. I was hoping to prove them wrong. Stepping past Seamus, I reached for the Templar's staff, which lay on the ground nearby. The men didn't hear, but the horses did.

They began to balk and shy, their ears pressed forward. I was terrified they would give me away, and without thinking, I spoke, the same way I had to the

Templar, reaching for the mind of his horse first. The mount was all impulse and feelings.

Hush ye now, laddie. I combined my words with thoughts of safety and peace, and he and the next quieted. I was pleased with the accomplishment.

In the clearing something was happening. I saw the shadow of the Templar rise. I held my breath, waiting. It seemed as if the night stopped: The crickets went silent, and the wind paused with me.

"Non nobis, Domine!" His war cry brought the guard and those who slept rushing across the clearing. He was unarmed, but in the moment it took for me to spy him out, he had already taken the sword from the nearest.

Wasting not a moment, I sprang to my feet and loosed the horses' reins. Swiping the nearest across the hindquarters, I mentally shouted *Go!* The horse took off, bolting straight through the camp toward the Templar and the men fighting him.

I didn't stop to watch further, but did as he'd instructed me. I took the next horse, his own, to Seamus's side, hauled the man to a sitting position, and tried to get him to stand.

He was heavy, more than I expected. I could barely move him. *Please, Seamus. Help,* I begged, sending the words directly into his sleeping brain. For a moment nothing happened but then, somehow, he seemed to hear. With a moan he came back to me.

"Hurry, Seamus. Just help me get ye into the saddle. Please, we have to get out o' here." The swordplay was loud behind us. I didn't know how many the Templar had engaged, but it was too much to hope that their attention would only be on him. Near me a soldier shouted. My breath came in gasps. "Now, Seamus, now." I put the whole of my strength into lifting him up over my shoulder. I know that he helped, though it didn't seem to be much or enough, but somehow I flung him over the saddle. He pulled himself forward using our bags as leverage, and at last lay sprawled along on the horse's neck. The mount jostled, forward and back, not sure of the weight that was suddenly on him.

I took the momentary boon to draw the slender sword from the sheath of the staff. It was a good thing I did.

Like images frozen in time, the memories of my training came back to me. Balanced with sheath in one hand and sword in the other I waited for the soldier that came on attack. It could only have been a moment, but it was as if everything stilled just so that I could equip myself. And then it started.

I swung my blade, bracing for the heaviness of the soldier's sword as it encountered my own. Then, changing balance, I countered and spun out of his way. His went wide and missed me, and I slipped past his guard.

My blade drew blood, cutting strongly through his clothing.

Infuriated, he hacked down from above. I sprang to my right, leaving him grappling with air. It was then that I saw the opening. As if we were sparring on the ship, I felt the deep knowledge that the next stroke would be mine. Without pause I took it, swiping my blade cleanly across his neck.

Exhilaration turned to horror as I watched the stripe of red well and gape. The bile rose in me, and I turned, blind, back to Seamus. The horse had been standing idle, shifting, trying to decide what it was supposed to do. My hands were on the saddle before I could think. Then from nowhere, I heard the Templar's voice in my head. *Go. Now!*

I sheathed the blade, tucked it under my arm, and vaulted into the saddle behind Seamus, nearly bringing us both down. With a great heave, I leaned onto Seamus, grasped the reins, and shouted like a man gone mad. "Go, go, go!"

RIDE LIKE THE WIND

The horse bolted just in time, plowing directly into the path of a soldier rushing us. I kicked out with my leg and caught the man in the chest, knocking him back and away. Then I tucked my legs tight to the horse's sides and mentally shouted to run like the wind.

He did. Past the clearing and out of the woods. There was nothing before us but hills and vales.

I was desperate to know how the Templar was faring, but I knew that I would do just as he said, get away and take the carving with me. I felt it then, as if the mere thought called it to life. Its burn scalded clear through the sporran, still tucked beneath my robe.

We rode like demons were on our tail, never looking back, never slowing, cutting east, then north, to make the trail difficult to follow. We slowed when I was sure no one was behind. Then, and only then, did I think about what had happened and what I had done.

This was not the first time I had killed, and I thought it should have been easier to bear. But it was not. I could not fool myself into believing I had acted on impulse.

That was a part of it, but I knew full well that, in the heat of the fight, I was in it all the way. It was kill or be killed, and somehow, right now, that seemed even worse.

I slid from the horse, careful not to take Seamus with me, and walked beside. The night air was cool on my hot skin. The sounds of nature loud. I heard the call of a wolf in the distance. A sennight ago it would have frightened me greatly, yet now, I could barely rouse myself to feel anything but the guilt and remorse filling my soul.

I led the horse deep into a copse. Morning was drawing near. I didn't deceive myself into thinking they would not come after us, but hoped and prayed that the Templar would find us first.

With as many soft fronds as I could gather, I made a pallet for Seamus. When it was right, I dragged him from the horse and laid him on it. His color was not encouraging: white like the lime we washed the great boulder with in the square at home so very long ago. Enormous dark circles ringed his eyes, and his cheeks were sunken and sallow.

I washed his face with water from the skin and checked the wounds on his body. The whippings he had endured left horrific marks I could never have imagined if I'd not seen them. His skin was purely stripped away in many places, and I could see beyond to the inside of him. I thought that the damage would make me sick, but oddly it didn't.

I had no salve like the one Brother Bertrand had used, but I did my best to clean the wounds as he had done, hoping that would help. My body was fit to drop when finally I finished. With everything in me I tried to stay awake, waiting for the Templar to come. He'd feel my soul's signature, I knew, as he had done from the beginning, and he would find us.

I fell asleep beside Seamus, with the horse tied to a nearby branch. It was not until I was deeply asleep that I had the vision that showed how very wrong I had been.

ALONE

A sword glinted in the moonlight, sweeping a path of destruction. Men were swarming. More than he could handle.

I woke shaking, terrified. He was not coming. He had not gotten away. Seamus was no help to me, and the Templar was somewhere, captured and beaten at the very least. I had to do something, but what?

I looked over at Seamus, so still, so frighteningly deathlike. I felt the slow, steady beat of the land beneath us. The carving was warm — not the glowing, burning fire of danger, but a steady, solid presence. I turned the sporran to the front and took the carving in my hand.

Its glow was heartening. As beaten down and discouraged as I was, the carving gave me hope. And it gave me something else. Suddenly I had a strange compulsion to lay my hands on Seamus. With nothing left to lose, I set the carving on his chest and rested my hands beside it.

Tingling heat ran through my fingers, and I felt myself drift, welcoming my other sense.

I saw deep into Seamus — beneath his skin to the very essence of bone and muscle. And without any doubt whatsoever, I knew how to make him whole once again and set about it.

Sweat rose on my skin and exhaustion weighted my limbs. What I was doing was taking its own toll on my body, but I continued knitting ripped and torn muscle, feeding blood to the places that were in need, healing the bones, speeding his body on its way to recovery.

As the sun set once again in the hot sky, I came to, lying half on, half off Seamus's chest, with the carving nestled safely in my hands.

"Get off, Tormod," I heard his weak voice say. "Ye're crushing me."

"Ye took yer time about waking," I said, rolling exhausted to his side. I slept then for so many marks of the candle I cannot even reckon them.

CONTRITION

I woke reaching for the carving, rooting around behind and under me. I was in a panic until I felt it pressing into my thigh beneath the fold of my robe.

"Here," Seamus said. "Eat."

He had foraged and found a variety of nuts and wild mushrooms. "Not much in the way o' a feast, but it fills the emptiness."

"Water?" I asked, groggily.

"Aye. Here." He handed me a skin, and I drank until I needed to come up for air.

"Ye healed me." Wonder filled his voice, but I sensed as well something was not as it should be. "Why did ye do it? Why did ye not let me die, as I should have?"

There was a darkness to him, a bleak despair that I felt coming off him in waves. As I was aware of the land, I now was aware of Seamus. Something in me had changed.

"No one should die when they are not destined to," I said. " 'Tis a sin to wish it on yerself."

His eyes turned to me. "I have betrayed him an' given us all over to death. I wish mine to come now."

"No. Speak not that way," I said. "The Templar is in need. Somehow we must work together to help him."

I looked to the night sky where a bright star to the north pointed the direction we would travel to follow the map, but we would not follow it as yet.

"How long did I sleep?" I was worried. The vision of the Templar's fight for our lives hung sharply in my mind's eye.

"A night an' a day. I tried to wake ye, but it was to no avail." There was a listlessness to Seamus that worried me.

"Tell me what has happened to ye, and I will do the same," I said. " 'Tis only with the full truth between us that we might hope to salvage this day."

He spoke of the night we disappeared. "They boarded the ship no' more than a candle mark after ye'd left. Not soldiers, but mercenaries. They had orders to keep us alive an' deliver us to Philippe." He spoke the tale without passion, as if it were nothing to him.

"We were taken to Paris for questioning." He shivered, and I noticed that he could not seem to stop. He clamped his hands together to try and still them. His face was white, and I could feel the fear and revulsion projecting from his mind.

"I gave them everything. All they could want an' more. I will pay for it with the price o' my soul." His head was low. Nothing I could say would have made a difference. I kept silent, feeling the press of his emotions beneath the surface of his mind.

"What did ye tell them, Seamus?"

"That Alex is following a map, seeking whatever lies a' its end." He took a short breath. "They know his safe places an' that the stars are the markers. They know he has a talisman that is helping him find his way."

My breath came out in a rush. "Ye gave him away! How could ye?"

"Do ye think for a moment that I don't ask myself that? Ye've no idea what Philippe is like, Tormod. So fair an' fine-looking, but he has the soul of a viper. The things that he did, the tortures he devised . . ." Beads of sweat gathered on his forehead. "An' now they have Alexander an' the carving. 'Tis over."

The bulk of the carving felt heavy in my sporran. Should I tell Seamus that Philippe's men did not have it? Should I give the carving over to him? Had he not already compromised our duty? Would he do it again?

The Templar's words echoed in my mind. *Trust no one. Safeguard it.*

A wash of fear crested in me. Would not these same tortures befall the Templar if he had survived the last encounter?

"We must go back," I said.

Seamus looked at me long and hard. I saw something flash in the depths of his eyes, and it frightened me. It was a longing, a longing for death.

PART THREE

RETURN

We took the chance that it was the last thing they would ever expect — that we would return. Seamus and I backtracked to the place we had been. The ash of the fire was long cold, but Seamus knew where they were going. He had been in and out of consciousness for many days before they found us, and had listened when they thought that he could not.

They were taking him to the walled city of Carcassonne, no more than a day from our last camp. Philippe waited there for word from his men on the ambush set for us.

We rode as fast as our burdened mount would take us, stopping only long enough to dismount and walk for stretches to relieve him. The land was easy. Slight slopes and valleys filled much of the trek, then gave way to a heavily forested wood. The wind was brisk. A seasonal storm was setting to open up on us. The skies were dark and overcast, and the hills a myriad of summer green.

My mind twisted and turned, thoughts whirling without beginning or end, all centered on how we could do anything to aid the Templar. He would be heavily guarded. And we were but two.

For all my thinking, I had come up with nothing by the time we arrived, and a feeling of despair settled over me. The city was a fortress. Its walls were great blocks of granite. Its windows were few and set high in the towers. Guards patrolled the gate, and sentries stood in the towers. How would we ever get inside, and what would we do then?

We camped in the woods, watching and timing the guards. I repeated the rotation aloud often in that first day, marking time with the progression of the sun across the sky. Seamus sat and watched silently. Where his mind had gone I had no idea, but late on the second day of our watch he spoke.

"There's got to be a way in."

I saw it just when he did. A single horse-drawn cart traveled the path to the gates.

We waited several candle marks. Time seemed to stretch on forever. Finally the cart reappeared, and it was no longer empty.

"Stay here," Seamus said. "I'll be back shortly. If anyone marks me, I rely on ye to cover my back."

He left me standing there wondering just how I was supposed to do that. I drew my dagger and crouched in the tree cover, the sword from the staff at my side. The wind blew down over the valley, rustling the branches, rattling my knees. Every noise made me jump. Every breath I took was labored.

Seamus appeared driving the wagon a short while later. Where the former driver and his passenger were, I didn't know, but he now wore a dull brown robe over his tunic. "Get in and pull yer hat low."

I climbed up and glanced back into the wagon. Fresh dark splotches stained the wooden planking.

He pulled the cart off to the side of the road. Waiting. Watching. I wanted to ask him what we were doing, but he had the look of the Templar — absolute concentration. A quarter mark of the candle later, he urged the wagon back onto the road.

"The new guards are in place. Let us hope they didn't speak much on the change." He flicked the reins. "Keep yer head down an' say nothing." I'd never seen him this way — solid, serious, deadly. I ducked my head and we rolled on across the drawbridge and boldly up to the gate.

"State yer business," called the guard.

"We're to pick up a body. Overdue, too," he added.

"You were supposed to be here earlier," the man said keenly.

My heart was beating triple time. Without thought I called up the power of the land and whispered a push of uncertainty. Immediately I felt the hum of another. Seamus had added his influence. The guard did not pause, just called for the gate to open, and the cart rolled inside with no fanfare.

Inside was a wide cobbled road. Seamus urged the horse with the reins and slowly we clopped up the slope, around the bend, and out of the sight of the guards.

"Ye've learned something while we were apart," said Seamus. This was as close to a compliment as ever I had received from him.

In a dark alleyway, in a seemingly less used part of the city, we tied up the horse and wagon and set out on foot. "They've got to have him in the citadel. They spoke o' cells in the bowels o' the city, where the inquisitor has free rein."

The thought made me move faster. I had been lagging, frightened by the silence around me and over the ease of our entrance. With barely a sound we slipped through the darkened alleys. Seamus moved with unerring accuracy. "How do ye know where ye're going?" I whispered.

"There is only one way, Tormod," he said. "Can ye no' feel his pain?"

I glanced quickly at Seamus. His face was pale.

I focused and found that I could feel the trace of the Templar's aura, mingling with the beat of the land. Pain rippled across the surface of my back. I hissed, wishing that I hadn't.

"Distance yerself," he commanded. I heard him but was too caught up in what I had tapped. "Focus. Ground. Shield!" he snapped. He sounded so like the Templar that I reacted and the pain receded. "Good. Ye need to practice that, Tormod. Ye cannot allow yerself to get trapped in a loop o' someone else's aura. Ye might never regain yer full faculties."

This Seamus was new to me. I didn't know what to say. I followed him without a word through the alleys and around corners as he tracked the Templar's pain. I did not, however, open myself to that trail again. Seamus led the way.

The citadel was a heavily protected keep built into the rock of the hillside in the lowest part of the city. Two guards stood at the front and one patrolled the roof. We crept around the perimeter looking for an entrance, but there was no other way in.

"No one goes in or out," Seamus murmured. "The guards are on high alert." I was stooped next to him beside the eastern wall of the keep. The ground beneath my feet was soft and smelled badly. I moved to Seamus's left to seek stronger purchase.

"God's thumbs, Tormod. What did ye step in?" He shook his head to clear the smell from his nose.

"I don't know, but it's making my eyes tear. Seems to be a stream o' it running right through here." I scraped my boots on the harder dirt trying to get rid of the filth. Then it hit me. "No one goes in, but something is getting out. Look!" It was hard to see in the dark when not seeking it, but once recognized, it was discernible. The stream of muck was leaching from a grate set low in the side of the keep. A gulley of runoff snaked directly to where I'd been standing. The privy pits.

THE PRIVY PITS

"Do ye think we could fit through?" I asked staring at the grate and dark space behind.

"Aye. It looks to be wide enough for two side by side, but 'tis only waist high. I don't know what's on the other side o' it, but 'tis worth a try, don't ye think?" A rotten smell wafted up my nose. It was all I could do to keep from answering no. This foul, disgusting discovery had been mine.

"Let's go," I said, anxious to be on our way.

"Hold," said Seamus. "If I've not offended the Lord, mayhap He will help us in our endeavor." He made the sign of the cross and I followed. "Our Father, who art in heaven . . ."

We clasped arms, as I'd seen him do with the Templar. "May the Lord guide our steps," he said.

"And our faith remain true," I replied. Seamus could not seem to meet my gaze, and I wondered for a moment what was wrong.

I didn't, however, have time to think on it, for it was time to move. The guards were leaving their post to brief the sentries coming on duty. We would only have moments, and we took the opportunity given, leaving our concealment at a sprint. We followed the path of the foul-smelling stream across the way and up to the wall. To avoid their eyes, we flattened ourselves against it and inched our way to the grate. Seamus leapt the small mouth of the gulley and positioned himself on one side. I stayed on the other. Then, as one, we met in the middle and tested its strength.

On the first tug it moved not at all, but on the second there was a wavering, and the mortar used to hold it in place crumbled beneath our onslaught. The grate was very old, and the constant flow of muck had eroded its metal edges. I could hear the guards moving into place. They were not directly above, but close enough that I thought I'd die then and there.

On the third try the grate came free with a soft rusted whine. Quickly we threw ourselves back, flat against the wall. I heard the guards approach, above.

Pressure blossomed in the back of my eyes, and I felt the hum coming from Seamus.

"Just a boar," said a guard.

"A nice meal that would make, eh?" spoke another.

"A sight better than the stale oats we've been given," replied the first.

The sound of their footsteps receding allowed me to breathe once again. Seamus motioned me in. With one last breath of somewhat fresh air, I ducked and darted in through the grate.

Ugh! It was all I could do not to shout the word aloud. The place was disgusting, as foul as ever I had smelled. In the black of the pits was the refuse of many. As we stepped into the depth of it, the slime slid past my ankles. I felt it squish beneath my boots, and when I forced myself to put my hands before me, I touched a wall that was coated.

"Gawd," I whispered, snatching my fingers back. I was at the base of a long shaft. The space was actually quite wide at the bottom. Seamus entered a moment later and I heard a slight gagging as he fought to keep from retching.

I had moved as far as the hole would allow me, to the left. Now, I hurried past him, to the right. Ahead there was a door. On it a small, rusted latch snapped off at my touch, leaving us locked out where we were.

"Great." Seamus's disgust was near on as annoying as it had been on the ship.

"Well, if ye've got a better way," I snapped.

"Shhh." He hissed. "Step back."

Inside the corridor a disturbing sound reverberated, a strange rustle and crack that chilled me to the bone. Beside me Seamus gagged.

"What?" I whispered.

"Cat-o'-nine." His voice was strangled. "The lash."

My body went cold as the sound came with an unrelenting rhythm. Without wanting to, I strained to hear the gasp of a prayer between the lash strokes.

In my mind I matched his prayers, sick in my heart and soul. Questions fell but none were answered. The lashing seemed as if it would go on an eternity.

"Back." Seamus's sudden whisper had me scrambling away from him. A soft thrum seemed to fill the space around us as he laid his hands on the door. It was black as pitch, but the edges of him faintly glowed. His body was stiff and still. Then from beyond the door the lashing and questions stopped. The door to a cell opened, and the sound of men passing came to me.

We waited in silence. I would not make the mistakes I had made with the Templar. Seamus moved first. "Give me yer dagger."

I fished it from my sporran and handed it to him.

He jammed it hard in the latch I had broken. It seemed impossible that it worked and no one heard, but moments later the door opened.

The light from a torch slowly filled the space, then waned as whoever had been there disappeared on their way.

"Others will not be far off. They'd not leave him alone." His voice was low and breathless. Slowly we crept out. The corridor bent a short distance away, and he held me back.

"Stay here a moment." I didn't even hear his steps, but a moment later came a dull thud, the sound of something large hitting the floor. In the dark silence I heard the soft rattle of keys.

"Tormod, come," he whispered loudly.

I moved quickly, stumbling, but righting myself when my feet encountered a body on the floor. "Is he dead?" I asked, sickened.

"No. Come, help me."

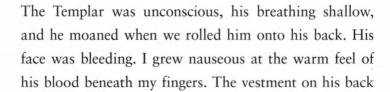

The Templar was unconscious, his breathing shallow, and he moaned when we rolled him onto his back. His face was bleeding. I grew nauseous at the warm feel of his blood beneath my fingers. The vestment on his back was shredded.

"What have they done to ye?" My voice was hollow. *Lord, help us, please. Help him.*

"Hurry, Tormod," Seamus said. "He's deadweight an' not walking out o' here on his own."

Seamus beneath one arm, and I the other, we dragged him, his head lolling forward in a faint.

Slowly we made our way back through the corridor and out of the doorway. The weight of his body was tremendous and the blood from his wounds slippery in my hands. The heavy, copper smell of it filled the dark space. His agony seemed to echo against the walls of my mind.

We came at last on the foul pit just as the carving began to flare.

"They're coming," I said breathlessly. "Hurry, Seamus."

We nearly dropped him in the struggle to get him through the grate. Seamus went first while I gripped the Templar's vestments, my arms aching with the strain. Then I pushed as Seamus pulled, dragging the Templar close against the wall to freedom. Waiting. Listening.

One. Two. Three. We counted the guard's steps overhead. *Four. Five. Six.* "Now," Seamus whispered, and we took off for the shelter of the darkened alleys. I thought there'd be an outcry, men at our back. There was nothing, but the trip was agonizing. The Templar remained unconscious, his tunic soaked clear through. My arms and back burned with the effort not to drop him.

"Get up," said Seamus, taking on the whole weight of the Templar's body.

I leapt into the wagon bed, and together we lifted the Templar and laid him in the straw. With a dark, filthy blanket that had seen much use, we covered him, hiding the white of his vestments.

"Get up in the seat and drive," Seamus ordered, handing me the dagger. "Take him through the front gate. Use the power on the guard if ye have to."

"Wait," I said. "What are ye going to do?"

"Do as I say and don't question it. It's vital that ye both go on an' finish as ye were destined. Follow the map."

I wavered. How could I leave him here?

"Go, before it's all for naught." He took the walking stick from the wagon and unsheathed the blade. "I'll keep them occupied an' run, as soon as I know ye're safe away." His face was white, pleading.

"No. I cannot leave ye," I said.

He looked at me one last time, and in his face I saw that the decision was out of my hands. "I'm sorry, Tormod. For everything." He slapped the horse's flank with the flat of the blade. "Heyah!" The animal took off faster than I had expected, and it was all I could do to rein him back in and direct us toward the gate at the sedate pace the healer I had replaced would have.

I dared not look back, but focused all my attention on the gate ahead and the aura of the guards pacing above. *They're o' no concern*, I whispered. *Let the wagon through.* My head pounded this time with the effort.

The gate dropped, and I crossed the drawbridge. On the far side I pushed again, even though my stomach now was heaving from the mental effort I'd expended already.

North. I urged the horse along the road and away.

⊕

Tuo da Gloriam.

The shout came at me across the distance of space and mind.

The clash of swords. Darkness. A yearning for death. Troubled eyes.

"No!" I snapped from the vision sense. "It was no' supposed to be this way! Ye said ye would leave. Ye said ye would escape."

Another life. Another cruel end. It was too much. This all was too much. I shook as if palsied, the tears rolling down my cheeks as I slumped over in the seat.

Hush ye now, Tormod. The Templar's soft Highland lilt whispered in my mind.

I sat up quickly and leapt into the back of the wagon beside him. "Seamus . . ." I whispered.

Let no' his sacrifice be in vain. His mind voice was full of grief. *We have yet a duty to fulfill.*

DESTINATION

I held a water skin to the Templar's lips, urging, willing him to drink. He did, but sparsely. It was almost more energy than he could expend. There was nowhere on the Templar's back that was not cut and welted.

"I can heal ye. Let me try," I pleaded.

"Ye've done too much already, Tormod. The power changes us, takes a toll every time it is used. Ye healed Seamus."

My head was pounding and my body felt drained. I hadn't realized why. "How did ye know?"

"I felt ye. It matters no'. We must leave here. The soldiers will be seeking us."

I didn't push the discussion. He was sorely injured. I got down from the wagon and watered the horse. How had this come to pass? I could not seem to make my mind work it through. The carving sat at my middle in the depths of my sporran, thankfully cool once again. I watched the Templar, sick with worry. Each time he shifted, the blood seemed to seep once more.

"Let's go." I let the horse have one last go at the water, then took it away and dumped the little left. "Do we still have the map?" he asked.

"Aye. They never took the saddlebags from yer mount." As he reached for it, he grimaced and his skin paled. "North and west from here."

We set out straightaway. In the quiet drone of the horse's tread, I thought about Seamus. Part of me wanted to talk to the Templar about what had happened, but another part of me was a coward whose throat filled with lumps and eyes filled with tears each time I tried to speak. It mattered not; the Templar had fallen into a pained sleep. I would not wake him. He needed rest and healing. I had to wonder if all that we'd been through, all that had happened, would be worth it in the end.

We traveled the low rolling hills for most of the day. Even in sleep, he winced each time the wagon jarred him. Exhaustion and pain issued from his body, and the feel of it twisted my insides. He woke several times, and at each interval I urged water on him.

By nightfall we were deep into a forest that marked the gradual ascent into a group of low-lying hills. The dark of the sky was a silken purple, the dots of the stars like fireflies above us. I decided to stop for a rest and drew up before a rippling basin of water, fed by a cascading fall over the jagged rock of the hillside. Cool mist surrounded the place.

Labored breath rang in my ears. I looked around disoriented. Steep rocks filled the space before my eyes. Feet stumbling. Climbing.

The carving in my sporran was burning. *Focus. Ground. Shield.*

"Templar Alexander . . ." I whispered. Fumbling, I drew the carving from the pouch as he woke and inched his way to the edge of the wagon bed.

He was pale and drawn, barely managing to sit as he followed the direction of my gaze. With a gasp that disappeared beneath the crash of the water, he crossed himself with reverence.

In the spray of the crystalline waterfall, a brilliant splayed cross was illuminated.

"What does it mean?" I whispered in awe.

"Look!"

I turned to find his gaze not ahead, but above. There in the sky directly atop us was the glow of the constellation that matched the one we had been staring at from the beginning. The constellation that marked the map.

"Behind the falls," I said. "An old man came this way."

With a torch made of a dried tree limb and a strip of my tunic, I led the way carrying the last of our supplies, his sword, and my dagger. The Templar had all he could handle lifting himself in his weakened state.

The climb was slow. In the dark, footing was unsure. The cool mist coated my skin, but I was warm beneath the carving's steady glow.

At the mouth of the cave I helped the Templar over the last of the climb. We stood on the ledge as he gathered strength, staring into the depths of the blackness. The crash of the water echoed with the beat of the land, and I listened, taking it deep inside me, then letting it drift out again.

The Templar stood beside me, suddenly stronger and steadier than he had been only moments before.

" 'Tis an ancient healing site," he said. "Can ye feel the power?"

"Aye," I said. "What is it?"

" 'Tis said that throughout our world there are places where the earth's power is concentrated, where the pulse beats strongest, and the heart of the land lives. This is one of them."

He took the torch and moved into the cave, shining the light on the walls. Images were scribed there, ancient and beautiful — older even than the ones on the astrolabe. I moved close, running my fingers along the nearest. There were symbols and pictures, and in the midst of it I saw a cross similar to that of the Templar Order. I saw things that were half man, half animal. And lines that ran in patterns with no beginning or end. "Can ye read it?" I asked.

"No. Perhaps if I had more time."

In the back of the cave we found the remnant of a long-dead fire. Twigs and old logs lay nearby. I stacked them and lit the bundle with the torch.

"Ye will need as many torches as we can make," he said. "The tunnels are black as pitch."

"I?"

He didn't speak for a moment. Then quietly he said, "They are coming, Tormod." He sat down beside the fire, staring into the orange glow of the flames. "We've spoken before o' the pebble dropped into the stream, aye?"

"Aye," I replied, remembering. "Ye said what we saw as the future could be changed."

"What I have seen has already begun to change, Tormod. Ye have changed it. This is yer legacy. Yer duty to fulfill." He reached for his sword, though the movement clearly sent pain cascading through him. He bared the blade from its sheath. "It is my duty to make sure ye have the chance."

"No," I protested. "This is no' a thing I can do alone. Ye cannot stay here." It was always all right when he was by my side, but I knew what he proposed.

"I must keep them from reaching ye. I have seen what is to come. It is vital that I protect ye. 'Tis my calling, though for a while I was no' very good a' it." He slowly began his exercises. "I don't have the endurance to travel the tunnels that lead off from here. There is no telling how far they twist beneath the mountain."

I had come far in overcoming my fear of the darkness, but this was different altogether.

"There is wood enough for several torches." He pointed his sword toward a pile of sticks in the corner. "Use the blanket. Make strips an' tie them to the top." He continued to work his body, readying for confrontation. His back was oozing fresh blood with movements that had to be painful, but he kept at it.

"How are ye feeling?" I asked.

He didn't answer immediately. "Tormod, our goal is within reach." His voice was strong and determined. "I will guard yer back an' do what I must."

I looked at the torch in my hand and dropped my head. "I am afraid," I said.

"Wise men fear, Tormod, but they don't let the fear stop them from accomplishing what they must."

"I am not worthy," I said. "I'm not like ye. I question His will. I'm no' good enough to be a Templar."

He looked up at me, compassion in his eyes. "O' course ye are, lad. A Templar is just one who believes, one who is called. Ye, Tormod, have been called. Do ye disbelieve that for a second?"

I thought on it. I felt the carving warm, now back inside my sporran, and remembered the many visions that had come to me over the past few months. "I know that I have been called. I just worry that when it comes time to do something about it, I will fail."

"We can only do our best, Tormod. 'Tis all that is asked o' us." It was so simple to him. His faith was stronger than any man I'd ever met.

"Are ye ready?" he asked, sheathing the blade.

I had enough food and water for several days. And as I lit the first torch from the embers of the fire, he approached.

I took a deep breath. "Aye," I said. "I am."

He nodded. "Pay heed to yer torch. If the light goes out it might mean the difference between life an' death. But if ye should lose it, look to yer other senses."

I gathered my things and he helped me bundle the rest of the torches into my plaid. I was ready, and yet so unready I wanted to beg him to come with me.

"Godspeed, lad." Something in his tone struck a strange chord in me.

"Ye will wait for me? Will ye not?" I asked, suddenly uneasy.

"Aye. As 'tis within my power to do so."

I should have been assured, but for some reason a dark shadow hung heavy between us.

"All will be as it should, Tormod. It will be as it must." He read my thoughts, just as he had always done, and that in and of itself was reassuring. I nodded and turned away. Holding the flaming torch before me, I began my journey into the belly of the mountain.

THE TUNNELS

The dark in the caves was different than any place I could ever remember. It surrounded me, pressing against the light of the torch. I could see no farther than the glowing gold of the flame. My first few steps were halting, as if there was no earth beyond the step I took; but as the sameness continued, I became, if not comfortable, less wary.

The smell of ripe earth and wetness in the air made my clothes damp on my body. The path I chose branched away from the main, yet I knew the way deep in my bones. An odd tug in my gut drove me forward.

Time passed with no way of accounting for it, save the burn of the torches and the curl of hunger in my stomach. I walked long, taking breaks when my legs were too tired to continue. I ate when I needed, slept when compelled, and woke when my body decided it was time.

The Templar was right. He would not have been able to make this journey. Though I was certain the carving was leading me along the correct path, I had no idea how far I had yet to go. I was down to one torch to which I tied strips of my tunic, but I knew there was coming a time when I would have nothing left to keep the torch alive. The thought made me extend my distance a little more each time I felt I could go no farther.

I pushed myself hard, making my way to the elusive place my body and the carving seemed to hunt. But during a rest I could delay no more, the flame that had become my only companion flickered and died.

When I awoke, it was to a blackness that was absolute. I cried out, feeling for my bundles and the staff that I had last used as a torch. Its end was warm, but there was no flame or ember. My light had gone. I could see nothing, not the walls of the cave around me, nor the tips of my fingers, though they were right before my eyes.

My heart beat so loud I could hear it in my ears, and my breath became short — as if along with the light, the air had suddenly disappeared.

It was then that I felt it, a sudden spark of warmth on my stomach, a heat so strong it was nearly pain. I scrambled to my knees and dug in my sporran. The glow of the carving was brilliant. It lit the space better than the best of my torches and gave off a path of sparkling light I knew to follow.

Moments later I stumbled into the cavern, barely able to believe my eyes; only in Heaven could there be such brilliance as this. The walls were lit from within.

In the center of the room an enormous pillar stood, one great stalagmite that seemed carved of ice. In a daze I moved toward it, holding the carving stretched out before me, prayer spilling from my lips. In the side of the pillar was a natural depression, a shelf that held something I knew eyes had not seen in over a thousand years.

To say that it was a bowl would be as like to describe the waterfall outside as a bit of rainfall. I placed the carving down on the ledge and, with a trembling hand, lifted the most fragile, beautiful vessel I had ever encountered.

Its brilliant white wood was hollowed and smoothed by loving hands. On the outer surface an intricate pattern of vines and roots wound in a delicate never-ending tracery. Tiny leaves covered bits and pieces, but never did they conceal or cut off the wonder of the curved vine.

While I held it, tingling warmth raced through me. Suddenly I knew what I was supposed to do. Slowly I placed the vessel into the upraised hands of the carving, and for a moment that lasted a lifetime I cradled them both.

CHOICE

From the tips of my fingers to the ends of my hair, energy crackled, whipping through my body like the wind.

Colors flared and swirled, taking my breath away. Beautiful. Vibrant. Life thrummed in and around me, and I was a part. Past, present, future — images flitted through my mind in a blur. Faces. Places. Births. Deaths. Generations of lives became my own.

They were protectors, linked in the duty this sacred vessel called me to fulfill. All were gifted, honest, dedicated, and strong. They were everything I longed to be, but knew I was not.

What was I doing? I was not brave nor strong. Everything I did was wrong. I would make a mistake, lose it or break it or give it to the wrong person. I was suddenly afraid. The responsibility was too much.

I willed my fingers to open, to break the hold the vessel had on me. As if in response, an image unfolded before me. A sword slack at the Templar's side. His eyes blank, caught in the vision state. A shadow on the wall grew large. A sword arced, a life-stealing blow.

No! It could not be. I had to go to him. He had to be warned. But how?

Focus. Details of the vision of the Templar came instantly at my call, clear and sharp. The sound of men moving up the rocks played in my ears, and the spicy smell of the herbs Ahram and his men used to clean their bodies filled my nose. I could not determine if the vision was of the present or future. Had it happened already or would it soon come to pass? All I wanted was to drop the vessel and rush to him, but I could not let go.

Ground. Gritting my teeth, I concentrated, seeking the still and silent place within the swirl of color. I locked mind and body into the depths of the earth. The power flowed through me from the ground at my feet, branching like a tree reaching for the heavens as the earth's magic filled my veins. Strong. Powerful. Potent. "What do Ye want of me?" I shouted.

And then it came to me. Choose. Accept or deny the duty set before me.

Shield. With a nearly effortless flick, I sent the well of power out toward the edges of my skin and looked down at the precious burden in my hands. Doubt fled. I needed the power of the vessel if I had any hope of saving him.

"I accept."

Two simple words brought the chaos to an end as my fingers slowly unfurled and the bowl and carving tumbled to the cave floor.

I woke to blackness, but there was no fear of the dark within me. With a start I realized that the holy vessel was not in my hands. Scrambling, I reached for the carving and tucked it in my sporran. Then I gently wrapped the bowl in my plaid.

With a sense of purpose and direction I left the cavern. The cool scent of damp earth hung in the air and a new awareness of the land's power filled me.

I ran, as I had when this whole trek began. The thud of my feet echoed in the tunnels and time passed in a blur. Fear for the Templar and terror that I would be too late pushed me nearly beyond my limits.

But then, from a distance I felt him. *Alexander!* I reached — joy and relief so heady I could barely breathe — and saw the vision that held him.

Me. I saw myself running through the dark of the tunnels. Now.

Tormod! Go back!

CONFRONTATION

I stumbled, feeling the lash of his anger. *Take it an' go. Damn ye, lad!*

But it was too late. I burst into the cave from a tunnel tucked in a fold of rock at his right, just as Philippe's soldiers rushed from beneath the falls. The Templar was as I'd seen him in the vision, his sword slack by his side, his eyes glazed, as battle cries bounced off the walls around us. I screamed and dove in front of him, my hand sweeping down and ripping the sword from his lax fingers.

It was heavy but felt right in my palm. I brought it up just as the first man came at me. The crack of his blade on mine brought me alive and I attacked with a vengeance, determined to protect the Templar until he could recover.

Ahram appeared at my side. Bakir and Fakih were at the cave's entrance heavily engaged. The Templar was suddenly behind me, out of his daze and shouting for his sword. I turned, distracted, and made to toss it to him just as the blade of the man before me snaked past my guard.

"No!" I screamed, filled with the knowledge of what would happen. As if time tried to reverse itself, the world slowed. Ahram dove toward us, his scimitar arcing down just as the sword of our attacker met its mark.

Blood from the man's arm splashed the runes on Ahram's face. I whirled and watched the Templar fall to his knees, clutching the blade in his chest.

"No! This will not be!" I drew the carving from my sporran, tossing off the plaid that covered the bowl. As the two reunited in my hands, the power of the land flared to life once more. Heat and color burst within me. Anger flooded my mind.

Men stopped midbattle, stumbling back, screaming in terror as a hot wind tore a circle around my body. I felt their fear and wanted them to suffer. I could think of nothing but destruction.

The blood in their bodies began to surge. I felt hearts pumping harder and faster and focused the power, unmoved by their screams.

Stop, Tormod! The Templar's weak command broke into my haze. *We are no' meant to use the power this way. Ye're a Templar. Ye're o' the light. Push it away.*

I was lost, confused. Staring around, I saw men cowering, white, bleeding. Others, released from my hold were clambering out of the cave.

"What have I done? Lord, what have I done?"

I turned to the Templar, begging for guidance,

dropping to his side. He was fading. Moving beyond. Leaving me.

"Please, Lord," I begged. "I'll do anything Ye ask, be anything Ye need. Please help me, just this once!"

Power rose again at my call, illuminating the cave with the brilliance of day. Heat suffused me and, as I had done before, I used the shield command to push it out to the edges of my skin. With the vessel still tight in my fingers, I laid it on his chest and focused on the wound.

No. His command was absolute. *The effort will steal yer strength. Take it from here, Tormod. This time ye will do as I say. Ye will change the outcome. I have seen it.*

And then, the Templar was no longer in my mind. He was closed off to me. Slowly I watched his body grow still.

"Ahhh!" My cry was that of a bairn torn from the arms of its mother. "No, Lord." I sobbed.

Ahram was beside me. "Tormod. More are coming. I'll see to him. There's nothing more you can do."

I could barely hear him through my grief. And then his hands were on me, heavy. Sharply, he dragged me to my feet. "Go, boy! He gave his life for you. Be gone from here, now!"

I stood, wavering, barely comprehending Ahram's dark eyes, snapping with anger. "Get out and run!"

Understanding came on me in a rush. I grabbed my plaid and threw it over the carving and bowl. I could feel the life pulse of men beyond the falls and bolted into the nearest corridor as darkness embraced me and I ran for my life.

AFTERMATH

Night was as day. I could sense nothing of the turning of time in the corridors beneath the mountain. And yet I moved through the blackness with ease. Tears streaked my cheeks, and the pain in my heart felt like a wound. He was gone.

His face hung in the dark of my mind, white and still. I would never see him again, never be his apprentice. The thought was a knife to my soul. I wanted nothing but to go back in time and erase what had happened, to die in his stead, or to stop running and lie on the floor of the cave and never rise again.

But even in this black hour, I would not. I had accepted the charge given me. The holy vessel and its power were mine to safeguard. I had seen what it could do, felt the awesome temptation to use it for evil, and understood how dangerous it was unguarded in the world.

I did not believe myself worthy, but I would do my best to ensure that not only the Templar's sacrifice, but that of Seamus and all of the others who had died in its service, were not in vain.

The beat of the land echoed in the wash of my blood. With a burdened heart I made my way through the dark, out into the light of a new day.

THE END

AUTHOR'S NOTE

The main characters in this novel are fictitious, and their resemblance to persons living or dead is purely coincidental. I did, however, bend facts with some of the historical characters, placing them in situations and geographical locations that helped the plot, and, in the case of Hughes de Payens, endowed him with the vision sense. Montségur was not a base for the Knights Hospitaller, but a twist of history I used to introduce readers to another important military body of the time, and also to explain the advanced system of checks and balances the Templars established. Please forgive my suggestion that the Popes Boniface and Benedict were part of a secret upper-echelon sect of the Templar Order. Although there is no evidence of this, imagining it adds depth to the mystery and makes a better story.

There was a group of warrior monks, the Poor Knights of the Temple of Solomon (or Knights Templar), who were an important and influential political and military body that functioned for nearly two centuries in the Holy Land and on three continents. Sworn to vows of poverty and chastity, they were nonetheless one of the wealthiest and most powerful governing bodies during the Middle Ages, with an impressive maritime presence. Their work in banking and finance was the precursor of many of the financial systems in use today. At their height they were the protectors of the treasuries and crown jewels of both France and England.

I came across the history of the Templars accidentally, while researching Scotland for an adult novel I was doing at the time. I was immediately drawn into their intrigue, and the more research I did, the more I felt the need to write about them. Their story demanded that I find and develop a knight of character and caring. Little did I know that I would find two.

ACKNOWLEDGMENTS

To my boys, Jim, James, and Conor: Your influence is clear on every page. You have my thanks and love, always.

To my fabulous editors Andrea Davis Pinkney and Eleni Beja: I can't thank you enough for taking a chance on a newcomer and embracing this completely insanely complicated little novel.

Special thanks are also given to Walter Lorraine, David Macaulay, Allen Say, and Fran Hodgkins, friends who each in their way, spearheaded this project into being. To Em S.K. Michael S. Kaulback, Grand Commander of Knights Templar of Massachusetts and Rhode Island, my Templar historian, for checking and rechecking all of the facts pertaining to the Templars, you have my undying gratitude. To Karen Brooks, for querying and calling me on the many details of fourteenth-century life. To Wolfman, for catching the porcupine and reminding me about the myths surrounding werewolves in the dark and superstitious time. And, finally, an enormous thank you to my favorite women: Eden Edwards, editorial coach extraordinaire, and Mary Plourde and Kim Biggs, whose constant and amazing insight into the detail of characters and place I could not have done without. To my mom and Ralph, thank you for always being there; I love you both. To my niece Amanda: You will love book two. It's all you, babe.

The adventure continues!

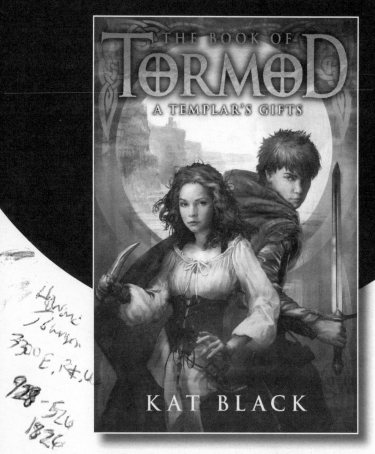

Something's wrong with Tormod. His visions are becoming unbearably intense, making him increasingly ill. Then he meets Aine, who has powers of her own. Together they must find the healer who can save Tormod's life—before the French king's ruthless soldiers find them.